Linda Ford
and
Dorothy Clark

The Journey Home
&
Family of the Heart

 HARLEQUIN® LOVE INSPIRED®CLASSICS

LOVE INSPIRED BOOKS

PLEASE RECYCLE
THIS PRODUCT IS RECYCLABLE

Recycling programs
for this product may
not exist in your area.

ISBN-13: 978-1-335-00757-5

The Journey Home & Family of the Heart

Copyright © 2018 by Harlequin Books S.A.

The publisher acknowledges the copyright holders
of the individual works as follows:

The Journey Home
Copyright © 2008 by Linda Ford

Family of the Heart
Copyright © 2008 by Dorothy Clark

www.Harlequin.com

Printed in U.S.A.

Linda Ford lives on a ranch in Alberta, Canada, near enough to the Rocky Mountains that she can enjoy them on a daily basis. She and her husband raised fourteen children—four homemade, ten adopted. She currently shares her home and life with her husband, a grown son, a live-in paraplegic client and a continual (and welcome) stream of kids, kids-in-law, grandkids and assorted friends and relatives.

Visit the Author Profile page
at Harlequin.com for more titles.

THE JOURNEY HOME

Linda Ford

This book would not be what it is without the help
of several key people.

First, my editor, Melissa, who saw what it needed.
Thank you for your guidance and encouragement.

And then two very dear critique partners who listen
to me whine and still find ways to point out what
I'm doing right and where I should reconsider my
direction. To Debbie and Carolyne, thank you both
for your continued support, your friendship and your
helpful suggestions. If I dedicate every book to you
it's because I couldn't do it without you.

Chapter One

South Dakota, 1934

He didn't know why God answered his prayers any more than he could explain why he still said them. But there it stood, the protection he'd moments ago begged God to provide, an old farmhouse, once proud, now with bare windows and a door hanging by one hinge. Deserted by the owners, as were so many places in the drought-stricken plains. The crash of '29 had left hundreds floundering financially. And years of too little rain resulted in numerous farms abandoned to the elements. He didn't hold out much hope of 1934 being any different.

Kody Douglas glanced upward. The black cloud towering high into the sky thundered toward him. An eerie yellow light filled the air. A noisy herald of birds flew ahead of the storm. Kody ducked his head against the stinging wind and nudged Sam into a trot. They'd better get inside before the dust storm engulfed them.

In front of the house, he leaped from the saddle, led Sam across the worn threshold and dropped the reins to the floor. Sam would remain where he was parked until Kody said otherwise, but still he felt compelled to make it clear. "You stay here, horse. And don't go leaving me any road apples. You can wait to do that business outside."

He grabbed the rattling door and pushed it shut. A hook hung from the frame. The eye remained in the door, and he latched it.

"Probably won't hold once the wind hits," he told his ever patient mount and companion. Man got so he talked to the only living, breathing thing he shared his day with.

Kody snorted. You'd think a man would get used to being alone. Seems he never could. Not that he cared a whole lot for the kind of company he encountered on the trail. Scoundrels and drifters willing to lift anything not tied down. Kody might be considered a drifter, but he'd never stoop to being a scoundrel. He had his standards.

He yanked off his hat and slapped it against his thigh, creating his own private cloud of dust. He jammed the hat back on his head and glanced around. Place couldn't have stood empty for long. No banks of dirt in the corners or bird droppings on the floor. The windows were even still intact.

The wind roared around the house. Sam tossed his head as the door banged in its crooked, uncertain state. Already the invading brown dust sifted across the linoleum. The air grew thick with it. The loose door wouldn't offer more than halfhearted protection, and Kody scanned the rest of the house, searching for something better.

"Don't go anywhere without me," he told Sam as he strode through the passageway into a second room. The drifting soil crunched under his boots.

Again, God provided more than he asked and certainly more than he deserved. A solid door stood closed on the interior wall to his right. He could shelter there until the duster passed. He yanked open the door.

"Hold it right there, mister. I've got a gun and I'm not afraid to use it," a voice cracked.

Kody's heart leaped to his throat and clutched at his tonsils. His nerves danced along his skin with sharp heels. Instinctively he raised his arms in the air, then slowly, cautiously, turned to locate the source of danger. He almost chuckled at the sight before him. A thin, brown-haired woman pressed into the corner, eyes steady, mouth set in a hard line. She held a rifle almost as long as she was tall.

The upward flight of his arms slowed and began a gradual descent. "You ain't gonna shoot me." It was about more'n she could do to keep the rifle level. The business end wobbled like one of those suffering trees in the wind outside.

"Back off or you'll see soon enough what I mean to do."

He lowered his right arm a few more inches, at the same time taking one swift step forward.

She gasped as he plucked the rifle from her.

He cracked it open to eject the bullet. The chamber was empty. He roared with laughter. "Lady, you got more guts than a cat stealing from a mother bear." Amusement made his words feel round and pleasant in his mouth. Unfamiliar, even. It'd been a long time since he'd done more than growl his words. He pulled his gaze from the woman who triggered the amusement, knowing his keen look made her uncomfortable.

She jutted out her chin. "This is my house. Get out."

She lived here? In this deserted house? Alone?

He stilled the questions pouring to his thoughts to deal with the immediate concern. "I don't intend to go out in a blinding dust storm. And no God-fearing, decent woman would expect me to."

She swallowed his accusation noisily. But nothing in her posture relented from her fierce protectiveness.

"I mean you no harm." Without seeking her permission, he sauntered to the corner farthest away, leaving her to plot her own actions. He made like he didn't care what she did, though his every nerve danced with alertness. Might be she had a hunk of wood hid beneath her skirts and would sneak up on him and smack him hard enough to give him a headache to regret. He didn't much figure she could overpower him even with a weighty length of two-by-four. He held back a heartfelt chuckle. Gotta admire a woman with so much spunk.

He heard her slight hiss and from the corner of his eyes saw her take a faltering step toward the door, maybe more intent on escape than anything.

The wind shook the house. The light faded. Through the window he watched the black cloud envelop them. Dust billowed through the cracks around the frame. They needed something to cover the window. In the dim light he made out a pile of material on the floor and, ignoring the woman's indrawn breath, went over to investigate. A ragged quilt. "Why don't you have this over the window? It might keep out some of the dirt."

"What a wonderful idea. I should have thought of it myself." Her sarcasm nearly melted the paint off the wall.

He snorted. "That is a most uncharitable attitude."

She put a rag to her nose. "How do you suggest I get it to stay there? Or do you propose to hold it in place?"

"Ma'am, where there's a will there's a way." What a sharp-tongued young woman. He held the quilt to the window. It greatly reduced the amount of dust coming through the cracks. A nail at one corner served as a hook. He felt around but could find no nail on the other corner. He pulled at the frame. It fit too tightly to allow him to stuff the material behind it. He stood with his arms over his head feeling as exposed as a deer in the middle of a bare field. And he was about to put himself into an even more vulnerable position. "You happen to have a fork or knife handy I could jab in behind the frame and hold this in place?"

She crossed the room and handed him a nail. "It fell out and I couldn't get it back in."

The quilt darkened the room, but even in the dim light he immediately saw her problem. She barely came up to his armpit. She'd need something to stand on to reach the top of the window. She probably needed a stool to brush her teeth. He grinned at his silly imagination and plucked the nail from her fingers. But how to drive it in? "Hold this."

He scooted over to make room for her. She lifted her arms and pressed the quilt as high as her short stature allowed. He felt around the window until he found a crack between the frame and the wall and wedged the nail in as firmly as he could. He caught a corner of the quilt over it and stepped back. "That should do."

"Thank you," she muttered as she headed back to the corner.

He chuckled. She sounded about as grateful as if he'd

handed her a bucket of sand. He returned to the opposite side of the room and hunkered down.

"Your house, hey?"

"My brother's. I'm watching it for him."

"Don't look like it needs much watching." The room was about as bare as the mile after mile of windswept fields he'd ridden by. It didn't take a lot of looking to see the place was vacant. Except for this woman. "What's anyone going to take?"

She made a sound that could have been anger or a signal of her intent to argue, but the storm increased in ferociousness. She ducked her head instead.

He pressed his hankie to his nose and prepared to wait it out.

Charlotte huddled into the corner. He'd accused her of being uncharitable. Her own thoughts rebuked her for being sharp-tongued. Normally she was neither, but her patience had worn thin, and her fears fueled by unexpected, unfair circumstances. Her faith had been sorely tested of late. Tested but not abandoned. What else did she have left but her trust in God?

Our Father, who art in heaven... She closed her eyes and silently repeated the words, mentally squeezing each for strength, determined to think of nothing but God's love and power.

But a dust storm raged outside, sifting fine particles of dirt through the air, threatening to dry-drown her, and inside sat a strange man. Her nerves twitched with anxiety greater than she'd known even on her first night alone in the empty house.

And not just any man. An Indian, complete with braids and a feather dangling from his cowboy hat.

I will not fear. God is with me. He will never forsake me.

The words had become her daily supplication since she'd walked into the house and found it empty—her brother, Harry, her sister-in-law, Nellie, and the two children had disappeared.

She'd been at the Hendersons' with instructions from Nellie to help with the new baby. Upon her return she discovered them gone—lock, stock and kitchen supplies—and a note from Harry saying he couldn't take the drought any longer. They were going farther west. No room in the truck for her. He'd send for her soon, within a week for sure. He'd arrange for Mr. Henderson to deliver a message.

They'd left barely enough food and water to last her.

"God will take care of me," she murmured.

The frightening man turned. "You say something?"

"God will take care of me." She spoke louder, firmer. After all, He'd led the children of Israel through the desert. Her situation wasn't any worse. Except she was alone. No, not alone. God was with her. So she had reminded herself over and over.

The house shook under the wind's attack. Dirt ground between her teeth. Her throat tickled. She breathed slowly to stop the urge to cough. She longed for a drink. Her last drink had been some unsatisfying mouthfuls this morning. The only place she could get more was at Lother's. She shuddered just thinking of her nearest neighbor.

Eligible young men were scarce as rain. Most had gone looking for work. Seemed wherever they went jobs were hard to come by. She saw them riding the rails every time she was in town, going from one end of the country to the other. Lother, one of the few bachelors still in the community, made it clear he'd be glad to marry Charlotte. He seemed to think she'd be equally pleased to accept the opportunity. If she had to choose between marriage to Lother or rotting on the manure pile, she'd gladly choose the latter. She shuddered again, harder.

"It will doubtless end soon."

Did he think she worried about the storm? That happened to be the least of her current concerns. "You can be certain? I heard tell they had a three-day duster over toward Bentley."

"Yeah, but it ended, didn't it? Even the flood ended eventually."

Despite her mental turmoil, she laughed. "I guess we should be grateful we haven't had a forty-day duster."

The wind increased in velocity.

The man raised his voice. "I sat by a railway track once while a train went by. Never figured wind could make more noise, but it does."

The roar made conversation impossible.

She hunkered down, prepared to wait out the storm. Just like she'd been waiting for Harry's message. Was she destined to spend her life waiting for one thing or another?

Kody glanced toward the woman. She sat with a rag of some sort pressed to her face. Above the gray cloth her eyes regarded him with wariness. Or was it determination? He guessed both. She'd already shown she had plenty of grit.

The wind grew louder. The room darkened like the dead of night. He buried his face against his knees and waited. Could be the storm would end soon, or not. No predicting the nature of nature. He smiled into his handkerchief. Ma would chuckle at his choice of words. Suddenly in the noisy gloom, he missed his mother and father, even though he knew they were better off with him out of the picture. Nor were they the only ones to benefit from his departure. He pushed aside the forbidden memory.

The woman opposite him coughed. Not a tickling sort of cough relieved with a clearing-your-throat kind of sound, but a dry cough that went on and on. He held his breath, waiting for it to end. She stopped and he let out a gust of relief. It was short-lived as she began again.

Poor woman needed some water to wash down the dust.

He slid across the floor until his elbow encountered the warm flesh of her arm, vibrating from her coughs. "Here, have a drink." He offered her the canteen he'd grabbed out of habit, having learned never to wait out a dust storm without water nearby to wash his throat.

She latched on to the canteen, lifted it to her mouth and drank greedily. For a fearful moment he thought she'd drain the contents. Not that it was a matter of life and death. He'd refill it from her well as soon as the storm ended. But nevertheless he swallowed hard. A duster could make a man mighty thirsty.

She capped the canteen and handed it back. "Thank you."

He stayed where he was and again buried his face in his handkerchief and let his thoughts drift back to Favor, South Dakota, where he'd been born and raised and where the only parents he'd ever known still lived.

He didn't want to think about all he'd left behind. Better to think about this woman huddled in the corner.

He turned his head a fraction, still protecting his face but making it possible to talk. "What's your name, ma'am?"

"What's yours?"

He chuckled. Got to admire a woman who showed no fear even in this awkward and potentially threatening situation. He knew many men who would take advantage of his position—alone with an unprotected woman. "Ma'am, my name is Kody Douglas. My father is a preacher man and I've been raised to be honorable and God-fearing." The "raised" part was true. Never mind he no longer had the faith he'd been raised with. Not that he could explain what he now believed. God's love had become so mixed up in his soul with man's unloving behavior he didn't know how to separate the two.

She uttered a sound full of disbelief.

He wasn't surprised. All his life he'd encountered the same reaction. As if a man like him could have a father like his, a home like his, a faith like he'd once had. For most people it defied explanation.

He hunkered down over his knees, preparing to ignore the woman. No doubt she likewise wished to ignore him. Besides, there was no reason to strike up a conversation. He'd be gone as soon as the storm ended. They'd never see each other again in this life or the one to come. That idea gave him pause. "You a believer?" he asked, even though he'd just told himself conversation was unnecessary.

"In God?"

He grunted affirmation.

"Most certainly I am. I have been since I was a child

at my mother's knee. In fact, He has been my strength and help all my life. He will continue to take care of me."

Kody wondered at the way she said the words. As if she expected him to argue. "Got no cause to disagree." God did seem to favor the likes of her, but Kody figured God regretted making the likes of him.

"My name is Charlotte Porter."

He thought of shaking her hand but refrained. He didn't want to put her in the position of having to choose whether or not to accept his offer nor did he want to shift his position and allow any more dirt to invade. Dust covered every bit of exposed skin, filling his pores until he envied the fish of the sea. He might head west to the ocean and sit in the water until he shriveled up like an old man just for the pleasure of having clean skin if he hadn't already decided to ride north into Canada and keep riding until he got to uninhabited land.

He settled for acknowledging her introduction with the proper words, though she perhaps expected nothing more than a grunt. "Pleased to meet you."

"You from round here?"

He guessed she felt the need of conversation more than he did. At least he wanted to believe so. Again he told himself a man should get used to being alone and sharing his thoughts with a faithful horse. "Not so's you'd notice." There was nothing about his past he wanted to share with this woman or anyone else on the face of the earth, and nothing about his future that held significance for anyone but himself.

"Where are you headed?"

"Just following my nose."

"Mr. Douglas, are you being purposely evasive?"

He chuckled. "Maybe I am. You might say it's a habit

of mine." Seemed no need to refuse the woman the information she sought. "I'm from Favor, South Dakota."

"I never heard of an Indian preacher man." Her voice was muffled.

"I ain't no preacher man." He jerked his eyes open, felt the sting of dust and closed them again.

"I mean your father."

He kept his handkerchief to his mouth, guessed she kept her eyes closed, too, so she couldn't see his smile. "My father is a white man."

She twitched. "But—"

"My mother is white, too. Kind of defies explanation, doesn't it?" He squinted at her, saw her regarding him through narrowed eyes.

"That's impossible."

He laughed, liking the way her eyes momentarily widened, then as quickly narrowed against the dust.

"Not if I'm adopted. Besides, my real mother is white. My father..." He paused. "One look at me is all it takes to know he was Indian."

"Adopted? Well, that explains it, doesn't it?"

Her voice said so much more than her words. As if it mattered about as much as fly sweat. As if he was already gone and forgotten. He settled back into his own thoughts, not sure he liked the way she silently dismissed him. Didn't she have any particular opinion about his heritage, the unnaturalness of being raised white while looking native? Everyone else seemed to.

He wrenched his thoughts to more practical matters. Had the light increased? Surely the wind roared with less vehemence. "It's letting up."

"Thank God. If this is the last duster I ever see, I would be eternally grateful."

"You and thousands of others."

Neither of them moved—gray dust particles in the air would fill their eyes and nose and lungs. No, they had to wait a bit longer. Kody glanced around the room, taking in more details. The only thing in the room was a bundled-up mattress in the corner.

"Why did your brother leave you here alone?"

"Who says I'm alone?"

He laughed. "I mean apart from me and my horse."

"I didn't mean you."

Again he laughed. This woman amazed him. Did she truly think he'd look around, see a virtually abandoned home and think she had a passel of brothers or sons or a husband to protect her? "What kind of brother leaves his sister alone?"

She studied him with narrow-eyed concentration. Weak light poked around the quilt at the window, but it didn't take morning sun on her face for him to know she resented his questions. But he couldn't dismiss his concern. Why would her brother leave her here alone? It didn't seem natural. For sure it wasn't safe. He wasn't the only man wandering about the countryside. Hundreds of them rode the rails every day looking for work or avoiding the realities of the Depression. Work was scarce. Pay even scarcer. He'd been trying for months to earn enough money to buy himself an outfit to start new in the North. He'd managed to save a few dollars. A few more and he'd be on his way.

"He's coming for me." She kept her face buried in her hands, the rag muffling her words. "Real soon."

"Until then you're here alone."

"I am not alone. God is with me. He has promised to be with me always."

Her words sifted through his thoughts, trickled down his nerves and pooled in his heart like something warm and alive. "I used to believe that."

"It's still true whether or not you believe it."

He laughed softly into his hands at the solid assurance in her voice. Could she really be so convinced? He stole a look at her. She regarded him. He wished he could see her mouth. Would it be all pruned up sourlike, or flat with determination?

She lowered her hand to speak and his eyes widened in surprise at the faint smile curving her lips. "One thing I know about God is He is unchanging. He doesn't have moods or regret or uncertainty as we often do." She turned enough to see the window and seemed to look right through the quilt and see something special beyond the fabric and glass. "'Fear not: for I have redeemed thee, I have called thee by thy name; thou art mine. When thou passest through the waters, I will be with thee; and through the rivers, they shall not overflow thee: when thou walkest through the fire, thou shalt not be burned; neither shall the flame kindle thee.'"

His heart burned within him. Had he not heard the words from his parents' lips time and again? *I have called thee by name. Thou art mine.* Yet somehow they sounded more convincing coming from this woman. He almost believed them.

Chapter Two

The man scrambled to his feet. Charlotte stood, as well, feeling as if every pore held a spoonful of irritating sandy dirt. Oh, for a good bath. Oh, for a quenching drink of water. For three days she'd metered out the last drops of her supply. Apart from a few swallows this morning, she'd had only the warm drink from the man's canteen.

She swiped at her hair, scrubbed the dirty rag over her face, shook her skirts and coughed.

The man slapped his hat against his leg and filled the air with a swirl of dust. She coughed again.

"Sorry," he muttered. "I should have waited until I was outside."

Charlotte threw open the door and choked on the thick air. The floor lay buried in several inches of dirt. The outside door must have ripped from its hinges. She closed the solid wood, blocking her only escape route. "Person can't breathe out there yet."

She kept her face toward the knob, thought of ushering the man out to his destiny. But his remark about the charity of a Christian woman still echoed in her head.

She'd give him a few more minutes, then she'd rush him on his way. Presuming he'd allow her to rush him. If he didn't... No point in threatening him with the rifle. Anger scalded her throat. If Harry had had the decency to leave her a bullet or two, she'd have had no trouble getting rid of the man in the first place.

Maybe she could appeal to his decency. After all, his parents were white folk and religious, so surely the man had been raised to know right from wrong. Of course the same could be said about a lot of men who nevertheless chose wrong. The thought erased every vestige of calmness.

She heard him move about the room and stiffened as he approached her bedroll. Harry and Nellie had left her bedding and enough food for a week. How very kind of them.

"Where are you headed from here, Mr. Douglas?" She hoped he'd hear the urgent suggestion in her words.

"Kody, if you please. I'm going wherever I can find work."

She ignored his suggestion she call him Kody. Father or son, made never mind to her. He'd soon be riding the tail of the wind out of her house and out of her life. Couldn't be too soon to suit her. "I expect you'll have to ride some to find work. It's mighty scarce around here. Lots of folks pulling up stakes and moving on."

"My sentiments exactly. It's an unfriendly country in my opinion."

At the harshness of his voice, she turned to study him. The typical angular high cheekbones, lips pulled into a hard, unyielding line that spoke of determination. "I take it you've been as disappointed in life as many of the folks around here." Harry and Nellie among them.

He faced her full on, his black eyes steady as if measuring her.

She met his gaze, knew they both had secrets bringing them to this place, this time and this house. She believed God cared for her, controlled every aspect of her life. Didn't the Scripture say all the days of her life were written before one of them came to be? But right now she struggled to believe it. How could God have planned for the country to blow from county to county? For Harry to abandon her? For a half-breed to be in her house? But she was being overly dramatic. Harry would send for her as he'd promised. He'd taken care of her since she was ten and their mother grew too ill to manage on her own. He'd provided her with a safe home since Mother died, as he'd sworn he would—apart from that time Nellie had demanded she be sent away. Charlotte shuddered. She would never forget her subsequent ordeal at the Appleby home.

Anxious to escape the past as much as the present, she opened the door again, breathing shallowly as she picked her way over the dirt on the floor.

Mr. Douglas followed close on her heels, whistling when he saw the damage in the front room. "Looks like your brother could plant a garden in here."

She ignored his comment. Her brother wouldn't be planting a garden anywhere near this house. And God willing, she'd shake off the dust of the place this very afternoon and be on her way to join him. Out of habit and desperation, she went to the window to see if Mr. Henderson rode her way with the promised letter from Harry. But she saw only the changed landscape—mounds of dirt in new places, fields scraped clean in others. A desolate, angry scene.

"Lady, could you point me to your well? I'd like to wash this storm off my face and refill my canteen."

She turned away from the hopeless view. His face looked as if he'd scrubbed in garden soil. She touched her cheeks, guessing she looked no better. "Well's out there." She pointed to the little shack Harry had built to store tools in.

Kody tromped into the kitchen.

Charlotte followed and screamed as she came face-to-face with a paint horse.

"This is Sam," Kody said. "He won't hurt you."

"You brought your horse into my house?" She sniffed. "Phew. He's stunk up the place like a barn."

Kody shook his head. "Sam, I told you not to do that in here."

The horse whinnied.

Charlotte thought the sound as unbelieving as her thoughts. "A horse answers the call of nature without regard to his surroundings."

"I'll clean it up."

"You certainly will." And she'd scoop out the dirt with the only tools Harry had left her—a tin can and a big spoon.

Kody grabbed the empty bucket from the old work-table left behind because it was nailed to the wall. He headed for the well. He had the decency to lead his horse outside with him and kick out the pile of manure as he left.

Charlotte stood at the door, praying for a miracle. God had brought water from a rock for His children in the desert. Didn't seem like water from the well ought to be any different. And while He was providing miracles, maybe He could see fit to send a message from

Harry and something to send Mr. Douglas hightailing it out of here.

Kody walked with a combination of roll and stride. He grabbed the handle and pumped up and down. The squealing protest caused Sam to sidle away and whinny. After several unproductive pumps, Kody called, "Well appears to be dry."

Charlotte sighed. Hoping against hope proved futile yet again. She couldn't imagine what lesson God meant for her to learn. "I know."

He sauntered over. "Been dry long?"

She shrugged. He didn't need to know the particulars, but they'd been going to Lother's for water for several months.

Kody shook the bone-dry pail. "Where was your brother getting water?"

Charlotte stared across the pasture indicating a well-worn path. In the distance she could make out the chimney, the roof of the barn and the life-saving windmill. "Lother Gross has been kind enough to let us use his well."

Kody touched his cheek with a brown finger. "I'd like to wash and refill my canteen." He waited, perhaps expecting her to lead the way.

Why couldn't the man take a hint? Desperately she sought for a way to persuade him to leave. The gun was out unless she used it as a club, and she didn't much fancy the idea of attacking him, knew she didn't stand a chance against his size and strength. She looked about the kitchen, hoping for some solution, finding nothing but emptiness and disappointment. Feeling his patient waiting, she sighed and turned back to face him.

"You could go across to the neighbor's and get water."

She nodded toward Lother's place. "I'll stay here and tidy up a bit." If he got so much as halfway across the pasture, she'd figure out some way to bar the broken door.

Kody's eyes narrowed.

She crossed her arms over her chest as if she hoped to protect her thoughts from his piercing gaze.

The man looked at the empty bucket, gave a long, considering study of the useless pump, then stared across the pasture. "How long you been out of water?" he asked, his voice soft but knowing.

Again she shrugged. Her problems were no concern of his.

He nodded toward the path. "Why don't you go get some?"

Her stomach lurched toward her heart, making her swallow hard to control the way her fear mixed with nausea. She didn't want Lother to know she was alone and had waited until dark two nights ago to slip over. She reasoned she could fill a pail and hurry away without detection. But his dog set up a din fit to wake the dead. Charlotte had tried to calm him. "It's me. You know me." She'd kept her voice low, but the dog wouldn't let up. Coming around after dark was a strange occurrence, not acceptable to the dog's sense of guard duty.

Charlotte had been forced to retreat without water in order to avoid being confronted by Lother.

"How long you been here alone?"

She pressed her lips together and jutted out her chin.

Kody adjusted his black cowboy hat and leaned back on worn cowboy boots. His gray shirt, laced at the neck, had seen better days. His pants were equally shabby. "Why ain't you walked out of this place?" He shook his head. "I don't get it. You've got the guts to face me with an empty gun, yet you hide in this derelict house without water."

How dare he? "What gives you the right—"

"Lady, despite the color of my skin—"

Which, Charlotte thought, had nothing to do with this whole conversation.

He continued in the same vein. "And the uncertainty of my heritage—"

One certainty he'd overlooked: this was none of his business. "I don't recall asking for your help," she said.

"I've been raised to care about the welfare of others."

That stumped her. How could she argue with something she also believed?

He continued. "You're out of water. And you're alone. It just plain ain't safe for a woman to be alone with so many drifters around."

"My brother is sending for me to join him."

"So you're going to sit here and wait?"

Why did he goad her? His words edged past her patience, her faith that Harry would indeed send for her, and dug cruel, angry fingers into her spine. "No, I'm not waiting." Why had she sat here for a whole week expecting the Hendersons to deliver a message? She spun on her heel and marched back to the dusty bedroom, threw her few things into the old carpetbag Nellie had left in the closet and rolled up the little bit of bedding. She stomped from the room, paused and grabbed the rifle. Not much good to her, but she'd return it to Harry, and when she did, she'd let him feel the sharp edge of her tongue for leaving her in such a position. Of course, she wouldn't. She wouldn't risk making him regret opening his home to her.

Ignoring the crunch of dirt under her shoes, she hurried out the door, gave one goodbye glance over her shoulder at the interior of the house and headed down the road. There was nothing for her here and no reason to stay. Besides, surely the Hendersons had a message by now and simply hadn't had time to deliver it.

Kody trailed after her.

She paused to glower at him. "Why are you following me?"

"Just wondering where you're going."

"To the neighbor. They might have a message from my brother, though I fail to see how it's any of your concern."

"I'll see you to this neighbor. My ma would have my hide if I didn't make sure you were safe." He pushed his hat farther back on his head and nodded as if she'd agreed.

"I'm quite capable of looking after myself. I don't need you keeping an eye on me. Go away." She steamed down the road, dragging her bundles and the rifle.

"I'm going the same direction. Why don't you let me put your things on Sam?"

She stubbornly plowed onward. When he sighed and fell in step with her, she paused. "Seems a shame to be wasting your time. You might find a job if you hurry to town."

"I ain't leaving you until I know you're safe. Ma would have my—"

"She'd have your hide. So you said."

"Are you always so contrary?"

"I'm the most compliant of persons." Except right now. "Normally."

"So it's just me."

"Yup. Now why don't you get on your horse and ride away?" She had never been sharp with anyone in her life, but this man prodded her the wrong way. "Sorry for being rude," she mumbled.

"I'm used to it."

Although he said this in a mild way, his words stopped her in her tracks and she turned to stare at him. His dark eyes gave nothing away. Nor did his blank expression, but she understood he meant he faced unkind comments because of his race.

"Huh," she finally said, unwilling to point out that not everyone felt the same way. She couldn't say how she felt about the man, but it had nothing to do with his race and everything to do with the way he got under her skin like a long, unyielding sliver. She hurried on, not surprised when he walked beside her.

"How far to this neighbor?"

"The Hendersons. Three miles. Big Rock is a few miles farther." She hoped the suggestion he might like to hurry in that direction would be clear.

"Yup."

The weight of the bag made her shoulder ache. The bedroll kept slipping from her arms and the rifle banged against her shins, but she paid them scant attention. She was used to working hard without complaining.

Kody caught the bedroll just as it threatened to escape her grasp.

"That's mine," she protested.

"So it is." He tied it to the saddle and reached for the rifle.

"That's Harry's and I intend to see he gets it back."

"Harry would be your brother?"

"Of course."

"Well, when you give it back, I suggest you do it like this." He waved the gun as if hitting someone with it, then rubbed his head, moaning.

Despite the fact she didn't want Kody to tie her meager belongings to the saddle, despite the fact she didn't want him accompanying her, she laughed because his action so accurately echoed her sentiments. Though she would never do it. No. She'd hand the gun to him meekly and promise to work hard and not argue with Nellie. She'd done so over and over just to make sure Harry wouldn't send her away. Like he'd done when she was twelve. How grateful she'd been when he took her back. Only with Harry did she have a safe place.

Remembering sucked away the last drops of anger, so when Kody reached for the carpetbag, she handed it to him without argument. And submissively followed him down the road.

A few minutes later, Charlotte pointed to the low house. "The Hendersons'." They paused at the turnoff. She reached for her things. "Thank you for your company."

Kody touched the brim of his hat and gave a slight nod. "My pleasure."

She wondered if he mocked her. She shrugged. What did it matter? She marched to the door and knocked. Mr. Henderson opened. Mrs. Henderson stood at his shoulder, holding the new baby. "I've come to see if there's any word from Harry."

Two older people stood by, watching curiously. The three other children eyed Charlotte.

"No, nothing. I would have ridden over if I heard anything. Haven't been to town for a couple of days. Not since I picked up my folks. They've come to help."

"Perhaps I could wait here." She knew as soon as she spoke it wasn't possible. They must be crowded to the rafters already. "Never mind. I'll go to town and see if there's a message waiting." *Please, God, let there be some word.* Her silent prayer grew urgent. What would she do if there wasn't?

Chapter Three

Kody waited at the side of the road. He didn't really want to help her, but if he ever saw Ma again he wanted to be able to face her without any guilty deed to hide. She'd raised him to see and respond to the needs of others. He only wished others had been taught the same and saw past his heritage to his heart. But it no longer mattered. He had a destination—northern Canada. He'd heard a man could get cheap land without the uncertain benefit of neighbors. It sounded like his kind of place.

He settled back out of sight behind a low drift of soil and watched as Charlotte made her way to the door and knocked.

A young man and woman opened to her. Kody strained but couldn't make out any words until the man nodded. "Certainly there might be something by now. I'm sorry I can't take you."

Charlotte murmured a reply, then turned and plodded back to the road. "We can fill the canteen and clean up."

He handed it to her. "You go ahead. I'll wait here."

"I thought you were anxious to wash."

He studied the house, the door now closed. "Your friends won't understand your keeping company with me."

"I'm not keeping company with anyone."

He didn't make a move toward the nearby water trough.

"They do understand the need for water."

Sam whinnied and nudged Kody. He could ignore his own thirst, but it hardly seemed fair to deprive Sam of a drink. "Lead on," he murmured, a sense of exposure causing him to put the horse between him and the windows of the house.

They both washed, then Kody pumped fresh water for them to drink. He filled the canteen and waited as Sam drank his fill.

Charlotte wiped the back of her hand across her mouth and smoothed her damp hair off her face. "I'm going on to town. Harry must have sent word by now." She hitched the rifle over her shoulder, tried to tuck the unwieldy bedroll under one arm as she struggled to carry the bulky bag in the other. Then she resolutely headed down the road.

Knowing he had to do what Ma would consider the right thing, Kody fell in beside her. "How far is it, did you say?"

"Didn't." She paused. "Five miles."

He swallowed a groan. He wasn't used to walking and had already used his feet for three miles while Sam plodded along with an empty saddle. "Seems a shame for Sam to be doing nothing."

"No need for you to go out of your way."

"I hadn't planned on going to Big Rock. Hadn't not planned it, either. I'm only passing through on the way to something better. Picking up work where I can find it on my way north."

"What's up north?"

"Canada and a new life." As soon as he earned some more money he'd be ready to start over. "Hear you can find places where you never see another soul for months at a time."

"I'm here to tell you it can get mighty lonely not seeing another person." She shot him a look so full of disgust he chuckled.

He understood her response to being alone differed vastly from his own reasons for wanting it, so he didn't say anything.

They walked onward a few steps.

"Seems a shame for Sam to be doing nothing."

"No one asked you to accompany me. Get on and ride for Canada."

He snorted. "My ma would give me a real dressing-down if she heard I'd done such an ungentlemanly thing."

"Your ma isn't going to know, now is she?"

"You can never be sure." His voice rang with a mixture of regret and pride.

She laughed. The sound made his insides happy. "I've heard of mothers having eyes in the back of their heads," she said. "But this is the first time I heard someone suspect their mother of having long-distance sight."

He smiled, liking how it eased his mind. He'd gotten too used to scowling. "It ain't so much she'll see me do something, but if I ever see her again, she'll see it in my eyes." He'd never been able to fool Ma. She seemed to see clear through him. Which was one more reason to stay away from Favor, and Ma and Pa and all that lay in that direction.

Charlotte stopped and considered him. "Do you know how fortunate you are to have such a mother? If I had such a mother I'd never leave her. What are you doing going to Canada to be alone?"

"I have my reasons. Now save me from my mother's displeasure and ride Sam to town."

She studied him for a long moment. His skin tightened at the way she looked at him. He saw the fear and caution in her eyes, knew she saw him as a redskin, someone to avoid.

With a hitch of one shoulder to persuade the rifle to stay in place, she turned her steps back down the road.

He'd met this kind of resistance before and sighed loudly enough for her to pause. "My horse ain't Indian. Or half-breed."

Her shoulders pulled up inside her faded brown dress. He could practically see her vibrate, but didn't know if from anger or fear or something else. She let her bag droop to her feet and turned to face him. The sky lightened, with the brassy sun poking through the remnants of the dust storm, and he saw her eyes were light brown.

"Are you accusing me of prejudice?" she demanded, her voice soft, her eyes flashing with challenge as if daring him to think it, let alone say it.

Could she really be free of such? His heart reared and bucked as long-buried hopes and dreams came to life—acceptance, belonging, so many things. He shoved them away, barricaded them from his thoughts. Best he be remembering who he was, how others saw him. "Nope. Just stating a fact."

"I couldn't care less if your horse is Indian, black,

pink or stubborn as a mule. I prefer to walk." She spun around and marched down the road, sidling sideways to capture the escaping bedroll with her hip.

He grinned at her attempts to manage her belongings. For a moment he stared after her. She said words of acceptance, but he doubted she meant them as anything more than argumentative.

He followed, leading Sam. "He ain't stubborn."

"How nice for you." She continued, unconcerned by the wind tugging at her skirt and dragging her coppery-brown hair back from her forehead, undaunted by her belongings banging against her shins with every step.

Mule-headed woman. She made him want to prod at her more, see what would surface. He tried to think of a way to challenge her insistence on walking, wanting to somehow force her to state her opinion on his race. No doubt she had the same reservations as—ha, ha, good word choice. Again, his mother would have been amused. The same reservations about Indians as most white folk. "My mother would want you to ride," he murmured.

Finally she nodded. "For your mother." He secured her things to the saddle, then she tucked her skirt around her legs and used his cupped hands to assist herself onto Sam's back. "I'll ride partway. You can ride the rest."

He didn't argue, but nothing under the brassy sun would allow him to ride while a white woman walked at his side. He could just imagine the comments if anyone saw them.

"Seems everyone wants a new life," she said from her perch on Sam's back. "Except me. I've been quite happy with the one God provided."

He wondered how being abandoned made her happy

or caused her to think God had provided for her. "How long since your brother left?"

She darted him a look, then shifted her gaze to some distant point down the road. "Near a week."

Kody had learned to let insults roll off him without response. In fact, he'd learned to ignore lots of things in life. But a week? Well, he figured she had to be made of pretty strong stuff to still be fighting.

They walked on for the distance of half a mile until Charlotte broke the silence. "Why are you so anxious to go where you never see another soul?"

Kody didn't answer at first. Wasn't sure how to. This woman had a family. Sure, her brother had left her behind. Maybe with the best of intentions. But she expected him to welcome her into his new home. What would she know about how it felt to be a half-breed? How it affected everyone and everything in his world? How people expected him to be a wild Indian? At times his frustration made him want to act like one. "Sometimes a man likes to be alone."

"Don't you feel the need to have someone to talk to?"

Always. Try as he might, he never got used to keeping his thoughts inside himself. "Sam here is a good listener."

She laughed, a sound like water rippling over rocks. A sound trickling through his senses like someone brushing his insides with a feather. "If you want only listening you could park a rock on your saddle and talk to it. Seems to me a person wants a bit more. Someone to agree or argue. Someone to acknowledge your presence."

He refused to let her words poke at his loneliness. He'd made his decision. There was no looking back.

They fell into quiet contemplation as they contin-

ued toward the town. Kody's thoughts always seemed
to have a mind of their own, and after talk about his
mother, there was no way to keep himself from remembering her. She loved him. As did his father. He'd never
doubted it. They treated him as their own and never
once made him feel inferior. For that he loved them
deeply, but life had created a solidly strong reason for
him to move on. He stopped himself from thinking further along those lines. He'd made his decision and he
wouldn't look back. Canada promised the sanctuary he
sought. He hoped it would also provide forgetfulness of
what he'd left behind.

Despite Charlotte's insistence she'd take her turn
walking, Kody did not allow Sam to stop until Big Rock
sat square in front of them. He pulled Sam off the road
and helped Charlotte dismount. He hung back behind
the low bushes at the side of the road. "You go on and
see if Harry has sent you a message."

She brushed the dust off her dress and smoothed back
her hair, which fell to her shoulders and trapped the
golden rays of sunshine, then she took the bedroll and
bag Kody handed her. He chuckled as she struggled to
carry the rifle. "Might as well leave it behind."

She ignored his suggestion. "Thank you again and
God bless you on your journey to Canada."

"You're welcome." He hunkered down behind the
bushes and waited. He'd make his way into town later
to assure himself she was okay, then he'd move on. He
plucked a dry blade of grass and rolled it between his fingers. Used to be he could occupy his mind with such useless activity, but not today. His thoughts had been willful
and troubling since he'd entered the house where Charlotte huddled alone. Something about her—her words

of faith, her belief in family and belonging—reminded him of what he'd left behind. He didn't thank her for bringing to his mind the very things he wanted to forget.

He turned to discuss the matter with Sam. "She thinks you're no better than a rock to talk to."

Sam snorted his disbelief.

"I know. I was offended, too. Shows what a woman knows. Sure, it's true you don't say much, but I know you understand."

Sam shook his head in agreement.

"Can't understand her brother abandoning her, though. She ain't so big she couldn't fit in somewhere."

Sam shook his head again.

"I sure hope the man has sent for her." He pushed to his feet and swung into the saddle. "Let's go see."

He pulled his hat low over his eyes and sat boldly upright, ready to face any challenge. He rode slowly through the wide streets of the suffering town, noted the vacant windows in several buildings. People pulled up and left everything behind as the drought and depression took their toll. A lone truck sat at the side of the street.

A man in the doorway of the feed store jerked to attention and watched Kody with narrowed eyes. Two old codgers leaned back on chairs in front of the mercantile. As Kody passed they crashed their chairs to all four legs. One spat on the sidewalk. Kody ignored them. He had no wish to start trouble. He only wanted to check on Charlotte and then he intended to head north as far as his empty stomach allowed before he tried to find some kind of work. It had become the pattern of his days. Sometimes, if the work was good or the pay promising, he stayed for days, even weeks. Other times, he earned a meal and moved on. Always north. Always toward his dream—Canada and forgetfulness. The journey had taken far longer than it should. He needed to make more effort to reach his goal.

He turned aside and stared at the display in the window of Johnson's General Store, though he only noted the post office sign. Charlotte would have gone inside to ask for her letter.

He waited, ignoring the stares from across the street. The two old men posed no threat, only annoyance and a reminder of what others saw when they looked at him.

Charlotte staggered out, a letter grasped in her hands. Her eyes had a faraway look as she stared past him, not seeing him, not, he guessed, seeing anything. At the shock on her face, he almost bolted off Sam, wanting to catch her before she stumbled and fell. Only the thunderous glance of a passing matron stopped him.

Charlotte collapsed on the nearby bench beside her belongings and shuddered.

Kody waited until the woman hurried on before he murmured, "You got your letter?" Seems she should have been a little more relieved to hear from her brother.

Slowly, as if it took all her mental energy, she pulled her gaze to him. She swallowed hard, her eyes seemed to focus and she shuddered again. "Harry says he's sorry, but they're still looking for a place. I'm to wait for further word from him. He suggested I stay with the Hendersons, but they're full with his parents there." Her eyes glazed. "I have no place to go."

The sound of someone on the sidewalk forced Kody to hold his tongue, though what could he tell her? Certainly she couldn't go back to the farm and no food or water, but she must have friends she could stay with for a few days.

A man stopped in front of Charlotte. "Well, if it isn't my neighbor. Haven't seen you in a few days, Charlotte. How are you doing?"

Charlotte folded the letter and tucked it into her bag. "I'm doing just fine, Lother. How about you?"

"A little lonely, my dear. But seeing you has fixed that right up."

Kody settled back, lowering his head and acting for all the world like he'd fallen asleep in the saddle. He didn't like the tone of proprietorship he heard in this Lother's voice, but it was none of his business and maybe the man would offer Charlotte the protection she needed.

Charlotte shuffled back, tucking her feet un-der the bench.

"What's this?" The man indicated the bedroll and car-petbag on the bench. "Planning a trip, are you?"

The storekeeper had moseyed out to take part in the conversation. "Harry and his wife moved out. Miss Charlotte's waiting for word to join them. That what your letter says?" he asked. "Harry sending for you?"

Charlotte shrank even farther back. She stared past Lother.

Kody lifted his chin just enough that their gazes con-nected. At the trapped look in her eyes he squeezed his hands into fists.

"No need for you to leave the country." Lother's words were low, his voice soft, yet Kody heard some-thing he didn't like. The sort of noise a rattler made be-fore it struck. "I'm willing to share my name and my home with you."

Charlotte's chin jutted out. "I have other plans."

"Joining your brother?" the storekeeper asked.

Charlotte flashed the man a defiant look. "That's my business, isn't it?"

"Mighty important business, too." The man snorted and returned inside.

Lother rocked back on his heels. "You're a strong young woman. 'Spect you could produce a whole lot of sons. Man needs sons to help on the farm. That brother of yours might be willing to sell me his land real cheap. Or I could wait a bit and get it for back taxes. With sons to help I could expand."

Kody wondered how soon he expected his sons to be big enough to help. Ma had taken in several babies while Kody lived at home, and he seemed to remember they were nothing but work for a couple of years and then they only ran around getting into mischief. Not much help, in his estimation. But this man had other plans for his babies. Plans including Charlotte as a broodmare. Kody twisted the reins until his hands hurt.

Lother touched Charlotte's cheek. "You'll do just fine," he said, his voice was as oily as the matted hair poking out from under the blackened edges of his hat. Kody could never understand a man who didn't wash up and comb his hair occasionally.

Charlotte twitched away from the man's touch, her eyes wide, dark with fear and something more, something Kody could only guess was loathing. It was plain she didn't much like this man.

Kody didn't like him at all.

Lother shoved Charlotte's belongings aside and sat very close, pushing his thigh against hers.

The man went too far. Kody leaned forward, preparing to spring to Charlotte's defense.

But Charlotte leaped to her feet. "Excuse me, I have

to get to the train station." She grabbed her belongings and hurried down the street.

Lother called after her, "You best be changing your mind soon and stop playing Miss High-and-Mighty. Ain't like you got other beaux." The man turned, saw Kody watching him. "What are you staring at, Injun? Move along."

Kody didn't need the man's permission, nor did he swing Sam into the street because he'd been ordered to. He had to see what Charlotte had up her sleeve. She'd said her brother had told her to wait. Did she have somewhere to go? Someplace safe from this Lother man?

He rode slowly to the end of the block and circled around by a back street to the train station. He dismounted and shuffled slowly to the platform, acting as if he had no reason in the world to be there other than aimless boredom. He didn't want to attract attention, nor have anyone suspect he had any interest in Charlotte.

She sat on a bench in the shade, slumped over her knees as if in pain.

He controlled the urge to hurry to her side and, instead, sauntered along the platform to stand near the edge, facing the tracks. His back to her, he said, "You figure out a place to go?"

She sniffed, a dry, determined sound that brought a slight smile to his lips. He'd expected tears, not this attitude of defiance. "I have no money. No family apart from Harry. No one here has room or ability to keep me. But I'm not stuck, if that's what you're thinking. I'm not alone. God is with me. He's promised to provide all I need. I'm sitting here praying."

"Waiting for a miracle?" Far as he could see, God had not smiled any more favorably on this woman than on himself. For his part, he'd given up waiting for miracles or, for that matter, evidence of God's love.

"I guess you don't believe in miracles or God's provision."

He crossed his arms over his chest and stared down the empty tracks. "Can't say one way or the other. Might be God sends them both your way."

"I'm counting on it."

There seemed nothing more to say after that. He could, having done his duty, rode away and leave her to God's care. Yet he didn't move. How often had he heard Ma say, "Son, what kind of people are we if we see a soul in need and turn our backs? Whatever the color of your skin, that uncaring attitude is savage." He wished he could shut off her voice, but it spoke softly in the back of his mind. She practiced what she preached, always helping those in need often without so much as a word of thanks. "I don't do it for the praise of men," she'd say. "I do it for God. He sees and knows my heart."

Kody had not one doubt what his mother would do in this situation. And what she would expect him to do. But she saw it in terms of black and white. He saw it in shades of red. He smiled, knowing Ma would appreciate the irony of his thoughts.

He uncurled his arms and let his fists hang at his sides. He could not walk away from his training. Again, he smiled, seeing the incongruity of his reasoning—unable to walk away from his training, yet determinedly riding away from his parents who had provided the training. His smile flattened. Best for those back home that he headed north, far, far from them all.

Except if he was to do what Ma expected, that might

change. "I know someplace where you can stay safely until you get word from your brother."

"You do?"

"With my mother and father." It totally fouled his plans, but he could not leave Charlotte here.

He heard her huff. Knew she would refuse.

"You got a better idea?"

"Yes. I'll wait back at the farm."

He spun around to face her. "You can't mean that. You have no water. No food."

Her stubborn look didn't change.

"And what about your friend Lother?"

"He's not my friend." She looked down the street as if fearing the man would follow her. Slowly, she brought her gaze back to Kody and stared at him for a full thirty seconds. "Seems I don't have a whole lot of choices."

He could hardly describe her reaction as grateful. "Maybe it's the miracle you've prayed for." He knew from the scowl on her lips that she didn't believe it any more than he did. "I need to get a few things. Why don't you go back to the store and arrange to have any messages forwarded care of Reverend Douglas in Favor, South Dakota?"

She nodded, reluctantly, he figured, and he left her to take care of that detail while he headed toward the livery barn. He patted his pocket, knowing his purse would be much lighter before he left town.

This decision of his meant he would be heading south, instead of north, heading back to the very place he'd vowed to leave behind forever.

Chapter Four

It took all Charlotte's self-control to keep from wailing with frustration and fear. A miracle? An answer to prayer? It certainly wasn't either in her estimation. She'd prayed for rescue, someone to offer her a home. The only person to do so was a half-breed. And Lother. She shuddered. She'd as soon sit on the step of Harry's empty house and wait to die of thirst as marry that man. Of the two, Kody seemed slightly less undesirable. At least he only wanted to escort her to his parents'. Or so he said. *God, I know You can't plan for me to ride out with this man. Please send someone else before he returns.*

Why couldn't some young mother needing help come along and see her? She'd willingly care for babies in exchange for a safe place to live. Or why couldn't an older couple shuffle by, the woman all crippled up and in pain and needing someone to run and fetch for her? Charlotte would put up with any amount of crankiness if it meant a roof over her head. Hadn't she been doing so for years, catering to Nellie's demands? And for what? To be thrown out or left behind at the slightest whim? God was in control. She knew that, but sometimes she found it hard to see how things could work out for good. But wasn't that when trust came in? When she couldn't comprehend circumstances?

Wait on the Lord. Wait and see His deliverance. She wished she could read the Bible and find appropriate words of comfort, but Harry had taken it with him.

She sat, waiting expectantly, until her skin began to twitch.

But the platform remained empty. So she trudged back to the store and made arrangements for the mail. Every step carried a prayer for God to intervene. No miracle occurred on her way to the store or her way back, and she resumed her position on the bench, pleading with God to do something. Surely there were people who would welcome her help in exchange for a warm corner to sleep in.

"Psst." The soft noise pulled her attention to the far end of the station, to a small cluster of trees where Kody waited. "Let's get out of here."

She didn't want to get out; she wanted to stay. She held her breath, praying for God to provide in the next two seconds something—someone—posing less risk than the man waiting for her.

Nothing.

Seems God had narrowed her choice down to this one option. Perhaps she'd displeased God, too, and He chose to ignore her. She pushed to her feet, taking her time about gathering her things, waiting for God to bestow better, praying with every breath. *God, help me. I trust You, even though things don't look good right now.*

Slowly she crossed the platform, her shoes thudding hollowly on the worn wood, the dusty air catching at her throat. She paused to glance in the window, saw Mr.

Sears at the wicket. He looked up, saw her and turned away dismissively.

"Hurry," Kody whispered.

The way he glanced about him sent warning skitters along the surface of her skin. "Why?" She spoke the word aloud, albeit softly.

"You're a white woman, I'm a half-breed. Need I say more?"

Caught up in his suspicions, she glanced over her shoulder to make sure no one saw her and then picked up her pace.

Kody took Harry's rifle, her bedroll and carpetbag—all her worldly possessions—and hung them neatly from the saddle, then helped her onto the old black mare he'd found somewhere.

Her doubts intensified. What did she know about this man apart from his own words? "Where'd you get the horse?"

He crossed his arms over his chest and stared up at her, his eyes hidden under the rim of his hat. "You figure I stole her?"

Her ears stung with heat that her caution had sounded accusing. She averted her gaze. "Just asking."

Kody grunted. "It might ease your mind to know I bought her fair and square from the livery barn. The owner seemed quite willing to part with her. He's running low on feed."

At his words a release of tension left Charlotte's spine weak. She didn't care to think the law would be after them.

Charlotte studied her mount—thin and probably as hungry as she was. She patted the mare's neck soothingly.

Kody pulled out of the trees and into the street, drew back as a truck putt-putted past, then flicked the reins and continued.

Charlotte started to follow, but when he headed away from the town to the north, her heart kicked in alarm. Did he expect her to follow him to Canada without protest? She pulled on the reins and turned the mare down Main Street. "Favor is to the south," she muttered.

Kody kicked Sam in the ribs and bolted to her side. "You can't ride through town."

"Why not? I'm a free woman. I've broken no laws."

He reached for her reins, but she jerked away from him.

"Again, I remind you, you're a white woman, I'm a—"

"So you said. But I am not riding north with you."

Kody grunted and fell back to her horse's rear. He pulled his hat lower over his face. "You're going to regret this," he murmured as he followed.

Charlotte kept her thoughts to herself, but she didn't intend to regret riding north when relief lay to the south, nor did she intend to ride out without giving God one more chance to send an alternative to riding into the unknown with a dark stranger.

As they traveled the three-block length of the street, Mrs. Williams stepped into view. The woman cleaned and cooked for Pastor Jones. Surely this was God's answer. The good Mrs. Williams would offer sanctuary to a stranded young woman. Charlotte edged her horse closer to the sidewalk and called out a greeting.

"Charlotte, how are you doing?"

"I'm actually in need of shelter. Harry has moved and until he sends for me, I am homeless. Perhaps you'll allow me to stay with you. I could find a job and provide for myself. I just need a place to sleep."

"I don't see how you could find work when hundreds of men are unemployed, and besides, with my husband being sick…" The older woman shook her head. "I'm sorry."

Charlotte nodded. "Thank you, anyway." She edged the horse back into the street, muttering to herself, "I wouldn't be in her way at all."

Kody grunted. "Times are hard."

Right then, Lother stepped out of the hotel. Charlotte shuddered as Lother glanced past her to Kody.

"You. Injun. What are you doing following my woman? Leave her alone." He waved his arms like he shooed chickens into the henhouse.

Kody didn't answer but said softly to Charlotte, "Make up your mind. Either ride on or stay with him."

"Some choice." She nudged her plodding horse onward, ignoring Lother's words following her down the street.

"No decent woman would keep company with an Injun of her own will." Anything more he had to say was lost in the clatter of horses' hooves.

Mrs. Craven peeked out her window as they passed, her eyes narrowing on Kody, then widening at Charlotte's riding with him. But she let the curtain drop without offering help.

As they rode out of town, Charlotte swallowed back the bitterness rising in her throat and resisted an urge to shake the dust from her skirts. She only asked for a little shelter. Instead, she was forced to accept the charity and kindness of a stranger. She prayed kindness guided this man's actions. *God, I need help. Please send someone.*

A mile down the road, Kody edged forward to ride at her side, but neither of them spoke. What could she possibly say? She'd accepted his help out of desperation. She felt no gratitude. Only a mile-wide hope that God would still see fit to send an alternative to accompanying this man into the unknown.

They had ridden perhaps an hour when the sound of an approaching car brought them to a stop at the side of the road. Charlotte expected the car to growl past and turned her head to avoid the cloud of dust. But the vehicle drew to a halt beside them and Sheriff Mack stepped out.

She wanted to laugh and cry and cheer all at once. God hadn't forgotten her. Why hadn't it occurred to her to consult the sheriff? "Sheriff, am I glad to see you. Perhaps you can help me."

"That's why I'm here." He pulled out his gun and leveled it at Kody. "Put your hands in the air and get down real slow."

For the second time in the same afternoon, Kody's arms went up and he dropped to the ground easily and gracefully.

Charlotte's heart stalled with alarm. Had she unwittingly accompanied a fugitive? She swallowed hard, trying to ease the gritty feeling inside, like she'd taken in too much dust in the last blow.

What had Kody done?

And why had she allowed herself to believe he wanted to help her? She'd been duped by talk about a God-fearing mother. She'd been taught you couldn't judge a man by the color of his skin. Seems you couldn't judge by his words or demeanor, either.

"Something wrong, Sheriff?" Kody asked in a low voice, apparently unconcerned.

She doubted he could be as indifferent as he appeared with the sheriff motioning him away from his horse.

"Charlotte, get in the car," Sheriff Mack said. "And you—" he kept his gun steady as he approached Kody "—turn around slow."

Charlotte sighed in relief as she got into the front seat of the sheriff's car. Sheriff Mack lived with his maiden sister. They'd be glad to take her in and she'd find a way to prove her value to them.

She watched as the sheriff handcuffed Kody and pushed him into the backseat. *I wonder what he's done. Too bad. He seemed like a nice enough fellow.*

The sheriff grabbed up the horses and tied them to the car. "Good thing Lother sent me after you," he said to Charlotte as he got behind the wheel.

A prickly sensation crawled along Charlotte's skin. She pulled her skirt down hard and tucked it around her legs. "Lother? What's he got to do with this?"

The sheriff chuckled. "No need to play coy with me, Charlotte. He told me you two were to marry. Said he saw this Indian take you out of town." Sheriff Mack started the car and edged down the road toward Big Rock. "But don't you worry. I'll take care of your kidnapper." He scowled over his shoulder at Kody. "Guess you know better than to expect any mercy. It's the rope for you." He turned and smiled at Charlotte. "I'll make sure you're safe with Lother before nightfall. Might even agree to stand up for him at his wedding." He nodded, seeming pleased with himself.

Charlotte stared at the sheriff. Nothing he said made

any sense. Safe with Lother? She shuddered. "Are you saying Lother thinks I've been kidnapped?"

"Good thing he saw your predicament."

"But I went of my own free will."

The sheriff stopped the car and faced her. "Didn't you just ask me for help?"

"I need someplace to stay until Harry sends for me." Her eyes stung with embarrassment as she prepared to beg. "I thought I could stay with you and your sister." She hated the desperate tone of her voice, but truth was, she had quickly dispensed with her pride about the time she walked off the train platform. "I could scrub up after the prisoners for you."

Sheriff Mack shook his head. "No can do. If I take you back, I'll turn you over to Lother. It's my duty." He patted Charlotte's hand. "Now don't you fret none. Many a young lady has been nervous on her wedding day. It's perfectly normal. But once it's done, you'll feel better."

Anger and disgust raged inside her at the way these men decided her future with absolutely no regard for her wishes. "I would not marry Lother if he was the last man on earth." She tipped her head toward Kody. "This man is the only one who has had the decency to offer to help."

Sheriff Mack looked uncomfortable. "Now, Miss Charlotte, no need to get all high and mighty on me."

"He's done nothing wrong. Release him at once."

"Now wait one cotton-pickin' minute."

"Now." She tilted her head toward Kody, indicating she wanted him released.

"You're making a mighty big mistake."

But Charlotte would not relent.

Muttering dark predictions about her future, Sheriff Mack took the handcuffs off Kody. "You're free to go."

Charlotte stepped out of the car as Kody backed away. He remained motionless as Sheriff Mack untied the horses. When Kody made no move to take the reins, Charlotte reached for them.

Sheriff Mack looked at her a moment, then scrunched up his lips on one side and made a sound of disgust. "Lother isn't going to be happy about this."

She didn't answer, although her brain burned with angry retorts. *Too bad about Lother. That's your problem, not mine. Next time you should...* There would be no next time for her. She intended to seek refuge with Kody's parents in Favor. What choice did she have? No one else offered sanctuary. *God, help me.*

She turned her head away as the dust whipped up around the departing vehicle.

Only after the gray cloud abated did Kody turn and in one smooth move, leap onto Sam's back. "Let's get out of here," he muttered as he urged Sam into a run.

Charlotte climbed onto the mare's back and kicked her sides, trying to catch Kody, but it seemed the mare's fastest pace was a bone-shuddering trot that practically shook Charlotte from her back. After several futile attempts to get the animal to gallop, Charlotte settled back into a slow walk as Kody and Sam disappeared over a hill. The puffs of dust swirling from Sam's hooves gave her direction.

Why would no one help her? *I wouldn't be a burden. I'd make them glad they'd taken me in.* But her silent arguments were a waste of time. She had to think about the future. *My times are in Your hands.* God had promised. He would not fail her.

With each exhalation she let out fear and disappointment. With every indrawn breath, she pulled assurance and peace into her heart. Certainly she couldn't understand why He would choose to send help in the form of a stranger and a half-breed. But she would not fear. She would trust. She'd allow Kody to take her to his parents, but she'd be on guard at all times to make sure she got there safely.

Courage and determination returned before she caught up to him twenty minutes later.

He lounged in the shade of a ragged rock, his legs outstretched, his head tipped back and his hat pulled over his eyes.

She dismounted, swaying a little with lightheadedness.

"Not used to riding?" Kody murmured.

How could he see with his hat pulled down? "I ride fine." It wasn't riding that made her weak but lack of food. Yesterday she'd eaten the last dry biscuit.

He sat up so quickly she jerked back, alarm skittering across the surface of her skin, eliciting goose bumps. She grabbed the saddle horn, preparing to mount up again and ride away if he threatened her. She sighed with defeat. He could probably outrun the mare on foot. She would have to find another way of protecting herself. Her mind blanked, her blood pooled in a cold puddle in the pit of her stomach as she admitted her defenselessness. In the middle of open country. In the company of a stranger. *God is with me. I will not fear.* Despite her assurance of God's protection, her mouth remained dry.

But Kody only pushed his hat back to study her.

She took a good hard look at him, hoping for something to ease her fears. Eyes blacker than coal. No surprise. Skin bronzed. Again, no surprise. But the kind gleam in his eyes caught her off guard. One thing her mother had said repeatedly before her death, "Charlotte, never judge a man by his looks. Always seek below the surface." Of course, even the look in his eyes revealed nothing of what lay beneath. Nevertheless, it eased her fear.

"You could have changed your mind back there."

She shuddered. "And go to Lother? I'd sooner be tied out in the sun and left to bake."

Kody's black eyes bored into her gaze.

The skin on her cheeks tightened as she realized she'd blurted out one of the ways Indians supposedly used to torture captives.

He nodded. "So be it." He strode over to Sam and dug into one of his packs.

Relieved to be free of his intense look, Charlotte sucked in the hot, dusty air and coughed.

"Here." He handed her a canteen. "It will have to last us the day, so ration yourself."

"Thank you." She tipped her head back and let the water fill her mouth, kept it there, savoring the relief to her parched tongue and throat before she swallowed. She allowed herself one more mouthful, then screwed the top back on and held the canteen toward Kody.

"It's yours. Hang it from your saddle."

"Thanks."

"Hold out your hand."

She hesitated as a spidery sensation crept up her spine. Was he trying to trick her? Take advantage of her?

"Look, you're going to have to trust me."

Trust him? No. She couldn't even trust her brother, her only living relative. She wasn't sure she would ever trust anyone again. Except God, of course.

Kody made an impatient sound. "Take it or leave it." He began to withdraw his hand.

She realized she'd made him angry and understood it made her even more vulnerable, so she opened her palm to him, keeping a careful distance between their hands.

Raisins dribbled into her hand.

Raisins? She'd expected… She didn't know what, but not this. Why had God chosen such an unusual way to satisfy her hunger? Her mouth watered in anticipation of the waiting treat and she decided to deal with her hunger first and her questions later.

"Thank you." Her voice rose in a squeak.

He grunted acknowledgment and swung up on Sam. "Best keep moving."

As Charlotte nibbled the raisins, savoring them one at a time, her thoughts returned to doubts about her decision. She blinked back tears. It wasn't her fault she'd been left with little choice but to ride across the country with a stranger. But who was she to blame? Lother? Now that he knew her to be alone, she would never be safe back at the farm. No one in Big Rock offered her shelter. Did they not believe in Christian charity? And what about Harry? He had promised to care for her always. Of course, he hadn't stopped caring. Things just hadn't panned out yet. They'd soon be together again as they should be. Perhaps she should blame Nellie with her whining and complaining. The last few weeks, it seemed no matter how hard she tried, Charlotte could not please her sister-in-law. But then many people, men and woman alike, found the continued drought more than they could bear. The drought? Surely that accounted for some of her problems? But who sent the rains or withheld them? God. Ultimately blaming anyone meant blaming God and she couldn't do that. She trusted Him, depended on His continuing care to see her safely returned to Harry's home. Relieved to have settled the matter, she glanced about her, seeing vaguely familiar landmarks. "We'll never make Favor by nightfall."

"Nope."

She glanced at him. He seemed unconcerned, but then, he was probably used to sleeping on the trail. The very thought filled her with fresh alarm. "Where will we spend the night?"

"With friends of mine." Kody slowed Sam so he could ride at her side. "Seems you have no choice but to accept hospitality where you can find it."

He'd pinpointed her hard feelings. She had no choice. She'd had none when her mother died and Harry became her sole guardian. She'd had none when Harry sent her to the Applebys, nor when he left her behind a few days ago. She had little choice now. She suddenly laughed. She didn't need to trust people to help her. "God will take care of me wherever we spend the night."

He turned in his saddle to give her a hard look. "Seems you're depending on me to help do God's work. Does that make me an instrument of God's using?" He paused but before she could answer, he continued, "Or does it make me an accidental encounter?"

She wondered if he mocked her faith. Or were his questions sincere? "Do you have cause to wonder which you are?"

"You better believe I have."

"And what would it be, if you don't mind my asking?"

Kody brought Sam to a stop and turned to stare at her.

Charlotte decided he looked surprised and disbelieving at the same time.

He rolled up his sleeve and pointed to his arm. "I'm sure you've noticed the color of my skin." He tugged at one braid. "And the color of my hair."

Indeed she had. And yes, she shrank back, knowing his heritage, but she trusted God to keep her safe. And whether or not He used a half-breed to serve His purposes, she would continue to trust Him. Besides, did God care about the color of a man's skin?

She turned to look Kody full in the face. "Doesn't the Scripture say there is no difference between people?"

"Words mean nothing to most people." He jerked forward and resumed their journey.

The sun beat down with unrelenting persistence. An hour or so later, Kody pulled off the road into the meager shelter of some trees. "We'll let the horses rest out of the sun for a while."

Charlotte kept her gaze on the trail ahead. She'd prefer to keep moving, the sooner to reach safety, but she understood the wisdom of giving the horses a break from the heat.

He settled down in the shade of a tree and pulled his hat over his face.

Slowly, Charlotte got down from her horse. She found a tree as far from Kody as she could and sank to the heated ground, trying unsuccessfully to pull both shoulders into the shade. The blazing sun sucked oxygen from the air. Lethargy seeped into her bones. She blinked, trying to keep her eyes open, knowing she'd be easy prey if she allowed herself to fall asleep. But sleep continued to threaten. Unwilling to succumb, she pushed to her feet and moved around slowly to keep herself awake. She leaned against a tree and stared across the parched fields.

"Get up real slow." A rough voice spoke behind her.

Charlotte stiffened and sucked in a gulp of oven-hot air. Slowly she turned. She couldn't see the speaker and edged a little to the right to see past the mare grazing placidly between her and Kody. What she saw made her blood jolt to her heart in a pounding pulse—two men, unshaven and unkempt, looking as appealing as last week's slop. One aimed a small handgun at Kody.

Kody folded his legs under him and rose in one slow movement.

"Hands above your head and don't try no funny stuff."

The shorter man, a menacing sneer slashing his face, held the gun. The taller man had a narrow face and beady eyes, reminding Charlotte of a rat. She pushed her fears to one side and tried to think what she should do.

"Looks like a good pair of boots. Them and the horses will come in mighty handy, don't ya think, Shorty?"

Charlotte sent up a prayer for help and then her brain kicked into gear. It seemed they hadn't noticed her. If she kept quiet, maybe they wouldn't. She glanced around, saw a boulder several feet away. If she hid behind it and didn't make a sound…

But what would happen to Kody? He'd been kind enough to rescue her. So far, he'd been nothing but a gentleman. She had lingering doubts about her safety with him, but she had no such doubts about these two. She would *not* be safe with them. And she couldn't imagine they'd have any compunction about killing Kody. She could run and hide, or—she gulped—she could do something to help. She fought the fear racing up her limbs and setting her teeth to chattering and made up her mind. *God, help me.*

Silently, as slow as a shadow following the sun, crouching low, she moved away from the shelter of the tree and edged toward the mare. She reached the horse just as Kody pulled off his first boot, and she cautiously removed Harry's rifle. Thankfully the placid mare paid no attention to her.

Charlotte put the rifle to her shoulder and tried to think how to be more convincing with this pair than she had been with Kody. She took a deep breath to stop the gun from wavering in her hands, forced a deep scowl to her face. She feared her eyes were wide with fright and concentrated on narrowing them. Only then did she step out from behind the mare.

"Drop your gun." She did her best to sound menacing. In truth, she was surprised any words escaped. It felt as if someone had tried to padlock her throat shut.

They stared at her in disbelief. "Where'd you come from?"

"God sent me."

The pair glanced heavenward and shuffled backward like they feared the wrath of God. She smiled at their frightened look and jerked the rifle upward slightly in what she hoped was a scary gesture. "Drop the gun."

"Do as she says," Ratface said.

"I am." Shorty tossed the gun aside.

Kody dived for it and turned it on the pair. "Best be on your way," he said.

Lifting their feet high as if afraid they might step on something, the two beat it down the road, glancing over their shoulders every few steps to see if anyone—or perhaps anything—followed them.

Charlotte moved to Kody's side and they kept both guns aimed toward the fleeing men until they disappeared from sight.

Only then did Charlotte let the heavy rifle drop. She leaned over and gasped for air.

Kody laughed. It started as a little burst of what Charlotte took for relief, then grew steadily to a deep belly laugh.

She shot him a look of disbelief. She saw no humor in the situation. They'd just been threatened by two men who surely would have had taken more than their belongings. She shuddered to think of what they might have done to her. And Kody. Surely he'd been aware of the danger. How could he laugh?

Kody sobered as she scowled at him, although his eyes continued to brim with amusement and his smile seemed as wide as a door. "They really thought you dropped out of heaven. Scared them good. And to think that old rifle has no ammo." He chuckled some more. "Apart from your bravado."

"I fail to see what's so funny." She pulled herself onto the mare's back. "I intend to ride as far and as fast from those two as I can."

Kody leaped to Sam's back. "Did you see the look on their faces as they ran off? As if they expected a whole flock of avenging angels to descend?" He laughed again.

Charlotte tried to urge the mare into a gallop. She only wanted a safe place with no more threatening men. No more wondering what lay around the next corner. But the mare had one gait and would not be pushed. Charlotte sighed and stopped fighting the horse.

Kody stayed at her side as if a short halter rope connected the two horses. His continued chuckling annoyed her almost as much as did the fact that she felt safer with him there.

"You saved us."

He tried, she guessed, to persuade her to see the humor in something she found too frightening to be amusing. "God saved us. I prayed. He answered. It's that simple."

"Didn't see God holding the empty rifle. Only saw you, though I'm thinking those two drifters saw more."

She turned to study him. Saw he teased, but his words had triggered an idea. "Maybe they did see something more. Maybe God sent angels to surround us and only those two men saw them. Like that story in the Bible." The idea made her feel better and she smiled.

"Could be your miracle." He grinned at her.

"I believe it is." For a moment she let herself forget she'd only just met this man and let her heart open a crack to enjoy a shared laugh.

But just for a moment. She hadn't forgotten her precarious state—riding across the dried-out prairie with a stranger, confronting dangers on the trail, facing a fearful, uncertain future. It provided little reason for amusement.

They rode on, for the most part in silence. The lonely days of worry, too little food, too little water and now a long ride took their toll. Charlotte grew weary, barely able to stay awake. She swayed in the saddle.

Kody grabbed her shoulder to stop her from falling. "Hang on. Just a little farther."

She could barely keep her eyes open. Her head kept falling to her chest. Kody stayed close to her side, steadying her several times.

"We're here," Kody said.

She realized they'd stopped at a picket fence before a low white house. "Where's here?" Her words felt stiff on her tongue.

"Where we will spend the night."

A robust-looking woman opened the door, drying her hands on a towel. "Claude, we have visitors." She shaded her eyes and studied Kody and Charlotte. A tall man joined her at the doorway.

Suddenly the woman's face broke into a huge smile. "Well, I'll be. It's Kody Douglas." She rushed down the pathway.

Charlotte saw it in fractured glimpses through eyelids refusing to open more than a crack. She felt Kody jump to the ground, felt his steadying hands on her arm as he introduced his friends as Ethel and Claude. She tried to remember how to dismount, but her limbs refused to obey her brain.

Kody lifted her from the saddle and eased her to her feet. When her legs buckled, he scooped her into his arms and headed for the door.

"I can walk."

"Not so good right now,"

"Put me down." Her protest was limp. "I need to get my things."

"I'll get them."

She didn't want to be a bother. She knew how people resented it.

"Stop fighting and let someone do for you for a change.

She ceased her weak struggles. He didn't sound annoyed at having to "do" for her. His arms tightened around her as he stepped over the threshold. He lowered her into a chair, pausing to murmur, "You saved my life. I guess that means I'm allowed to do things for you."

She opened her eyes and stared at him.

He hovered at her side, making sure she wasn't going

to tip over, then slowly straightened, his dark gaze never leaving her face. She couldn't break away from his look.

"I'll get you something to drink and arrange for our accommodation."

She hadn't done anything to earn his favor except point a useless gun at two cowardly men and trust God to do the rest. But this appreciation, this attentive care to her needs, caught her off guard. The way it made her feel valued snuck right past her anger and fear, side-stepped the feeling she must make herself useful and settled down beside her heart like it meant to stay.

But it couldn't be.

She rested her elbows on the table and held her chin in her upturned palms, and despite the sluggishness of her sleep-hungry brain, she faced the hard, undeniable truth. Kody said he knew who he was—a half-breed. And she knew well who she was—a charity case who must prove her worth to keep from being tossed out on her ear.

It had been much too easy for Harry to leave her behind. She'd been getting complacent. Not working as hard as she should. When she rejoined them she would work doubly hard to make sure she had a place to live.

Chapter Five

The following afternoon, Kody reined Sam in at the fork in the road. If he kept pushing they could reach Favor before nightfall.

He glanced down the narrower road. Four years ago he'd said his final goodbye to what lay down there, promising himself and others he would never return. But all his noble intentions were powerless to stop him from turning aside, away from town and in the wrong direction.

Charlotte followed meekly. He already noticed she automatically did as told. In fact, she practically leaped to comply with the barest suggestion and she seemed to think she had to help with every chore. This morning she'd insisted on saddling her own horse.

He laughed, remembering how the saddle kept rolling under the mare's belly.

"What's so funny?" she demanded.

"Just thinking."

"Huh." She sounded suspicious.

Could be because he often and unexpectedly laughed as he recalled some of her little exploits. Like chasing off those two scoundrels yesterday. Just recollecting that made him laugh again. Come to think of it, he'd laughed more in the past two days than in the past two years. Or longer. Only two days ago he'd settled low in his saddle, with nothing on his mind but getting to Canada. Now his whole life had turned around.

He sobered. The sooner he returned to his original plans, the better. But seeing as he'd come this far, he might as well take one more detour. Somewhere deep inside his brain, a mocking voice called, *You're only making excuses and mighty glad you are of them, too.*

"You're laughing at me again, I suppose." She didn't sound overjoyed.

Glad of the diversion from his unwanted thoughts, his grin returned. "I gotta admit it was a lot of fun watching you try and saddle that old thing you're riding."

"I could've figured it out myself if you'd given me a chance."

He chuckled softly. "Thought you were anxious to get to Favor."

"You know I am now I have no choice, but I only came along with you because you pushed me to."

He snorted. What a stubborn woman. Several times she'd blamed him for making her leave that dried-out old house. "Don't I recall you stomping off down the road ahead of me?"

"Only 'cause you made it plain you planned to be a pain in the neck if I tried to stay."

He glanced over. She gave him a look full of balky defiance.

He laughed. "You and that mare make a good pair."

She blinked with surprise and then narrowed her eyes. "What's that supposed to mean?"

"That old mare picks her own pace and ain't about to let anyone convince her to change it. Seems you do same."

They plodded on. Sam had stopped trying to pick up the pace, accepting the mare's slower one. Kody itched to ride faster. The sooner he delivered Charlotte to his parents, the sooner he would turn around and head north.

Yeah? So why are you riding down this trail?

Did God have a hand in bringing him back?

"You implying I'm slow?"

"No, ma'am, not in the least." He restrained the laughter tickling his throat and turned to grin at her.

She gave him a look fit to slice bread. "You can stop staring now. I know you're meaning I'm stubborn. But you're wrong. I'm not stubborn. In fact, quite the opposite."

He shook his head. "Can't think what's the opposite of stubborn. Compliant?"

"Submissive." She spoke matter-of-factly. "Why are we riding this direction? I thought Favor lay down the other road."

He'd wondered how long it would take her to voice an objection. Seemed she could only shake the compliant attitude when pushed and pushed hard. And going the wrong direction was a hard push.

"We'll stay with friends of mine tonight. Safer than being on the road after dark. 'Course if not for that stubborn thing under you, we might have a chance of getting to Favor before nightfall. But…" He shrugged.

Charlotte patted the mare's neck. "She's faithful and gentle. Seems she should get a little credit for that."

Kody wondered if she thought the same of herself. He didn't know this Harry fellow and didn't want to. Far as he was concerned any man who rode off and left his sister to manage on her own ranked lower than worm juice. They'd talked some as they rode. When he learned she was only eighteen, he teased her about being young.

Upon getting him to confess to being twenty-one, she laughed. "Indeed, you are so aged."

He hadn't told her he felt too old for his years and yet not wise enough. He held on to the hope Canada would give him the distance to deal with both problems.

His destination lay around the next bend in the road. He reined in his horse and lounged in the saddle as if he had nothing better to do than stare out at the rolling hills. Toward Favor they would enter the irrigated area, which made the town prosperous even in the drought. A dam built earlier in the century ensured good crops. "You can always find work in the hills," people said, meaning both the irrigated flats and the hills surrounding the town, which supported a brick factory and a sugar-beet factory. Ranchers struggled a bit because of the low price for beef, but the hills with their copses of trees provided decent enough grazing.

"What are you waiting for?" Charlotte asked.

"Just looking around."

She settled back, uttering not one word of complaint, which didn't surprise him. She had not complained once about the discomforts of the trail even though she'd hardly been able to walk when they stopped for a noon break.

He supposed he should prepare her for what lay ahead. "My friends, who we'll spend the night with, are Indians, the Eaglefeathers. They live on a reservation."

She nodded. "Do they like it?"

He blinked. He'd expected protest, or hastily disguised shock. "Like what?"

"Living on the reservation."

"They don't have much choice."

"No choice about living there, maybe. But don't they have a choice about whether or not they like it?"

He had the feeling she wasn't just curious about his friends. More like exploring how other people dealt with events in their lives helped her find a way to deal with hers. And thinking that made him want to prod her. Force her to look at her own situation with both eyes wide-open, rather than through the filter of how others reacted.

"I think they have decided to make the best of it. Which doesn't mean they are sitting around waiting for life to happen to them."

He saw a flash of acknowledgment in her eyes and knew his words struck pay dirt.

"Is that what you think I'm doing? Sitting around waiting for something to happen?" Her soft words gave away little of her feelings, though he wondered if she could be as unaffected as she tried to appear. She hadn't been quick enough to stop the little gasp of surprise when she realized what he meant.

"You were just sitting in that empty house."

"I'm not anymore."

"Nope. But I get the feeling you're only planning to move the place where you sit and wait for Harry to invite you back into his family."

She looked away, letting her gaze follow the distant hills. "Sometimes the alternatives aren't too appealing."

He thought of Lother and had to agree.

She clucked the old mare into slow-motion forward. "Let's go."

He hesitated. He should probably have said more about where they were going. But then, what could he say? Some things could not be shared. Or admitted. No one must know his secret.

He should call her back. Return to the main road. Forget this little side trip. But he could not deny himself the chance to see how things were. He knew they would be fine, but once he saw, he could ride north again with a clear conscience.

Finally he reined in Sam behind Charlotte and the plodding mare.

From this direction, they reached the Eaglefeather home before the other homes on the reservation.

The low shack looked weary and worn since he'd last seen it, the unpainted wood weathered to gray. One lone, spindly tree struggled to survive beside the house. Two boxes sat against one wall. Kody knew they served as stools. A skitter of dust crossed the bare yard. The yard would have been swept that morning, every morning, in fact. A fire pit glowed in the center of the yard. He shifted his gaze away from the meager living quarters, but what he saw farther along didn't ease his sense that the Eaglefeathers, like many on reservations, struggled to eke out an existence. A thin horse stood in a tiny corral. A small garden struggled against the oppressive heat.

"Hello," he called.

John ducked out of the low house and squinted into the light. "Kody, my friend. Long time no see."

Kody dropped to the ground and crossed to grasp John's forearm as they squeezed each other's arms in greeting. John wore a faded red shirt and gray trousers, his hair braided much the same as Kody's.

"My friend," said Kody, "I have missed you."

"And I you."

And then Morning stepped from the house. She had dusky, flawless skin and wore a sandy-brown dress that would have been shapeless on another woman, but tied at her waist, it emphasized this woman's willowy frame.

She rushed to Kody's side. "It is good to see you."

Kody's gaze slipped past the pair to the open doorway. "Where is she?"

Morning turned and called softly. "Star, come and greet a friend."

A dark-haired child appeared in the doorway.

Kody stared. "She's grown."

"She's four years old now." Morning's voice held a touch of humor.

"She's beautiful." Kody couldn't take his eyes off her.

Morning held out her hand and the child hobbled toward her.

Kody's response was so sudden, so intense, it took his breath away. His gut twisted like he'd eaten something tainted. He took a step toward the child. John's hand on his arm stopped him. He forced air into wooden lungs.

"Her foot." He managed to grate the words past clenched teeth. He hadn't seen her since she was a baby. Had never seen her try to walk.

"It has always been crooked," John explained in low tones so the child wouldn't hear. "We hoped it would get better when she started to walk. You can see it hasn't."

Kody had noticed when she was tiny that her foot curled but he figured it was normal and as she grew it would straighten.

Star reached Morning and took her hand. "Momma?"

Her sweet, innocent voice grabbed Kody by the throat. He should have thought about this more. But he would never have guessed how it affected him to see Star again.

"Star, this is our good friend, Kody Douglas. Say hello."

"Hello, Mr. Kody Douglas."

Kody knelt on rubbery knees, his heart ready to burst from his chest with emotions so totally unfamiliar and unexpected he had no idea how to contain them or tame them.

"Hello, Miss Star. I'm pleased to see you." He touched her shoulder, let his hand linger for a moment, but as the ache inside him grew, he pulled his hand back and put two more inches between them. Immediately he changed his mind and leaned closer. This child had dark eyes, laced through and through with golden highlights. Unusual in an Indian. He supposed others noticed it, too.

"We knew you would return." John's voice pulled him back to reality.

He pushed to his feet. "I didn't intend to." He remembered Charlotte. She stood at the mare's side, watching with narrowed eyes.

A tremor snaked across his skin. She couldn't have guessed the truth. "This is Miss Charlotte Porter. I'm taking her to my folks."

The Eaglefeathers welcomed Charlotte. John brought two chairs from the house and insisted they sit while he added bits of wood to the fire. Morning hustled about preparing something to eat. Charlotte followed Morning, begging to be allowed to help, until Morning gave her the job of frying bannock.

Star settled on the ground nearby, playing with a corncob doll.

"How are your folks?" John asked.

"Haven't heard from them since I left."

John and Morning exchanged looks.

"Have not seen them in some time." John chased away a fly.

"Don't they still come out here for Bible lessons?" His attention clung to the child, happily playing.

"Leland got sick. He could not come."

Kody pulled his gaze to John. "Sick?" He couldn't remember Pa ever being sick.

John shrugged. "Probably fine now."

Morning and Charlotte passed around the simple food. The stew had no meat. Kody wondered what happened to the government's promise to provide beef. He took a closer look around, noted how thin the material in John's shirt was, the color faded to pink in many spots. Morning's dress seemed to be crafted from material not meant for a garment. Even Star's little dress showed signs of being rather worn.

Purple shadows filled the hollows. A golden sun hovered at the horizon.

"Another beautiful day gone." John's low voice filled with pleasure. "Another day of God's goodness. And now we have the pleasure of Kody and Miss Charlotte's company."

Kody nodded, glad the drought and depression hadn't affected his friend's faith. Neither John nor Morning would presume to question Charlotte about how she and Kody met. And Charlotte didn't seem about to explain. That left Kody and he sketched the details.

"God has a plan for you," Morning said when he finished.

Charlotte looked startled.

Morning turned to Kody. "And you, too, my friend. He has brought you together for His purpose."

Kody and Charlotte looked at each other. They met by accident, each of them compelled to change their plans because of the other. He figured neither saw it as a blessing. Charlotte flashed a quick smile filled with triumph, then ducked her head. Kody understood Morning's simple faith echoed her own.

He would not express his doubts to Morning. The good woman had been so hospitable. It would be downright rude to argue with her.

The sun flashed its last light in dying pinks, and then the sky turned the color of water where the fishing was best, then indigo. In a few minutes the only light came from the fire, closing them in. The best time for sharing secrets, admitting intimate details that remained hidden in the light of day.

Only, Kody didn't intend to let any secrets pour forth.

At least not until Charlotte slept soundly out of earshot.

Morning rose gracefully. "Come, Miss Charlotte. I will show you where you can sleep." She scooped up the drowsy Star and carried her inside.

Kody and John sat in companionable silence, listening to the rustle of the women and child preparing for bed. Kody waited until they grew quiet. He waited some longer, but knowing Charlotte must be exhausted after riding all day, he figured she'd fall asleep as soon as her bones settled.

He turned to John and spoke softly yet urgently. "How is she? Really. Do the others accept her?"

"Everyone knows she isn't our child. And her eyes are light. They wonder who she is. They ask questions. But no one says anything bad."

"No one has guessed she's my child?"

"No one has said that's what they think. I see them whispering behind their hands, though."

"They must never know."

John sat in silence for some time. Kody knew he had more to say on the subject. He could keep talking, trying to keep John from speaking his piece. It would be futile in the end. John would sit quietly, nonjudgmental, until Kody grew silent, then say what was on his mind. So Kody waited. Might as well get it over with.

"What do you have to hide?" John's soft voice gave away nothing, but Kody knew his friend did not approve of his choice, although he would never come right out and say so.

"I don't fit in the white world or the Indian one. I don't want that for Star. I want her raised to belong here."

"We love her as our own."

That went without saying, so Kody didn't bother responding. Instead, he asked, "What about her foot? Has a doctor looked at it?"

John poked at the fire for a few minutes, sending sparks into the air. Finally he sat back. "I try once to take her to doctor in Favor. Big fat nurse chase me away. 'No Indians allowed,' she say. Government send doctor to reservation. I take Star to him. He look at foot and say only we can do nothing. 'Be satisfied she happy.'"

Kody gave a long sigh. She'd already borne the brunt of prejudice, then. Weariness filled his bones. He knew he couldn't expect anything more. Not many people were like Ma and Pa, who didn't care about Kody's heritage.

"So there's absolutely nothing you can do?"

"One thing. Doctor say there are special shoes. They cost much money."

Kody nodded. "I will get her those shoes."

"And then you will be gone again?"

"It is for the best."

John grunted. "For you?"

The question skidded along Kody's nerves. It was for Star, of course. She was better off without him. "She can't belong to two worlds. It doesn't work. Take it from someone who knows."

John grunted again but didn't speak. Just when Kody decided he didn't intend to, John murmured, "You are man with much war inside your head."

It was Kody's turn to grunt. John might have a point but this was not about his own needs. He had to do what he thought best for Star.

Chapter Six

The next morning, Charlotte thanked Morning and John for their hospitality. They were a kind couple, generous Christians willing to share what little they had. And Star was a sweet child, loved and cherished by them. She'd brought her cornhusk doll to Charlotte and told her about her doll being lost and found again. Charlotte didn't know if the story was imaginary or real, but she heard the underlying themes of loss and uncertainty. Perhaps common enough in a child, but poignantly more real in this little girl.

It was about more than she could do to keep from shooting an accusing look at Kody.

She restrained her confrontation until they rode away from the Eaglefeather home, until they both turned and waved for the last time. Then, as they rounded a bend blocking them from sight, she turned on him. "I overheard your conversation last night."

Shock widened his eyes, revealed itself on his face.

She didn't give him a chance to offer useless explanations. "I can't believe you would deny your own daughter."

His face turned into an expressionless mask. "I want your promise to never reveal this secret."

She shook her head. "How can you treat her like this? Is it because she's crippled? I heard John say nothing could be done. Are you ashamed of her?"

He allowed Sam to pick up the pace so he rode several feet in front of her, making further conversation impossible.

But Charlotte's anger had been building throughout the night and this morning as they drank tea and ate breakfast. She kicked the black mare. "Come on, Blackie, hurry up."

Kody snorted and glanced over his shoulder. "Since when did the old thing have a name?"

"Since right now. Even an animal deserves recognition." She managed to narrow the distance between them. "Do you have any idea how that child will feel when she finds out her father abandoned her? And where is her mother?"

"Her mother died shortly after her birth."

"I'm sorry." So Kody was Star's only parent. He needed to give that some importance in his plans. "It's simply not fair to ride off and leave someone behind like you're doing."

He reined in Sam and faced her. "I can never figure out if you mean yourself when you say such things."

"Me? This isn't about me. It's about Star. And you."

"Is it? Are you sure? Aren't you the least bit angry with Harry for leaving you behind?"

"Of course I'm upset." Harry had promised Charlotte would always have a home with him—a promise he seemed to forget on occasion. "I've done my best to always be pleasing and obedient." She swallowed back the torrent of words rushing from her memories of how she'd bent over backward trying to help and please. It hadn't seemed to make a difference in the long run. She shifted her thoughts to the most promising one—Mother's admonitions to be quick to obey, eager to help, easy to get along with. "That way," Mother said, "Harry will always be glad to provide you a home." When she rejoined Harry, Charlotte vowed he would never have cause to dismiss her.

Kody lifted his eyebrows and waited as if expecting more explanation, which, she decided, he wouldn't be getting.

"You don't have to walk away. You can try and change things. I envy you your choices."

"What's stopping you from making choices? You're white and free."

"You're male and free. That gives you choices I'm not allowed. Harry and his family are my only relatives."

He snorted. "Why don't you grow up and admit you're old enough to move on? Forget Harry. It seems he hasn't any trouble forgetting you."

Anger, so gut level and undeniable, roared through her like a duster with no barrier to break the wind. It sucked at her defenses, left her weak with fear and uncertainty. "He's not forgotten. I'll be joining him soon." She said it out of habit and desperation, unable to contemplate an alternative. But Kody's words forced her to face the unwelcome truth. Harry had left her behind. He'd easily abandoned her. Where had she failed? Was God really protecting her? Working out things for her good? Questions with no answers, and she didn't care one bit for Kody constantly poking at this sore spot.

She sucked in hot, dusty air. She wouldn't let Kody

make this about her. "Sooner or later Star will realize Morning and John aren't her parents. John said himself people know she isn't their daughter. After all, a baby doesn't appear without some warning. And she had those light eyes. Was her mother white?"

"Half-breed like me."

"Can you imagine the questions and doubts Star will have when she figures out the truth? Where is my father? Why doesn't he care about me? What did I do wrong? As if a baby could be responsible for what an adult does. Poor little girl." She'd never expressed such vehement feelings before. Good little Charlotte. Always subservient. Always obedient and quiet, exactly like her mother said. Where did all this rage come from? She hardly recognized herself as she rushed on, unable to stem the frenzy of anger-driven words. "Doesn't she have enough to deal with—her mixed heritage, her crippled foot—without dealing with abandonment?" Her fury spent, she grew silent.

Kody pulled Sam to a halt, blocking Blackie's progress.

"She is better off on a reservation than with me. She will be accepted as an Indian. She would never be accepted as a half-breed in a white world. I forbid you to mention again that I am her father."

She sniffed disdainfully.

He continued to block her escape. "Your word."

She struggled with the instinct to comply. Good Charlotte always agreed. Readily. Quickly. Without argument. But good Charlotte seemed to have gone into hiding. "I will agree to no such thing."

He reached for the bridle, but she saw his intent to

hold her there until she gave in and jerked Blackie to one side, laughing at the surprise on Kody's face.

He lunged after her, but slow-moving Blackie astonished them both by sidestepping out of his reach.

He moved Sam after her. "I will not allow you to cause my daughter—" He stopped. "I will not allow you to cause Star problems. Like you say, she has enough already."

"As you kindly pointed out, I know what it's like to be abandoned. This isn't the first time I've experienced it. And I have to say it doesn't get easier even when you get older. If there is anything I can say to make you care about Star…"

"I care about her," he shouted. "Can't you see that? Leaving her is the hardest thing I've ever done, but it's for her good."

She turned and faced him. "Then I guess someone needs to prove to you it isn't the best thing for her."

He laughed mirthlessly. "Ought to be quite a challenge." He looked at her steadily as if measuring and assessing, then he flicked the reins and Sam trotted down the road leaving Blackie and Charlotte to suck in his dust.

Charlotte settled into her slower pace. She'd tried. She could only pray Kody would think about her words. That someone would convince him he was wrong.

Too bad he planned to head to Canada as soon as he was rid of her. If they had some time together, she might be the one to do it.

She watched him, relaxed in the saddle, his braids swinging across his shoulders. Even from the back she read his defiance. She figured he challenged the world. No doubt he'd faced prejudice. But running hardly seemed the answer, especially when he had a sweet little daughter to keep him here.

Thinking of him leaving pinched her stomach as if a pin had come open and jabbed in her gut. He was the only person she knew. Everything else familiar and safe had been taken from her.

She laughed softly. Only two days ago she hadn't felt the least bit safe with him. Now she did. She'd miss Kody when he left, and acknowledging it gave her a vacant sensation—a different sort of feeling than the one of the past week as she struggled with missing Harry.

But how she felt didn't matter. She had until they reached Favor to convince him to be a father to little Star.

She nudged Blackie to go faster so she rode at Kody's side. He glanced at her as she jogged up to him. His eyes narrowed with annoyance and probably a liberal dose of anger. She could hardly expect to win him over if he was mad. So she smiled and said nothing. She'd wait. For now. Just not long. Every step brought them closer to Favor, where he would deliver her to his parents and turn back north.

After a few minutes, he sighed, and relaxed into his saddle.

Did he think she'd forgotten the whole thing? Strangely enough, not many days ago she would have, rather than risk offending someone. But she had nothing to lose in this situation. And Star did. *Lord, guide me. Give me words that will change his mind.*

Suddenly he grabbed her horse and turned from the trail.

"What do you think—"

"Shh." The urgency in his voice filled her with alarm,

and she kicked Blackie to follow Sam into the cluster of trees.

"Get down," he whispered, catching her before her feet hit the ground and rushing her behind some rocks.

He pulled off his hat and slowly peered out. Then he motioned her to keep low and look. She edged over until she glimpsed around the rocks. They were a few yards from joining the main road, and two men slouching on horses headed toward Favor.

She dropped out of sight and sank to the ground. "Ratface and Shorty," she whispered.

"You named them?" He shook his head, no doubt recalling her words that even animals deserved recognition.

She rolled her eyes to indicate it didn't mean the same thing.

He hunkered down beside her. She wasn't fooled by his relaxed posture. She sensed his alert readiness. She glanced to where he'd hastily tied the horses and wished she'd thought to grab Harry's rifle. But she dared not move now and give away their hiding place.

Ratface and Shorty drew closer. She made out their words.

"We're gonna find that Injun and his white squaw, and when we do, we're gonna make them pay."

"Something about that woman don't sit right. Where'd she come from?"

"She was hiding. Probably didn't want anyone to see her with a savage."

Charlotte held her breath and prayed as never before. If the pair turned this direction, heading for the reservation, they would surely see Kody and her. And if they somehow didn't, then John, Morning and Star would be at risk.

Obviously thinking the same thing, Kody leaned forward, preparing to spring into action.

"Let's see what we find in this here town first."

"Something to drink maybe."

"Maybe."

Charlotte's breath eased out as the men continued on the main road.

Their conversation faded, but neither Kody nor Charlotte moved.

Finally Kody rose and edged up so he could see past the rock. "They're gone, but I guess we'll wait here awhile."

"Suits me just fine." She sucked in a few steadying breaths, then chuckled.

"What's so funny?"

"Shorty's still wondering where I came from. Scared him good."

"You hear the rest of what they said?"

She knew what he meant, figured he wanted to hear how she felt about it. "About me being a squaw?" She shrugged. "Silly, scared, evil men. Of course they think evil of others. Did you see the horses they're riding? And the guns? Where do you suppose they got them?"

"Probably stole 'em."

"What if they killed someone?"

"Not much we can do about it."

She sighed. There were far too many things a person couldn't do anything about.

Kody sank to the ground beside her.

There was one thing that could be changed. One thing she might be able to do something about. She prayed again for wisdom to use her words wisely, then began talking as if interested only in passing time. "I was ten when my mother died. Harry is eleven years older than me and as my only living relative, became my guardian. Mother knew she was dying and did her best to prepare me."

Kody shifted so he looked into her face. "Hard to prepare a child for such a thing."

Charlotte smiled. "Mother did a good job. I knew Harry was stuck with me, and it was up to me to make sure he didn't regret it."

"By being compliant?"

For some reason she disliked that word, probably because he said it with such contempt. "By helping and being agreeable."

He nodded. "Compliant. Submissive."

She'd always thought those characteristics highly desirable, but he made them sound less than ashes from yesterday's fire. She wanted to argue. Totally not a Charlotte reaction. She dismissed the desire and continued with her story, intent on her reason for telling of her hurtful past. "Harry married Nellie when I was barely twelve. I tried so hard to please her. But instead, I only seemed to succeed in making her angry." She drew in a deep breath. It still hurt to think of that troubled time. "Finally she insisted Harry find me a position somewhere else. He sent me to work for the Applebys." She tried to keep the bitterness from her voice, tried to stop the memories from hurting. She closed her eyes for a moment. *God, help me say what I want to say without having to live those feelings again.*

She opened her eyes, saw Kody watching her carefully and lowered her gaze. Had he seemed sympathetic, understanding? That might serve her well. She looked at him again. His dark eyes were steady, filled with bottomless concern. Something jolted through her in a rush, like a hot wind blowing away debris, sweeping clean the land. She wanted him to understand, to care about what happened to her. Unable to break from this unexpected sensation, she picked up her story. "The Applebys didn't consider me a part of their family. I served them, then ate my meals alone in the kitchen. I wasn't allowed to visit with either of the girls, who were around my age." She stopped, unable to say anything more, unwilling to share her shame at the rest of what happened. "It was the hardest time of my life. I'd lost my mother and now I might as well have lost my brother. I loved him and needed to be with him. I needed to know someone cared about me."

Kody grunted. "Seems rather cruel to send you away."

She leaned forward, eager to make him see how his case bore similarities. "He had his reasons, just like you think you do. He had a new wife who resented me in her home. I suppose I annoyed her. I know I argued with her a time or two." She'd quickly learned to avoid doing so, though it seemed very little she did pleased Nellie.

"Still, he is your brother and guardian."

She sat back. "And you are Star's father. How is it any different?"

He sighed. "It is. In so many ways. You're just too wrapped up in your own experiences to be willing to admit it."

Charlotte jutted out her jaw. "I suppose you expect her to understand all your very noble reasons?"

"She'll never need to know them because—" he grabbed her hand, resolve blazing from his eyes "—

because she will never know she has a father other than John."

Charlotte pulled her gaze from his demanding stare. She rolled her head back and forth. "She will know someday. It's inevitable. As is the pain of rejection she will feel." She faced him squarely, boldly, determination making her voice hard. "You are the only one who can prevent that." She extricated her fingers from his grasp.

"You know nothing about what she'll have to deal with." He stalked over to the horses, led Blackie to her, helped her up, then jumped on Sam's back and kicked him into a trot.

Charlotte followed at Blackie's slower pace. She'd failed to convince Kody to change his mind. How long before Star realized she wasn't Morning and John's daughter? Before someone pointed out the impossibility and began speculating who her parents really were?

The poor child deserved to be spared the pain of such uncertainty and rejection.

As Blackie plodded along, Charlotte prayed for a miracle. She saw a town in the distance. Favor. *Lord, I've about run out of time.*

Kody reined Sam about and trotted to her side. "We're almost there. You have to promise not to say anything about Star to my ma and pa."

Shock like a cold drenching shivered down her skin. "They don't know they have a granddaughter?"

"No one knows about Star but Morning and John. And my secret is safe with them."

Charlotte stared at him. She realized her mouth hung open and she stiffly closed it. "You can't—"

"No. You can't. You can't say anything. Give me your word."

She narrowed her eyes and met his hard look. Compliant, he'd called her, making it sound like something small and annoying. Well, he was about to find out she could be *non*-compliant. "I will make no such promise." The heat of her words surprised her. She didn't know she had it in her to argue so vehemently.

"Then I won't take you to my parents." He waited, expecting her to give in.

"I never asked you to in the first place." She jerked Blackie away and rode onward.

Muttering, he caught up and rode at her side. "What do you plan to do?"

She had no plan, but she wasn't about to confess it to him. "First, I'll check and see if a letter has arrived from Harry." One couldn't have arrived yet, but she said it airily as if her heart didn't quake with fear of being on her own. As if she didn't shudder at the thought of seeing Ratface and Shorty.

She pushed away her scaredy-cat thoughts. She knew how to work. She'd find someone and throw herself at their mercy. Likely that was what he thought she should do. "You're right. I've been far too compliant and submissive. It's time I stepped out of my safe little world." She sucked in hot, dry air. "I'm sure I can find a position somewhere—chambermaid at a hotel, waitress, nanny…" It sounded easy, but she couldn't imagine walking up to a stranger and asking for work.

He snorted. "I can just see it. You'll jump at the first opportunity someone hands you, even if it's a wolf in sheep's clothing."

She stared straight ahead. Not even in exchange for a promise of rain would she let him see her fear of finding her way in an unfamiliar world. It was his fault she was in this situation. "If you'd just left me waiting for Harry... But no. You had to badger me until I agreed to leave with you, promising I'd be safe with your parents." She might have left out a few details like being out of water, like having Lother expect she'd marry him, like having the sheriff offer her a ride back to Big Rock. She shuddered. The sheriff actually thought she'd be glad to go with him straight into Lother's arms.

Kody rode at her side. "I really don't have a choice." He sounded as exasperated as she felt. "I'll take you to my parents as I promised. What you do after is up to you. But only on one condition—you promise not to tell them about Star."

The horses stopped moving as Kody and Charlotte stared at each other, measuring, challenging, considering.

Charlotte did not want to agree. She understood too well the pain the child would feel when she learned the truth or guessed parts of it. But she couldn't face riding into a strange town on her own. Her inner turmoil raged for several minutes. Then she nodded. "I'll leave it to you to tell them."

"Fine."

She noticed the irrigation ditches and the green fields fed by the life-giving water. If Harry had settled here, life would have been very different for them. Of course, Harry did not have money to buy land in such a prosperous area.

An hour later, they rose into the outskirts of Favor. She leaned forward. A pulse of life and activity radiated from the town. It had been so long since she'd felt the sense of hope the busy town expressed. She smoothed her hair and gave her dress a good study—wrinkled and dirty from wearing it for days and covered with evidence of the dusty trail. Suddenly she wasn't anxious to be seen by others. Not in this condition.

She ducked her head and wished she had a wide-brimmed hat to pull down to hide her face.

Kody sat up straight, facing ahead. "No point in trying to hide. People will look twice to see who is accompanying the savage."

"This has nothing to do with you. I don't want people to see me so dusty and untidy. Besides, how do you know they think that? Seems being the preacher's son would prove otherwise."

"You might think so."

He looked as if a stick had been shoved the length of his spine, so rigid was his posture.

They passed a big house with a tended yard and picket fence. An older man worked on the flower beds. He glanced up at the sound of their passing. Slowly he straightened, pushed his hat back and stared.

"Don't think he's thinking *preacher's son*. Nope. He's thinking *savage*. No doubt wondering if you've been captured."

"Well, I've not." She smiled and waved at the man. "Your flowers are pretty," she called.

The man beamed. "Thank you." He squinted in Kody's direction. "Aren't you Kody Douglas?"

Kody muttered to Charlotte, "You couldn't just ride on? No. You had to call attention to me being here." He touched the brim of his hat. "Hello, Mr. Blake."

Mr. Blake stared after them as Kody urged Sam forward.

"Seems like a nice man," Charlotte said.

"Huh."

"Has he treated you unfairly in the past?" She couldn't explain why she wanted to goad him. Unless to pay him back for how he pushed at her about sitting in the house waiting for Harry. Seemed like a good enough reason. "Is that the school?" She studied a two-story brick building with wide stairs leading to the double front doors. "I went to a school like that back in Kansas. Did you attend there?"

"A few years."

"You didn't finish?"

"Nope."

"This have anything to do with being part Indian?"

"Might have."

"I might as well squeeze the sky for water as try talking to you."

"Yup."

"What are you running from?"

"Who's running? Couldn't go much slower and still call it moving, now could we?"

She sniffed, annoyed beyond patience that he thought he could drag information from her and make a judgment on it, yet remain tight-lipped when it came to sharing anything about himself. "Some are accused of sitting around waiting for life to happen to them. Others seem to think it's superior to run from life."

They sauntered down Main Street past stately brick buildings. Cars and trucks lined the side of the street. A couple of wagons stood in front of a store. She read the sign: Benson's Feed and Mercantile. People hurried along the sidewalk. Another horseback rider pulled his mount to the hitching post in front of the post office. Despite her haughty words to Kody, she knew there would be no letter from Harry yet.

"Isn't that our friends, Ratface and Shorty?" He directed her gaze toward a pair skulking around the back of the bank. "Think they're planning to rob the place?"

Charlotte snorted. "Don't think they have the brains for anything that sophisticated."

The pair disappeared from sight and Charlotte relaxed again.

"This way." He turned down a side street.

She followed. She'd told him so much about herself. She wished she'd learned more about him, but it was too late to prod any more information from him.

She was about to meet her future.

Chapter Seven

Kody took in all the details of the town he hadn't seen in five years. A new store on Main Street. More houses past where the town used to end. More automobiles. Fewer horses.

Probably the same attitudes and prejudices.

He tightened his grip on the reins, forced himself to remain outwardly calm, giving no sign of emotion. Within minutes everyone in town would know he had returned. He steeled himself not to turn and ride away.

Then there it stood. The home where he'd been loved and welcomed. Emotions—long denied—choked him, clouding his vision. He blinked and stared, noted a bare patch on the roof where the shingles needed repairing. Then he widened his eyes and gave the place a hard look. It could do with a paint job. And an overhanging tree branch threatened the back porch. Strange Pa hadn't trimmed it. He'd always been mighty particular about such things. John said Pa had been sick. Kody narrowed his eyes. A ready, waiting tension tightened his muscles. What if Pa had died? Or Ma? He had to find out. He jumped from Sam and reached over to help Charlotte off the mare.

She smoothed her dress and hair. "I'm afraid I don't look my best. I feel like I'm wearing a coat of dust."

"Won't matter to Ma." Ma never judged a person by their clothes or their situation.

Or the color of their skin.

Not everyone proved so charitable. Ma and Pa had been hurt many times because of comments about Kody. Many people didn't understand how they could give a half-breed a home, a name and their love.

He hesitated at the gate. Why bring that pain back into their lives? He could simply leave Charlotte with instructions to find her way into the house and introduce herself. Ma would welcome her without question. He could jump back on Sam and...

But he wasn't strong enough to deny himself a chance to see his parents. To assure himself they were both okay. To receive again their love and acceptance. He despised his weakness.

The gate squealed a protest and dragged on the ground as he pushed it open. The top hinge needed fixing. His muscles twitched. Something was very, very wrong with the whole picture.

He waved for Charlotte to follow him and quietly crossed the yard, every nerve at attention, taking in every shadow, every corner. The only sound as they reached the door came from the birds in the trees. His boots echoed on the wooden steps. He paused. Did he knock or burst through the door as he had as a child? Not knowing what awaited him on the other side, he decided to knock.

The door opened slowly. "Yes?"

"Ma." He stepped into full view. "Ma." He hoped his voice didn't sound as rough as it felt.

"Kody, my son." Her arms went around him in the way he remembered, her hair tickling his cheek, her hands patting his back.

He hugged her tight, let himself be her boy again for just a few seconds, then pushed away to study her face. Lines had deepened around her eyes, creasing her cheeks. She seemed thinner. Her hair had turned gray before he left home—probably because of the worry he caused her. "Ma, how are you?"

"Dakota Douglas, it's been almost five years." Her voice tightened and tears wet her cheeks.

Kody didn't know if he should retreat or wait for the dressing-down he knew he deserved. He chose the latter.

"Five years, Kody, without a word. I didn't know if you were even alive. Where have you been?" She shook him gently. "Never mind. You're here now. An answer to my prayers." She hugged him again. "It's so good to have you back."

"Ma, I'm not staying."

"Why not? This is your home."

"It's better if I leave."

Her eyes clouded with what he supposed was sadness. "I guess you have to do what you think best." She tugged at his arm. "Come in." Then she saw Charlotte. "You've brought company?"

"Ma, this is Charlotte Porter. She needs someplace to stay until she can join her brother."

Ma took Charlotte's hand and pulled her inside. "Any friend of Kody's is more than welcome."

Charlotte's expression grew cautious. "We aren't really friends. He just found me and said—"

"Well, you're welcome, anyway." Ma's look at Kody suggested he'd somehow been amiss. He couldn't imagine how. He'd brought Charlotte here despite his reservations—the word again brought a smile to his lips.

Ma drew them into the kitchen. "Sit down and tell me everything," she said to Kody. "Wait, I'll make tea. Everything is better over a cup of tea." As she bustled around filling the kettle and pulling out teacups, Charlotte went to her side.

"How can I help, Mrs. Douglas?" She hesitated then in a softer voice, added, "If you're to provide me shelter, then I intend to repay it by helping as much as I can."

Ma gave Charlotte a gentle smile. "I appreciate your offer, but we'll settle that later. I'm sure there will be lots of ways you can prove yourself useful."

Kody stood in the middle of the room, his insides so tight it would have been impossible to bend enough to sit. "Where's Pa?" He couldn't imagine how he'd deal with an announcement that something had happened to the man who taught him most everything he knew.

"Resting. He had a hard night."

Kody's breath went out in a noisy rush. He sat down quickly to hide the relief leaving him weak in the knees. Pa sometimes sat with the sick and dying and troubled. But he didn't nap long even when he'd missed a night or more of sleep. He'd be striding through the door any minute, calling to Ma to put the kettle on. Kody filled his lungs with heart-calming air for the first time since he'd noticed the disrepair of the house. Pa had been busy, was all.

Ma poured tea and sat down. "How did you meet Charlotte?"

Kody filled in the details with some help from Charlotte. Ma laughed as Charlotte described her anger at her brother for leaving her a gun with no ammunition.

"Sounds to me like you've got lots of spunk," Ma said.

Kody grinned widely. "You don't know the half of it." As he told of Charlotte chasing off the two robbers with the same empty gun, his heart swelled with admiration.

"I trust God to take care of me and He does," she said with perfect calm and assurance.

Good thing she trusted God because it seemed she couldn't trust her brother. He wondered, not for the first time, what sort of man Harry was. To think of Charlotte there alone, Lother only a mile away. If the man had realized...

Ma squeezed Charlotte's hand. "I can truthfully say the same for myself. He has never failed me." Ma turned to Kody. "I pray you continue to believe it, too."

Kody shifted his gaze toward the front-room door, hoping to see his father, but he felt Ma's expectant waiting. Finally her silence forced him to look back. "Ma, I know what you believe is true. But I'm not sure it's for me."

He wished he could pull the words back as Ma's expression registered shock, sadness and pain. "Oh, Kody. You once believed. I know you did. What happened? Where have I failed?"

"Ma, you didn't fail, but my life just doesn't fit into neat little packages like yours and Pa's do."

"Are you suggesting we believe because we haven't faced difficulties?"

"Of course not. No one has a life without troubles. But you know who you are." He wished she'd let it go. He didn't want to hurt her. Nor did he want Charlotte to witness this.

"You know who you are, too. You are Dakota Douglas. My son. You are loved and special."

He sighed. "I've never doubted your love. But there are things outside of that. Let's not discuss it anymore." He had avoided Charlotte's eyes, but now sent her what he hoped passed as an apologetic look. When he saw the challenge in her eyes, he doubly wished he'd sidestepped the conversation. He suspected she'd somehow take this whole scenario and twist it to mean something more than it did. Somehow she'd make it about Star. "Where's Pa? Shouldn't he be up by now?"

Ma pushed her chair back and sighed. "I guess it's time for you to see him."

Kody did not like the way Ma's voice seemed so tired. Something simply wasn't right.

"Come along."

Charlotte remained seated.

"You, too," Ma insisted. She led them past the living room into his parents' bedroom.

Pa lay in bed, staring at the ceiling, covered by a patchwork quilt Kody remembered, made of fabric Ma had salvaged from worn-out trousers.

"Leland, Kody's home."

Pa didn't move. Didn't even blink. His skin had never been such a washed-out pasty color, nor his mouth so slack.

Kody stared. "What's wrong with him?"

Ma sat on the edge of the bed and took one of Pa's hands. "He's had a stroke. He's improving every day, though."

Kody did not want to know what he'd been like before the improvement.

"Come," Ma said. "Sit where he can see you."

Kody hesitated. This unresponsive, shrunken man was not his father. He was a stranger, a frightening shell of a man. Looking at him made Kody want to run upstairs to the bed where he'd slept as a child and hide his face in the pillow. Pretend things were exactly as he remembered them. That nothing had changed since he left. But he couldn't hide from the facts, so he crossed to the bed and sat where Ma indicated.

His father turned slowly and, with what seemed like great effort, pulled his gaze to Kody. He mumbled something that might have been "Hello."

Kody tried not to think of the man his father had been last time he saw him and smiled in spite of the tightness starting in his toes and spiraling upward to the corners of his mouth. "Hello, Pa. It's been a while."

Pa lifted one hand a few inches from the bedcovers and mumbled. Kody thought it sounded like his name. Suddenly his love for this man overcame his shock. He bent over and hugged his father, breathing in the smell of soap and mothballs.

When he straightened, his father's cheeks were damp with tears.

Ma grabbed a hankie and dried them. "He's so glad to see you. As am I."

Pa struggled with wanting to say something. Finally he got out the words, "You stay?"

Kody wished he didn't understand his father's question, but he did. He wished he could give the answer his father wanted, but staying this close to Star made it impossibly hard to pretend his daughter didn't exist. If people learned she was his, their prejudice would undo the four years of sacrifice he'd already endured.

Yet how could he leave his parents under these circumstances? "I'll stay a few days, then I must be on my way." Long enough to fix the roof and prune the tree, if nothing else.

He waited until they were back in the kitchen before he bombarded Ma with questions. "When did this happen? How have you managed? Is he going to get better?"

Ma bustled about pulling potatoes from the bin in the pantry. "It's been a couple of months now. But he started to have weak spells before that." She seemed distracted by meal preparations, so Kody waited. He'd get his answers sooner or later.

Charlotte stood by offering to help.

Ma gave her a knife and a basin of potatoes. "I don't mind if you peel these." She opened the icebox and pulled out an already cooked roast. "I wondered how I'd use this all up when I cooked it yesterday. The Johnsons brought it. People have been so good to us. Even though your father hasn't been able to perform his preaching duties, many still make sure we have enough."

Kody wondered how true that was or if Ma maintained her positive attitude out of habit. As he recalled, even when Pa preached every Sunday, the offerings were skimpy. Most people gave in the way of food. He choked back his anger. Ma and Pa were good, kind people. They didn't deserve this misfortune.

Charlotte put the potatoes on to boil, then quietly went to Kody's side. "I'd like to bring in my belongings."

"I'll help you." He needed to get his mind on other things besides the unfairness of this situation.

When they reached the horses, Charlotte grabbed his arm and forced him to face her. Tears clung to her eyelashes. Her smile quivered. "What a blessing you returned. See how God works things out? He knew you were needed at home."

The approval in her voice gave him a warm feeling; the weight of her hand on his arm, the way she touched him without aversion, sent a sudden skitter of pleasure to his heart. But it didn't change the facts of life.

He looked at her hand on his arm and backed away, forcing her to drop her arm to her side.

He knew he'd embarrassed her, made her think she minded her touching him. It wasn't the case. If things were different, if he was a different person... But he wasn't. And he couldn't change the facts. He didn't belong in the white world, wasn't accepted on the reservation. And anyone associated with him would be marked for the same narrow-mindedness. How often had he heard people whisper cruel things about Ma and Pa? Some didn't even bother lowering their voices.

Charlotte took her things when he handed them to her, but set them on the ground. "I'll help with the horses."

He couldn't be bothered to argue, so she carried the bridles to the garage housing Pa's old car. At least Pa still had it so he could get out and around. Kody stopped so suddenly Charlotte jolted into his back.

"What's wrong?" she asked.

"Nothing." Perhaps Pa would never again need the car. Good thing he'd insisted Ma learn to drive, too. Kody took a deep breath. "Why does God allow such things? It just isn't fair."

Her eyes grew wide, but he didn't want to hear any more platitudes. He hurried to hang the saddles before she could come up with any sort of answer.

Chapter Eight

Charlotte followed Kody into the house. "I'm glad you're staying here for a bit."

He spun around so fast she stopped. She didn't much care for the way his eyes flashed, and she fell back a step.

"And why should you be glad?"

His voice had dropped to deeper tones, full of quiet warning, but she didn't let it stop her from speaking her thoughts.

"It will give you time to reconsider your decision to ride out of Star's life." God had provided her another chance to convince him. Perhaps this had been His plan all along, the reason she'd been left by Harry—in order to serve a purpose here. She'd known God had a plan, that He would turn things out for good. And if it helped Star, well, it was quite fine with her.

"You promised you wouldn't say anything about her."

"To your parents. Not to you."

He grunted. "Don't expect me to be sitting around making small talk."

"Nope. But surely you wouldn't deny me the pleasure of your company once in a while." She felt telltale heat race up her cheeks, felt it burn deeper by the sudden awareness she wouldn't be averse to spending time in his company, and not for the sole purpose of discussing Star. Something about him proved both unsettling and steadying.

He quirked one eyebrow in mocking disbelief. His eyes narrowed as he took in the way her cheeks flared. Then he smiled, the gesture beginning at the corners of his mouth and working upward to his eyes.

At the way he looked at her, the heat in her cheeks spread to her chest, making her heart beat against her ribs in a most alarming way. Something alive, vibrant and vital, passed between them. She didn't know what to call it—interest, friendship or something exceeding both. She only knew the moment shifted her world, changed the way she looked at life, enticed her toward something new, exciting and deliciously frightening.

And then he grunted. "You are joking, of course." And he took the last two steps toward the door.

She didn't move, waiting for dizziness to pass. They'd shared a few special days and she embarrassingly admitted to a growing regard for him, yet he'd dismissed her feelings. Obviously he didn't return them. Yet how dare he toss her feelings aside as if they had no value? Anger stole past her usual complacent attitude. Why would he be any different from Harry and Nellie, or the Applebys, or Lother? Seems people treated her like a commodity. Use Charlotte or leave her. Whatever suits you.

She closed her eyes. *Lord forgive me. I belong to You, not people, no matter what they think. Help me be patient and cooperative.* Her anger fled as quickly as it came.

Only when peace settled back into her soul did she follow Kody indoors.

Mrs. Douglas wiped her hands on a worn towel. "The doctor said there's no reason he shouldn't do more. But he doesn't seem to have any interest in anything but lying in bed staring at the ceiling." She chuckled. "But I think having you here will make him want to get up. He won't want you to think he's laid down and quit."

"Is that what he's done?"

Mrs. Douglas sighed. "I've thought so a few times. I'm so glad God brought you back to us. It's bound to make a big difference. I think we should persuade him to join us for supper."

Charlotte understood they spoke of Kody's father. She hurried to the cupboard and took the towel from Mrs. Douglas. "Let me finish the supper preparations while you and Kody tend to your husband."

"Thank you, child."

Kody and his mother left the room, set on stirring Mr. Douglas from his comfortable bed. She smiled, thinking how persuasive Kody could be. Not with sweet talk, but with prodding and badgering. She tried to imagine him sweet-talking her, praising her, appreciating her. She grabbed the edge of the cupboard as an ache as wide as the South Dakota prairie tore through her. Then she pushed the idea from her mind. She wasn't so needy she hungered for approval from everyone she encountered. She drained the potatoes, mashed them to a creamy texture and spooned them high into the serving bowl, hoping Mrs. Douglas would appreciate her efforts.

She hummed as she worked. What a pleasure to be in a house with water as close as the turn of a tap, with a window overlooking a yard with trees, and filled with a spirit of joy and faith. She took the potatoes to the table. A piece of oilcloth in blue and yellow squares covered the wooden table. Crocheted pads, alternately blue and yellow, covered the seats of the six wooden chairs. Yellow medallions marched in straight lines up the pale-blue wallpaper. Several calendars hung in various places; one had pictures of mountains, another of an English landscape and two showed bright bouquets of flowers. Charlotte smiled, thinking if Nellie had hung such cheery pictures, instead of the stern likeness of her parents and a calendar boasting the latest threshing machine, they might all have benefited.

Charlotte set the bowl in the middle of the table between the platter of thinly sliced roast beef and the divided dish with four kinds of pickles and relish, and thanked God for the bounty.

The trio edged into the room, Mr. Douglas leaning heavily on Kody's arm. Charlotte hurried to hold a chair for the man. He wore a tan sweater buttoned over a dark blue shirt. His black trousers hung on his tall frame. His thinning white hair had been combed back by either Mrs. Douglas or Kody.

"Thank you, child," Mrs. Douglas said, breathing heavily as she bent over her husband. "That was a long walk for you. Are you okay?"

Mr. Douglas gave a crooked smile. "I'm fine." His speech was slurred yet discernible.

Mrs. Douglas sat down. "Let's pray."

Charlotte closed her eyes, as the woman folded her hands to say grace.

"Your gifts are so bountiful. My son is back home. My Leland walked to the table. We have a beautiful young woman to share with, and You have blessed us with plenty of food. My heart is full." Her voice thickened. "Too full for words," she whispered. "Amen."

Charlotte stole a glance at Kody. His eyes narrowed, his expression tightened as if forcing himself to mentally refute the words. He seemed determined to believe God's love and care did not extend to him. He blamed his race and people's prejudice, yet how could he deny this outpouring of love from God's heart through his parents and into his life?

Mrs. Douglas cut her husband's food into bite-size pieces, then wrapped his fingers around the fork handle and guided it toward the food.

He let his hand fall to the table and looked confused at the idea of feeding himself.

"You can do it, dear," Mrs. Douglas encouraged.

Her husband mumbled, sounding angry.

Charlotte caught her breath as he tried to capture a piece of meat. She let her lungs exhale when he succeeded in getting the meat into his mouth. His eyes glistened with angry defiance. Charlotte ducked her head to hide her amusement, knowing either anger or determination were healthy emotions to spur the man into fighting his way back from the ravages of his stroke.

Mrs. Douglas faced Kody. "Now tell me what you've done since you left home. I want to know everything."

Kody laughed. "Ma, we only have three hours until dark."

"Start with the condensed version and fill in the details later."

"Well, I worked in an irrigation ditch for a season. Didn't like mucking in the mud. Helped build some roads. The machinery's too noisy. I helped on a ranch for most of a year. I liked that work the best. But I needed to move on."

"Where? Where are you going, Kody? What are you looking for you can't find here where you belong?" Mrs. Douglas asked the questions, but Charlotte saw how Mr. Douglas focused on Kody, waiting for his answers.

"I'm heading for Canada."

"Why? What's in Canada?"

Kody's smile looked strained. "Space, Ma. They say there's places where a man can live and not see another human being for months."

Mrs. Douglas shook her head. "Sounds like a lonely place to me. And I know you wouldn't be happy there. You've always been the sort to have lots of friends."

"Sometimes a man is better off alone."

Mrs. Douglas put her fork down and reached for Kody's hand. "We were sorry to hear Winnoa died. I know how that must have hurt. I figured that's why you disappeared. You needed time to get over that. We understood. But that's almost four years ago. Surely it's time to come home."

Kody shrugged. "I can never come home."

"Why?" Mrs. Douglas demanded, her voice thin with what Charlotte took for sorrow over her son's attitude. "What happened to make you change? We have always loved you and still do. You know that."

Charlotte watched the play of emotions in Kody's face—the desire to ease his mother's concern warring against his belief he belonged nowhere. She wanted to shout for him to notice how clearly he belonged here surrounded by his parents' love.

"Ma, this has nothing to do with you. You and Pa are the best parents anyone could wish for. This is about who

I am. I said I'd stay a few days. I'll fix a few things and then I'm moving on."

Charlotte ducked her head because she knew Kody might be running from his life, but God had turned him around and brought him back—perhaps to give him a chance to see how much Star needed him, even for him to discover how much he loved the child. It satisfied her to think God might have chosen her to bring Kody back to his family. It almost made it worthwhile to have suffered fear, hunger and thirst, and to endure missing Harry and the family with such an ache.

A draft of loneliness blew through and left her empty and tired. She'd cared for five-year-old Ricky since his birth, reading him stories and playing little games to amuse him when Nellie was occupied. As he grew older she taught him how to tie his shoes, how to build a little farm out of sticks and marbles. And when Mandy came along eighteen months later, she'd done the same for the little girl.

Pain hit her with cruel force. Kody had what she wanted so badly it filled her mouth with a dry, dusty taste. He had love and a home.

She suddenly had difficulty breathing and kept her head down, struggling to control her emotions, grateful the Douglas family focused their attention on Kody.

"Charlotte?" Kody said.

Maybe they weren't as distracted as she hoped. She sucked in air, slowly filled her lungs, willed herself to cover her emotions with a smile and then she looked up.

"Are you all right?"

The concern in his face caused her smile to slip. Her eyes stung.

"Something's wrong."

She shook her head and lifted her hand to indicate she didn't want to talk about it. She dared not try to speak for fear of losing control.

Mrs. Douglas watched, her face full of concern, which further threatened Charlotte's self-restraint. She shifted, met Mr. Douglas's eyes and almost broke down at the compassion in them.

He nodded. "Sad," he said, as plain as if Kody had said the word. "Why?"

She might have ignored Kody's questions and side-stepped his mother's silent ones, but she couldn't ignore Mr. Douglas's.

"I miss my brother and his family," she managed to choke out. It wasn't the whole source of her sadness, only the beginning of it. Knowing Harry could walk away from her so easily reinforced an idea she'd been fighting since her mother's death. Harry didn't really want her, even though she'd done her best to follow Mother's in-structions to be useful. No matter how hard she worked, how quickly she obeyed, how useful she tried to be, she was tolerated rather than welcomed.

Mrs. Douglas reached for her hand. "My dear, forgive me. I've been so busy rejoicing over my own blessings, I've forgotten your troubles."

Charlotte managed a shaky smile. "It's okay. He's sending for me." He had to. She had no other home, no other family. She belonged with him, whether tolerated or welcomed.

Mrs. Douglas patted Charlotte's hand. "Well, you're more than welcome to stay here as long as you need. I'm mighty glad for the company."

There was the word she longed for—welcome. It hurt that it came from a stranger. How could Mrs. Douglas care about her when her only surviving family member so obviously didn't?

Mrs. Douglas leaned back and smiled at everyone around the table. "I think I owe it to you that Kody has returned. God works in mysterious ways."

"You and Charlotte both talk the same," Kody said. "As if bad things are a blessing in disguise."

Charlotte and Mrs. Douglas exchanged wide smiles. It had been a long time since Charlotte had known the pleasure of a shared faith with an older woman. Not since her mother's death. The idea of her being a stranger vanished. They were sisters in Christ.

Kody's mother voiced a thought for both of them. "Sometimes they are."

Mr. Douglas tried to speak. They waited as he struggled with his words. "God's ways are always good. We have to believe that."

"Fine," Kody said. "God's ways might be good, but man's ways leave much to be desired."

Charlotte ached to point out God's love wasn't controlled by man's actions, but she struggled with sorting out the difference in her own mind and had no words of assurance to offer except those that expressed the faith she clung to. "God uses all things for our good."

"Amen," both Kody's parents said.

The pleasure of their shared faith was a balm to Charlotte's soul. She wished they would share ways they'd seen God turn things around, knew it would bolster her own struggling faith, but Mr. Douglas tried to push his chair back. "Bed."

Charlotte filled the basin with hot water and tackled the wall behind the stove. Mrs. Douglas had protested when Charlotte insisted she wanted to work, then confessed she could use help with the spring cleaning.

"I know it's long overdue, but somehow I haven't had the heart to do it."

Charlotte gladly took on the job. She loved to help, even without Mother's warning ringing in her ears. *There's nothing harder to tolerate than a homeless relative who contributes nothing.* Charlotte figured it applied equally to an uninvited guest.

As she worked, Charlotte listened to the sound of Kody repairing the roof.

He'd begun the job before breakfast as if he couldn't wait to get done so he could be on his way.

Somehow she had to devise some way to convince him otherwise and learn to deal with being Star's father. That required a chance to talk to him in private. And she knew he wasn't going to make it easy for her.

She didn't know how long she had. Perhaps today a letter from Harry had been forwarded to Favor.

But Mrs. Douglas returned from the post office without a letter for Charlotte. Charlotte smiled despite her disappointment. "Maybe tomorrow. In the meantime I have lots to keep me busy." And something she wanted to accomplish before she left.

By lunchtime, she'd washed the walls in the kitchen. Over the meal of thick, homemade tomato soup and hot biscuits, she said, "If I had a ladder I could wash the ceiling."

"I'll get something," Kody said, and after the meal, brought in a stepladder and set it in place. "Be careful."

She stared at his back as he retreated. He hadn't worn his hat since he returned home, and the sun glistened on his hair as he stepped out the door.

His caution was only polite words with no particular significance, yet she couldn't stop herself from thinking he might care a little about her safety. As she stood on the ladder and scrubbed the smoke and flyspecks off the ceiling, she smiled, remembering how frightened she'd been of him just a few days ago. But he'd proved to be a gentleman, a loving son and a hardworking man.

She paused and looked at her work. She'd missed a spot and she leaned over, grabbing the top of the ladder as she stretched.

"Is this your idea of being careful?"

Kody's demanding voice startled her. She swayed, tried to steady herself but found only air to cling to. "No," she wailed as the ladder began to tip.

She closed her eyes, waiting for the crash, waiting to feel her body hit the hard floor. She gasped as, instead, she felt a warm, solid chest and strong arms holding her.

"Are you okay?" The breath of his soft words brushed her cheek.

She kept her eyes shut, too embarrassed to risk meeting his eyes. "I'm fine." She tried to step away but still off balance, succeeded in leaning into him more heavily. She grabbed for his chest.

His arms tightened around her. "Take it easy."

"I'm fine," she said again and managed to right herself and step back, then realized she held a scrap of paper. She must have caught it when she clutched his shirt for support. She glanced at it, then looked closer at the advertisement for special shoes for children with clubfeet. "Straighten your child's feet," it read.

He quietly took the paper from her fingers and re-

Chapter Nine

Kody kept his hand over his pocket. John had given him the ad for the shoes. Kody intended to order a pair for Star before he left. In fact, he planned to do so this afternoon.

And get some supplies for the folks. He'd been to the basement to clean out the vegetable bins and noticed the shelves held only a few canning jars from last summer and one lone can of beans. Ma usually kept the shelves well stocked. Always said you never knew when you might have unexpected company or some emergency.

Charlotte waited as if expecting an explanation for the scrap of paper. No doubt she'd figured out what the shoes were for.

"Star needs a pair of special shoes."

"And you're going to get them?"

"Ain't like John can afford it."

"They appear to live a pretty meager life."

Her words seemed to slice through any defense. As if he was somehow to blame. But she didn't need to point out he had a responsibility to see Star had all she needed. Which meant seeing John and Morning had their needs met.

"I figured on getting a few things for them while I'm here."

"I'll help."

He finally relaxed at her eagerness. "How?"

"If I had some fabric I could make dresses for Morning and Star. And a shirt for John."

Her unexpected generosity made him look at her with fresh interest. She'd already impressed him with her gumption and her good humor. Again, he wondered how she really felt about Indians—and half-breeds. Was she only being charitable because they were poor unfortunates, or because she saw them as people like her with the same needs and wants and concerns? "The store has yard goods. If you go with me, I can buy what you need."

"Great. When do you want to go?"

"When will you be finished here?"

"Another hour?"

"I should finish the roof by then, too."

She nodded and began to turn away, then stopped. "You care about your daughter more than you want to admit."

He gave her a warning look, silently reminding her of her promise, and glanced over his shoulder half expecting to see Ma standing in the front-room doorway. She wasn't, of course. He could trust Charlotte to be careful not to give away his secret.

An hour later, they headed toward the business section of town.

As they stepped inside the mercantile store, he noticed the way the room grew quiet. He expected as much.

It had been the same since he was big enough to attract attention.

Charlotte didn't seem to notice, however. She rushed toward the yard goods and started to examine the bolts. "Look, this would be perfect for John." She held out a bolt of deep blue.

Ignoring the way Mr. Boulter watched his every move, Kody went to Charlotte's side. "He'd like that."

Within minutes, Charlotte picked out a fawn-colored material for Morning. She went through the stacks twice. "I don't see anything that's just right for Star." Charlotte signaled to the young woman hovering behind the counter and she hurried over. "Do you have anything else? I want something for a little girl."

"I do believe I have a couple more bolts in the back." She looked closely at Kody. "It's Kody Douglas, isn't it?"

Kody raised his eyes to the girl. "Amy Boulter?"

She nodded.

"You've grown up since I last saw you."

"I bet your parents are glad to see you."

"Amy—" Mr. Boulter spoke sternly "—is there something you should be doing?"

"Yes, Father." She leaned toward Charlotte. "I'll be right back." She flashed a smile at Kody. "It's good to see you." She scampered away and returned with two bolts of material. Charlotte oohed over the brown with little pink flowers. "That's perfect. Don't you think so?" She waited for Kody's approval.

Keenly aware several customers hung around watching the proceedings and no doubt drawing their own uncharitable conclusions, he readily agreed.

Amy cut off the requested lengths and carried them to the till.

Kody hung back and spoke low to Charlotte. "I want to get some things for Ma and Pa, too. Can you help?"

"Of course." She flashed him a smile. "I love shopping."

Together, with input from Amy, they decided what to buy. When Amy began to total the bill, her father edged her aside. "We can't give you credit. And I've given your parents all I can allow."

"Father!" Amy gasped.

"How much do they owe?" Kody demanded.

Mr. Boutler did some figuring. When he gave the total, Kody realized he wouldn't be able to order the shoes for Star until he earned more money. He pulled out his purse and practically emptied it.

Behind him, he heard a hoarse whisper. "Where do you suppose he got so much money?"

Mr. Boulter took the cash with undue haste as if expecting Kody to snatch it back. Only then did the storekeeper step aside to let Amy finish the order.

"I'm sorry," she said, her voice cracking. "Don't pay any attention. Not everyone is so close-minded." She sent a look at her father, clearly informing him who she considered to be exactly what.

Kody began to gather up the bundles.

Amy stopped him. "We'll deliver the order, won't we, Father?"

The man glowered at the three of them but didn't refuse.

Kody headed for escape, but Charlotte paused at the door.

"Thank you. It's been a pleasure doing business in your fine store."

He glanced over his shoulder to see she included Mr.

Boulter in her smile. Then she nodded to the hovering customers.

"I'm sure I'm going to enjoy your beautiful town." Still smiling, she joined Kody.

He let his breath *whoosh* out as they headed for the post office. "Now you see the way it is."

"They have a good selection of most everything. I am really happy about the yard goods we chose."

Was she being purposely thick-headed? "You don't think I mean the things on the shelves, do you?"

She stopped and faced him with narrowed eyes. "What else would you mean?"

"I mean the way they acted, of course."

"Amy was very pleasant."

"Unlike her father."

"Some people are naturally more cheerful that others."

He stopped walking to stare at her. "You must have heard the people muttering behind us."

"Nothing wrong with my hearing as far as I know. But why let a few unjustified comments rob you of enjoying the fun we had or the welcome Amy extended?"

"That's a little nearsighted in my opinion."

She shrugged. "I learned a long time ago it was best to overlook insults. Otherwise I would be walking around all day nursing hurt feelings."

He jammed his hands into his trouser pockets and strode toward the post office. No point in trying to reason with someone who ignored anything that didn't fit into her belief that everything had a good and noble purpose. And perhaps it was best to let her cling to her idealized way of thinking. He didn't want her to deal with the harsher realities he faced.

He waited outside while she went in to check for a letter from Harry. When she came out empty-handed he expected her to be disappointed, but she smiled.

"It gives me time to make those garments, time to see you get those little shoes for Star and—" she looked away and finished airily "—time to see you change your mind about being her father."

"I don't think you'll be around long enough. Because, lady, you will be long in your grave and still waiting."

"We'll see. In the meantime, I have some sewing to do."

"How come you argue with me all the time? Aren't you supposed to be cooperative?"

"Oh, yes. Good little Charlotte, meek and mild. Poke her hard and see her smile."

Her quiet tone did not deceive him. He'd touched a nerve. He didn't mean to hurt her, yet he enjoyed seeing her with a little spark.

"This something you heard before?"

"Only inside my head. Sometimes it's hard to be obedient and cooperative."

They turned off Main Street toward home. No longer did he feel as if eyes followed his every move. And he relaxed. "I like you better when you show some spunk, instead of sitting around waiting to be rescued." Then he began to laugh low and quiet so as not to attract attention from anyone who might be passing. "I'll never forget how you threatened me with a useless gun and sent those two scoundrels racing down the road with the same gun."

She grinned at him. "They deserved to be scared."

They stopped walking and faced each other. They didn't touch. Didn't make any gesture toward it. Yet the way she looked at him felt as real as if she'd brushed her hand over his cheek or squeezed his shoulder, friendly and reassuring with a hint of something unsettling, as if the imagined touch eased him toward the edge of a precipice.

He should step back from the force that seemed to bind him to her. He knew he ought to run as fast and far away from this woman as possible.

But he knew he wouldn't. Couldn't. Didn't want to. He had Star and his parents to think about, but only by dint of extreme concentration did they even enter his thoughts. It wasn't any of them holding him here on this spot, making him want to stay in Favor where he seemed unlikely to gain favor from anyone. Charlotte pretended to be all docile and cooperative. He guessed she'd been taught so by a mother who feared for her future. But he had seen glimpses of something fierce and strong in her. He wouldn't mind seeing what happened when that side finally escaped into the open. He figured it would, given time and some encouragement. He just might be the one to give her a little prod in that direction.

That evening, Pa agreed to sit in the front room after supper. Charlotte had a little dress almost sewn together. "You mother has a sewing machine. It makes things go quickly." She attached buttons as Ma read to Pa from the Bible. Kody wished he had something to do with his hands. Something to occupy his mind, to keep him from watching Charlotte and enable him to block the words from Ma's mouth. He relaxed significantly when Ma closed the Bible. Not that he didn't believe it. But he couldn't believe it included him.

Ma looked at Charlotte. "I expected you would be

making a dress for yourself when you asked to use the sewing machine, but that's a child's dress."

Kody's lungs grabbed at his ribs and refused to operate. He didn't move, fearing his face would register his worry. But he gave Charlotte a look he wished could burn her face, make her glance at him and see his silent warning. But she kept her eyes on knotting a thread, then held up the little garment.

"We stopped at the reservation before we got here. I met some of Kody's friends."

Kody kept his eyes on her. *Be careful what you say.*

She flashed a quick smile as she continued, "They have so little. I offered to make a garment for each of them and Kody bought the goods."

Kody tilted his head a fraction. She'd done well. "They know the Eaglefeathers from teaching out there." He turned to Ma. "They befriended me when I went to the reservation."

"Good people. Sincere Christians. They always ask after you when we go. Of course we haven't been able to make it in some time. I was always glad to know you'd made some friends there."

He didn't bother saying how few he'd made. The Indians hadn't cared for a half-breed with white ways.

"When Kody left home, he went to the reservation," Ma explained to Charlotte. "I understood how he wanted to connect with that part or himself."

Kody watched Charlotte. Would she reveal any revulsion at being confronted with the facts? But she met Ma's eyes with open interest. "Kody says you adopted him?"

"He was ours from his first breath."

The way Ma said it always gave Kody a sense of well-being. But he wondered what Charlotte really thought of his mixed race. And what would she think if she knew his uncertain heritage? "Ma, tell her how you came to be stuck with me."

"Kody, what a dreadful thing to say. We weren't stuck. We were blessed." She turned to pat Pa's hand. "Weren't we, Leland?"

Pa waved a trembling hand at Kody. "Good boy."

The slurred words blessed Kody.

"You're right," Ma said. "He's always been a good boy."

Kody darted a look at Charlotte, found her accusing gaze on him. Knew she figured a "good boy" would not walk away from his daughter. She had no idea how difficult the decision had been. Leaving again would be even harder. He should never have come back.

"Kody?" Ma pulled his attention back to her. "Why don't you tell Charlotte your story."

"Go ahead and tell her, Ma. You know it better than I do." He chuckled. "I was too young to remember most of it."

"Very well." She turned to Charlotte. "One day more than twenty-one years ago, a girl came to our door, so sick and weak she couldn't talk. And about to have a baby. I helped her as best I could. It was all she could do to bring her little son into the world. She died without telling us her name or anything about herself. But the baby was healthy and strong. We've never been able to have children and thanked God for this little gift. We named him Dakota and he grew into the fine young man sitting in that chair."

Charlotte's eyes glistened. "That's beautiful. So all your life your parents have delighted in you." She choked up and couldn't continue.

Kody blinked. Yes, he was loved by his parents. He'd never doubted it. But the words, the accusations, the nasty comments of others were a raging flood covering his parents' love and pride with their dirty, muddy waters. He'd heard the story of his birth many times. As a child it made him feel special, a miracle gift to his ma and pa, but he grew up, discovered others looked upon his birth as less than a blessing. He learned to reason and as he did, he despised the details.

Charlotte widened her eyes and sent him a look full of something he could only describe as longing. Hadn't she once said something about wishing she had a mother like his? What a strange world. He envied her the way people accepted her, rushing to fill her order at the store and extending her little courtesies. It appeared she envied his loving parents. Seems like a person always wanted the things out of their reach.

He could tell her that what she wanted and envied him for might not satisfy what she seemed to ache for—a place where she felt accepted or...

He suddenly realized what she longed for—appreciation for who she was as a person.

"I've been working on a quilt," Ma said. "I'll finish it up and donate it to the cause."

Kody couldn't look at Ma. Avoided meeting Charlotte's gaze knowing the silent messages she'd be sending. She'd already accused him of robbing his parents of a granddaughter. But Ma and Pa must never know about Star.

Pa tried to get up from his big chair and Kody hurried to assist him. He helped Pa prepare for bed, then left Ma to tuck him in. "I'll say good night," she said as she headed out of the room.

Kody bid them both good night and hurried back to the front room. Somehow he had to explain his insight to Charlotte and make her understand how, if people didn't appreciate her, they were blind, ignorant and unworthy of her efforts to please them.

"I'm almost finished Star's dress. Do you think she'll like it?"

Kody faltered. Through no fault of her own, Star would face many of the same questions, doubts and prejudices Kody had never grown accustomed to. He had to stay away from her and give her a chance to be Indian and nothing else. She might also feel the same needs Charlotte did—a need for appreciation. Charlotte thought a parent's love would outweigh all those other things. But it didn't. He knew from experience.

"She'll like it just fine." He'd intended to sit down and talk to her. But now he wanted only to end this evening before his thoughts grew any more confused. "I'm going to see about finding work tomorrow."

"Can I help in any way?"

He chuckled at her eagerness. "Always trying to prove yourself indispensable, aren't you?" At the wounded look in her eyes, he wished he had enough brains to keep his thoughts to himself. She had no idea of the things causing him to say that. "You don't need so try so hard. Some people appreciate you just fine."

She opened her mouth, but not a sound escaped. Her gaze clung to his, expectant and unbelieving.

"I like you just fine." A poor way to say all he felt, but no other words came to his befuddled mind.

Twin spots of pink showed on her cheeks.

He'd embarrassed her. "You don't have to prove anything to me." The color in her face deepened. What was he trying to say? He rubbed his chin and tried again. "I appreciate your help. Making this dress for Star is a generous gesture. But, Charlotte, you don't have to work to gain my approval."

Her color heightened. She looked down, slowly folded the little dress, and got to her feet. "If you think I am doing this to make you like me, you are so wrong. I'm doing this because it's not fair how you're treating Star, and I want to show her that people can and do care about her." She pushed past him and headed for the stairs. "Even if her father doesn't."

He grabbed her elbow and stopped her escape. "You don't believe that. I do care about her. I'm trying to do what's best for her."

She turned slowly and fixed him with a hard stare. "And how do you expect to explain that to her? 'Cause I can guarantee soon or later she's going to want to know why her father left her."

"Charlotte, I don't want to argue about what I think is best for her."

"You're saying it's none of my business." She sighed. "You're right. I have no call to interfere." She climbed the stairs.

Kody ought to be grateful she'd given up the fight. But for some perverse reason it wasn't gratitude he felt. He stared at Charlotte's back. He didn't like this compliant, passive Charlotte.

Good little Charlotte, meek and mild
Poke her hard and see her smile.

He grinned. He knew one sure way to shake her from

her meek and mild state. "Guess you'll just sit around and wait for Harry to send for you."

He stopped.

His grin widened as she lifted her chin.

Slowly she turned. "Kody Douglas, you are so wrong. I don't intend to do any such thing. I'll have the garments finished by the end of the week and then I expect you to take me to the reservation so I can deliver them. And I will prove to you that you need to take care of your daughter yourself." She spun around and strode down the hall.

Kody leaned back on his heels and chuckled softly. He loved to see Charlotte all feisty and ready to do battle. A sobering thought failed to quench his smile—her battle seemed to be always with him. It had been from the first. But somehow he didn't mind. Not that she had a chance of changing his mind. He'd already made that clear.

Kody pinned his note to the board next to the post-office door. "Willing to break horses for a fair price. Buck 'em out or gentle train them. Never been thrown."

A lanky cowboy sidled up to him and peered at the notice. "Never been throwed, huh? You ought to go by the Cartwell place. He's got a rank horse there. He's promised twenty bucks to anyone who can ride him."

Twenty dollars would buy a pair of little shoes and add some to his travel fund. "Cartwell, you say? They the ranch back in the hills?"

"Cross the river and up the trail." He shifted to look at Kody more carefully.

Kody stiffened, hoping the man wasn't going to create a scene in the post office.

"Say, I'll bet you're Kody Douglas."

Kody looked the other man up and down. Tall, slightly bow-legged, with a twinkle in his blue eyes. "Do I know you?"

"Don't suppose you do. I married Bess Macleod. She told me about you. Jed Hawkes." He shoved out his hand.

Kody shook it. "Nice to meet you." What a pleasant change to be welcomed.

Jed pushed aside a couple of notices. "Old Lady Murphy is looking for a man again."

"The Widow Murphy? I can't believe she's still alive. I thought she was old as Methuselah when I was a kid." He read the notice aloud. "'Need hardworking man willing to stay a spell. Top wages. Bonuses.' She really pay top wages?"

"Hear she pays good but not many men willing to stay."

"Why's that?"

"She's mighty particular that things are done exactly as they've been done for the past fifty years. She don't hold much for letting the men have days off. And on top of it, she lives so far back it's a hard ride to town. Man ends up stuck there with little to amuse 'im. Most just don't stay."

Kody studied the notice. It sounded like his kind of place, except for one thing—he needed to be close to town so he could help with Pa's care and see his folks were doing okay.

And he wasn't averse to seeing more of little Miss Charlotte, especially when she wasn't meek and mild. After she left, after Pa was doing better...well, he wouldn't need a job, because he'd be on his way to Canada again.

Chapter Ten

Charlotte glanced to the backseat of the car at the boxes of supplies they carried. The shirt and two dresses were finished. They had turned out rather well, she thought. She hoped the Eaglefeather family would receive them gladly.

Kody borrowed his pa's car for this trip to the reservation. "Car's faster than horseback and I want to be back in good time."

They bounced along, breathing in dust and hot air. "Sure could use rain," Charlotte said. The reservation was in the hills beyond irrigation and bereft of any sort of advantage.

"Yup."

He sounded cheerful, almost pleased with life. And she couldn't figure out why. She'd warned him yet again she had one goal—to persuade him to be a father to his little girl. But rather than being annoyed or defensive, he seemed almost glad about it, which made her wonder if he was up to something. She shifted so she could study him, hoping to get a clue.

"What?" he asked.

"What what?"

"You're staring."

She jerked her attention back to the road. "Sorry."

"Did you want to ask something?"

"No. Well, now that you mention it…why are you being so pleasant about this?"

"About what?"

She didn't miss the flash of amusement in his eyes. "You know I intend to make you change your mind."

He chuckled. "As I already told you, that will be impossible." He waggled his eyebrows. "But it's kind of fun to see you try."

She flicked him a warning look. "You ain't seen nothin' yet."

He laughed and slapped the steering wheel. "Like I said…" He slowed as they passed a spindly group of trees. "Isn't that smoke?"

"Looks like someone has set up camp."

"They shouldn't leave a fire unattended."

She saw a flash and followed it. "Someone's there." A face peeked around a rock. The man saw the car and ducked out of sight. She laughed. "It's Ratface. And there's Shorty trying to hide behind a tree."

"I expect they're up to no good."

"They sure have a lot of junk scattered about."

They passed the camp and Charlotte turned her attention back to the road.

"I don't like them hanging about," Kody said.

"At least they aren't bothering us."

He grunted. "I hope it stays that way."

For several days Charlotte had tried to think of convincing words to present to Kody, something to make him see how much Star needed him. She knew without a doubt how the child would feel as bits of truth came out, and they would. She had prayed for guidance. But they were only a few miles from their destination and still she had no idea what she should say. But if she didn't say something soon, she'd have to wait until after their visit.

"Where did you meet Star's mother?"

"On the reservation. Winnoa had been fathered by a soldier. She had light eyes and freckles and knew what it felt like to be an outcast. I guess we gravitated toward each other because of our common half-breed status."

"Winnoa. What a lovely name. So you married and lived on the reservation?"

His short burst of laughter rang with bitterness. "We ran away and got married and tried to find work with anyone who would hire me. One half-breed is bad enough. Two is more than most people want to deal with."

"Did Star's birth have anything to do with her death?" Maybe he blamed the baby and, despite his best intentions, that affected his attitude toward his daughter.

"No. She got some kind of infection and…" He shrugged.

So he didn't blame Star. Hesitantly she asked, "Did you take her to a doctor?"

"He couldn't do anything to help her."

She exhaled noisily. And he couldn't blame her death on a doctor who refused to treat a half-breed. "Did you love her very much?"

He grinned at her. "What I loved most about her was she was a half-breed like me. That's about all we had in common."

For some reason his statement made Charlotte grin so widely she looked out the side window to hide her face. Not that she had anything in common with him. Mentally she listed their differences: he had the love of parents, yet it didn't seem to count, whereas she would do anything to make Harry continue to love her; Kody claimed to have left the faith he'd embraced as a child, and she clung to it for dear life; she thought he should be involved as a father to Star, and he seemed to think he should pretend he wasn't her father; and most of all, he was headed for Canada and she waited for Harry to send for her.

Yet none of those facts stopped her from being glad neither of them meant to move on yet.

The reservation came into view. Kody pulled to a stop in front of the Eaglefeathers' home. John and Morning waved. Star sat contentedly in John's arms.

Charlotte turned to see if Kody's face revealed any emotion at seeing his daughter held by another man. She thought she caught a flash of surprise, which he quickly masked. He hesitated a heartbeat before he opened the door. She could only pray he'd begun to see what he stood to lose by pretending Star wasn't his daughter.

John reached Kody's side and shook his hand. "Welcome, my friend. Star, say hello to Kody and Miss Charlotte."

"Hello." She had such an innocent huskiness to her voice. "He here with that lady before. She like my baby."

Morning welcomed them, then Kody opened the back door. "We brought you a few things." He pulled out a box.

No one moved. Charlotte feared the gifts offended their pride.

"Allow me to do something while I can." Kody's gaze lingered on Star.

John nodded and Kody carried the box to the house.

Morning followed. "It is very generous of you, Kody." She rested her hand on his arm. "We accept." She paused. "I understand how you need to feel you give something." She examined the contents of the box—oatmeal, oats, flour, canned goods.

Kody didn't move. A casual observer might think he was watching Morning lift out the items, but Charlotte stood where she could see his face and saw he looked past Morning, his eyes bleak, empty. It was as if Morning's words sucked away his determination, his so-called good reasons, and left him with nothing to replace them.

He spun back to the car to get the second box.

John stood in his way. "I'll get it." He handed Star to Kody.

Charlotte felt his hesitation more than she saw it. For a moment she thought he would refuse, then Star leaned toward Kody and he had no choice but to raise his arms and take his daughter. Emotions raced across his face—resistance, then surprise, then pleasure, as Star stared into his face with intent concentration. "What do you see, little one?" he asked.

"You."

He laughed. "Am I okay?"

She nodded. "You okay."

"Why, thank you." Kody's voice deepened.

John returned with a box and stopped to look at the pair. Morning straightened to watch them. Charlotte guessed the other two were as aware as she was that something special took place before their eyes. Kody would deny it, but he certainly had to feel it.

He glanced up, saw her watching him. "Let's see what else we have."

Charlotte nodded, went to get her own parcel from the back and opened it. She handed the dress to Morning, the shirt to John.

John grinned widely. "Nice shirt."

"Thank you." Morning spoke softly, shyly.

"And for you, little miss." Charlotte held out the dress, anxious to see Star's reaction.

Star's eyes grew wide. "For me?" She demanded to be put down. Kody did so, reluctantly, Charlotte thought, and kept his hands at her back until she balanced on her uneven legs. She held the dress before her. "Look, Momma. Just for me." Then she folded it into a rough bundle and pressed it to her chest.

Charlotte blinked back tears. She dared not look at Kody.

She had one more thing to give Star. A rag doll. Mrs. Douglas made them for Christmas gifts for the Sunday school. She'd helped Charlotte make this one. Charlotte had given the doll black yarn hair and braided it. She'd made dark brown eyes, rather than black, to match Star's. She'd made a little dress out of scraps from Star's dress.

She held the doll out to Star.

"Ooh, a new baby." Star handed her dress to Kody so she could take the doll. She examined it carefully, then sighed and cradled it close. "I love my baby. I love her forever."

"What do you say, Star?" Morning prompted her.

Star turned to Charlotte. "I love you very, very much."

Charlotte smiled even as her eyes filled with tears. What a precious child.

Star turned to Kody. "I love you very, very much, too."

Kody looked as if someone had put him through the wringer and hung him to dry.

"You should say, 'Thank you,'" Morning corrected.

Charlotte laughed. "That's better than a thank-you."

Kody turned away and stared out at the dry hills.

Charlotte took a step toward him, but Morning stopped her. "You know about…?" She dipped her head toward Star.

"I know."

"That is good. But it is best to let Kody work things out in his own way."

Charlotte nodded and allowed Morning to lead her to the house, where she helped prepare lunch. However, she had no intention of sitting around waiting for Kody to do things in his own way. Because his way meant riding away from this special child.

They sat in the shade of the little house and ate a simple meal, drank copious amounts of tea and visited.

Star played at their feet, enjoying her new doll. She took the dress off and wrapped the doll in a scrap of material, then dressed it again. She examined the doll's feet for several minutes until Charlotte wondered if she should do something.

She turned her attention to Kody, who couldn't seem to stop watching the child. And she prayed he would be moved to reconsider his decision.

"Too bad about your foot," Star murmured to the doll.

Charlotte shifted her gaze back to Star. The impact of what the little girl had done would have knocked Charlotte backward if she wasn't sitting pressed to the wall. Instead, the sight hit her with the force of a dust storm, sucking at her lungs, stinging her eyes, echoing in her brain with the power of thunder over her head, reverberating through her with resounding waves.

Star had tied one cloth foot of the doll back with a thread. She cuddled the doll for a moment, making soothing noises. "It doesn't matter. I love you and you can still walk." She walked the doll around her in a limp that couldn't be disguised or explained away.

The wind made a sighing sound around the cabin, pulled at Charlotte's hair and tugged her scalp. The sun beat brittle light around them, flashing bright lights in Star's dark hair, drawing sharp angles across her face, giving her an older, more mature, more careworn look.

Charlotte ached to jump up and break the thread crippling the doll, but her limbs refused to do her bidding. She sat riveted to her perch.

"I fix it for you," Star said, and broke the thread, freeing the bent foot. "See, all better." In her hands, the doll danced and jumped.

Charlotte sucked in the hot air, heavy with so much sorrow, so much unnecessary pain. This child was made for loving even if her foot couldn't be fixed. Certainly John and Morning loved her unconditionally. Otherwise she wouldn't be such a happy, outgoing child. But she deserved more. The love of grandparents who would dote on this child. The love of her only living parent to carry her through the tough times ahead.

She shifted her gaze away from the wonder and pain and amazement of Star to Kody. An expert at masking his emotions, he hadn't been able to hide the pain of seeing Star act out the truth of her crippled foot. His eyes were wide, darker than the blackest of night. His mouth pulled to a hard line.

How could he pretend this child didn't need him?

How long before her sweet innocence turned sour? About as long as it took her to overhear some of the remarks already said regarding her. About as long as it took for her to realize she'd been abandoned. How could Kody not see how she would feel?

Charlotte shook her head. There had to be a way she could convince him to reconsider his decision and save such needless pain.

Star struggled to her feet. Watching her limp toward Morning on her crooked foot filled Charlotte with fresh, pulsating pain.

Star leaned against Morning's knees. "Jesus will make my leg better when I see Him." She nodded, her eyes questioning.

Morning brushed her hand over Star's head. "In heaven you will run and jump like a deer." Her voice was soft and reassuring.

Star nodded. "I like that."

Kody watched Star, as did Charlotte. As the child moved away, he shifted. Their gazes brushed and stalled. She saw the tightness around his eyes, the way he pulled his mouth in as if he could contain his feelings, perhaps even deny them.

She'd hoped for, prayed for, something to change his mind, but she hadn't hoped for the pain she saw etched in his face. His pain became her pain, knifing into her heart with cruel abandon. She pressed her palm to her chest as if she could end it. She lifted her other hand toward Kody, wanting to end his suffering.

He sucked in a noisy gust of air, blinked, and suddenly his mask fell into place again, his eyes grew cool and indifferent, his mouth a mocking smile.

But she knew what she'd seen.

Chapter Eleven

Kody patted his pocket. He'd been to the Cartwell ranch. He'd clung to the back of that rank horse until they both knew he couldn't be thrown. He'd earned the twenty bucks. His first stop—the post office, where he intended to order those special shoes for Star.

Thinking of Star, he squinted, held his breath, preparing for the avalanche of emotion to thunder through him. There'd been too many deluges in the past three days to count. They'd started as he watched Star play with her doll, tying one foot back and then freeing it. The first avalanche almost swept him off his feet, literally. He would have given his own limbs if they could have fixed hers.

The second came hard on its heels when she'd gone to Morning wanting reassurance she would walk and run in heaven. Why should she have to wait until then to be free? He vowed he would earn money and order those shoes as quickly as humanly possible. He wanted to do more, but some things were out of the world of possibility. Charlotte declared she would pray for a miracle. He knew she didn't mean only Star's foot. He wished he believed in miracles as readily as Charlotte did. Right now he'd give his right arm for one.

He couldn't stop his thoughts from returning to another avalanche. Something grabbed his heart and squeezed it cruelly as he remembered Star's words: "I love you very, very much." He wished he could hear those words every day of his life. Just wasn't possible. Although the words twisted his gut, their sweetness soothed the sting.

He slowed his steps, waiting for the roar of emotions to pass before he entered the post office. One thing he appreciated, Charlotte hadn't mentioned the incident on the trip home. He couldn't have handled her pointing out how much Star needed him. He pretty much figured he'd end up telling her he needed the child even more than she needed him. He wanted to be the one to encourage Star through each day, to tell her he loved her very much and her crooked foot only made him love her more. He wanted to hear her sweet words of love every day he lived. But acknowledging his love for her did not change one thing—she would be better off raised as an Indian than facing rejection in a white world. Or worse, sharing his half-breed world, fitting with neither race.

He'd been glad of Charlotte's quiet presence beside him on the trip back to town, and when she squeezed his arm, he gripped the steering wheel extra hard to stop himself from reaching for her. He wanted to hold her close and breathe in the sweet, fresh scent of her hair and skin, like the breeze off the mountains on a spring day. He kept himself from opening his arms to her, but he couldn't stop the new cleft forming in his heart that let in the pure sunshine of her presence. She knew how it felt to be rejected. It made her sweet, kind and understanding. For the first time he felt safe with someone besides his parents and the Eaglefeathers.

He reached the post office and firmly pushed his distracting thoughts out of the way. He threw open the door and jerked to a halt.

Charlotte stood halfway across the room.

He hadn't seen her since yesterday when, glad of the excuse, he'd stayed home with Pa while Charlotte and Ma went to church. He'd left this morning before anyone else awoke.

She turned, saw him, and her eyes flared with welcome. Her mouth curved in a smile, making him long for things not possible for a man like him—home and family and permanency.

"Hi." Her voice filled with the sound of happiness—he let himself think she was glad to see him.

He nodded and grinned. She indicated he should do his business first, so he asked for an envelope, addressed it and made out the money order for an amount to cover the cost of the shoes.

Charlotte stood close behind, watching. "I hope they help," she murmured.

"Me, too." His voice sounded thick and he cleared his throat.

"You want the mail?" Mr. Scofield asked.

"Sure thing."

Mr. Scofield handed him three thin envelopes. He checked them. Two were for Pa. The third for Miss Charlotte Porter. The expected letter from Harry? For a moment he thought of pretending it wasn't there. The minute she opened it she would be off to join her brother without a thought in any other direction. Belonging was more important to her than anything else. Certainly more than something as uncertain and bound to be full of rejection as staying with him would be.

No, he didn't mean him. He had other plans.

And even if he did mean her, he couldn't think of her being treated like a white squaw.

He handed her the letter.

"It's from Harry." She pressed it to her chest. "Finally."

Kody knew how she'd react—nothing mattered but rejoining Harry, the brother who didn't mind deserting her on the farm.

She stepped back to a corner by the window, carefully ran her thumbnail under the flap and pulled out one page. She looked inside the envelope and shook it.

"I thought he would send a money order."

She unfolded the page, torn from an old school scribbler, and read the letter aloud. "'We are in a tiny shack. Can't find work. You must wait. I will send for you at first opportunity.'" She gave a tiny cry of distress and read the letter again, her mouth silently repeating the words.

Kody stepped closer, aching to comfort her, assure her he didn't mind if she stayed around Favor for a while.

She folded the page, placed it carefully back in the envelope and pushed it into her pocket. "How could Harry simply abandon me? I haven't even been able to write and inform him I'm with your parents. For all he knows I've starved to death on poverty acres. The house could have fallen down around my head." She flung an angry look at Kody. "Maybe he hopes I've decided to marry Lother out of desperation." She shuddered. "If you'd turned out to be a scoundrel, I could be on my way to

Canada without leaving a trace. But does Harry care? Apparently not. He didn't even ask how I was."

She pushed past Kody and stormed from the building.

Kody followed on her heels, hoping she didn't intend to do something foolish. He'd seen how her anger fueled her to do things she wouldn't normally consider.

"Charlotte—"

"Don't talk to me. I'm not in the mood." She headed down Main Street, then reconsidered and spun around.

He leaped out of her way.

"I do all I can do to please both him and Nellie. I run errands, do the dirty jobs, all—" she flung him an accusing look as if he was personally at fault "—without complaining. But does it count? No. I'm his sister. You'd think it would make me part of the family, but it doesn't seem to."

She made a sharp right and steamed onward. She drew in a long breath and slowed. "Sometimes it's mighty hard to see God's hand in these things."

They walked on at a slower pace, passing the newer houses.

"I told you about being sent to the Applebys."

He felt angry just thinking about how she'd been treated. "I gather it wasn't a happy experience for you."

"He had no right to send me away, but Nellie… Never mind. The reasons no longer matter. But I was a kid, a babe in the woods. I needed someone to protect me. I had no one." She stopped and fixed Kody with a look so full of pain and confusion that he took her hand and pulled her off the street into a little park. He led her to a bench and waited for her to sit, then dropped down beside her.

He wanted to hold her in his arms, make all the bad things go away, but he didn't know how she'd react to such a bold move. So he hesitantly took her hand and let out a tense breath when she gripped it.

"Jerrod, the oldest Appleby boy, eighteen years old, thought himself pretty special and so did his parents. What Jerrod wanted, Jerrod got. And when he decided he wanted me, they turned a blind eye. They had to see the way he watched me, how he made excuses to come into the kitchen when I was alone. But who was I? Just a servant girl. His sister, Viola, was the only one who showed me any kindness. And she saw. She watched Jerrod and when he came to my bed one night, she followed him. She called her parents to confront him. But of course, he wasn't at fault. *I* was. They wanted to turn me into the street, but Viola took me to a friend and contacted Harry." Her voice filled with bitterness. "I'm surprised he came to get me."

"Let me guess. That's when Nellie had a baby."

"Yes. Ricky. But I didn't care why they'd let me come back. I was that glad to be safe." She squeezed his hand so hard he wondered where she got the strength.

The wind whined around the trees, carrying with it the never-ending supply of dust that stung Kody's cheeks. He lifted his face to the bite of each particle. He dared the wind to do more, cut his skin with its tiny, sharp weapons, shred it; he would let blood gush from each torn pore. Even that would not equal the way Charlotte's words tore at his insides. He hoped he'd meet Harry someday. His muscles clenched. Best for both of them if he never did.

Charlotte sighed and leaned back, still clinging to his hand. "You see, I know what it's like to be forsaken by your only living relative."

Her silent accusation iced his veins. He withdrew his

hand. "How can you make this about Star? She's in a safe place. Morning and John love her."

"Yes, they do, but will it be enough when she discovers the truth, or at least cruel hints of it?"

"Why should she?"

"Let's see." She held up one finger. "First, everyone knows she isn't Morning's child." She held up another finger. "People can figure out who might be the parents by simple deduction. Or by gossip and guesswork." She held up a third finger. "As I'm sure you've noticed, she doesn't have Indian eyes."

"They're pretty dark."

She made a disbelieving sound.

He faced her squarely. "You also discovered what it's like for people not to accept you. It makes you afraid, vulnerable. It hurts."

She took his hand. "I'm sorry you've been hurt by what people say. But how can it turn you from your own child? She needs you. You need her."

He wanted to pull away from Charlotte. He hadn't meant himself when he said rejection hurt. He wanted to deny what she said. He couldn't. Neither could he escape the knowledge Morning and John might be able to give Star what he could not—a place where she'd be accepted. "She's safe with them. They would never send her away or put her in a position like Harry did to you."

Charlotte's shoulders sagged. "Yes, at least she'll be safe."

Kody's anger fled. "You no longer need Harry to keep you safe." He ached to promise her he would be willing to do it, but he couldn't. He didn't plan to stay. "Besides—" he started to grin "—you're no longer a child and quite capable of taking care of yourself. Haven't you proved it several times since Harry left? Maybe it's served a good purpose—you have learned how strong you are."

Her gaze clung to him as if seeking truth and reassurance from him.

He smiled, quite willing to give her whatever she needed.

Slowly, the tension in her face faded. "I have done some surprising things since I met you." Her eyes widened. "I guess I have you to blame." Her voice dropped to a whisper. "Or should I thank you?"

"You can thank me if you want." He studied her lips and thought of a time-honored way of expressing thanks. He jerked his attention back to something he needed to say. If he could only remember what it was. Oh, yeah. "But you don't need me to goad you into being strong. That's what you are and you need to realize it."

She searched his face. Her gaze delved deep into his eyes. "You might not like me strong, ready to defend and protect."

He wondered if her cheek was as smooth as he imagined and touched it. His heart leaped to his fingertips at the warm, soft texture. Slowly, giving her lots of chance to duck away, he lowered his head and touched her lips in the softest form of a kiss.

A pair of women passed. One tsked loudly. "Did you see that?" she proclaimed in a loud whisper. "Some people have no decency. You expect it from his sort, but her?" She sniffed loud enough to suck the dust from a thirty-foot radius.

Kody jerked back. He would have bolted to his feet, but Charlotte grabbed his hand. She grinned at him.

"Didn't you just point out I need no protecting? I'm a strong person, remember?"

She rose slowly, seemingly unaffected by the way the women glanced over their shoulders, and she held his hand firmly. He could have easily broken away if he tried. He didn't.

"Where are we going?" Charlotte asked. She seemed happy in spite of her letter from Harry.

Kody hoped he might have something to do with it. At his invitation, after supper they left Ma reading to Pa in the front room and headed outside for a walk. "Do you want to see where I used to play?"

"Sure"

He'd hardly been able to keep his eyes off her throughout the meal and had to force himself to pay attention to Ma as she told how Pa walked from the bedroom without any help. He was glad Pa showed improvement, but it paled in comparison to the idea of spending time with Charlotte.

He took her hand, liking how it fit perfectly into his palm, liking how she moved closer to his side as they walked down the alley. They cut across an empty lot and were soon out of town. Half a mile later he helped her up a steep hill to a rugged crop of rocks. "One of my favorite places to play when I was a kid."

She looked about, then flashed a smile that warmed him deep inside. "What did you play?"

"Depends if I was alone or with a friend." He'd almost forgotten those happy times, allowed them to be swallowed up by the other stuff—the cruel remarks, the whispers not meant to be secret and his growing resentment.

"What did you play alone?"

"I would make little hideouts in the rocks and pretend to be a real Indian." He led her to a hollowed-out spot. "See, here's one of the places. Sometimes Ma even let me spend the night. That was great. I'd lie on my back staring at the stars and thinking."

She leaned against a nearby rock and watched him poke through the dirt. "What did you think about?"

"Mostly about what it would have been like to be the first man to see this place, how big the ocean is, what makes the stars twinkle. Does God love everyone the same—" He stopped. He hadn't meant to say the last part, but now that he had, he wondered if Charlotte would try to answer it.

"I've wondered, too, and I've decided He loves everyone, but some people see more of it."

"What do you mean?"

"I think people who have hard things to deal with know more about God's love, don't you?"

Kody stared at her. He wasn't sure he agreed with her. In his case, had his difficulties turned him to God? No, they'd turned him away. But Charlotte...

"I guess I'd have to say it seems to have made you cling to God."

She smiled so serenely it caressed his heart just watching her. Something sweet and good, something gentle and healing, slipped into his heart. "I know He loves me but no more or less than He loves you."

He believed her. For the first time in years, Kody felt as if God cared about him. Not that it changed anything. People would still treat him the same. But rather than spoil the moment by pointing out the unchangeable realities of life, he turned the talk to other things.

"My friends and I loved to play hide-and-seek or—" he slanted her a look, wanting to see her reaction "—cowboys and Indians. Guess who had to fight not to be the Indian?"

She blinked as if having trouble following his change of subject, then slowly her eyes widened and she laughed. "I can't imagine who got picked to be the Indian. I suppose the most unruly friend."

He laughed. "I was always a good kid, but it didn't make any difference. I still had to be the Indian. Most times I didn't mind. I liked sneaking up on them and scaring them. I even tried to scalp Tommy Tompson once."

She looked suitably shocked. "You didn't."

"With a pretend knife."

She laughed. "It sounds like you had a lot of fun as a kid."

Telling Charlotte about those happy times filled him with sweet pleasure. "I did. Didn't you?"

"My father died when I was a baby and Harry left home to work when I was only eight, so Mother and I were alone. As long as I can remember, Mother was sick. I had little time for play. I learned early to help out as much as I could."

"Maybe it's time you had a little fun."

She looked vaguely uninterested.

"You *are* familiar with the idea, aren't you?"

"Of course."

Suddenly he dashed behind some rocks to a place he remembered hiding. The place didn't quite accommodate his size anymore, but he tucked himself deep into the crevice and waited. He didn't have to wait long.

"Kody, where are you?"

"Find me," he growled deep in his throat.

"Kody. Stop it."

"It's called play," he called, and then hunkered down further as he heard her start around the rocks.

"Where are you?" she called, drawing closer.

He hoped she couldn't see him.

She called again, closer, called yet again, this time just inches away. Unless she turned she could pass by and not see him. She paused. "Kody. This isn't funny."

He hadn't enjoyed anything this much in a long time. Maybe he was the one who'd forgotten how to play. He counted—one, two, three—and as she took another step, leaped out with a yell rivaling any uttered by an Indian, imagined or real.

She screamed and took off like a shot.

"Yiiiie, yiiie, yiii!" He raced after her.

She glanced back, saw him and turned around. "That's not funny. You scared me out of ten years."

He bent over his knees, laughing. "It was priceless."

"Why you…" She began a measured stalk toward him.

Still chuckling, he straightened, tensed and when she almost reached him, jumped away.

She broke into a run, trying to catch him.

He darted back and forth, taunting her, tempting her to catch him before he ducked away.

She stopped, plucked a blade of grass, examined it as she edged toward him, pretending the grass held her attention, trying to make him think she didn't want to catch him, but he wasn't fooled and leaped away as she lunged for him. His foot caught on a rock and with a yell, he fell on his back.

She pounced, pressing her hands to his chest. "Serves you right, you crazy man."

He didn't move to escape. Instead, he locked eyes with her. Her gaze went on and on. Beyond his past, over his feelings of inadequacy, straight to the cracks and scars on his heart, and in that moment, by some spiritual miracle, they began to heal.

"You caught me," he whispered, meaning far more than pinning him to the ground.

"I'm trying to decide what to do with you."

"I can tell you."

"Really?"

"This." He cupped her head and lifted his head to meet her mouth with his.

He felt her surprise and then a quiet yielding. Then he pulled back and looked into eyes full of dark emotion. He wished he could believe it to be acceptance and caring, when most likely it was nothing more than surprise at his boldness. He'd kissed her twice in one day. And she'd let him. He guessed that meant something, thought he couldn't say for sure what. Nor what he wanted it to mean. This was getting way too complicated.

She sat back on her heels, looking out over the hills, but didn't say anything.

Glad not to have to deal with his confusion, he scrambled up and sat beside her, his legs stretched out on the brittle grass. The sun sank low in the west. The air, foggy with dust, turned pink. He waited for her to speak, wondering if she would scold him or…

He wouldn't let himself dream of other possibilities. Yet all the reasons he could hope flashed through his mind. She never seemed to notice he had Indian blood in him until he reminded her. Could it be possible? His heart rattled against his ribs like a rock tossed by turbulent water. He could love this woman if he let himself. The realization hit him like a full-force gale, sucking away his breath, turning his insides into a whirlwind of warm, delightful thoughts—the joy of sharing every moment with her, the fun of teasing and making her laugh, the pleasure of seeing her grow feisty and defensive...

"It's a pretty evening," she said. "I wish life could always be like this—soft and pleasant."

"Huh." Not much he could say to something like that, because wishing didn't change the harsh realities of life—something he would do well to remember.

He pushed to his feet, dismissing his delightful, totally unrealistic dreams. "We better get back." For a few delicious moments, he'd let himself think—but even if she did care about him he knew the censure she'd face if she acknowledged it. The best thing he could do was get himself out of this town as fast as possible and ride for Canada like he was driven by the relentless wind.

Only, he had to see Star with her new shoes first.

He had to make sure Pa would be able to take care of himself.

He wanted to enjoy a few more days of Charlotte's company.

Chapter Twelve

Martha, as Mrs. Douglas had insisted she be called, said she needed nothing more done. The walls were scrubbed, the windows gleamed and a batch of rhubarb jam lined a shelf in the cellar.

Charlotte left the house and headed toward the park where she and Kody had sat a few days ago. The day he told her she was a strong woman, the day he kissed her.

She needed to think, figure out what it all meant. She sat on the bench and prayed. *God, I think I love Kody, but I'm confused. I don't know if it's real or if it's returned. Keep me from dong anything foolish.*

He thinks I'm strong.

Could it be possible? She'd been so busy trying to please she hadn't thought of anything else. Until Harry left her, she'd gladly, willingly, let him or Nellie dictate her every move. She chuckled, thinking it had been fun to make some of her own decisions and even exert a little defiance. She'd managed to scare off Ratface and Shorty. For a moment she wondered if they'd moved on, then she forgot the pair as she cherished the memory of how she and Kody had played a game of tag ending in a kiss.

Her feelings for Kody were so fresh and unfamiliar she could hardly think what they meant. She only knew she felt safe with him in a way completely different from the way she felt with Harry. She trusted Kody. He would always be honest and sincere. Even when he didn't want to be. Even when she didn't want to hear what he had to say because she preferred not to face the truth.

But was she simply looking for someone to replace Harry?

It was all so convoluted and confusing.

She could only again pray that God would guide her and keep her from being foolish.

She left the park, but took her troubling thoughts with her as she walked the streets of Favor. Eventually she ended up in one of the stores. She bent over a display case to admire a tiny hand mirror. She wished she had the money to purchase it for Star. The child got so much pleasure out of simple things. She imagined her enjoying the little mirror.

She left off staring at the mirror and wandered around the store, aimless and bored. She wasn't used to having nothing to do. But she recognized her restlessness went deeper than boredom. Kody rode off early every day, gone to some ranch to break horses. She'd seen men ride wild horses to a standstill. Or more often, get tossed to the ground trying. Some suffered more than surface injuries. She tried not to think of Kody being hurt.

But until he returned each evening, she missed him and worried about him.

She left the store and sauntered over to the post office to ask for the mail. She stopped to poke through the notices on the bulletin board, not looking for anything, simply passing time.

A woman hurried through the door and over to the wicket. "Give me my mail, Matt."

"On your way to the hospital, are you?"

"I am. I hadn't expected to work today, but Matron practically begged me to come in. We're run off our feet with cases of dust pneumonia. We could sure use some help."

Charlotte turned to see who spoke. The woman appeared to be in her thirties and wore a crisp white uniform and white cap with stiff, starched wings. Could they use *her?* It would be nice to be needed again. She drew in a deep, courage-giving breath and approached the woman. "What kind of help do you need?"

The woman looked her up and down with sharp eyes, taking in every detail. "Are you volunteering?"

"Could I? I mean, I have no nursing experience."

"Can you run and fetch? Follow orders?"

"As well as most, better than some." Something about this woman made Charlotte speak briskly.

"Then go down to the hospital and ask to speak to Matron Morrow. Tell her Helen Chester sent you. And be prepared to start work immediately. Wear a big apron and pin your hair up." Mrs. Chester smiled. "You'll be welcomed with open arms. Of course, you'll be paid a fair wage."

"I'll be there as soon as I deliver the mail to the Douglases."

"You're living with them?"

Charlotte nodded. "For now." For how long she didn't dare venture a guess.

Mrs. Chester's smile widened. "They're good folk. Anyone associated with them needs no other recommendation. Now hurry. I can use your help."

Charlotte dashed from the building and hurried up the street. Breathless by the time she reached the Douglas home, she clattered into the house, raced upstairs and into the sewing room, where she knew Martha would be.

Martha looked up, startled by her rushed entrance. "Charlotte, what is it?"

"I have a job." She told of her conversation with Mrs. Chester. "I guess I'm going to need one if I have to support myself."

"You'll always be welcome here."

"I know." She also knew how desperately short of cash Martha and Leland were. "I appreciate it, but I'll feel better contributing something."

She changed into a clean cotton dress Nellie had given her when she gained weight with Mandy. It wasn't material Charlotte would have chosen. The pale pink color looked faded even when new, the flowers unnatural. Nellie made the dress plain as bread, but Charlotte had prettied it up with a daisy stitch around the collar. According to Mrs. Chester's instructions, she pinned her hair back and twisted it into a little bun. She borrowed a big white apron from Martha. Not certain how long she'd be there or what arrangements had been made for the staff to eat, she packed a small lunch and set off. From the bottom of her stomach crept an uneasy feeling she tried to ignore. She'd never spent any time in a hospital. Could she handle the sight of so many sick people?

Matron Morrow greeted her as if expecting her. "Nurse Chester said you might show up. You look sturdy enough. Now let me tell you what you will encounter. Most of our patients right now are here with dust pneumonia. Many are quietly struggling to avoid the inevitable. We do all we can to ease their suffering. Others, thank God, are recovering."

Charlotte tried not to think of the despair of those dying and vowed she would do all she could to help both them and the recovering ones. "What do you want me to do?"

"Assist the weaker ones. Get them to eat or drink if you can. Take water to the thirsty. I don't think you'll have any trouble keeping busy if you are at all industrious."

Charlotte decided then and there she would prove to Matron Morrow and every nurse on the staff how useful she could be. Matron led her down the hall and into the wards. The whole building rattled with coughing—loud, hacking coughs, as well as gasping, struggling ones. Charlotte remembered the lung-deep irritation of breathing in too much dust and longed to be able to ease each sufferer.

She stepped into the women's ward and noticed that the patients were thin, pale and out of breath. Most were elderly. Or mere children. Within minutes she was busy. She carried water to everyone. She spent an hour rubbing the back of a small boy while his parents sat on two metal chairs, their feelings so clear in their eyes—fear, dread, worry and a tiny shred of hope their child would survive.

She paused at noon, following Nurse Chester's instructions to join the nurses in the kitchen. Cook presented them with steaming cups of coffee while the nurses opened their sacks of food. Charlotte gratefully opened the lunch she'd packed.

Matron's prediction proved right. The afternoon passed so quickly Charlotte could hardly believe it when one of the nurses tapped her on the shoulder. "It's time to go home."

Matron stepped out of her office. "Can we count on you tomorrow morning?"

"If you want me." She'd scurried around from patient to patient, she'd helped measure out medications, she'd tried to comfort an old, old man so wrinkled and shrunken he might have been a hundred. Only, he comforted her. "Don't worry about the drought and dust— every day means we're a day closer to it raining." Charlotte laughed at his philosophy.

"You did well," Matron said. "I'll be glad to see you regularly."

Although her feet hurt clear up to her knees and weariness swept over her, Charlotte reveled in Matron's praise as she headed home. For the first time in ages she'd done something of significance. Her footsteps slowed. This was the *first* time she'd done something *she'd* decided to do, and it felt good right down to the soles of her very sore feet.

Martha had supper prepared when Charlotte got back, and guilt swept away some of her joy. She rushed forward. "I'm sorry I wasn't here to help."

Kody came into the house in time to hear Charlotte's apology. He quirked an eyebrow and his silent look asked many questions.

She could barely contain her excitement. She wanted to tell him, tell them all, how much she enjoyed her new job, but first she had to make sure she did her share of the work here. "Next time wait until I get home."

Martha fluttered a hand at her. "I can manage to prepare a meal. You sit down and put your feet up."

But Charlotte could not. She helped carry the bowls of vegetables to the table.

Leland waited for everyone to be seated, then lifted a hand. "I will pray." His words slurred, he nevertheless managed a quiet, heartfelt prayer full of gratitude. "Lord of all creation, You have made each of us. You have blessed us. Thank you. Amen."

Charlotte glanced at Kody, wondering if he shared Leland's gratitude. He smiled, and the smile fell into her heart with an unexpected burst of pleasure. She ducked her head. How silly to think she might be part of the reason he seemed happy. Yet she hoped...

"I got a job," she said.

"Good for you. Who had the good sense to hire you?"

His ready approval pleased her more than she cared to admit. "I'm an aide at the hospital."

Over the meal she told them about her work. She repeated the old man's remarks about every day of drought being closer to the end of it, and everyone laughed. "I'm to go back tomorrow." She stopped and looked at Martha. "Of course, if you need me—"

Martha laughed. "You go to work. It's the best thing for you."

"She's right," Kody said. "This is just what you need to get your mind off waiting for life to happen."

He probably meant his words to be encouraging, but they stung. Did he think she sat around waiting? No. She worked while she waited. She grinned, silently acknowledging the truth of his words.

"They need strong people like you to help with the sick."

His reminder that he thought her strong made her sit taller. "I enjoy the work."

They exchanged quick smiles, then she ducked away before Martha and Leland could think her too bold with their son.

"How did your day go?" she asked of everyone, but looked at Kody, wanting to hear what he'd done since she last saw him. Seems Leland and Martha felt the same, as they turned to him and waited for his answer.

"Nothing exciting about my day. Broke a few horses. Saw a baby hawk learning to fly. Outrode a dust storm." He said it with such calm, bored, flat tones that for a minute Charlotte thought he might have been reading a list of supplies. She saw the twinkle in his eye at the same time as she realized how out of the ordinary the events had been, and she laughed.

Leland and Martha laughed, too.

Kody grinned and seemed pleased he'd amused them.

Charlotte worked ten days before she got a day off. She picked up her first pay and before she headed home, stopped at the store to buy the mirror she'd admired.

Kody continued to work on nearby ranches, mostly breaking horses but doing odd jobs, as well. "Anything to make a few bucks."

She didn't ask what he planned to do with the money—it wasn't any of her business—but she knew it would finance his Canada trip. He never said anything to suggest he'd changed his mind. She knew he waited for the shoes for Star, and hung about to help Leland. But every day Leland grew stronger, and once the shoes came...

What would keep him there after that?

How could she hope she might be a reason for him to stay? Sure, they found more and more excuses to spend time together. She very much enjoyed walking and talking with him, and sharing stories after Martha and Leland went to bed. But was it enough to convince him to abandon his plan to head to Canada?

She glanced at the package she carried. She'd made little progress toward convincing him to become Star's father. To her shame, she'd been distracted with her own interests. Her work at the hospital was both satisfying and demanding.

A sense of urgency made her walk faster. She didn't know how much time she had left to accomplish her goal. She only knew she didn't dare waste another minute.

Kody returned for the evening meal. When she'd helped clean up afterward, he asked if she wanted to go with him to check on the horses kept in the small pen in the back of the yard. He rode Sam almost everywhere he went and threw out some feed for Blackie before he left each morning.

She agreed to accompany him, reminding herself she must use this opportunity to work on him about Star.

They leaned on the top rail of the fence. "I suppose we ought to sell Blackie," Kody said. "She's nothing but a hay burner."

"I hate to see her go." The horse had been so patient with Charlotte on the ride to Favor.

"It's not like anyone rides her."

"I might decide to."

"What for?"

"Something to do."

"Aren't you pretty busy with the hospital and all?"

"Didn't you remind me the other day that a person should play, too?"

His head jerked up and their gazes locked. "Showed you how, too." His voice seemed husky.

She couldn't look away from his black eyes. She couldn't get a sound past her constricted throat. Yes, she'd enjoyed the kiss. Even more, she'd been thrilled to think he cared about her, had forgotten for just a few minutes he was both Indian and white and yet neither, remembered only he was a man and she was a woman and something good and strong and right had been growing between them since he'd walked into Harry's house in the middle of a dust storm. He'd blown her right out of her complacent frame of mind as cleanly as the wind swept bare the dried-out prairie.

"You've been showing me lots of things." She finally managed to squeeze out the words.

He looked deep into her eyes, searching past her words, past her smile to something deeper, something she wasn't sure she wanted to expose. "Like what?" he asked.

"How to be strong. I'm liking it."

"You would have discovered it yourself sooner or later."

"Maybe." She hovered between taking another step toward what he thought she could be, and clinging to his strength. Yet neither was safe. Being independent felt good but scared her. She was used to someone else taking care of problems. However, leaning on him would be futile. He'd ride out as quickly as Harry had when he finished here. That brought her sharply back to her real purpose for wanting to talk to Kody alone. She'd decided coming directly at the subject of Star only caused him to throw up instant, automatic resistance. So she would try something indirect.

She knew he'd visited the reservation several times since she'd been there last—surely a good sign. "Shouldn't those shoes have been here by now?"

"They have to be specially made. John gave me an outline of her feet to send with the order. I suppose it takes time."

"I wonder if you'd give me a ride out to the reservation so I can give Star a little present."

"Sure. I planned to go tomorrow, anyway."

Chapter Thirteen

Kody again borrowed Pa's car to drive to the reservation. The sun shone with brittle determination. But it only made Kody smile. "One day closer to rain," he murmured, reminding Charlotte of the old man in the hospital.

"One more day of God's blessing."

He didn't argue. Seems God had been giving Kody many gifts lately, which made him nervous, suspicious, cautious. He wondered when the rug would be yanked out from under him.

But Charlotte seemed bent on itemizing her blessings. "I am so grateful for my job. I love the work. And your father is getting better every day. I'm sure if I look around I can think of more things to rejoice about."

He glanced at her, saw the way her eyes caressed him, wondered if she counted him among the things she was grateful for. Her cheeks blossomed pink and then she jerked her attention to something out the window. He'd been staring, drinking in her smile and gentle spirit. He had no right to allow himself such thoughts. Not that he didn't like to believe she might return his feelings of welcome, connection, acceptance, but love? No way. He couldn't allow himself to love her. Even as he couldn't admit he was Star's father. Because nothing changed. Nothing ever changed. It never would. He would forever remain a half-breed, hated by most of the whites because he was too Indian, shunned by most of the Indians because he was too white. And anyone who loved him got the same cold shoulder from others. He would never do that to Charlotte. Yet he smiled, recalling how she'd purposely ignored the women in the park on that day when he'd admitted he had very deep feelings for her, when he'd kissed her and reveled in her acceptance. For a few delicious moments, he'd let himself think about what it would be like...

He knew better than to even think about it.

He shifted the conversation to Pa's announcement he intended to go to church tomorrow. "I expect next thing we know Pa will be wanting to start preaching again."

Charlotte chuckled. "Your mother says he's finally started to fight back from this stroke, and now she wonders if it isn't as bad as having him lie there and do nothing. She said she doesn't dare leave the house because the minute she does, he tries to do something she doesn't think he should. Yesterday he climbed the stairs. She came home to find him sitting in the rocker in her sewing room. Said she almost had a heart attack."

They laughed, their eyes connecting with shared pleasure and amusement.

"Its good to see Pa more like his old self."

"He's been reading the Bible and making notes, but he complains to Martha he can't read his own writing anymore. He asked her to make notes for him. She refused. 'If I do,' she said, 'the next thing, you'll be wanting me to hold you up while you stand at the pulpit.'"

Again they laughed.

"He'll be standing there on his own before we know it if I know my pa."

"Are you going to accompany him to church tomorrow?"

Pa had asked him, but Kody murmured something about having an important task to take care of.

"Do you plan to give him some weak excuse?"

He shot her a look. "Sometimes I think I liked you better complacent and submissive."

She lifted her chin. "Well, thanks to you, I'm not anymore."

"Me?"

"Yes, you. You stomped into my safe little house and literally forced me to leave."

He laughed. "How can you call that a safe place?"

"Because it was familiar and where Harry told me to wait."

Harry! Kody had no use for the man. How could he ride off and leave the woman in his charge? Kody's thoughts did a sudden turn. But leaving Star with Morning and John was not the same. Not even close.

Thankfully they arrived at the Eaglefeathers', sparing him having to argue further with himself or answer the challenge in Charlotte's eyes.

He'd brought more supplies, including some tinned beef. Charlotte and Morning made a stew with it. Charlotte waited until they sat back with cups of tea, helping themselves to biscuits from a tin he'd brought, before she got the package from the car.

"Star, this is for you."

Star held the unopened parcel, her eyes sparkling. "Oh, goody! Just what I always wanted."

The adults laughed.

Kody said, "Shouldn't you open it first and see what it is?"

Star carefully pulled the ends of the bow and removed the string. She scrunched it into a bundle and handed it to Morning. "I save it."

"I'll put in a safe place."

Star folded back the paper. The sun flashed in the mirror and she jerked back, looking frightened.

Charlotte knelt at her side. "It's a mirror. You look in it and see yourself." She held it to her face first and patted her hair. Then turned it to Star. "See."

Star stared openmouthed, then took the mirror. She touched her hair. Made faces and giggled.

Kody laughed at her antics. And he pushed away the pain he would never quite get used to, even though he knew he did the right thing in leaving her here.

He joined the conversation, but kept his eyes on Star. She struggled to her feet and hobbled toward him. He prayed God would use those special shoes to straighten her foot. He didn't even bother to question why he felt he would pray for someone else but not himself.

Star leaned her bony elbows on his knees. Although it hurt, he welcomed it. When he was alone in Canada, he would touch those twin spots and remember her looking up at him like this.

She held the mirror for him to look into. Then she pulled it away and looked into his eyes so demandingly he almost shifted his gaze. "Eyes black," she announced, and moved to John, where she did the same thing.

"Eyes black," she said, and moved to Morning's

knees. "Eyes black," she announced again, then shifted to Charlotte's knees. She looked into Charlotte's face a long time. "Light eyes."

She sat down in the middle of the yard again and looked into the mirror. "Light eyes." She lay the mirror down. "I get baby." She hobbled into the small house.

Kody's insides curled like an angry fist. Charlotte was right. Star already recognized she was different.

"Some of the children call her Light Eyes," John murmured.

Kody's fists balled. His shoulder muscles tensed. Was his daughter to face prejudice even here? Because of something she couldn't help or change? He leaned forward to the balls of his feet. He wanted to run. But where would he run? To Canada? Even there he would not be able to escape the pain this knowledge gave him.

"They are not unkind," John said, as if suspecting Kody's fear. "Just stating a fact."

Slowly the tension seeped from Kody's limbs, leaving him feeling beaten and chewed.

He felt Charlotte's gaze on him but couldn't look at her. She would see his pain. She would guess his fears and use them to fuel her arguments.

Star returned with her rag doll and played happily for the rest of the afternoon. Two black-eyed girls about Star's age came over and squatted beside her. Star let them play with the mirror and shared her doll. The three of them giggled together like any little girls would.

Kody smiled. She was accepted here, had friends. He was right to leave her. Even if it hurt all the way to the depths of his marrow and to the ends of every nerve in his body.

Later he held the car door for Charlotte as they prepared to leave. She gave him a long, demanding look, which he ignored. She would have something to say about the afternoon on the ride home, but he figured if he had his say first, she wouldn't get a chance to poke at his pain.

"I remember when I was young," he began, determined to show Charlotte how prevailing prejudice was, even toward children, hoping it would silence her campaign to make him agree otherwise. "Ma had some ladies over for tea. I remember the little cakes they had and how they all managed to hold tiny little cups so daintily. They sat in the front room discussing some missionary project. I recall the door being open to let in a breeze, and I sat by it, looking outside, wishing I could be out there running and playing, but Ma insisted I dress up like a little man and sit through the visit. I watched a tall Indian walking down the street and thought how proud he seemed. His wife hurried after him, a papoose in her arms, a small child at her skirts. We didn't often see Indians in town and I was fascinated by the buckskins and beads." He laughed. "I thought they looked a lot more comfortable than my jacket and trousers. Then one of the women said Ma should send me with them. There were my kind. I had no idea what she meant. It was the first time I realized I was somehow different." The first but not the last time he'd been sharply reminded how people saw him.

He hadn't gotten used to it. Every time he heard a similar comment, his heart shriveled. He'd meant for Charlotte to see how it felt to be always on the outside, but perhaps he should have chosen another story. One that didn't remind him, didn't fill him with dread that Star might experience the same thing.

Charlotte made a sympathetic sound. "How utterly cruel of that woman."

Kody chuckled. "Ma was very angry. I knew it even though she didn't show it. She picked me up and held me on her lap and hugged me tight and said to the woman, 'Dakota is my son. He's my kind of boy. He belongs right here.'" Remembering how safe he'd felt in her lap, he swallowed hard.

Charlotte squeezed his arm. "You ma was right. You belong right here." She seemed to promise so much with her simple words.

He let the car creep to the edge of the road and crawl to a halt.

He let himself look at Charlotte, let himself be drawn into her gaze, let the warmth in her look reach deep into his soul where he kept secret things locked away, where they'd been so long they were buried in a tangle of webs. It seemed her look eased open the door and as she talked, the cobwebs peeled back just a little.

He couldn't turn from Charlotte's gaze. It offered the same kind of acceptance his ma's arms had provided. A man could feel safe with her.

He could no longer deny his feelings. He loved her. Somewhere in the distant recesses of his mind, he remembered they didn't belong to the same world. He had no right to even think of loving her, but right now he wanted to let his thoughts drown in the warm depths of her eyes.

The pressure of her hand on his arm had a gentle yet reassuring weight to it. Her touch made him want to confront people who dared say anything about his heritage. He leaned closer, breathed in her sweet, flowery scent, drank in her welcoming smile. He brushed his knuckles along her chin, enjoying the softness of her skin and the way her gaze clung to his. As if she accepted him just as Ma and Pa did. He wanted to believe it possible.

He kissed her gently, then pulled back and smiled into her eyes. He could live like this, enjoying her presence.

But the reality of who he was could not be avoided. He'd take it with him no matter how far north he rode. He'd live with it every day of his life. He had to accept how it affected his choices. And how it affected everyone he cared about.

"I don't belong anywhere." His voice rasped. "I don't know who I am. I don't know my real mother's name. Or who my father was." His voice dropped to a croak. "Maybe he forced himself on her." He meant to shock Charlotte. But the confession tore his deepest secret, his worst fear from him. "I could be just like him."

Tears glistening in her eyes, she rubbed her hand along his arm. "I think you mean you don't know who your parents are. We all know who *you* are."

Her touch made him want so many things—the chance to be someone, the right to ask for a woman's caress, to marry and have a family. But how could he hope for such things? He didn't belong anywhere. Didn't have anything to offer but an uncertain heritage. "Who am I?"

She smiled. "That's easy. You're a good, kind man with a sense of humor who helps others even when it means a sacrifice."

He ached to believe her. He touched her cheek, her skin as soft as the petals on a wild rose.

And white.

He jerked back. "That's what I do. But who *am* I? I don't belong in the white man's world. I tried living on a reservation and found out I don't belong in the Indian world, either. I am neither. I belong nowhere. Except maybe in Canada."

The warmth of her hand on his arm threatened his determination. "Kody, you can't keep running from who you are. What's more, one of these days you'll discover you have no reason to. You'll realize a man is what's in his heart, and you have a good heart." As if to drive the point home, she pressed her palm to his chest, then red crept up her neck and she drew back, ducking her head.

He wavered, torn between wanting to believe her words and the reality of what he'd seen and heard and lived all his life.

Charlotte sensed his withdrawal and knew it came from years of being conditioned to believe he didn't belong. Even though Martha and Leland loved him and accepted him wholly and freely, in Kody's mind it didn't outweigh what others said and how they'd acted toward him.

She ached to be able to convince him not everyone cared about his heritage. She wished for a way to make him admit those who loved him had more value in his life than those who showed such unkind prejudice. But she knew her words would fall on deaf ears. She could only pray, and she did, fervently, the rest of the way back to Favor.

She'd intended to point out how Star needed him to help her face the comments already coming her way. But Charlotte couldn't contemplate adding to Kody's distress and kept silent on the subject.

They arrived at the Douglas home and Kody parked the car. Charlotte waited outside as he straightened things in the garage. She wanted to say something to bring back the closeness she'd felt in the car before he confessed how he didn't know who he was, but Kody came out carrying his saddle.

"I'm going to take Sam for a ride. He needs the exercise."

Charlotte watched as he cinched the saddle and rode away. This wasn't about Sam needing exercise. This was about Kody dealing with his feelings. *Lord, God, please send healing into his heart. Show him how he is valued by so many people. Help him to see there will always be unkind people. Lord, I love him. Bring him back to me. As always, I submit to Your plan.*

Kody slipped out of the house Sunday morning before anyone stirred. He had almost decided to go to church for the pleasure of seeing Pa enjoy it. But it wasn't Pa he pictured. It was Charlotte. And he could not walk into church for the sole purpose of sitting next to the woman he loved but could not have.

He saddled Sam and rode out of town.

A few minutes later, he passed a very untidy campsite. He stopped to look around, found no one in the vicinity, although the ashes from the fire were still warm.

The general filth reminded him of Shorty and Ratface, but he hadn't seen them in days and figured they'd moved on.

With a shrug of indifference he returned to Sam. "Don't suppose those two are still hanging around, do you?"

Sam snorted.

"Yeah, you're right. A person better be a little cautious just in case."

Sam lifted his head and whinnied.

"You think they're still looking for revenge?" He jumped into the saddle. "Maybe I won't ride out of town, just in case." He would make sure no one hurt Charlotte.

He reined Sam around and headed back to Favor. "I kind of like having an excuse to hang about."

He could only describe Sam's response as a hearty horse-laugh.

He rose through town, checking the back alleys and hiding places—he knew most of them from childhood games. He saw nothing of the two men. It seemed they had gone elsewhere to conduct their mischief. He headed home. Ma and Pa and Charlotte would soon be back from church. He wasn't any more averse to Ma's cooking than he was to spending the afternoon in Charlotte's company.

Yeah, he knew he played dangerously close to the flames. But he could handle it for a few days. As soon as the shoes for Star came, he would leave. "Won't hurt any to allow myself a little enjoyment," he muttered, and earned a snort from Sam.

Chapter Fourteen

Charlotte was glad for her work at the hospital. Not only did she enjoy it, not only did it make her feel useful and appreciated, it kept her too busy to dwell on her relationship with Kody.

She cherished every minute they spent together and wished it could be more, but Kody left early every morning, working at various ranches earning money. He said he wanted to provide John and Morning with enough supplies for the winter before he rode north.

"I have to check on my pack and see what I still need," he said as they finished supper one day. "Care to help me?"

"As soon as I clean the kitchen."

Martha shooed her away. "I'll do it. You've put in a long day. Besides, how many nice evenings do we get? Go enjoy."

Charlotte fought a short-lived battle with her conscience. But Martha was right. How many evenings would she get to enjoy Kody's company? Each day she sensed his growing restlessness.

"I need to think of being on the road again soon."

He shook his bedroll and hung it over the wooden fence to air.

Charlotte didn't bother to respond. He said it so often she'd begun to think he was trying to convince himself.

"I can't imagine what's taking those people so long to send Star's shoes."

Charlotte leaned against the fence and smiled as she watched him. "It's giving you lots of time to get to know your daughter." They went to the reservation as often as Charlotte could get away. She knew Kody went even more often.

Kody paused from sorting through his things and smiled at her. "Can't complain about that."

"She's one sweet child."

He nodded. "You won't get any argument from me. John and Morning have done well with her."

Charlotte did not miss the flash of pain in his face before he bent over to examine his ax. "She's grown very fond of you. She's going to miss you when you go." She turned and stared across the alley, seeing nothing as pain pinched the back of her heart so cruelly she almost cried out. Star wouldn't be the only one who missed him when he left.

"Still no word from Harry?"

She recognized his intent in asking the question. *You'll be leaving first chance you get, too.* "I showed you his last letter."

It had read: "Glad you found someplace safe. Still looking for a suitable place for us. I'll send for you when I do."

"Huh," said Kody, as if nothing more needed to be said.

But Charlotte's heart burst with things to say. She

wanted to beg him to change his mind. But she knew unless something inside him changed, he would be headed to Canada.

As if to confirm her thoughts, he said, "I need to get there in time to find a place before winter. Get some sort of shelter erected, if only a tent of sorts."

She spun around. "You'd live in a tent for the winter? You'll freeze to death."

He leaned back and laughed. "You forget my ancestors have lived in various forms of tents for centuries."

She closed the distance between them and leaned over to give him a hard look. "I don't care how your ancestors lived. All I care about is you." No. She hadn't blurted out those words. Heat scorched up her cheeks and her eyes watered, but she refused to turn from his surprised look. "Promise me you won't do anything so foolish as to try and survive the winter in a tent." Her words fell to a whisper.

He continued to stare at her, his eyes dark and bottomless, drawing sweetness from her heart. She had said more than she ought, but she meant it and would not take back one word.

She kept her eyes locked on his. She could hear the tick of her heart.

He pushed to his feet. "How can you care for the likes of me?" He sounded doubtful, surprised and pleased at the same time.

She smiled, feeling the sweetness pouring from her heart to her lips. "How can I not?"

He stood motionless. "Don't you know what people will say?"

"Maybe I don't care."

He laughed mockingly. "What would your mother

think? Didn't she teach you how you must please people?"

She wanted to refute the suggestion, say it didn't matter. But didn't it? Didn't a person need approval in order to be safe? But approval from whom? Wasn't that the more important question? Surely the opinion of people who loved her and whom she loved should outweigh what others thought.

Kody stepped away. "I need to get this packed up again."

"Wait. You didn't give me a chance to answer."

"I think I did."

"It's hard to get over what's been drummed into your head for years."

He snorted. "Ain't that the truth?"

"But, Kody, I am. You pushed me to take the first step toward making a decision on my own. Now look at me. I have a job I get paid for. I am not sitting around waiting to be told what I should do." She realized there was more to it. "I'm not waiting to be told who I am."

He spared her a glance. "That's good." He rolled up his pack and tied it securely. "You're a strong woman. You don't need anyone to tell you anything." He strode into the garage.

She followed. "Why do you let people tell you who you are?"

He kept his back to her and took his time stowing his pack. She stubbornly waited. She wanted an answer.

Finally he faced her, his expression hard. "It doesn't matter what anyone thinks about me. But I won't let anyone I care about be branded so they face the same prejudice."

She jumped out of his way as he strode past her. "If you think you're protecting me…"

But he swung onto Sam's back and rode away.

She slumped against the fence as pain emptied her heart. Had he meant her among those he cared for or only Star? She wanted him to admit he cared, but not like this. Not in such a dismissive way.

She feared he might avoid her after that, but the next evening, he offered to go walking with her. They wandered back to the park where he'd kissed her. She wondered if he took her there for that reason, but they only walked through without stopping at the bench, even though she'd slowed her steps, giving him plenty of opportunity to do so.

The next evening, the wind blew ferociously and they stayed indoors playing checkers. Charlotte wasn't good at planning her moves. So she played recklessly, carelessly, eliciting hoots of laughter from Kody as he captured her kings as fast as she earned them.

The following evening burned so hot they sat in the shade of the house and listened to the sounds of summer. Martha and Leland sat beside them. Leland said, "I have agreed to take the pulpit the first of the month."

"Good for you, Pa."

"I want you to be there."

Charlotte saw the way Kody's muscles tightened even though he didn't move.

"Could you not do this one thing for your Pa?" Leland begged.

"I'll see."

After Martha and Leland went inside, Charlotte sat quietly at Kody's side. She sensed his struggle. She knew he wanted to please his pa, yet he had his own internal battles to fight. Wanting him to know she cared, she reached for his hand.

He stiffened and she expected him to pull away. Instead, he turned his hand so their palms rested against each other and their fingers twined. "Whatever I decide, someone is going to be hurt."

"Your pa will be hurt if you don't go. This is important to him."

"I know how people will react to me being there."

"I should hope most of them would rejoice. After all, isn't church supposed to be a place of healing?"

He snorted.

Suddenly, something she'd struggled with the past several days seemed so clear. "I've been trying to understand an important truth. I think it's more important to listen to what people who care about us think than to give weight to what people who don't care about us might say. But what's even more important is what we think about ourselves as people God created."

He considered her words. "I'm glad you've come to that conclusion. It seems like a good one for you."

She wanted to point out it might well apply to him, but he squeezed her hand gently, sending her a silent warning to let it go, and she knew now was not the time. She would continue to pray for God to teach him the same truth in His way.

Charlotte was weeding the garden a few days later when Kody rode into the yard. He barely let Sam stop before he leaped from the saddle and rushed to her side. "They've come." He waved a parcel, then glanced toward the house and lowered both his voice and the parcel. "I don't want Ma and Pa to know about this. It would make them wonder." He nodded toward the garage.

She pulled off her gloves as she joined him inside. "Open it. Let's see how they look."

He had the package half-open before she finished. From the box he lifted a pair of white boots fixed together with a metal bar. "How's she supposed to walk in these?"

Charlotte pulled a sheet of paper from the box. "Here's instructions." She glanced through them. "It says she's to wear them day and night and there are directions of how to adjust the bar to turn her foot a little more each day."

He tossed the shoes back in the box. "They look like instruments of torture. How can I do this to Star?"

'There's a handwritten note on the bottom that says her clubfoot is only moderate and should respond well to correction."

"I guess I have to try it. She deserves a chance to see if this will help." He put everything back in the box and hid it behind his saddle. "I'll go out tomorrow." He faced her. "Are you working tomorrow?"

She shook her head. He already knew she had the day off.

"Will you come with me?"

"I'd love to." She enjoyed visiting John and Morning and loved Star's bright spirit. But the biggest reason for going was to spend more time with Kody. Maybe tomorrow would be the day he let go of his hurts from the past and became willing to face a future with her. She dreamed and prayed he would come to that decision. Now that the shoes were here, he would be leaving any day. The idea he might leave without changing his mind… She took a deep breath to stop the way her insides threatened to wither. She considered her options. She could pack up and go with him. She gladly would endure the hardships of the North. But unless he stopped running from who he was, he would not take her along. He would never consider making her his wife. *Please, God, show him Your great love. Let him see it's enough.*

She got up early the next morning and took special pains with her hair. She'd been wearing it in a bun since she started work at the hospital, but today she left it down and held back from her face with pretty little combs. She chose her nicest cotton dress—nothing fancy about it, but the blue fabric brought out the color in her eyes. She needed nothing to bring out the color in her cheeks. That came from anticipation.

Both she and Kody hurried through breakfast. As they went outside, Kody said, "I suppose she'll need some stockings to wear inside them."

"I saw some at Boulter's."

"Let's go get them." He checked the time. "It's early. Let's walk."

Several people were at the store when they arrived. Charlotte waved at Amy and hurried toward the display of children's clothing.

Amy left her father serving a man and wife to assist Charlotte and Kody.

The woman at the counter turned to stare rudely and spoke loudly enough for all to hear. "We aren't the only ones with things gone missing. Seems to have started about the time he rode back into town."

Charlotte stared at the woman. She heard a rumble of comments and shifted her gaze around the room. Most people refused to meet her look. Mr. Boulter, however, didn't mind sending her a very pointed look.

She felt Kody stiffen, didn't need to look at him to know he'd heard.

Amy touched his arm. "Don't pay them any attention. Some people have nothing better to do than gossip and speculate. Now, how can I help you?"

Charlotte stole a glance at Kody, not surprised he kept his face as expressionless as a wooden mask. But she knew beneath his indifferent demeanor lay hurt.

"Thank you, Amy." She appreciated the girl's defense of Kody. "Are those what you want?" She pointed to the stockings and waited for Kody to decide.

"Fine." He followed Amy to the register, Charlotte on his heels. Glowering, the outspoken woman stepped back as if afraid he'd get too close.

"I have cash." Kody's low, measured tones were meant for everyone to hear as they strained forward to see what he would do.

Amy wrapped the stockings carefully in pretty tissue paper as if to show her father and everyone else she didn't agree with their censure, and then she grabbed some candy. "My gift."

"Thanks." Kody nodded and marched for the door, his stride long but his steps unhurried.

Charlotte paused at the doorway. She wanted to say something, but what could she say that wouldn't make this worse? She was no good at defying people like Amy did. But she gave the woman and Mr. Boulter a hard, accusing look before she followed Kody.

It took them far less time to make it back to the house than it had taken to get to the store. Charlotte gasped to catch her breath as they stepped into the yard. They wasted no time climbing into the car and driving away.

Not until the town was behind them did either of them speak.

"Now you know what it's like." Kody sounded as if it hurt to push the words out.

"Like Amy said, some people don't have anything better to do. They're ignorant. Amy was kind, though." She wanted him to acknowledge that not everyone used the same paint in their brush.

"Nothing ever changes."

She smiled. "I beg to differ. Lots of things have changed recently."

He darted her a look, saw her smile and relaxed slightly. "You mean *you've* changed?"

"Does it show?"

He glanced at her again. "I don't think you've changed so much as you finally see who you really are."

"And what is that?"

"Are you begging for compliments?"

"I don't think so." She considered it. "Nope. I just want to hear what you think."

He chuckled.

She didn't care about anything else after she'd brought the sunshine back to his face.

"You are a strong, brave woman who is willing to face challenges."

"You really think so?"

"I know so."

"Then why don't you give me a chance to do it?"

His glance seemed puzzled. "I'm not stopping you."

She wanted him to see that he was. He wouldn't give

her a chance to prove she had enough strength to face the kind of remarks she'd heard in the store. "Yes, you are. And the sad thing is, you think you're protecting me."

He stared straight ahead.

She knew he understood her comments and chose to ignore them. But perhaps he would think about her words. And maybe, God willing, they would make him change.

"Was that the first time you heard things have been stolen around here?" he asked.

"No. Some of the women at the hospital say things have been taken off their clotheslines or from their woodsheds. The matron said things were missing from the storeroom. I can't imagine stealing from a hospital."

"I wonder…"

She waited, and when he didn't seem inclined to finish, she prodded, "What?"

"Well, if I'm not stealing things, then someone else must be."

"Obviously."

He nodded and look thoughtful.

"You think you might know who it is?" she asked.

"I have my suspicions."

"Then tell the sheriff."

"Huh. You think he'd believe me? But there's more than one way to skin a skunk."

"What are you going to do?"

"Catch them. Prove I'm not the one."

She sat back and stared out the window. "What if they're dangerous? You might be hurt."

He grunted. "Not if it's who I think it is."

They arrived at the reservation then, and the conversation came to an end. She wanted him to promise not to try to stop these men on his own. "Be careful," she murmured before they got out.

Chapter Fifteen

It tickled Kody right down to his toes that Charlotte cared about his safety. He sobered instantly. She made it plain she cared about him in other ways, too. But she had no idea how cruel people could be and he had no desire for her to find out. As soon as he got these shoes on Star, he would head out.

But first, he had to stop whoever was stealing from people around here. Whether or not Ratface and Shorty were the culprits as he suspected, he couldn't be certain Charlotte was safe as long as they hung around. He wouldn't leave until they were locked up or he was certain they'd left the area. He preferred the former over the latter.

He grabbed the box holding the shoes from the back-seat and went to greet the Eaglefeathers.

A few minutes later he'd shown the shoes to Morning and John, who looked doubtful. John touched them. "They are very hard."

"Will they not hurt?" Morning asked.

Kody didn't like the idea one bit better than they did. "It's the only way to straighten her foot."

They had stayed a distance from Star as they examined and discussed the shoes, and now they went over and Kody sat on the ground in front of her. "See what I brought you." He let her examine the shoes.

The little girl took her time doing so, then handed them back to him. "No, thank you."

"Star, don't you want to walk and run like the other children?"

"Yes."

"These will straighten your foot so you can."

She searched his eyes, demanding in her unblinking intensity. He wanted to be everything she needed. He wanted her to trust him as her—he faltered—father.

Finally she nodded. "I do as you say."

He helped her put on the new stockings. The shoes weren't easy to put on. She stiffened. Tears filled her eyes as he forced her crooked foot into the boot, but she didn't protest. She fixed him with a hard look that seemed to say, *I'm trusting you to do what is best.*

He hoped and prayed this would work. Finally he got both shoes tied. The bar allowed some movement and he put her on her feet. She couldn't balance and he caught her as she tipped over.

She pushed from his hands and plopped onto her bottom. "I can't walk now." Her voice rang with accusation.

Kody flung a desperate look to Charlotte, saw the glisten of tears in her eyes before she knelt beside Star.

"It takes a long time for your foot to get better." She held out the instruction page. "It says here it's a slow process. It also says you can *learn* to walk in these shoes. Why don't you try again?"

Star gave them each a disbelieving look. Morning and John had backed away but now joined them.

Morning squatted in front of Star. "You must learn to walk again."

John reached for her hands. "I'll help you."

Star turned her unblinking gaze back to Kody. "You help me."

"I'd like to." Though his inclination was to take those wretched boots and throw them as far as he could. Star had been quite happy hobbling around with her crooked foot. How could she understand this was for her good? He felt he needed to explain it and pulled his daughter onto his lap. "Star, it's not that we don't all love you just the way you are." So bright and keen and sweet, what was not to love? "But if this will fix your foot, well, I think you should try it. Don't you?"

She nodded. "I will walk."

He held her hands and helped her to her feet. His heart twisted as she grimaced and her face paled. She struggled a few yards.

"I not walk." She yanked away from him and dropped to her hands and knees. "I not want to walk anymore."

John scooped up the child and pressed her to his chest.

Kody closed his eyes as Star buried her face against John's shoulder. He didn't want to do this any more than Star did. But didn't she deserve a chance?

Charlotte touched his arm. "Give her time to get used to them."

He reached for her hand and held it, willingly accepting her sympathy and understanding.

"We'll give it a fair try. Is everyone agreed?" he asked.

John and Morning nodded, though their eyes filled with distress.

Charlotte squeezed Kody's hand. He knew she understood how much it hurt to have to do this and he clung to her strength.

Morning prepared lunch, but Kody had no appetite. He couldn't bear to watch Star crawl about on her hands and knees, her face drawn with pain and determination.

He put aside his plate and sat on the ground beside her. "Sometimes people have to hurt you because they love you." He didn't expect that made any more sense to her than it did to him. "I only want to see your foot better. That's what we all want."

The other three murmured agreement.

He remembered the candy Amy had given him and pulled it from his pocket. He handed it to Star.

"Thank you," she said, but stared at it with little interest. Finally, she popped it into her mouth all the while staring into Kody's face with an accusing look. "Good," she murmured without enthusiasm.

His heart ached clear to his toes.

They didn't stay long after that. It was too difficult watching Star struggle.

"You will see that she wears them?" Kody asked John as he walked with them to the car.

"Yes. It is the only way to fix her foot." The resignation in his friend's voice echoed Kody's own feelings.

He slipped out after supper while Charlotte helped clean up, hoping to ride away before she discovered his purpose. But as he tossed the saddle onto Sam's back, he heard the door shut and knew he wouldn't succeed.

"Oh. You're going somewhere."

He ducked his head to hide his smile at how disappointed she sounded. Could be she had come to enjoy their evening hours together as much as he did. His smile fled. He walked in dangerous territory, allowing himself this forbidden pleasure—loving her, but knowing he had to ride away. "I've got something to tend to."

She came around Sam so she could see him. "You're going to try and catch whoever is stealing things around here, aren't you?"

"Huh."

She grabbed his arm, forcing him to face her. "Tell me you aren't going alone."

Her concern was honey to his soul. Oh, to have this interest in his welfare for the rest of his life. He sucked in the smell of horseflesh and forced resolve into his thoughts. "Matter of fact, Jed Hawkes is going with me. I figured no one would believe me if *I* turned in two scoundrels."

"Two? You're going after two?" She sucked in air and seemed to struggle to control her reaction. "Jed's a good man. I know him and Bess from church, but two evil men? Won't you need more help than that?"

He touched her cheek, wanting to ease her worry. "This pair won't be more than the two of us can handle."

Her expression relaxed as he rubbed his knuckles against her kitten-soft skin. Then she grabbed his hand and squeezed it between hers. "How can you be so sure?"

He couldn't stand her distress. "I think it's Shorty and Ratface. We both know they're halfways cowards."

"You think they're still around here? That campsite on the way to the reservation has long been abandoned."

"I saw another campsite that looked like it had exploded. Guessed it was probably them." He reluctantly extricated his hand so he could tighten the cinch.

She touched his shoulder. "Kody, be careful."

Her words held more power than a loaded gun, and he

straightened and faced her, knowing it was probably the most dangerous thing he'd ever done in his life. "Charlotte, I ain't no fool. I don't take chances."

She nodded, but her eyes remained troubled.

He leaned over and kissed her gently, longingly. If only... But there could be no *if only*s. He let his lips linger a heartbeat, excusing himself, saying he had to reassure her, but promising it would be the last time he kissed her. Soon as he completed tonight's task, he would have no further excuse for staying.

He'd been right. The campsite belonged to Shorty and Ratface. And the pair was there. Kody and Jed stayed out of sight, watching them. Then followed as the the scoundrels set out at dusk. Shorty and Ratface made no attempt to be quiet, nor did they check the trail to see if anyone followed.

"Like I told Charlotte, they aren't the reddest apples on the tree," Kody murmured. But smart or not, if these two were guilty of what he suspected, they had to be stopped, and he didn't suppose they would take kindly to someone putting an end to their free pickin's. Cowards could be deadly when cornered. He knew enough to be careful.

They followed the pair to town, then down a back alley to a darkened house.

"The Sloans," Jed whispered. "It's no secret they've gone to visit their daughter in Missoula."

Jed and Kody hung back, watching, as the other two prowled around the house, gunny sacks draped over their shoulders. They waited as Shorty tried the back door, found it wasn't locked and tossed aside his crowbar. When the two scuttled inside, Jed and Kody dropped

silently from their mounts and eased up to the yawning
door. When the pair returned with their arms full, Kody
and Jed greeted them with drawn guns.

"Put that stuff down real slow and get your hands
in the air."

"I'll hold them. You go get the sheriff," Jed said.

Kody nodded. Any other way and suspicion would
be cast on him.

He returned in a few minutes with the sheriff and
sighed with satisfaction as the pair were cuffed and
dragged off to jail.

The sheriff leaned back in his chair as Kody and Jed
gave their statements. "I thank you for your help." He
fixed Kody with an appraising look. "The town could
use more men like you."

Kody shook hands with the lawman and strode out. It
felt good to hear such words. He wished he could stay,
put down roots here, marry a certain young woman and
be a father to his daughter, but in the end, nothing had
changed. He was still a half-breed. He still had no idea
who he was or what he'd come from. Nor would the sheriff's approval change the way Mr. Boulter treated him.
He did not intend to share the realities of his life with
Charlotte or Star. It wouldn't be fair to either of them.
He'd let Charlotte know Ratface and Shorty wouldn't
be bothering her. And then…

He pulled his hat down over his eyes. He'd about run
out of excuses for not leaving.

Pa was to preach this morning. Kody planned to go
to church and hear him. He didn't have a whole lot of
choice, seeing as he'd hung around long after he should

have gone, telling himself he had to see Pa well enough to take over his regular tasks before he left.

He'd intended to spend less time with Charlotte, knowing he might as well get used to living without her company. Instead, he spent every possible moment with her. Evenings after they both finished work for the day were gentle, satisfying hours he knew he would relive over and over when he settled in Canada, but her days off were...

He closed his eyes at the bittersweetness of them.

They usually went to the reservation. It provided a handy excuse for spending the day with her. But seeing Star grow more and more frustrated with those torturous shoes was like a lance straight through his heart. The cheerful, outgoing, sweet child grew unhappy and discontent. Her eyes filled with dark accusation when he visited. Not even the toys he took erased it. He hated being the cause of her pain. He wanted nothing more than to take those shoes off and burn them. Only the hope she might one day walk properly gave him the strength to endure her misery.

Charlotte understood his pain, perhaps even shared it, for she, too, loved Star. He found comfort in her presence, in the way she touched his arm. And yes, despite his vow otherwise, he kissed her again. Almost every time they left the reservation. He needed to feel her love and accept it for a few minutes. The memory of those kisses and her sweet love would have to last him a long, long time. He would finish packing today. He would leave first thing tomorrow morning.

He stood in the middle of his bedroom, holding several Western novels, trying to decide which ones to pack for reading material and which to leave behind. If he wasn't such a sentimental fool he would simply buy new ones, but he wanted the memories associated with these familiar ones. He randomly selected the one in his right hand and dropped it on the bed, along with the picture of him taken with his parents when he started school and the Bible presented to him for perfect attendance in Sunday school. He snorted. Wasn't hard to be there every Sunday when your father was the preacher. He would probably never read it, but again, sentimental value made him decide to take it.

He looked around the room. What else did he want to take? Nothing. He meant to start over.

Groaning, he sank to the edge of his bed.

He didn't want to leave.

But he'd run out of excuses to stay.

He had to go. The sooner, the better. His feet like lead on every step, he made his way downstairs for breakfast.

They drove to church, so Pa wouldn't be worn-out by the time they arrived. Kody hung back as they stepped into the churchyard. "Best if I wait a bit and sit in the back."

Ma and Pa paused, exchanged a look and Ma turned to argue.

"Go ahead. Everyone will want to greet Pa."

Reluctantly they left him. Charlotte stayed beside Kody and slipped her hand through the crook of his arm. He squeezed his elbow to his side, pressing her hard to him, and fought an urge to declare his undying love. He noted many surprised glances in his direction. They convinced him to keep his mouth shut on the matter. Charlotte deserved acceptance, not the kind of looks several of the women sent his way. Then Jed saw him and waved. He and Bess hurried to join them.

"Glad to see you," Jed said. "I hoped you'd be here. I have a favor to ask."

"I'll do whatever I can. What is it?"

"I'm rounding up some horses tomorrow. They've been running free all year. I could sure use help from a man like you."

Kody kept his face expressionless, but Jed's words raced through him with a force sucking at his lungs. *A man like you.* Jed meant it as a good thing. "I'll be there first light." Another delay. And how he welcomed it.

They hurried inside. Jed and Bess indicated they should sit in the same pew and Kody gratefully accepted, sliding in beside Charlotte.

The congregation stood to sing the first hymn. He didn't bother opening the hymnal but sang words as familiar as Pa's face. Charlotte's clear, sweet voice joined his. A deep joy filled his heart. This felt as good as coming home.

And then Pa took his place at the pulpit, and Kody strained toward his words. Pa's speech was still slightly slurred. He spoke slower than he once had and he paused often as he struggled to find a word, but the same familiar power drove the words deep into Kody's heart.

The sermon reminded everyone God's love didn't change. It didn't depend on circumstances, health or what other people said or did. It didn't depend on wealth or belongings. It depended on God's word. His unchanging word.

"We are reminded in Hebrews, chapter thirteen, verse eight, that 'Jesus Christ is the same yesterday, and today and forever.' He has taught us to pray, 'Give us today our daily bread.' My prayer for myself and each of you is we will accept God's promise of love, trust in Him for what we need today and stop fretting about yesterday and tomorrow."

Kody drank in Pa's words like a drought-stricken land would suck in water. He had always believed. He was tired of denying it. *God, You are my God. I have faltered and failed so much. Give me the strength to do as You want, and the wisdom to know what it is.*

He squeezed Charlotte's hand briefly, wanting to share his feelings with her. She smiled, and he knew from the glistening in her eyes she understood this moment was special.

Chapter Sixteen

Charlotte rushed home with her exciting news, hoping Kody would be back from helping Jed Hawkes. She laughed out of sheer joy. Yesterday had been more than she dreamed possible in her prayers. She'd sensed Kody's doubts disappearing as his father preached, been aware of the change in him even before he turned to her and smiled. She rejoiced when he'd gone to his father after the sermon. They'd spoken quietly, then Leland hugged Kody. Even from where she stood, Charlotte had seen the glisten of tears in Leland's eyes. Her own vision blurred as Martha joined them, and Kody hugged her. She'd prayed for Kody's healing and it thrilled her to be able to watch it.

And now news like she'd never expected. God certainly knew how to answer above and beyond her wildest dreams.

She went in the back gate and almost cheered when she saw Kody coming from the corral. She hurried to his side. "I have the best news!"

He quirked an eyebrow. "I can't even begin to guess what it might be."

"You wouldn't in a hundred years!"

"Then maybe you should just tell me."

She grabbed his hand. "Matron told us today a special doctor is coming to visit."

"Uh-huh."

"He can fix bones."

Kody again quirked an eyebrow. He obviously wasn't getting how great an opportunity this could be.

She slowed down and spelled it out carefully. "Matron told us how he's fixed broken arms that weren't set correctly, how he's helped people with something wrong with their hips and—" she squeezed his hand hard "—he's had very good success with fixing club-feet. He could fix Star."

Kody jerked back, pulling his hand from her grasp. "Are you joking?"

"No." Why wasn't he excited about this possibility?

"Then let me point out a few facts. For starters she's an Indian and won't be allowed to see the doctor. Besides, the doctor told John her foot couldn't be fixed."

"This doctor *is* fixing them."

He stared at her like he'd never seen her before. "White children, maybe."

"A clubfoot is the same whatever the color of your skin."

"Except the color of your skin makes people treat you differently."

She jutted out her chin. "Not everyone. Do I treat you differently? Do your parents? Bess and Jed? And probably hundreds of others if you care to pay attention."

"You expect Star to understand that?"

She couldn't believe his resistance. "Kody, she deserves a chance. You know those shoes aren't working."

He took off the saddle and pushed past her to carry it to the garage.

She followed. He had to see that Star needed this. "Couldn't you at least take her to this doctor and get his opinion?"

He draped his saddle over the stand before he answered. "I have no intention of giving people a chance to tell me to take her back to the reservation where she belongs."

Anger erupted from Charlotte's brain, erasing caution, fueling her words with fire. "Kody Douglas, you know something? This isn't about Star and her facing negative comments—"

"Prejudice."

"I don't care what you call it, because I realize something. This isn't about her. This is about you. You don't want to face those unkind, untrue remarks. You'd sooner run. How far do you think you'll have to run to outrun yourself? Canada won't be far enough. Alaska wouldn't be. Isn't it time you stopped running and faced life? Your life?" She stomped away, not caring if she'd offended him. Partway out the door, she paused. "You know, Kody, I almost thought I loved you." Her anger shifted so suddenly to pain she cried out. She loved him whether or not he would ever accept it.

She ran to her room and threw herself on her bed.

He talked about being strong, expecting her to be so, yet he ran from his own problems.

She breathed slowly, calming her anger, letting her pain dissipate. Then she turned to prayer. *God, I know You've sent this doctor. Please make Kody see how it could be the best thing for Star. She deserves this chance. Please, let Kody love me as I love him.*

She remained there for a few minutes, then hurried downstairs determined to find a way to convince Kody to change his mind.

The look he gave her as he sat down to supper warned her he would hear nothing more on the subject. She ducked her head. She would find a way to say more.

However, he made it impossible to talk to him that night. He played checkers with Leland, then held a skein of yarn as Martha rolled it into a ball.

Charlotte sent him pleading looks and sighed heavily.

Martha looked up. "Is there something wrong, dear?"

"No, I'm fine." She crossed to the window. "It looks so lovely out. It'd be nice to go for a walk."

"Go right ahead," Martha said kindly, unaware of the tension between Charlotte and Kody. "I'm almost done here. Kody, why don't you go with her?"

Kody yawned loudly. "I'm tired, Ma. I think I'll go to bed early."

"Another time, then?" Charlotte knew he understood the warning in her voice, but he only gave her a dark look that said he would not give her another chance to mention this subject.

She sent him an equally hard look, silently informing him she wasn't prepared to give up. She didn't know how she'd convince him, but she would do so if humanly possible.

But next morning she still hadn't come up with a way to do so, let alone how to get the chance. He wasn't at breakfast. Her heart stopped working when she saw his empty place. Had he gone to Canada without saying goodbye?

"Gone back to the Hawkes'," Martha said. "Says he promised to break some horses for Jed."

Charlotte thanked God she would get another chance.

* * *

Kody sat at the table when she returned from the hospital that afternoon.

"We must talk," she murmured.

"Nothing left to say."

"I think there is."

He simply shook his head.

Martha hurried in from the front room. "There's a letter for you." She handed it to Charlotte.

Charlotte recognized Harry's writing and opened the envelope, pulled out the sheet of paper and unfolded it. She read the message twice, wondering that she felt nothing.

"Let me guess," Kody's voice rasped. "He still doesn't have any room for you."

"Listen to what he says. 'We've found a house finally. I've enclosed a money order for a ticket for you to join us. We've missed you. The children ask after you constantly.'" She shook the envelope and a money order fell out.

"You'll be leaving, then?"

She stared at the letter she'd been waiting for since she'd been abandoned.

"I miss the children." She could go and help Nellie, make herself indispensable, as Mother had advised. Certainly Nellie would appreciate her now. "Listen to the rest. He signs himself, 'Lovingly, Harry,' and 'P.S. Nellie is expecting another baby.'" She slowly folded the page and returned it to the envelope, along with the money order.

She waited for Kody to say something, anything to convince her she shouldn't go, but he stared into his cup of tea as if he hoped to discover all the secrets of the world there.

"Kody, can you give me one reason I shouldn't buy a ticket and leave?" She loved him. Guessed he must know it by now. But her love meant nothing unless he returned it.

Slowly, he brought his head up and stared at her, his eyes dark, revealing nothing. Nothing at all. Finally he shook his head. "You should go to Harry. It's what you wanted from the start. It's where you belong."

Her insides tensed. She gathered up every ounce of her courage. "I could belong anywhere I'm wanted."

"He's family. Where else should you be?"

His words swept clean her heart, cleansing it of hope, leaving her empty and hurting. She pushed back from the table and fled to her room, where she stared out the window. She tried to pray, but her empty heart yielded no words.

"Supper," Martha called up the stairs, and Charlotte forced resolve into her heart. She could face this. Wasn't Kody always telling her she was strong?

Her head high, she marched into the kitchen and took her place, thankful Leland was full of talk about a visit he'd had with the church elders, arranging for him to resume his role as pastor.

The meal over, Charlotte rose to clear the table.

"Ma, Pa."

The sound of something both hard and reluctant in Kody's voice stopped her in her tracks.

"I'll be leaving tomorrow morning."

"Leaving?" Martha sounded surprised.

"For Canada."

"But I thought…" Leland grabbed Kody's arm.

"After…" He struggled to get his words out. "Sunday. I thought you would be staying." Leland sent Martha a pleading look.

Martha nodded and voiced the words Leland couldn't pull from his shocked mind. "We both thought you had accepted who you are, who God made you to be."

"I can't deny my faith. But my reality is still the same. I don't fit."

Charlotte gripped the plate she held so hard her fingers cramped. She wanted to grab him, shake him hard until he admitted he was accepted by some, not by others. But what mattered most was what he thought of himself.

"Kody, my son—" Martha's voice rang with pain "—when will you ever forgive those who have been cruel to you?"

He pushed from the table. "Ma, I can forgive them all I want, but it won't change them. I can handle what they say about me, but—" he shot Charlotte a look so full of pain she almost cried out in protest "—I won't let others be branded the same way. This is goodbye. I'll be gone before anyone is up tomorrow."

"No," Charlotte called, but he slipped out the door before she could say anything to change his mind. She wanted to say she didn't care what people said. She loved him enough to ignore it. People who mattered knew he was a good man.

Martha took Leland into the front room. They spoke quietly, but Charlotte didn't need to hear their words to know they sought ways to deal with Kody's impending departure.

As she washed dishes, she sought her own way. Found nothing to ease the twisting of her insides. She didn't

cry, her pain beyond tears. Somehow she had to go on
from here. She could only do it with God's help. She remembered Leland's sermon. She had only to trust God
one day at a time.

Charlotte lay in bed. Kody had ridden away yesterday
morning as she'd watched from her bedroom window.
He'd glanced back, seen her there, gave the barest tilt of
his head, then kicked Sam into a gallop.

She moaned. The house shuddered. She smiled crook-
edly. Even the house missed him. She bolted upright. The
house rattled. She raced to the window. The air looked
gray as shameful laundry. The northern horizon rolled
with a gigantic black cloud.

Kody was out there somewhere. She prayed he'd
found shelter.

She tried to block out the sound of the wind as she
prepared for work.

It blew all day, through the night and all the next day.
Charlotte thought of the Eaglefeathers and prayed they
would be okay. She thought of the people living in the
drought-stricken area and prayed for their safety. She
tried not to remember stories of people lost in such a
storm. How their bodies had been found buried in dirt.
She shuddered. What an awful way to die. She wouldn't
think Kody could suffer such a fate. He knew enough to
find shelter. But what if…? She wouldn't let her thoughts
go there and prayed even as she helped clean the hospital.

Next morning people suffering dust pneumonia
started to flock to the hospital. The wards were full of
coughing. Charlotte raced from patient to patient with
water, urging them to drink more. She spoon-fed broth

to those too weak to help themselves. She stayed late, knowing how desperately these people needed care.

Long past dark she made her weary way home. Martha had left a plate of food in the oven for her. She tried to eat it, but hardly had the energy to lift the fork to her mouth.

She dragged herself upstairs and sank onto the edge of the bed. Her gaze fell on Harry's letter. He'd asked her to join them. She shook her head. She couldn't leave Matron and the nurses when they needed every pair of hands they could find.

They needed her. It felt good, but it had nothing to do with her need to be needed. This was about doing something of value. She sat straighter. What she did had importance. She considered the idea. For the first time she considered who she was, what she wanted.

She'd been raised to think she must trust Harry to take care of her. She must work to ensure he would, but she didn't need Harry's protection. She'd proved it. She didn't need to kowtow to Nellie in order to have a home. She'd found a perfectly good home here. And even though she couldn't expect to continue to live with Martha and Leland, she could move into the nurses' residence. She had value and purpose. Right here—she pressed her hand to her chest—in her heart, accepting the life God so graciously provided her. *God, thank You for who I am.*

If only she could tell Kody. *Please keep him safe wherever he is.*

Renewed, she quickly penned a note to Harry saying she couldn't leave her job. She put the money order and letter in an envelope and sealed them. She would mail it tomorrow.

Smiling so hard her cheeks hurt, she prepared for bed and fell asleep instantly.

When, next day, she mentioned moving to the nurses' residence, Martha and Leland begged her to board with them. She agreed readily.

Her newfound joy filled her with a bubble of continuous laughter the next few days, marred only by missing Kody and her wish that Star could see the special doctor. Often she gazed to the north, wondering how far Kody had gone. Would he ever stop running? Would he ever come back?

Chapter Seventeen

Kody had every intention of riding hard and fast for Canada when he left Favor, but he had one thing to do first. He rode to the reservation to say goodbye to John and Morning and to give Star one last hug. It took every ounce of his strength to keep from showing any emotion as he held his little daughter. He would never see her again, but he could do one last thing for her. He unlaced those hateful, hurtful boots and tied them to Sam's saddle. "I'll dump them in a ravine somewhere."

He squatted before Star. "You be happy, hear?"

"I don't want you go." She sobbed. "Why you have to?"

"It's for the best." Seems he had to say it so often when it should have been obvious to everyone. "I have to go."

"No, you don't."

He brushed his hand over her hair and stroked her cheek, then pushed to his feet and nodded a last goodbye to Morning and John. But when he returned to the main road he stopped. Somehow, despite his determination to ride fast and far, he couldn't head north. Instead, he turned south, rode a mile, then chose a road to the west. He needed a place far enough from town he could disappear for all intents and purposes. Yet he could be close enough to keep an eye on both Charlotte and Star. And he knew just the place. The Widow Murphy needed a man.

He rode until he reached the Murphy place. Widow Murphy hired him instantly, accepting him without reservation. He chuckled. He like the old lady. Admired her spunk. But it was way past time for her to give up her hard life. He said so every chance he got. She was so crippled she could barely walk. He carried water to the house for her. She moaned as she hobbled to the stove.

"Ma'am, why are you clinging to this ranch? Sell it and move to town, where you can have a few comforts."

"Can't, boy. Who'd I sell it to?"

"Lot of people would be glad of this place." It was a beautiful ranch with lots of grass and water and a big log house her husband had built. "This house is way too big for one woman."

She sighed. "We planned to fill it with kids. Didn't plan for Cyrus to get hisself killed."

"So let someone else fill it with kids. Ain't it time to let it go?"

"Boy, I vowed I would keep this ranch after my good man died. I haven't quit anything in my life. Figure I ain't going to now."

"Sometimes it's okay to change your mind."

"Next you'll be telling me I'm too old to run this place."

He gave her a hard look. "You *are* too old. Stop being so stubborn."

"I ain't old if I don't want to be."

He snorted and stalked from the room. How could she be so blind? She seemed to figure if she chose to believe she wasn't old, she wasn't old. But pretending it wasn't so didn't change the facts.

He faltered on his next step as one thought caught another and twisted together like tangled rope. Widow Murphy ignored the fact of her age. Kody Douglas ignored the fact people cared about him despite his heritage.

He took an uncertain step. He knew Charlotte cared for him. He cared for her. He loved her.

But did she love him enough to face prejudice? Accept his uncertain heritage? Did he want to face it? He knew people could be cruel. Who knew what sort of people the future might bring into his life?

Pa's words blasted through his mind. *Joyfully take what God gives us today. Let Him take care of yesterday and tomorrow.*

Kody's today included a woman he loved and who, he hoped, loved him back.

It included a little girl he wanted to be there for.

He raced back to the house. "I'll be gone a day or two, but I'll be back." He carried in enough water to last Widow Murphy while he was away and filled her wood box to overflowing. "Don't do something stupid while I'm gone, like climb into the loft to see if it needs repair. I'll look after everything when I get back."

He reached Favor at suppertime, turned Sam into the little corral and hurried to the house. He hoped he wasn't too late to stop Charlotte from leaving to join Harry.

He burst through the door.

Three pairs of eyes jerked in his direction. "Ma, Pa,

Charlotte. I've come back." He saw only one face—
Charlotte's. Something sweet and joyous and completely
welcoming flared in her eyes. He couldn't believe how
close he'd come to riding away from that.

She set a place at the table for him. Ma and Pa plied
him with questions he hoped he answered in a reasonable fashion. He wouldn't be able to think straight until
he dealt with two important items.

After supper, he waited until Ma and Pa had left the
room before he said to Charlotte, "Did that special doctor come yet?"

"He's coming tomorrow."

"Good. I want to take Star. Will you come with me
to the reservation to get her?"

She nodded.

"I'm going to tell her I'm her father."

Charlotte laughed. "Thank God. One prayer answered."

"One?"

She ducked her head. "I have more, but let's deal
with this first."

He agreed, even though he wanted to sweep her into
his arms and declare his love right there on the spot. But
he wanted to do it right. He wanted to allow her to see
exactly what he was and have a chance to decide how
much it mattered.

Charlotte had the day off, so they left early next
morning. He wanted to get Star to the doctor as soon
as possible.

It wasn't until he stopped the car at the Eaglefeathers' home that he realized he had no idea what to say.
He said as much to Charlotte.

"Seems to me the plain and simple truth is best."

He nodded. He took Morning and John aside first and told them his plan. John squeezed his arm. "It is for the best. We have hoped you would do this."

But Kody feared his confession would upset Star. After all, he intended to turn her world upside down. He grabbed Charlotte's hand as he went to face his daughter.

Charlotte squeezed reassuringly. "I'll pray," she whispered.

He had her support and God's help. He could do this.

He sat cross-legged in front of Star, liking how she looked in the dress Charlotte had made her, seeing her light eyes, knowing they set her apart, yet her eyes were beautiful. He would teach her to be proud of how she looked and her heritage. Just as Ma and Pa had taught him. It had taken a while for it to get through his stubborn resistance, but it finally had. He took a deep breath, glad when Charlotte stood close by, offering encouragement yet understanding he and Star had to deal with this alone.

"Star, I have something important to tell you."

She squinted at him. "No more boots."

He laughed. "This isn't about your foot. It's about who you are."

"I am Star."

His bright, shining child. He wanted to hug her close, but needed to face her to make this announcement, needed to give her room to react however she chose. "Star, you have light eyes because your mommy had light eyes."

She stared at him.

"Her name was Winnoa and she died when you were a baby. That's why I left you with Morning and John."

She didn't blink. Her intense gaze made his eyes sting.

"I am your father."

Her eyes widened. She looked to John and Morning. "They are my momma and poppa."

"They both love you very much and will always love you. But I am your father."

"Why you leave me?"

All his arguments became dust before her accusations. "I thought it best."

"Not best."

"I know that now. I want to take care of you. I want you and I to be together."

She nodded. "Like a real father?"

"Yes. Like a real father."

Her smile rivaled the sun for brightness. "I like that." She shifted her gaze back to Morning and John. "I not want to leave my momma and poppa."

"You won't have to until you're ready." He didn't have a place for her yet. There were so many things to work out.

Star scrambled to her feet and threw her arms around his neck. "My real own daddy."

Behind him, Charlotte sniffed.

He laughed and hugged his little daughter. "I love you, Star Douglas."

She hugged her arms around his neck so tight he almost choked, but he didn't mind. Not in the least.

She leaned back against his arms. "I know'd you was my father."

"You did? Who told you?"

"Nobody. I know'd 'cause you made me wear bad boots. Only a father would make a little girl do it."

He crushed her to his chest. "It is because I love you."

Her warm little arms stole around his neck and she pressed her face to his cheek. "Me, too."

Charlotte, eyes gleaming, knelt at his side and patted Star's back.

After a few minutes he shifted Star so he could look into her face. "Because I love you, I have one more thing I want you to do."

She nodded slowly, her eyes so full of trust it hurt his heart.

"I want to take you to see a special doctor who might be able to fix your foot."

"Will it hurt?"

"I can't say. You'll have to ask the doctor."

She nodded. "Okay."

Kody didn't want to rush away, but Morning and John encouraged him to get her to the doctor.

Charlotte led them down the hall of the hospital to the waiting room.

A nurse rose from behind a wooden desk. "Why have you brought that child in here?"

"Nurse Sampson—" Charlotte began.

Many grown men quaked at the way she spoke. He was finished with quaking and running and for Star he would face someone ten times Nurse Sampson's size and noise. "My daughter needs to see the doctor."

Behind him he heard words like *dirty Indian*. But one woman, who stood to his right, mumbled, "Poor thing."

The nurse jerked her head back and seemed to get six inches taller. "Indians are not welcome here." She shooed at them.

"I will see the doctor," Kody insisted.

"Ain't that why he's here?" the woman to his right demanded.

Several others added their vocal support. The nurse sat down. "Very well. You can stay, but I can't promise the doctor will see you." She sniffed.

The doctor not only saw her, he said, "This is a fairly simple thing. I think it can be fixed."

Star give him one of her intense looks. "You can make me so I can walk right?"

The doctor leaned over until eye level with Star. "I think so."

"It hurt?"

"You'll have to wear a cast for a while. You'll be stiff and sore as you learn to walk again, but it won't be much for a brave girl like you. Not for someone who has walked on this crooked foot for four years."

"Not like bad boots?" she demanded.

Kody explained about the special shoes. The doctor assured Star it wouldn't be like that at all.

Star nodded soberly. "I want to walk right."

"Then let's do it."

Kody signed papers and discussed payment. His Canada fund, no longer needed for that purpose, would do.

Then he and Charlotte took Star to meet her grandpa and grandma.

Ma and Pa were thrilled to know they had a granddaughter. Kody understood he'd robbed them of four precious years, but they would never point it out. They would take what they had now and enjoy it. As Pa said, enjoying what the present offered.

Star hung back shyly for about two minutes, then started in on a long story about her doll. Ma and Pa couldn't keep their eyes off her.

"Can I leave her with you while Charlotte and I go for a walk?" Kody asked.

No one protested.

Charlotte let him take her hand as they walked down the street. He didn't speak and she waited, knowing this walk had a purpose. She'd seen a difference in Kody from the moment he rode back to town. His eyes were clearer, his face had lost those hard lines. She rejoiced that Star would get her foot straightened and Kody was prepared to be Star's father, but she hoped his return had another purpose. One including her.

He led her past the church and through the little gate into the cemetery. They passed several monuments. Kody stopped before a small marker under a big elm tree. He pulled her close to his side. "My mother's grave."

She read the inscription: *Mother of Dakoka Charles Douglas.* A long, bony finger of shock scratched up her spine. She'd known Kody didn't know his mother's name, but to look at cold, hard proof made it real in a way she hadn't accepted until now.

"I'm sorry," she whispered.

"For what?"

So many things. The fact he didn't know his mother's name or who his father was. That it seemed to matter so much to him.

"I thought I'd learn to live with it, but instead, I've been running from it, as you pointed out."

"I had no right." She'd never intended to hurt him.

"I'm glad you did. I thought I could pretend it didn't matter if I kept running from who I am. But I don't want to run anymore. I want to stay right here and raise Star."

He turned and put his arms around her—his strong, loving arms.

She looked up, letting everything she felt fill her smile.

He drank it in as he studied her eyes, ran his gaze down her cheek, settled on her mouth. She waited for him to confess his love and kiss her.

Instead, he eased back fractionally. It felt like he'd moved ten feet. Cold lumped in the bottom of her stomach. He'd said nothing about including her in his change of plans.

He glanced toward the grave marker. "You see my past—uncertain in so many ways. I can't promise people won't judge you poorly because of me. But I love you, and if you'll have me I can promise to love you as long as I live."

Her insides sang with joy. "Kody Douglas, I love you. I can't change my past. I can't guarantee anything about the future except my undying love. But today is ours. Let's take God's good gifts and enjoy them."

"I would like to share today and whatever the future holds with you and Star and any children—"

She laughed. "One step at a time."

"One day at a time." He kissed her then. Gently, sweetly, a kiss full of love and promise and joy.

Epilogue

Four months later

The October day was perfect. Shimmering yellow leaves danced on the poplar trees. The air glowed in the golden light peculiar to autumn.

Charlotte breathed in deeply, inhaling the rich scent of the season. She wanted to hold the smells, devour the sights, cherish each feeling so she would never forget one detail of this, her wedding day.

She'd chosen a pale pink taffeta for the simple tailored dress Martha helped her make. It would serve her for special occasions for years to come. Her bouquet was a generous spray of tiny sunflowers from Nurse Chester's garden.

"Is it time?" Star demanded, pulling Charlotte's attention back to the small room where they waited for the ceremony to begin.

"Any minute now." Her words were soft, confident. Over the past few months she and Kody had grown in their love for and understanding of each other. She'd thrilled to see how he started to walk down the sidewalks with the confidence of a man who belonged. His growing faith challenged her own spiritual growth. How she enjoyed praying together with him, sharing her doubts, her triumphs and the ordinary events of her day. She loved having him share his life with her.

She felt the smile fill her eyes with joy, felt it wrap around her heart with assurance at the depth of her love for Kody, of his for her.

"Do I look pretty?" Star's voice reminded Charlotte of the presence of others.

Star wore a rose-pink dress. Her cast had come off two weeks ago. She could barely contain her pleasure and pride at being able to walk with a barely noticeable limp. Charlotte leaned over and hugged her. "You are beautiful. I hope your daddy can stop staring at you long enough to notice me."

Star giggled, then turned serious. "Now you'll be my momma?"

"Indeed I will and I'm so happy about it." She hugged the child. Star whispered, "Momma," in her ear. Charlotte wondered if her heart could hold any more joy.

She turned to Emma, her bridesmaid. "You'll be stealing hearts left and right yourself." Emma had joined the hospital staff during the summer, and she and Charlotte had soon become fast friends. Emma, practical to the core, seldom bothered to dress up. She wore a uniform for work and simple cotton dresses for church. She usually kept her thick blond hair in a tight bun, as suited a nurse, she insisted when Charlotte tried to talk her into letting it hang loose. But Emma had allowed Charlotte to have her way for the wedding and her hair hung in shimmering waves halfway down her back.

The pianist played the processional and Star headed down the aisle.

Emma grinned at Charlotte. "You are positively glowing. I hope you don't ignite before you get properly hitched." She kissed Charlotte on the cheek and hugged her, then followed Star. She'd refused to do the prissy half-step considered appropriate for weddings.

Charlotte smiled as her friend swung down the aisle with the boldness and assurance of the strong woman she was. Charlotte took a deep breath to still her demanding heart, which urged her to run to Kody's arms. She stepped to the doorway. Harry had been unable to come, saying Nellie needed him in the last stages of confinement, so Charlotte had asked Jed to accompany her down the aisle. She and Kody had become good friends with Jed and Bess. Clinging to Jed's arm, she stepped into the sanctuary. The church was full. John and Morning sat by Kody's parents. She didn't take time to identify any of the others but shifted her gaze to the front.

Her lungs refused to work when she saw Kody standing at the front, resplendent in a black suit his father had persuaded him to wear. He'd recently cut his hair and he looked very debonair. He could pass for a successful businessman. In the last few months he had continued to work for Widow Murphy. Star had divided her time between the Eaglefeathers and her new grandma and grandpa. In a few days, she would join Kody and Charlotte at the Murphy ranch.

"It suits me," Kody often said of the ranch. "Wild and free. Besides, what would Mrs. Murphy do without me?"

He smiled from the front of the church, and Charlotte's lungs remembered to work. She held his gaze as she made her way up the aisle. She heard the whispers and aahs as she passed those in attendance, but she had eyes for no one but Kody.

She reached his side, took his hand and let her breath ease out.

As in a dream, she repeated her vows. Not until Leland told Kody he could kiss his bride and Kody's lips met hers in a vow of eternal love, did she feel like the dream ended. Or had it just begun?

Martha, with the help of the church ladies, had prepared a tea for afterward. Kody seemed perfectly at home with everyone. She could hardly believe how distant he'd kept himself not so long ago.

And then the tea things were cleared away and gifts piled in front of them. Together they opened them—towels, fancy dishes, sheets and other essentials.

Later, dusk settled like a pale gray cloak as they climbed into the black truck Kody had purchased, insisting they needed better transportation than horses to take them back and forth to the Murphy ranch.

Someone had left a light burning in the living room of the ranch house, and it beamed a golden welcome as they drove into the yard.

Kody leaned over and kissed Charlotte thoroughly before he jumped from the truck and hurried around to help her out. She looked around, expecting to be led to the small house Mrs. Murphy provided her hired man, but Kody led her up the path toward the big house.

"What…?" Then she realized Mrs. Murphy must have given them access to the house for their wedding night.

Kody allowed her to walk as far as the door, then swept her off her feet and carried her over the threshold. He kissed her again without putting her down. He crossed to the middle of the great room rising open to the second story.

"Welcome home, Mrs. Douglas," Kody whispered as he set her on her feet. "I have a wedding present for you." He reached into his breast pocket and pulled out a sheaf of official-looking papers, which he unfolded and handed to her.

She read them, tried to make sense of them. "This looks like some kind of business deal."

"Mrs. Murphy offered to sell me the ranch. I can pay it off month by month."

She gaped at him. "She did?"

"Yeah. I guess she likes me."

Chuckling, she kissed him, then tore herself away and turned full circle. "This is to be our home?"

"Think you'll like it?"

She laughed. "It's beautiful. I can hardly wait to see the view through those long windows in daylight."

He pulled her into his arms.

She wrapped her arms around him and hugged him tight. "God is so good."

"That He is." His gentle kiss promised more than enough joy for every day.

* * * * *

Award-winning author **Dorothy Clark** lives in rural New York. Dorothy enjoys traveling with her husband throughout the United States doing research and gaining inspiration for future books. Dorothy believes in God, love, family and happy endings, which explains why she feels so at home writing stories for Love Inspired. Dorothy enjoys hearing from her readers and may be contacted at dorothyjclark@hotmail.com.

Books by Dorothy Clark

Love Inspired Historical

Stand-In Brides

His Substitute Wife
Wedded for the Baby
Mail-Order Bride Switch

Pinewood Weddings

Wooing the Schoolmarm
Courting Miss Callie
Falling for the Teacher
A Season of the Heart

An Unlikely Love
His Precious Inheritance

Visit the Author Profile page
at Harlequin.com for more titles.

FAMILY OF THE HEART

Dorothy Clark

This book is dedicated with boundless gratitude to my extremely talented writer friend and critique partner Sam Pakan, who read every chapter (though there is not a fistfight or dead body in any of them), encouraged me and prayed for me when "life" happened and interfered with my writing time and stuck with me through the last two weeks of my writing marathon, though he was racing to meet his own book deadline. You sure know how to go the "second mile," cowboy. Thank you.

"Commit thy works unto the Lord, and thy thoughts shall be established."
—*Proverbs* 16:3

Your word is truth. Thank You, Jesus.
To You be the glory.

of her day dresses, but none of her gowns were really appropriate for a nanny. If only there had been time to obtain more suitable attire.

Sarah let out a sigh and closed her mind to the concern. It was of no matter now—her gowns would simply have to do. She glanced down, shook out her long bottle-green velvet skirt, smoothed down the tab-cut leaves at the waist edge of her matching spencer, then lifted her head and appraised the house in front of her. It was well named. The rectangular stone house, with its set-back kitchen ell, sat square in the middle of the point of land that forced the road to curve.

It was an attractive house. Not large, compared to the homes of the elite of Philadelphia, but two stories of generous and pleasing proportion. And, though there was nothing ornate or fancy about the place, it had charm. Shutters, painted the dark green of the pines on the hill-side, embraced the home's symmetrically placed multi-paned windows and framed its solid wood-plank front door. Ivy spread clinging arms in profuse abandon on the front and climbed the gable end, stretching a few tentacles toward the wood shingles of the roof.

"Ready, miss." The driver, holding her large trunk balanced on one beefy shoulder, appeared beside her.

Sarah stepped back, giving him room to open the gate sandwiched between the two lamp-topped stone pillars that anchored the low stone walls enclosing the home's front yard. She ignored the *maaaa* of one of the sheep grazing on the lawn and followed him up the slate walk. Hope quickened her pulse. Her new life was starting. Surely tending a toddler would keep her too busy to dwell on the past, to remember the loss of her dream of being Aaron's wife. Surely it would fill the emptiness and make the pain ease. *Oh, if only the pain would ease.*

The driver banged the brass knocker against the plate on the front door, and Sarah straightened her back and curved her lips into a smile. Everything would be better now. Soon, everything would be better.

The solid wood door opened. A stout woman stepped forward and stood centered in the frame. She looked at the driver, noted the trunk he carried and dipped her head toward the left. "Take that o'er t' the side door. Quincy'll let you in." She shifted her gaze. Surprise, then doubt swept over her face. "You *are* the new nanny?"

Sarah felt her smile slip away at the woman's tone. She pasted it firmly back in place and nodded. "Yes. I am—"

"Late! We expected you this morning." The woman stepped aside and waved a pudgy arm toward the interior of the house. "Don't stand there, come in, come in!"

Sarah hesitated a moment, debating the wisdom in pursuing her decision to accept the position. But the challenge was exactly what she needed. And she'd never had a problem getting along with her family's servants. Perhaps the housekeeper was simply feeling the need to establish her authority. She squared her shoulders, climbed the three stone steps and crossed the small stoop. A child's unhappy wails fell on her ears as she entered the small entry.

The woman closed the door and gave a brief nod toward the stairs. "'Tis that we've been sufferin' all day! The little miss is cryin' an' in no mood to be quieted. And Mr. Bainbridge is—" Her words came to an abrupt halt as a door on their left flew open.

"Eldora! Can Lucy not *stop* the child from cry—"

Sarah stiffened as the man in the doorway snapped off his words and swiveled his head her direction. He swept an assessing gaze over her, and his dark-brown brows lowered in a frown. "I was not aware we had a visitor." He made a small, polite bow in her direction. "Forgive me my outburst, Miss...er..."

"Randolph—Miss Sarah Randolph, of Philadelphia."

The man's brows shot skyward. "*You* are the new nanny?" He skimmed another gaze over her. Doubt flashed into his eyes. The frown deepened.

The man's reaction rasped against her tense nerves. Was he going to judge her on appearance only? Did he deem that stylish clothes meant she could not care for a child? Sarah's back stiffened. She gave him a cool nod. "I am. And it sounds as if I am sorely needed." She lifted a meaningful glance toward the top of the stairs. The toddler's cries were gaining in volume.

"Indeed." The man gave her a piercing look. "You seem confident of your abilities."

"And you seem highly dubious of them." Sarah lifted her chin and looked right back. "I would not have written requesting to be considered for the position of nanny were I not competent to handle the child."

The man's eyes darkened. "It will take more than words to convince me of that, Miss Randolph. Competency is a thing that is proven, not—" he winced as a loud wail echoed down the stairs "—declared." His face tightened. "And the first test of yours will begin now. I shall postpone your interview until later this evening. Please see to the child immediately. It's impossible for me to work in this din." Her prospective employer shifted his gaze back to the stout woman. "Mrs. Quincy, show Miss

Randolph to the nursery. Immediately!" He stepped back into the room behind him and closed the door.

"This way, Miss Randolph." The hem of the housekeeper's long, gray skirt swished back and forth as she turned and headed toward the stairs.

Can Lucy not stop the child? The man's words were still ringing a warning alarm in her head. Sarah shot a quick glance at the closed door beside her. What sort of man called his daughter *the child?* A tiny frisson of apprehension tingled through her. Perhaps this nanny position would not be as easy as she expected. But she could always go home. She hugged the comfort of that thought close, lifted her long skirts slightly and followed Mrs. Quincy up the stairs.

"Here we are." Mrs. Quincy opened a door at the end of a short hallway.

Sarah stepped forward into a well-furnished, sunny nursery. At least, that was her initial impression. She hadn't time for more with her attention centered on the squalling, squirming toddler trying to twist free of the grip of the young maid sitting in a rocking chair. The maid rocked furiously, jiggling the toddler up and down and making soothing noises.

Sarah froze. Mrs. Quincy stepped forward and looked at her in demand. The maid—Lucy was it?—looked at her in relief and stood to her feet. Oh, dear! They expected her to— What? Sarah's stomach flopped. Her first thought was to turn about, run down the stairs and not stop until she reached the hotel where Ellen awaited her instructions. Perhaps they would both be making the journey back to Philadelphia. But the unhappiness apparent in the toddler's cries held her frozen in place. Perhaps if she could get the child's attention… She moved closer and leaned down to place her hand on the toddler's back. "Hello, little one. I'm your new nanny."

The child didn't even look at her, only squalled louder and squirmed harder. What now? An idea popped into her head. An absolutely absurd idea—but she had nothing to lose. Sarah undid the satin ties of her bonnet and tossed it on the rocking chair, opened her mouth and let out a wail that made both Mrs. Quincy and Lucy jump. The toddler stopped squirming and crying and stared up at her out of big blue eyes. *It worked!*

"There now, that's better." Sarah spoke softly, but firmly. She lifted the startled toddler out of Lucy's arms and started toward the window in the wall on the opposite side of the room. She had no idea what next to do, but movement seemed a good idea. She glanced at the child in her arms and burst out laughing. The little girl was staring at her as if she didn't know what to think of her. That, too, seemed a good thing. "And do you have a name, little one?"

"Nora. Nora Blessing Bainbridge." Mrs. Quincy's answer was followed by the click of the door opening and closing.

Sarah glanced over her shoulder. The room was empty. She looked back at the toddler. "Well, Nora Blessing Bainbridge, it seems you and I are on our own." The child's lips quivered, pulled down at the corners. She placed her tiny hands against Sarah's chest and pushed. "Except for that squirrel. Look!"

Sarah quickly turned Nora so she faced outward, holding her so Nora's small back rested against her chest. "See?" She pointed at a large gray squirrel sitting on a branch of the tree outside the window, nibbling on some sort of bud. The distraction worked. The toddler's tensed muscles relaxed. She stared at the squirrel, caught a broken breath, then another, stuck her thumb in her mouth and began sucking. Her little legs, dangling over Sarah's supporting arm, stilled their kicking.

Thank goodness for the squirrel! Sarah swayed side to side, humming softly, ignoring the child except for an occasional downward glance. After a few minutes, Nora's eyelids drooped, opened, drooped again. A moment later her little head dropped forward until her chin rested on her chest.

Sarah looked down and smiled. Nora had lost her battle against sleep. The toddler's light-brown eyelashes rested on her round rosy cheeks and her little mouth was relaxed, no longer sucking at the tiny thumb. She looked adorable…asleep. Now, if only she could keep her that way until she could collect herself.

Sarah continued to sway and hum as she turned and scanned the room. A cherrywood crib with turned spindles and a white, crocheted canopy stood against the far wall. She carried Nora over, laid her on the blanket-covered down mattress and pulled the woven coverlet over her. She held her breath and stood poised, waiting… Little Nora blinked her eyes, sucked on her thumb and slept on.

Sarah let out a long sigh of relief and glanced around the room. Time to familiarize herself. She stripped off her gloves and tossed them on the rocker with her bonnet, tiptoed to a large, handsomely carved wardrobe and pulled open the double doors. Small dresses, aprons and coats with matching bonnets hung in colorful array on the right side. Little shoes and slippers marched beneath and, on the left, undergarments filled drawers. She noted the fine workmanship on Nora's clothes, shut the wardrobe doors and looked around the room. Shelves, full of books, toys and stuffed animals, filled the alcove formed by the stone fireplace. An exquisitely detailed dollhouse sat beneath a window. A child-size table, set for a tea party, its matching chairs holding the attending dolls, sat in front of the shelves.

Sarah smiled at the evidence of the father's love for his daughter. Obviously, that twinge of warning she had felt on meeting the man was wrong. She had simply misinterpreted his perturbation over Nora's unhappy cries. Thankfully, she had been able to quiet the child. She skirted the chair on the hearth and opened a door onto a dressing room. Sight of the pipe traveling along the stone wall to the wash basin and tub brought a rush of relief. Running water! She had been prepared to give up that luxury. It was wonderful to know that sacrifice wouldn't be required.

She glanced back to check on Nora, moved to another door and peeked inside. A cool draft flowed out of the dark room. Sarah shivered and stepped back, hesitant to enter the gloomy space. There was enough darkness in her life. She pulled the door closed—froze—opened it again. Yes. That was *her* trunk sitting on the rug of braided rags on the wide plank floor.

So this dismal place was to be her bedroom. Disappointment morphed into the barely controlled despair that was always with her. Why had she been so foolish as to think taking this position as nanny would help her over her grief? She should go home where she had every luxury, where she was cosseted and pampered, and…and *wretched*.

Unwanted memories impelled Sarah into the room. Her gaze skittered from the stone fireplace centered on the interior paneled wall, to a writing desk and chair, to the four-poster bed situated between two shuttered windows. She rushed forward, threw open the shutters and tugged up the bottom sashes. Light and warmth flooded into the room. The scent of lilacs floated in on a gentle breeze.

The horrid tightness in her throat and chest eased. Sarah lifted her face to the waning sunshine and took a deep breath. The tears that had been so close to flowing receded. Another battle won.

The victory gave her courage. Sarah marched to her trunk, unfastened the hasp and lifted the lid. She needed to change out of her travel outfit before Nora's father summoned her. A sigh escaped. How she longed for Ellen. The woman had been her confidante as well as her personal maid since she outgrew her own nanny. She looked down at the trunk's contents, and the victory she had won dissolved. She touched the cool silk fabric of the top dress and tears flooded her eyes. The gown had been designed for her to wear on her honeymoon. She should be aboard ship with Aaron and halfway around the world right now. A sob caught in her throat.

Sarah wrenched her thoughts from what should have been, wiped the tears from her face and lifted out the top dress. She shook out the blue and white silk gown, held it up and gave it a critical once-over, focusing all her attention on choosing an appropriate gown. Were the four flounces that decorated the bottom of the skirt too fancy? Would the gold, watered taffeta with the rolled silk ribbon trim be a better choice? What did one wear to an interview with an employer?

* * *

Clayton Bainbridge stared at Sarah Randolph. She was unlike any nanny he had ever seen. Her gown was the equal of those his wife had owned—and there was certainly nothing subservient in her manner. Indeed, her demeanor was more that of a guest than of a woman being interviewed for a position. It had him a little out of kilter. As did her latest revelation. He frowned down at her. "So you are telling me you have no actual experience as a nanny."

"That is correct. However, as I wrote in my letter, I have abundant experience in caring for children." She smiled up at him. "My aunt has an orphanage and I often helped with the babies and small children. She is my reference." She handed him a sealed letter.

"I see." Clayton scowled at the letter, tapped it against his palm. *He would have to start the search for a nanny for the child all over again!* He tossed the unopened letter on the table beside him. "I'm afraid you have made a long journey in vain, Miss Randolph. A reference from a family member is unacceptable."

"Laina Allen may be my aunt, Mr. Bainbridge, but I assure you, she is a woman of great integrity. She is highly respected in Philadelphia—as are all members of my family. You can trust her word."

Sarah Randolph's stiff posture and the gold sparks in her brown eyes belied the coolness of her voice. Clayton hesitated, then yielded to an inner prompting, picked up the letter and broke the seal. Silence, invaded only by the crackle of the fire that had been started to ward off the chill of the evening air, settled around them as he read.

"Your aunt recommends you highly as one skilled in caring for toddlers and young children." Clayton folded the letter, slipped it in his jacket pocket and fastened his gaze on Sarah. She looked regal, with her erect posture, lifted chin and light-brown hair swept high on the crown of her head. And wealthy. That gold gown she wore would cost more than his month's wages. Why had she applied for the post of nanny?

Clayton frowned, continued his assessment. It was certain Sarah Randolph had never done a day's work. Her hands were soft and white, the nails long and neatly shaped. And her face was the face of a pampered woman. He drifted his gaze over the small lifted chin, narrow nose and shapely high cheekbones to the brown eyes under delicately arched light-brown brows. He stiffened. There was a challenge in those eyes. And something else. Pain. He recognized it easily. He should. He saw it his own eyes every morning when he shaved.

Clayton averted his gaze. Sarah Randolph was hurting, vulnerable, despite the bravado of that lifted chin. But she had courage. That was apparent. She was not yielding to her pain. She seemed to be a fighter. Perhaps she was suitable for the post in spite of her delicate, pampered appearance. He cleared his throat. "I believe you aptly demonstrated the skill of which your aunt speaks by quickly silencing the child's cries on your arrival. Because of that, Miss Randolph, the position is yours—should you still wish it after learning of your duties and responsibilities. They exceed the normal ones." He turned and walked to the hearth, giving her time to absorb that information.

The silence settled around them again.

Sarah stared at Clayton Bainbridge's back. He'd done it again. He'd referred to Nora as "the child." And what did "They exceed the normal duties" mean? Her stomach quivered, tightened.

"Should you stay, Miss Randolph, the child will be fully in your charge. While I shall provide all that is needed for its care, I will have no personal contact with it. Is that clear?"

Shock held her mute.

He pivoted to face her. "Do you understand?"

Sarah found her voice hiding behind a huge lump of anger in her throat. She lifted her chin and met his gaze full with her own. "Your *words*...yes. But—"

"There is no *but,* Miss Randolph. Those are the special conditions of your employment. I realize you will require some personal time, and *that* need will be met by having Lucy sit with the child while she naps in the afternoon. And, of course, your evenings will be free. Other than that, you will spend all of your time with the child. Your wages will, of course, reflect the added responsibility. Do you wish to accept the position?"

Incredible! Sarah clasped her hands in her lap to keep from reaching out and pinching Clayton Bainbridge to find out if he was flesh and blood. The man might as well be a marble statue. His face was expressionless, his voice void of emotion. Had he no feelings? An image of the toddler sleeping upstairs flashed into her head. "Yes, Mr. Randolph, I accept the position." She fought the anger that had brought her to her feet, lost the battle and gave voice to the words clamoring to be spoken. "I must, sir. Because your *daughter* is a little girl, not an *it.*"

Sarah squared her shoulders, whirled away from the look of astonishment on Clayton Bainbridge's face and swept from the room.

Chapter Two

He would dismiss her first thing in the morning! Clayton stormed into his bedroom, removed his jacket and threw it onto the chair beside the window. His fingers worked at the buttons on his waistcoat as his long strides ate up the distance to the highboy on the other side of the room.

Your daughter is a little girl, not an it!

And he had felt sorry for her. Ha! His sympathy had certainly been misplaced. How dare that woman offer him such a rebuke! Clayton grabbed the silver fob dangling from his waistcoat pocket, jerked his watch free, dropped it into one of the small drawers, pivoted and paced back toward the window.

And for her to walk out of the room and leave him standing there like…like some servant! He shrugged out of the vest and yanked his cravat free. And what did he do? Nothing! Shock had kept him frozen in place. By the time he'd made his feet move, she had disappeared up the stairs. Well, he was not shocked now. And in the morning he would tell Miss Sarah Randolph she was completely unsuited for the nanny position, give her a stipend for her time and have Quincy arrange for her transportation back to Philadelphia.

Because she spoke the truth?

The voice in his head stayed his hand, cooled his anger. Clayton frowned. He refused to consider that question. What did Miss Sarah Randolph know of his truth? Nothing. And, truth or not, she had overstepped her place in speaking it.

Clayton tossed the vest and cravat on top of his jacket and sat in the chair to remove his shoes. Finding another nanny took so much *time.* And meanwhile chaos would again reign in the household. For some reason Lucy was unable to keep the child from crying all day. And the first nanny had not been that successful at it, either. But at least she had known her place.

Clayton scowled, tugged a shoe off, dropped it to the floor and wiggled his freed toes, weighing the situation in the light of that last thought. Perhaps he should give Sarah Randolph another chance. Perhaps that outburst was only because she didn't yet fully realize what her position was. Her erect posture and lifted chin as she faced him down, proved she wasn't accustomed to servitude. No, Sarah Randolph was a lady. Every inch of her. A *beautiful* lady. So why was she here?

Clayton rested his elbows on his knees and stared down at the floor. The anomaly was intriguing. It was obvious Miss Randolph was not impoverished. And it could not be a case of familial division—she had spoken well of her family, and they of her. At least in the letter. Of course there was the matter of her temper.

A vision of Sarah's face, brown eyes flashing, burst into his head. She *was* spirited. And beautiful. Clayton's face tightened. He grabbed the shoe he had removed, tugged it back on and lunged out of the chair. Bed could wait. Right now he would go to his study and work on his progress report of the needed repairs on the canal locks here in Cincinnati. And on the estimated repairs required on the rest of the southern section of the Miami Canal. He was due to report to the commissioners next week. And the plans had to be perfected, as well. An hour or two spent staring at blueprints would drive away that unwelcome image.

Sarah looked toward the foot of the bed. Her trunk sat there…waiting. She did not dare pack the few items she had taken out for fear of waking little Nora. It would have to wait until morning—or until an angry fist pounded on her door and Mr. Bainbridge told her she was dismissed. She sighed and looked around the bedroom. She had held her post as nanny for what…a few hours? Well, it was her own fault. She should have controlled her temper. But—

No buts! It was too late for buts. Too late to take back her outburst. And too late to leave this house to-night. Sarah removed her silk gown, hung it in the cup-board beside the fireplace and tugged the soft comfort of an embroidered cotton nightgown over her head. She pushed her feet into her warm, fur-trimmed slippers and shoved her arms into the sleeves of her quilted cotton dressing gown.

What had caused her to act in such an unaccustomed way? She had gained nothing by giving vent to her out-rage over Clayton Bainbridge's callus attitude toward his daughter. Except for the momentary satisfaction of that look of utter astonishment on his face. Her lips curved at the memory of his widened deep-blue eyes and raised, thick, dark-brown brows, the flare of the nostrils on his long, masculine nose. That had been a gratifying moment. Of course, an instant later anger had replaced the astonishment. His brows had lowered, his eyes had darkened and the full lower lip of his mouth had thinned to match the top one. And that square jaw of his! Gracious! It had firmed to the appearance of granite. No, her outburst had done nothing to help little Nora. Or herself.

Sarah caught her breath at a sudden onrush of memories, fastened the ties at the neck of her dressing gown and hurried into the nursery. The oil lamp she had left burning with its wick turned low warmed the moonlight pouring in the windows to a soft gold. Tears welled into her eyes as she straightened the coverlet that had become twisted when Nora turned over. She had thought by now she and Aaron might be expecting a child of their own. The tears overflowed. She brushed them away, smoothed a silky golden curl off the toddler's cheek and, unable to stop herself, bent and kissed the soft smooth skin. Nora stirred, her little lips worked as she sucked on her thumb, went still again.

Sarah's heart melted. She resisted the urge to lift the little girl into her arms and cradle her close to her painfully tight chest. The hem of her dressing gown whispered against the wide planks of the floor as she walked back to her own room. What was *wrong* with Clayton Bainbridge? How could he not want anything to do with his own child? How could he not love her?

Sarah glanced at her trunk, halted in the doorway. Would whoever took over this position of nanny love little Nora? Would she give her the affection every child deserved? Or would she simply take care of her physical needs and keep her quiet so Mr. Clayton Bainbridge was not disturbed? Oh, why had she ever challenged the man's cold, detached attitude toward his child? She should have kept quiet—for Nora's sake. The little girl needed her.

And *she* needed this post.

Sarah blinked back another rush of tears and walked to her bed. She removed her dressing gown, stepped out of her slippers and slid beneath the covers, fighting the impulse to bury her face in the pillow and sob away the hurt inside. Crying wouldn't stop the aching. It never did. But everyone said time would bring healing.

If only it were possible to hurry time.

Sarah breathed out slowly, reached over and turned down the wick of the lamp on her bedside table. She couldn't bring herself to snuff out the flame. She could do nothing about the darkness inside her, but she could keep the darkness of night at bay. She rested back against the pillow, pulled the covers up to her chin and stared up at the tester overhead, willing time to pass.

Birdsong coaxed her from her exhausted slumber. Sarah opened her eyes and came awake with a start. She shoved to a sitting position, blinked to clear her vision and gazed around the strange room. Where was she?

Her open trunk provided the answer. The moment she saw it, the events of yesterday came pouring back. She sighed and swung her legs over the side of the bed, searching for the floor with her bare feet. Her toes touched fur and she pushed her feet into the warm softness of her slippers and gave another sigh. She wasn't accustomed to rising with the dawn, but she had better get ready to face the day. Mr. Bainbridge was most likely an early riser. Even when he wasn't angry.

She tiptoed to the door of the nursery, glanced in to make sure Nora was still sleeping and yawned her way to the dressing room to perform her morning toilette. How was she to manage without Ellen?

Soft stirrings emanated from the nursery.

Sarah gathered her long hair into a pile at the crown of her head the way Ellen had shown her, wrapped the wide silk ribbon that matched her gown around the thick mass and tied it into a bow. When she removed her hands, a few of her soft curls cascaded down the back of her head to the nape of her neck. She frowned and reached to retie the ribbon.

The stirrings grew louder.

She had run out of time. Her hair would have to do. Sarah took another look in the mirror to make sure her efforts would hold and hurried from the dressing room into the nursery, smiling at sight of the toddler who was sitting in the middle of the crib, her cheeks rosy with warmth, her blue eyes still heavy with sleep.

"Good morning, Nora. I'm Nanny Sarah—" *at least until I'm summoned downstairs for dismissal* "—do you remember me?"

"'Quirrel."

Sarah's smile widened. "That's right. We watched the squirrel together yesterday. Aren't you clever to remember." She moved closer to the crib and held out her arms. "Are you ready to get up and have some breakfast?" She held her breath, waiting.

Nora stared up at her. "Cookie." She scrambled to her feet and held up her arms.

"Cookie?" Sarah laughed and scooped her up. "I'm afraid cookies are not acceptable breakfast fare for lit-

tle girls. Would a biscuit with some lovely strawberry jam suit?"

Nora's golden curls bounced as she bobbed her head. "Me like jam!"

"Yes, I thought you might." Sarah looked around for a bellpull. There was none. She hurried to her bedroom, glanced around, frowned. Where was— The truth burst upon her, rooted her in place. Servants did not have bellpulls. And in this house she was a servant. She tightened her grip on Nora and sank to the edge of the bed, absorbing the ramifications of that truth. Perhaps it was just as well she would be going home. She had no idea what to do. Someone had to prepare Nora's breakfast. But without a bellpull how did she summon—

"Bisit."

Sarah looked into her charge's big blue eyes and sighed. "Biscuit?... Yes. You shall have your biscuit and jam, Nora." She took a deep breath, made her decision. She would take Nora to the kitchen—wherever that was—and have cook prepare breakfast for both of them. "But first I must get you washed and brushed and ready for the day."

Nora squirmed. "Go potty."

"Oh. Of course. Wait a moment." Sarah tightened her arms around the toddler, rose and hurried toward the dressing room.

"Good morning." Sarah smiled as Mrs. Quincy spun around from the iron cooking stove and gaped at her. The woman's flushed face registered surprise, then censure.

"You're not to be using the main stairs." The housekeeper tossed the piece of wood she was holding into the stove, replaced the iron plate and hung the tool she'd used to lift the lid on a hook on the wall. Her long skirts swished as she moved around a large center table and pulled open a door. "These back stairs are the ones you're to use."

Sarah glanced at the narrow stairway with the pie-wedge-shaped winding steps.

"Remember that in future." Mrs. Quincy closed the door, went back to the stove, picked up a spoon and swirled it through the contents in a large iron pot. "Is there somethin' you needed?"

"Yes." Sarah's stomach clenched at the smell of apples and cinnamon that wafted her way. She ignored the reminder that she had been too nervous to eat supper yesterday and carried Nora toward the table. "I am unfamiliar with the way you run the house, and I wondered if you would be so good as to tell me where and when Nora's meals—and mine—are served."

Mrs. Quincy put down the spoon, picked up a griddle covered with slices of bacon and placed it on the stove. "Miss Thompson came down, give me orders for what she wanted for herself and the child and went back upstairs. Lucy toted and fetched their trays."

Sarah winced at the cold, offended note in the housekeeper's voice. Miss Thompson must have been overbearing in flaunting her elevated position as nanny to the daughter of the house. No wonder Mrs. Quincy was less than welcoming. "I see. Well, I do not wish to be an intrusion in your kitchen, Mrs. Quincy. Miss Nora and I will partake of whatever fare is being offered." She gave a delicate sniff. "Breakfast smells wonderful." She paused, rushed ahead, braving the woman's ire. "However, I do wonder if it might include a biscuit with jam for Miss Nora? I promised her one this morning." She offered an apologetic smile. "I shan't make rash promises about meals to her again."

The starch went out of Mrs. Quincy's spine. She nodded, broke an egg onto the griddle beside the sizzling bacon, tossed away the shell and reached for another. "I've biscuits made. And there's strawberry jam in the pantry. I'll put one on the child's tray. And on yours as well." She grated pepper onto the eggs, added salt. "Lucy will bring them up directly."

"Thank you, Mrs. Quincy." Sarah glanced toward the door that opened on the winder stairs. She didn't feel safe climbing them with Nora in her arms. She waited until the housekeeper was busy turning the bacon and eggs and walked back the way she had come through the butler's pantry and into the dining room.

"Bisit-jam." Nora's lower lip pushed out in a trembling pout. She twisted around and stretched her pudgy little arm back toward the kitchen.

"Yes, sweetie. You shall have your biscuit. But first we have to go back upstairs."

"Bisit! Jam!"

"In a moment, Nora."

The toddler stiffened and let out an irate howl.

Sarah took a firmer hold on the rigid little body and howled louder. Nora stopped yelling and gaped at her. Clearly, the child did not know what to think of an adult who yelled back. How long would that ploy work? Judging from the storm cloud gathering on the small face, Nora was not going to give up easily. The little mouth opened. Sarah shifted her grasp, lifted the toddler into the air and whirled across the dining room. By the time she reached the doorway they were both laughing.

"That is much better." Sarah stepped through the dining-room doorway into the hall and came to an abrupt halt. It appeared her concern over breakfast was in vain. Clayton Bainbridge was striding down the hall toward her, and she had no doubt she would be dismissed as soon as he saw her. Lucy would be the one caring for Nora today. She squared her shoulders as best she could with Nora in her arms and curved her lips into a polite smile. "Good morning."

Clayton Bainbridge stopped in midstride and lifted his gaze from the paper he held. Surprise flickered across his face, was quickly replaced by displeasure. He gave a curt nod in acknowledgment of her greeting. His gaze locked on hers, didn't even flicker toward the toddler she held. "Did I hear yelling, Miss Randolph?"

His tone made her go as rigid as Nora had only moments ago. "Yes, Mr. Bainbridge, you did. Nora and I were playing." That was true. There was no need to tell him the yelling occurred first. Or that the play was to prevent it from happening again.

"I see. In the future, please confine your 'play' to the nursery." His scowl deepened. "There are back stairs directly to the kitchen, Miss Randolph. It is unnecessary for you to bring the child into this part of the house." He gestured behind her. "If you go through the dining room to the kitchen, Mrs. Quincy will show you the stairs' location."

He was completely ignoring his daughter! Sarah resisted the urge to lift little Nora up into Clayton Bainbridge's line of sight where he could not dismiss her. "She has already done so." She matched his cool tone. "But the steps are narrow and winding, and I feel they are unsafe to use when I am carrying your daughter."

And how can you object to that, Mr. Bainbridge? "Now, if you will excuse us, our breakfast trays are waiting."

Sarah sailed by Clayton to the forbidden staircase and began to ascend, defiance in her every step. What had she to lose? He could not dismiss her twice.

Clayton stared after Sarah Randolph. The woman had an unpleasant and inappropriate autocratic manner. But he would not tolerate her presence much longer. He would dismiss her as soon as she had given the child her breakfast. He pivoted, strode to the dining room, took his seat, glanced at the paper in his hand. A moment later he threw the paper on the table and stormed into the kitchen. The heels of his boots clacked against the stones of the floor as he marched over and yanked open the door enclosing the back stairs. The narrow, wedge-shaped steps wound upward in a tight spiral. His anger burst like a puffball under a foot. Sarah Randolph was right. The winder stairs were unsafe for a woman burdened with a child.

"Was there something you needed, sir?"

Clayton turned to face Mrs. Quincy. She looked a bit undone by his unusual appearance in the kitchen. "Only my breakfast, Eldora." He closed the door on the happy little giggle floating down the stairway. "And to tell you Miss Randolph will be using the main stairs." He turned his back on her startled face and returned to the dining room, feeling irritated, yet, beneath it all, cheered by his sudden decision to keep Miss Randolph on as the child's nanny. There was not a hint of crying from upstairs, and it had been a long time since he had been able to read his paper and enjoy his breakfast in silence.

Chapter Three

Lucy sat in the rocker and pulled the linen she had brought to mend onto her lap. Sarah gave the young maid a grateful smile and tiptoed from the bedroom. Her time was now her own until Nora awoke from her nap—and she had caught only the briefest glimpse of Cincinnati when she arrived.

She hurried down the stairs, crossed the entry hall to the front door and stepped out onto the stoop. The afternoon sun warmed the flower-scented air. She took an appreciative sniff. *Lilacs.* She loved their fragrance. And what a beautiful view. She descended the front steps, hurried down the slate walk toward the gate and swept her gaze down the flat, dusty ribbon of road toward town.

Clayton stared down at the paper spread out on his desk. The blueprint had turned into a drawing with no meaning. The sight of Sarah Randolph holding the child had seared itself into his brain and had his thoughts twisting and turning over the same useless ground.

He put down his calipers, shoved his chair back and

rose to his feet. What sort of man was he to betray a deathbed promise to his mentor and friend, and endanger, through his weakness, the life of the very person he had promised to marry and care for and keep safe? Andrew had trusted him with his daughter's life, and now, because of him, because of one night, Deborah was dead.

Clayton balled his hand and slammed the side of his fist against the window frame so hard the panes rattled. He would give anything if he could take back that night of weakness. He had even volunteered his life in Deborah's stead, but God had not accepted his offer. Instead God had given him a living, breathing symbol of his human failings—his guilt.

A splash of yellow outside the window caught his eye. Clayton looked to his left. The new nanny moved into view, walking toward the front gate. There was a healthy vigor in the way she moved. If only Deborah could have enjoyed such health. If only she had not had a weak heart...

Clayton's face drew taut. He stared out the window, fighting the tide of emotions sight of the child had brought to the fore. Sarah Randolph seemed an excellent nanny. He had not once been disturbed by the child's crying since she arrived, and he was reluctant to let her go. But he would if she did not obey his dictates. He would not tolerate the child in his presence. He needed to make that abundantly clear. And he would. Right now.

He crossed to his desk, grabbed his suit coat from the back of the chair and shrugged into it as he headed out the door.

Sarah rested her hands on the top of the gate and studied the scene below. Cincinnati, fronted by the wide, sparkling blue water of the Ohio River, sat within the caress of forested hills that formed an amphitheater around its clustered buildings. For a moment she watched the busy parade of ships and boats plying the Ohio River waters, but the sight reminded her of Aaron and all she wanted to forget. She drew her gaze up the sloped bank away from the waterfront warehouses, factories and ships massed along the river's shore. People the size of ants bustled around the business establishments, shops and inns that greeted disembarking passengers and crews. Farther inland, churches, scattered here and there among the other shops and homes that lined the connecting streets, announced their presence with gleaming spires. Throughout the town, an occasional tree arched its green branches over a street, or stood sentinel by a home dotted with brilliant splashes of color in window boxes or around doorways. Smoke rose from the chimneys of several larger buildings.

A sudden longing to go and explore the town came over her. Visiting the familiar shops in Philadelphia had become a bitter experience, but there was nothing in Cincinnati to make her remember. No one in the town knew her. Or of—

"What do you think of our city?"

Sarah started and glanced over her shoulder. Clayton Bainbridge was striding down the walk toward her. She braced herself for what was to come and turned back to the vista spread out before her. "I think it is beautiful. I like the way it nestles among these hills with the river streaming by. And it certainly looks industrious."

"It is that." Clayton stopped beside her, staring down at the town. "And it will become even more so when the northern section of the Miami Canal is finished."

She glanced up at him. "Forgive my ignorance, but what is the Miami Canal? And how does it affect Cincinnati?"

A warmth and excitement swept over his face that completely transformed his countenance. Sarah fought to keep her own face from reflecting her surprise. Clayton Bainbridge was a very handsome man when he wasn't scowling. She shifted her attention back to his words.

"—is a man-made waterway that, when finished, will connect Cincinnati to Lake Erie. It is already in use from here to Dayton." He lifted his hands shoulder-width apart and slashed them down at a slant toward each other. "Cincinnati is like a huge funnel that takes in the farm produce of Ohio for shipment downriver. And that will only increase when the canal is finished." A frown knit his dark brows together. "That is why it is vital that I make an inspection trip over the entire southern section soon to check on weak or damaged areas. But first I must oversee repairs to the locks here at Cincinnati."

"Locks?"

Clayton shifted his gaze to her and she immediately became aware of the breeze riffling the curls resting against her temples and flowing down her back. She should have taken the time to fetch her bonnet. She would have to guard against her impulsiveness—it was such an unflattering trait. Sarah held back a frown of her own, reached up and tucked a loosened strand of her hair back where it belonged.

"Yes, locks. There are a series of them on the canal that lift or lower boats to the needed level. Unfortunately, the contractor who won the bid on the locks here at Cincinnati scanted on materials and construction practices to make it a profitable venture. Hence the locks were unequal to the demand placed on them and must now be either repaired or strengthened."

"And that is your responsibility?"

He nodded. "I am the engineer in charge, yes."

"Of the repairs over the entire southern section of the canal?

"Yes."

"That must be daunting."

"It could be, were I not educated and trained to handle the work."

Sarah's cheeks warmed. "Of course. I meant no—" His lifted hand stopped her apology. She looked down at the city.

"I understood your meaning, Miss Randolph. And I wish you to understand mine." His gaze captured hers. "If you recall, during your interview, I told you I do not wish to have any personal contact with the child. Not *any*. I will overlook the incident in the hallway this morning, but I do not want it repeated. See that it is not."

Sarah's budding respect for Clayton Bainbridge plummeted. She drew breath to speak, glanced up and bit back the retort teetering on her tongue. His face had a cold, closed look, but there was something in his eyes she couldn't identify. Something that held her silent.

"I also wanted to tell you I have given Quincy orders to drive you to town whenever you wish."

He was not going to dimiss her? "That is most kind of you."

"It is a necessity." He glanced at the road that led into the city below. "The grade of the hill is mild, but it is, nonetheless, a hill. Now, if you will excuse me, I must get back to my work." He gave her a polite nod and started back toward the house.

Sarah watched him for a moment then pushed open the gate, stepped out into the road and, holding her long skirts above the dusty surface, walked to the carriage entrance and followed the graveled way out beyond the kitchen ell. A stone carriage house snuggled against the rising hill at the end of the way. A gravel walk led off to her left and she turned and followed the path, walking along fenced-in kitchen gardens to another gate set in pillars.

She stopped, gazing in delight at the small formal garden on the other side of the gate. Trimmed lawns cozied up to boxwood hedges lining a brick walk that led from a large back porch to form a circle around a birdbath, sundial and pergola surrounded by blooming flowers. Lilacs and other shrubs, their feet buried in lush green ivy, threw splashes of color against the high stone walls that defined the garden area. Daffodils and other spring flowers bloomed among the ivy. It was a perfect place for little Nora to play in and explore.

Sarah lifted the latch, stepped through the gate and let it swing shut behind her. Birds drinking and bathing or feeding on the ground fluttered up to rest on the spreading branches of the bushes. For a moment silence fell, then the birds started their twittering again. Sarah smiled and moved slowly toward the porch. What a lovely place to sit and read or have an afternoon tea. All of Stony Point was lovely. Though it was much smaller than her home.

Home.

Her pleasure in exploring Stony Point dissolved. Sarah blinked away a rush of tears, lifted her long skirts and climbed the porch steps. She glanced at the table and chairs on her left, walked to a wood bench with padded cushions and sat staring off into the distance. When would the pain of Aaron's death go away? A year? Two? When would she be able to face going home again?

Sarah moved around the nursery straightening a doll's dress here, adjusting the position of a stuffed animal on a chair there—anything to keep busy. The afternoon had been a challenging time with the toddler, who seemed to think she should have a cookie every few minutes. It had left her no time to think or feel. But Nora was now in bed for the night, the demands of caring for the toddler were over for today, and the night was hers. The dark, idle time that had become her enemy.

Sarah looked around, stepped to the shelves and rearranged the few picture books, fixing her thoughts firmly on the present. Why hadn't Clayton Bainbridge dismissed her? He had certainly been angry with her. The scowl that sprang so readily to his face testified to that. Aaron had never—

No! She would *not* think about Aaron. Sarah spun away from the shelf and searched the room for something else to do. There was nothing. Everything was tidied and in its proper place. She had unpacked and her own bedroom was in order. And she wasn't ready to write her mother and father and tell them she had been accepted in this position as a nanny in Cincinnati. They thought she was still visiting Judith in Pittsburgh. And when they learned what she'd done… Oh, they would be so *worried.* And she didn't want to cause them more distress. They were already concerned for her.

Sarah blinked away a rush of tears, walked to the windows and closed the shutters on the deepening shadow of the coming night. How she hated the dark! She shivered and started toward her bedroom, listening to the light pad of her footsteps, the soft rustle of her long skirts. The quietness, the solitude pressed in on her. She stopped, fought for the breath being squeezed from her lungs by a familiar cold hand. She couldn't do it. She couldn't face the long night with nothing to do, with no weapon with which to hold off the memories. She cast a glance at the sleeping toddler, hurried to the door and slipped out into the hall. There must be a library, or study, or some-place in this house where she could find a book to read.

Sarah hurried to the stairs, lifted the front of her skirts and started down. Light shone out of an open door on the left side of the small entrance hall below. She paused. The room was only a few feet from the bottom of the stairs, and she had a strong intuition it was Clayton Bain-bridge's study. Would he hear her? She had no doubt it would anger him to find her snooping about his house in search of reading material. Of course, if she asked his permission there was no need for such clandestine measures.

Sarah descended the last few steps and marched over to rap on the frame of the open door. "Excuse me for in-terrupting, but—" She stopped, scanned the empty room. It was Clayton Bainbridge's study all right. Blueprints littered a table. Papers with mathematical equations on them covered his desk with some sort of reference book open beside them. More books were stacked helter-skel-ter on the thick beam that formed the mantel on the stone fireplace. Her hands itched to straighten them. Instead, she turned back to the hall. The drawing room, where she had been interviewed, was on the opposite side, door open, lamps aglow, inviting one in to its comfort—un-less one was a servant, of course.

Sarah shook her head, turned and walked down the hall toward the rear of the house, retracing the way she had taken that morning. What a strange position she had placed herself in. Whoever had heard of a wealthy, socially elite servant? Perhaps if she wrote of it in an amusing vein to her parents, they would be less concerned with her decision to accept this post. Surely they would understand she had to get away from all the reminders of her loss.

She halted, glanced at the dining room, now dark and uninviting. But candlelight poured through an open door on her left, tempted her into the yet unexplored room. She paused just inside the door, ready to apologize for intruding and make a hasty retreat. But this room, too, was empty.

She relaxed and looked around, admiring the room's slate-green plastered walls, the deep mustard color of the woodwork and window shutters. An old, one-drawer table holding a flaming candle in a large pewter candlestick and a family Bible snuggled into the recess created by the fireplace. A framed needlepoint sampler hung on the wall above the table. Two tapestry-covered chairs sided a settee with a candlestand at one end. She moved to her right, stepped around a tea table and entered a large alcove lined with shelves of books. In its center stood a pedestal game table with a game of Draughts displayed on its surface.

Sarah smiled, slid one of the pieces forward on the board, moved it back to its starting place. How Mary and James loved to challenge and bait each other while playing Draughts—while doing anything. Her younger sister and brother were fiercely competitive. Who was mediating their clashes of wills now that she was gone from home?

A sound of footsteps startled her from her reverie. The door in the outside wall swung inward, exposing the night. The candlelight flickered wildly in a gust of wind that carried a strong scent of rain. The breath froze in her lungs. Sarah stared at the dark gap of the open door, pressed her hand to the base of her throat and took a step back toward the safety of the hall.

Clayton Bainbridge stepped out of the darkness, halting her flight. Surprise flitted across his face. He gave her a small nod. "Good evening."

Sarah stood in place, acutely aware of her pulse pounding beneath her hand, the tightness spreading through her chest. She inclined her head.

"Sorry if I gave you a start, I did not realize you were in here." Clayton pulled the door closed, faced her. "It seems we are in for a bit of weather. The wind is coming up fast."

The sighing moan of wind seeking entrance at the windowpanes accompanied by a distant rumble of thunder testified to the truth of his prediction. Sarah darted her gaze toward the window, fought back a shudder. She would have to hurry. Get back to her room before the storm broke upon them.

"Were you looking for me? Is there a problem?"

She jerked her attention back to Clayton Bainbridge. "No. No problem. I… I was searching for something to read." She lowered her hand, squared her shoulders. "I hope you do not mind?"

"Not at all." Clayton's gaze shifted to the books. "Were you looking for anything in particular?"

"No." Lightning lit the sky in the distance. Sarah

winced and turned her back to the windows, focusing on the books in front of her. "I only wanted something to read until I can fall asleep." *Little chance of that now.* She edged in the direction of the door.

Clayton strode up beside her, reached out and pulled a book off the shelf. "The music of Robert Burns's poetry always works for me." His thumb slid back and forth over the black leather cover then stilled.

She was trapped. Sarah watched him, held fear at bay by trying to identify the myriad emotions that shadowed his eyes. Sadness...anger...loneliness...and something— He lifted his head, looked at her. She flicked her gaze back to the books. Warmth crawled into her cheeks. Had she been fast enough? Or had he caught her staring at him?

"Do you like poetry, Miss Randolph?"

She nodded. "Yes, I do." The wind moaned louder, raindrops spattered against the windows at the far end of the room. The warmth drained from her cheeks. The tightness in her chest increased. If only he would move out of her way!

"Do you enjoy Burns? Or perhaps you prefer Blake or Wordsworth?"

"I have no preference. I like them all." Lightning flashed, throwing light against the walls. There was a loud, sharp crack. Sarah flinched and bit down on her lower lip to stop the scream that rose in her throat.

"But not thunderstorms?"

She glanced up at Clayton. He was studying her. And she knew exactly how she looked—face pale, mouth taut, eyes wide and fearful. No point in trying to deny it. "No. Not thunderstorms. Not anymore." There was a brilliant flash, a sizzle and crack, the burst of thunder. "Excuse me."

Sarah pushed her way between Clayton and the game table, rushed into the hallway and sagged against the wall, struggling to catch a breath. She could still hear the thunder, but its rumble was muffled by the walls, and there were no windows to show the lightning. If only she could get to her room! But her legs were trembling so hard she was afraid to move away from the support of the wall. If she could *breathe*—

"Are you all right, Miss Randolph?"

He had followed her! Sarah nodded, gathered her meager strength and pushed away from the wall. Her knees gave way. Clayton Bainbridge's quick grip on her elbow kept her from falling. She turned her face away from his perusal. "Thank you." She struggled for breath to speak. Panted out words. "If you will…excuse me, I need to…go upstairs. Nora may wake and be…frightened by the storm."

"In a moment. You are in no condition to climb stairs." He half carried her the few steps to a Windsor chair. "You are very pale." His eyes darkened. His face drew taut. "Rest here while I get you some brandy. A swallow always helped my wife when she had one of her spells." He turned toward the drawing room.

"No, please. That isn't necessary." Sarah pushed to her feet, forced her trembling legs to support her. "Thank you for your kindness, but I need to go upstairs to Nora." *And to hide from the storm.*

Thunder boomed. Sarah winced and rushed to the stairs. She heard him come to stand at the bottom, felt his gaze on her as she climbed. He must think her insane to react so fearfully to a simple thunderstorm. Would he judge her unsafe to care for his child because of it?

The sound of rain pelting the roof and throwing itself in a suicidal frenzy against the shuttered windows of the nursery drove the worry from her mind. "Sufficient unto the day are the troubles thereof…" Tomorrow would take care of itself. She had the night to get through.

Sarah tucked the covers more snugly around the peacefully slumbering Nora and ran tiptoe to the dressing room to prepare for bed. Prayers formed in her mind in automatic response to every howl of the wind, every flash of lightning and clap of thunder, but she left them unspoken. She had learned not to waste her time uttering cries for mercy to a God who did not hear or did not care. It would profit her more to hide beneath her covers and wait for the tempest to pass.

She shivered her way to bed, slid beneath the coverlet and pulled the pillow over her head to block out the sights and sounds of the foul weather, but it was too late. The storm had brought back all the memories, and she was powerless to stop the terrifying images that flashed one after the other across the window of her mind.

Lightning flashed. Thunder cracked, rumbled away. Clayton pushed away from his desk and crossed to the window. Rain coursed down the small panes of glass in torrents, making the barely visible trunks of the trees in the yard look liquid and flowing. He had not seen a storm this bad in years. He frowned and rubbed at the tense muscles at the back of his neck. Hopefully it would pass over soon. If not, the weak wall they were working to reinforce at the lock might not hold. And if it collapsed it would put them weeks behind the time he had scheduled for the repairs.

Clayton shook his head and turned from the window. There was no sense in worrying—or praying. He knew that from all those wasted prayers he uttered when he found out Deborah was expecting his child. What would be, would be. And he could do nothing until morning. He might better spend his time sleeping because, one way or another, tomorrow was going to be a hard day. He snuffed out the lamps, left his study and headed for the stairs. The sight of his hand on the banister evoked the memory of Sarah Randolph's white-knuckled grip as she had climbed. She had trembled so beneath his hand, he had expected her strength to give out after a few steps, had worried she might fall. But she had made it to the top. And to the nursery. He had listened to make sure.

Clayton cast a quick glance down the hallway to the nursery door. All was quiet. He entered his bedroom and crossed to the dressing room to prepare for bed. What could have happened to make Sarah Randolph so terrified of a storm? Something had. When he noticed her pale face and asked if she liked thunderstorms she had answered, Not anymore. Yes, something frightening had definitely happened to Miss Sarah Randolph during a thunderstorm. But what?

Clayton puzzled over the question, created possible scenarios to answer it while he listened to the sounds of the storm's fury. It was better than dwelling on the possible damage the weak locks were sustaining.

Chapter Four

"Tompkins, start those men digging a runoff ditch five feet back from the top of the bank, then follow me." Clayton slipped and slid his way down the muddy slope and turned left to inspect the lock under repair. One quick look was enough. He squinted up through the driving rain at his foreman and cupped his hands around his mouth. "Tompkins, get some men and timbers down here! We need to shore up this wall."

His foreman waved a hand to indicate he had heard him above the howling wind and ran off to do as ordered.

Clayton swiped the back of his arm across his eyes to clear away the raindrops, tugged his hat lower and sloshed his way across the bottom of the lock to check the other side. The pouring rain sluiced down the fifteen-foot-high wall to add depth to the water swirling around his ankles. He turned and slogged along the length of the wall, checking for cracks or weak spots, but the gravel and clay loam they'd used to reinforce it was holding up well beneath the deluge.

Lightning rent the dark, roiling sky and sizzled to earth with a snap that hurt his ears. Thunder crashed and rolled. Sarah Randolph's pale, frightened face flashed into his head. He frowned, irritated by the break in his concentration, but could not stop himself from wondering how she was handling the storm. Perhaps it was only at night—

"Look out below!"

Clayton pivoted, squinted through the rain to see a heavy timber come tumbling down the wall on the other side. Men at the edge were poised to drop another. He cupped his mouth. "Stop! Hold that beam!"

His voice was lost in another loud clap of thunder. The two men holding the beam upright at the top of the lock wall gave a mighty shove and leaped aside. The beam tumbled down end-over-end, hit one of the horizontal beams of the form for the new stone wall and knocked it askew. Clayton broke into a run, shouting and waving his arms, trying to catch the attention of someone on the opposite bank before the carelessness of the unskilled laborers caused the unfinished wall to collapse.

Water splashed over the top of his boots, soaked his pant legs and socks as he ran. Rain pelted his upturned face, coursed down his neck and wet his shirt. Lightning flashed. Another beam came tumbling down the wall. No one was paying him any attention.

He ran faster, angling toward the bank where he could climb in safety. His hands and feet slipped and slid as he scaled the slope, adding the offense of mud to his sodden clothes. He heard a loud crash and rumble, stopped climbing and looked to his left. There was a gaping hole where a section of the newly placed, but unsecured, stones of the wall under repair had collapsed.

Clayton glanced up, saw the men who had pushed the last beam over the wall waving other men forward and pointing down at the damage it had caused. He sucked a long breath of cold, damp air into his laboring lungs and resumed his climb, wishing, not for the first time, he had personal fortune enough to hire ten men knowledgeable about engineering work and skilled in the performance of it.

"What a good girl you are, Nora." Sarah smiled approval. "You ate all of your lunch."

"Soup."

"Yes, you liked the soup, didn't you?"

Nora's answering nod set her golden curls bouncing. "Cookie?"

Sarah shook her head, wet a cloth and washed the toddler's face and hands. "No cookie today. You had pudding for dessert."

"Cookie!"

Sarah looked at the toddler's determined expression. It seemed a battle of wills was about to ensue. At least the sound of the storm would cover Nora's squalls. She lifted her charge into her arms. "No cookie. It is time for your nap."

Nora let out an irate wail. Sarah lifted the yelling, kicking toddler into her arms and walked to the rocker on the hearth.

"Cookie!" Nora howled the word, pushed and twisted, trying to free herself.

"No cookie. Not today." Sarah tightened her grip enough so the child would not hurt herself and began to rock. She hummed softly, ignoring the fighting, crying toddler. Nora's storm was as furious as the one outside, but she lacked the strength to sustain her effort to get her own way. After a few minutes of futile exertion, she gave up the fight, stuck her thumb in her mouth and began to suck.

Sarah watched the tiny eyelids drift closed as the toddler succumbed to the rhythmic motion, the steady whisper of the wood rockers against the floor. She wiped away Nora's tears, studied the dainty brown brows, the tiny nose and soft contours of her baby face. She was a beautiful child. Spoiled but beautiful. Why did Clayton Bainbridge refuse to allow her in his presence? Refuse to even acknowledge her by name? Was she not his?

Sarah's pulse quickened. She stared down at Nora, thinking, remembering, drawing a parallel between her childhood and Nora's. Even if Nora *was* Clayton's natural child, it could be that he didn't know how to be a father. Perhaps he only needed to be encouraged in his relationship with his daughter—the way Elizabeth had encouraged her father to love her and Mary.

Her father.

Sarah leaned her head against the chair back and closed her eyes. She had never told anyone, including Mary, that she knew Justin Randolph was not their real father. Justin, his servants, *everyone* thought she had been too young to remember, but the day that man had come to Randolph Court and taken her mother away was indelibly etched in her memory. And she remembered how the servants had gossiped about how Justin Randolph had gone after them and found the man dead and her mother severely injured from a carriage accident.

She had been only three years old, but she vividly recalled Justin bringing her mother back home, and the horrible whispering when she died. She remembered it well because her nanny had taunted her by telling her the man who died was her real father, and that he and her mother were both evil and that's why they had died, that she would die, too, if she wasn't good. She had been so terrified she had decided not to talk for fear she would say something wrong that would make her die. But when Justin Randolph had married Elizabeth, everything had changed.

Sarah opened her eyes and looked down at Nora asleep in her lap. She had never thought it through before, but Elizabeth had changed everything because she had brought love into their house. Elizabeth had taken her and Mary—two orphans forced upon Justin's care by the death of their mother and real father—into her heart. She had loved them and treated them as daughters. And Justin Randolph had followed her example.

Her *example*. Excitement tingled along Sarah's nerves. The situations were entirely different, of course. Elizabeth had married Justin Randolph. And she had no intention of ever marrying. Aaron had been her dream, her love; she would not betray his memory. But still... If she could only bring Nora into Clayton Bainbridge's presence... Resolve replaced the excitement. There had to be a way. And she would find it. Or she would make a way.

Sarah hugged Nora close, kissed her soft baby cheek, put her in the crib and hummed her way to her bedroom. The brilliance of a lightning flash flickered through the small cracks between the window shutters. Thunder boomed. She flinched, started to back out of her room, then squared her shoulders, marched to the writing desk and pulled it into the center of the room, turning it so her back was to the windows. She was ready to write her parents now, and no storm was going to stop her. Determination brought her inspiration. She opened the clothing cupboard, pulled her green-velvet coal-scuttle bonnet off its hook and put it on, letting the wide silk ties dangle free. There was a loud thunderclap.

Sarah flinched, then smiled. It worked. The deep brim shielding her face prevented her from seeing the lightning flashes from the corners of her eyes. Feeling both cowardly and clever, not to mention a little like a horse with blinders on, she seated herself and took up paper and pen.

The afternoon had passed quickly. Too quickly. Sarah picked up the children's picture books she had used to entertain Nora and put them back on the shelf. She would have to make up more simple baby games. Little Nora caught on to them quickly. She was a very bright little girl—with quite a temper.

Sarah glanced at the toddler now asleep in her crib and shook her head. Supper had been a real challenge. Who would think that such a small body could house such a mass of determination. It had taken all of her ingenuity to get Nora to eat her meat and vegetables before her dessert.

Sarah's smile slipped into a frown. She had a suspicion, based on Nora's frequent requests for sweets and her unpleasant behavior when they were not forthcoming, that the former nanny may have used sweets to quiet her. But Nora's bout of bad temper at supper had soon dissipated, her sunny disposition had returned and they had played quietly until her evening bedtime. She really was an adorable child.

Sarah tucked the blankets more closely around the little girl and roamed into her bedroom seeking distraction. She glanced at the desk that was again in its proper place beneath the window on the far wall. Her letter to her parents rested on the cleared surface, folded and addressed, sealed and ready to be posted. Perhaps she would do that tomorrow afternoon if the weather cleared. She had considered giving it to Ellen to carry home with her, but the post would be faster. And she had been thinking of going to town to visit the shops. Of course Nora's hour or two of nap time did not allow for much exploring. Still, she should have time enough to accomplish all she needed to do, including visiting Ellen to send her on her way.

A clap of thunder invaded her thoughts, reminded her the storm was still raging, though awareness of it was never far away. It hovered like a dark cloud in the background, ready to carry forward painful memories at every flash of lightning or howl of the wind. Sarah shivered, adjusted the wick on the oil lamp and smoothed a wrinkle from the lindsey-woolsey coverlet on the bed. This was not working out as she had planned. She had counted on the demands of a toddler keeping her too busy to remember—or to feel the pain of her loss. But with Nora's afternoon nap and early bedtime that hope had proven false. She had too much free time, especially with the storm adding to her unrest. If only…

Sarah lifted her gaze to the door at the right of the fireplace and absently tapped her thumbnail against her lips. Why not? What had she to lose? She opened the door wide, in order to hear Nora if she woke, and started down the winder stairs, longing for a hot cup of tea and some adult company. The storm had lessened in ferocity, but it still had her shaken and overwrought. She opened the door at the bottom, stepped into the kitchen and turned toward the table. Mrs. Quincy looked across the room, staring at her, most likely resenting this uninvited invasion of her domain. "Good evening." She smiled and moved forward into the room.

The older woman nodded, leaned her direction and squinted her eyes. "Are you feeling all right, Miss Randolph? You look a bit under the weather."

Sarah forced a laugh. "An apt description, Mrs. Quincy. I do not care for thunderstorms." She glanced toward the stove, noted the pots steaming there and looked back. "I wondered if I might have some tea? And if you would care to share it with me? I would be glad of the company."

The housekeeper studied her for a long moment, then walked to a cupboard standing against the wall, took out a tin of tea and headed for the stove. "This storm's been a bad one. Guess you're thankful it's about wore itself out." She measured tea into a red and white china teapot and added hot water from the kettle on the stove.

"Yes, I am." Sarah moved closer to the long worktable and changed the subject. "I apologize for making extra work for you. Is there anything I can do to help?"

Mrs. Quincy gave a snort of laughter. "Lands, this ain't work! My feet and I are grateful for the chance to sit down." She placed the teapot on its tray, added some biscuits from a tin box sitting on the cupboard beside the stove and inclined her head toward the shelves hanging on the wall. "You can get two of them cups if you're of a mind to help."

Sarah hastened to do as she was bid. She had been accepted. At least for the moment. No doubt because of Mrs. Quincy's tired feet.

Clayton dismounted in front of the carriage house, opened one of the wide double doors and led Pacer inside, the argument he had been waging with himself on the long, miserable ride home still engaging his mind. It was the storm. The ceaseless tempest coupled with his inherent protective instinct toward women was what had brought the image of Sarah Randolph's pale, frightened face returning to him throughout the day. It had nothing to do with the woman herself. It was only that he had never known anyone so terrified of a thunderstorm. He had been pondering the possible causes of that fear since last night. Most likely it was some long-remembered childhood fright.

A gust of wind drove the rain into his face, splattered the deluge against the building and tried to rip the door from his grasp. He battled the wind for possession, managed to pull the door closed and headed toward Pacer's stall. Sassy nickered softly, welcoming her barn mate home. Pacer tossed his head and snorted, nudged his back.

"Easy, boy, you will have some oats soon enough. But first we have to get you dry."

The door opened. The wind howled through the breach, lifted hay and dust from the plank floor, swirling it through the air to stick to his wet face and clothes. Clayton blinked, blew a bit of straw off his upper lip.

Alfred Quincy wrestled the door closed. "Saw you ride in." He walked over and held out his hand for the reins. "There's hot venison stew waiting for you."

Clayton nodded. Droplets of water clinging to his hat brim broke free and slithered down his cheeks and neck. He swiped them away. "A plate of hot stew is exactly what I need after the cold soaking I have had today." He gave his mount a solid pat on the shoulder. "And Pacer deserves a long rubdown and a double scoop of oats. He earned them today."

"I'll see to it."

Clayton nodded, stepped outside, lowered his head against the wind and pelting rain and ran toward the house. That stew was going to taste good tonight. There had been no time to eat today and his stomach was growling so fiercely he could not tell its rumblings from the distant thunder.

The kitchen door opened. Cold, damp air gusted across the room. The lamps flickered. Sarah turned, saw the rain-soaked figure standing against the blackness of the stormy night and gasped. The cup she held slipped from her grasp and smashed against the slate floor. The sound of the breaking china brought her back to her senses. "Oh, I... I am sorry." Her voice quavered. She clamped her teeth down on her lower lip and crouched to pick up the pieces of broken cup, grateful for the table that hid her as she struggled to compose herself.

The door closed. The light steadied. Boot heels clacked on the floor. A shadow fell across her. Sarah closed her eyes, wished she were up in her room. She did not want Clayton Bainbridge to see her like this again. She tried to will herself to stop trembling.

"You look...unwell... Miss Randolph. Leave the cup."

Sarah shook her head, opened her eyes. "That would not be fair to Mrs. Quincy. I broke it and I shall clear it away." She cleared the sound of tears from her voice. "And I am not 'unwell.' I am fine." She reached for a jagged piece of cup and stabbed her finger. Blood welled up to form a bright droplet against her flesh. She gathered another piece, started to rise to throw them away, wobbled and resumed her crouch, reaching for another piece of the cup to disguise the unsuccessful effort. "It was only that you startled me."

The shadow covered her. Clayton Bainbridge's hands closed around her upper arms. He lifted her to her feet. She looked up and met his gaze. Her knees quivered. She dropped her gaze to the pieces of china in her hand.

"You have hurt yourself."

His voice was as warm as his hands.

"A mere prick." She firmed her knees, stepped back. He released his grip. She ignored the sudden cold where his hands had been and brushed with her fingertip at the tiny rivulet of blood before it dropped onto her gown. "I apologize for breaking the cup." She glanced up. "I will replace it, of course."

A frown drew his brows down to shadow his eyes. "That is not necessary. It was an accident. And as you pointed out, the fault was mine for startling you." He swiped his hand across the nape of his neck and turned away.

"Nonetheless—"

"*Miss* Randolph—" he turned back, frustration glinting in his eyes "—*must* you be so fractious? My clothes and boots are sodden and mud-caked. I am weary, chilled to the bone and hungry as a bear emerging from hibernation. I have no desire to stand here arguing with you over a broken cup."

The heat of embarrassment chased the chill from her body. Sarah straightened her shoulders. "I was not being fractious, Mr. Bainbridge, only…steadfast. However, you are right, it would be inconsiderate to continue this discussion while you are in discomfort. We can resolve the issue of my replacing the cup tomorrow."

A scowl darkened his face. "No, Miss Randolph, we will not. This discussion is over." He looked down the long table. "Eldora, I shall be down for my supper directly after a hot bath." He crossed to the winder stairs and began to climb.

Sarah's cheeks burned. How dare he speak to her in such a fashion! Let alone dismiss her as if she were a servant! Truth struck. Of course, she *was* a servant.

She fought down the desire to march to the stairs and demand an apology and watched until her employer disappeared from view. Even in his rain-soaked, muddy clothes Clayton Bainbridge had a presence, an air of authority about him. He was a strong, determined man and getting him to accept and love his daughter suddenly seemed a daunting task. But she had more than a little determination herself *and* a strong, worthwhile purpose. The little girl upstairs deserved her father's love and attention.

"Are you still wanting tea, Miss Randolph?"

Sarah jerked out of her thoughts and glanced at the housekeeper. "I am indeed, Mrs. Quincy. And please, call me Sarah." She threw the broken cup in a basket holding bits of trash, walked to the shelves and took down another. Tea with the housekeeper had taken on a new importance. It might help her bring father and daughter together if she knew why Clayton Bainbridge held himself indifferent toward Nora, and servants always knew every household secret.

The storm had finally ceased. Sarah opened the window sash and stood listening to the quiet sounds of the night. Moisture dripped from the leaves of the trees, the drops from the higher branches hitting the leaves

on those below before sliding off in a sibilant whisper
to fall to the ground. There were muted rustlings of
grasses and flowers disturbed by the passage of small,
nocturnal animals. Somewhere an owl hooted, another
answered. But concentrate as she would on the sounds,
she could not blot out her tumbling thoughts, could not
stop the images that were flashing, one after the other,
into her head.

She shivered and wrapped her arms around herself,
more for comfort than for warmth. The cold was inside.
If only she had not gone downstairs for tea. The sight
of Clayton Bainbridge's rain-drenched figure against
the darkness had whisked her back to the night Aaron
had died.

Sarah gave a quick shake of her head to dislodge the
memories—to no avail. She closed the shutters, adjusted
the slats to let the cool night air flow into the bedroom
and hurried to the nightstand. The gold embossed letters on the black leather cover of the book resting there
glowed softly in the candlelight. *Robert Burns.* She slid
into bed, took the poetry volume into her hands and let
it fall open where it would. All she wanted was words
to read to chase the pictures from her head. She pulled
the lamp closer and looked down at the page.

"Oppress'd with grief, oppress'd with care,

A burden more than I can bear,"

Sarah slapped the book shut, tossed it aside and
slipped from bed. She didn't need to read about grief,
she was *living* grief! She rushed, barefoot, into the nursery, ran to the crib and scooped Nora into her arms. The
toddler blinked her eyes and yawned. "Nanny?"

"Yes, Nora, it's Nanny Sarah. Close your eyes and
go back to sleep."

Sarah walked to the rocker, sat and wiped away the tears blurring her vision. She covered Nora's small bare feet with part of the skirt of her long nightgown, took hold of one little hand and began to hum a lullaby. Quietness settled over her as she rocked, her tense nerves calmed. She kissed Nora's warm, baby-smooth forehead, touched a strand of silky golden curl, then leaned back and closed her eyes. She had been unsuccessful in her attempt to get Mrs. Quincy to talk about Clayton Bainbridge or his wife over tea. Maybe tomorrow.

The thought of him brought the memory of Clayton Bainbridge helping her to her feet. The feel of his hands, so warm, so strong yet gentle on her arms. The way his eyes had looked as he gazed down at her.

Sarah opened her eyes and stared down at the child in her arms, disquieted and troubled. Clayton Bainbridge had made her feel…what? She searched for the right word for the unfamiliar emotion that had made her want to turn and run from him, then frowned and gave up. What did it matter? It was of no importance. It had been only a momentary aberration caused by her fear of the storm that had quickly disappeared when Clayton Bainbridge had returned to his customary, unpleasant anger.

Chapter Five

What a beautiful day! The only reminders of the thunderstorm were the areas of damp, dark earth beneath the bushes where the sun's rays hadn't yet reached, and the colorful memory of flowers that littered the ground. Sarah sighed and crossed the back porch to the stairs. The storm had stripped the beauty from every branch and stalk in the enclosed garden. Not one flower was left intact. Still, the storm was over and the horrible constriction in her chest had eased. She took a deep breath of the clean fresh air and helped Nora down the steps to the brick pathway.

"Well, Nora, what shall we do first?" She reached down and straightened the pinafore that protected the toddler's yellow dress. "Do you want to go sit in the pergola and watch the birds take their baths?"

"Birds!" Nora's lace-trimmed sunbonnet slipped awry at her emphatic nod. Sarah laughed, adjusted the bonnet and took hold of her charge's tiny hand. Hoofs crunched against gravel. She looked toward the carriage house, saw Clayton Bainbridge mount his horse and start down the path toward them. She smiled as he neared. "Good morning, Mr. Bainbridge."

"Miss Randolph." Clayton gave her a brief nod, touched his fingers to the brim of his hat and rode on.

Not so much as a glance at his daughter. Sarah stared after him, anger flashing. But as she watched him ride toward the road, her anger dissipated, vanquished by an odd sort of sadness. It was almost as if she could feel his unhappiness, his loneliness.

"'Quirrel!"

Nora's tiny hand pulled from her grasp. Sarah brushed the strange sensation aside and watched Nora run, as fast as her little legs would carry her, toward the squirrel that was scampering along the railing of the pergola. Her anger sparked anew. If Mr. Clayton Bainbridge was lonely, he had no one but himself to blame. She would not waste sympathy on a man who wouldn't even look at his own daughter. But despite her adamant avowal, a remnant of that odd, sad feeling lingered. And irritation at his abrupt departure. She stepped to the gate and looked down the empty gravel path. "You could have stopped a moment to bid us good morning, Mr. Bainbridge."

"What's that, miss?"

Sarah started, turned to see Mr. Quincy emerge from the shadow at the far end of the carriage house. He was pushing a wheelbarrow. Her stomach flopped. Thank goodness he had not heard her clearly. She shook her head. "Nothing, Mr. Quincy." Her nose identified the rotted stable leavings in the wheelbarrow when he drew near. "Is that for here in the garden?"

"Yep." He glanced over the shoulder-high wall and a smile deepened the lines radiating from the corners of his piercing blue eyes, poked dimples in the leathery skin covering the hollows of his cheeks. "'Pears like the little miss is enjoyin' this fine day." He dropped the back legs of the wheelbarrow to the ground and straightened. "I'll come back later and spread this mongst the flowers an' such. I don't want to ruin Miss Nora's playtime. Young'uns need to be outside where they can learn about God's creations, not be—" He clamped his lips shut, gave her a brief nod and turned away.

Not be—what? Sarah took a breath. "A moment, Mr. Quincy."

"Yes, miss?"

The set look on his face told her he had said more than he intended—and did not mean to compound the error. The question hovering on her lips died. She would get no information from him. "Do you know when Mr. Bainbridge will return?"

"Not till supper, miss. Leastwise, he had Mrs. Quincy fix him a box lunch, so he must be figurin' on a long day."

"I see. Then—" Sarah spun at a sudden squeal from Nora.

"'Quirrel, all gone." Nora's lower lip pouted out, trembled.

"'Pears like you've got a problem." Mr. Quincy chuckled and walked away.

"It will be all right, Nora." Sarah hurried down the path and scooped the little girl into her arms for a hug. "You frightened the squirrel when you yelled." She walked to the pergola, sat on the wooden bench and settled Nora on her lap. "Shh." She laid her finger across her lips and softened her voice to a whisper. "If we sit still and are very quiet, the squirrel will come back."

The admonition worked until the disturbed birds returned to their bathing and feeding.

"Bird." Nora pointed and squirmed to get down. Sarah helped her off her lap, then sat watching as Nora ran from one bird to another, squealing with delight when they fluttered into the air only to land a few feet away and resume their feeding.

The toddler's laughter brought a smile to her own lips. One that disappeared in a small gasp when Nora stumbled and tumbled facedown onto the grass. She rushed to the railing, waited. Nora pushed to her hands and knees, got her feet under her and ran after another bird, her sunbonnet now flopping against her back, her blond curls bobbing free.

Sarah relaxed. It seemed the only damage done by the fall was the smear of green on the pristine white pinafore and that bit of torn lace dangling from the bottom of Nora's pantalettes. The laundress would not be happy. But what did any of that matter in the face of the child's happiness?

Sarah frowned and returned to her seat. *Young'uns need to be outside where they can learn about God's creations, not be*— Kept quiet in the nursery all day? Is that what the former nanny had done to Nora? Of course, the woman was probably following orders. But still, how could she treat Nora like that? It was unnatural to keep a child hidden away like...like some unwanted possession. Did the child's happiness count for nothing?

Sarah's thoughts leaped backward, focused on the cruel woman her mother had hired to care for her when she was Nora's age. Nanny Brown had cared nothing for her happiness. The woman had made her life a misery. And her mother and father had not cared about her happiness, either. They had left her behind with Justin Randolph when they ran off. How could parents disregard the needs of their children?

Sarah took a deep breath and wrapped her arms around her waist. She had struggled for so long after her mother abandoned her to overcome the horrid, empty feeling of being forsaken and unloved. She could not let Nora feel that way. And the little girl *would* if something did not happen to change Clayton Bainbridge's cold, callus treatment of her. Because, though he provided for Nora's every physical need, he had abandoned her in his heart. Why? He seemed considerate of others. What caused him to treat his child this way? There had to be a reason.

Sarah pushed the question aside to concentrate her attention on Nora. The toddler was no longer chasing the birds but had squatted on the brick path and was poking at something on the ground. She rose and hurried down the steps to discover what had captured the little girl's attention. "Oh. You found a worm."

"Worm." Nora's tiny finger poked at the pink, squiggling worm trying to escape.

Sarah bit back an admonition to not touch the thing, and squatted down. "Be careful, Nora. You will hurt the worm. Do it like this." She squelched her repugnance, took hold of Nora's hand and gently touched the tip of the child's tiny finger to the worm. It wiggled. Nora giggled and touched it again.

"Here are the biscuits you asked for, Miss Randolph."

"Bisit!" Nora pushed to her feet and ran toward the house.

Mrs. Quincy stepped onto the porch, holding a tray. The door banged closed behind her.

Sarah caught up to Nora, lifted into her arms and carried her up the steps. "Bless you for the interruption, Mrs. Quincy." She settled Nora on a chair and gave the stout woman a grateful smile. "She found a worm."

The housekeeper nodded. "At least 'tis better than a bumblebee. Worms don't sting." She set the tray on the table.

"Gracious! I forgot about bees." Sarah wiped Nora's small hands with the bottom of the grass-stained pinafore then folded them together. "Close your eyes, Nora."

The toddler's lips pulled down. "Bisit."

"You shall have your biscuit after we ask the blessing." Nora let out a screech. Sarah folded her own hands and waited. The child's acts of rebellion were getting shorter. The toddler stopped yelling, stared up at her, then closed her eyes. Sarah bowed her head. "Dear gracious, heavenly Father, we thank Thee for this food. Amen." She handed Nora a biscuit and glanced up. There was a distinct look of approval in Mrs. Quincy's eyes. What had brought about her change of attitude?

"I brought lemonade for you, Miss Randolph. Mrs. Bainbridge liked to sip lemonade while she rested here on the porch. But if it's not to your liking I could bring you some tea."

"Lemonade is fine, Mrs. Quincy. Have you time to join me?"

The housekeeper shot a yearning glance at the padded bench and shook her head. "There's cleaning to oversee, and the baking to be done. Another time, mayhap." She turned toward the door.

"Of course." Sarah took a breath and seized her opportunity. "You said Mrs. Bainbridge *rested* here on the porch. And Mr. Bainbridge mentioned she had 'spells.' Was she unwell?"

The stout woman stopped, nodded. "'Twas some sort of weakness in her heart stole her breath from her if she moved about. Oft times till she swooned." She looked down at Nora and her voice took on a reflective tone. "She was too frail for childbearin'. She died shortly after this one was born. Nora has the look of her."

Sarah studied Nora's delicate features. "Mrs. Bainbridge must have been a beautiful woman. It's a pity Nora will never know her."

"She was beautiful…an' spoiled. An' the little one was followin' along after her, till now." Mrs. Quincy looked up, blinked and gave a little shake of her head. "But 'tis not my place to speak of such things. Don't know why I'm standin' here wastin' time when there's work to be done." She hurried across the porch. "I'll send Lucy to fetch the tray." The door banged shut behind her.

"Bisit?"

"No, Nora. No more biscuits." Sarah gave her a sip of lemonade and lifted her off the chair. "Come with me. I am going to teach you to do a somersault." She helped her down the steps onto the grass, knelt down and placed one hand on the toddler's tummy, the other on her upper back. "All right, we are ready. Now bend waaaay over…"

"Here we are, miss."

Sarah glanced at the building on her right, noted the Post Office sign above the large multipaned window and climbed from the buggy. "Thank you for bringing me along to town, Mr. Quincy. I shan't delay your return home. I will meet you here in one hour." She watched him drive off down the street, shook out the three braid-trimmed tiers of the long skirt of her rose-colored silk dress, checked the time on the locket watch pinned to her bodice and crossed the sidewalk to the door. A gentleman passing by hastened to open it for her.

Sarah smiled her thanks, entered, then paused inside the door waiting for her eyes to adjust to the dimmer light after the brightness of the afternoon sunshine.

"—mark my words, Edith dear, this sickness going around will increase because of the foul weather during that storm—" The two women approaching the door broke off their conversation to give her a polite nod as they passed.

Sarah returned the politeness.

"May I help you, miss?"

She looked toward the sound of the voice. "I should like to post a letter." She pulled the folded and sealed missive from her reticule and walked to the table where a man stood sorting a large bag of letters into small piles.

He took the letter into his ink-stained hand and squinted down at the address. "Randolph Court, Philadelphia." He moved to a high desk standing at right angles to the table, glanced at her. "That will be twenty-five cents. You going to pay?"

Sarah shook her head. "No, Father will pay." She watched him write the charge, date and Cincinnati on the top corner of the folded letter. Her stomach tightened in protest. Her parents thought she was still in Pittsburgh. Well, there was no help for it. And any fears the city name engendered would be allayed when they read the letter. "I expect a reply. Will you please direct it to Stony Point? My name is Sarah Randolph."

"Of course, Miss Randolph." The man pulled a ledger from a shelf below the desk surface and jotted down the information. "How long will you be visiting at Stony Point?"

"Oh, no. You misunderstood. I am not visiting. I am the new nanny." The man's mouth gaped open. Sarah gave him another smile and turned; her silk dress rustled softly as she headed for the exit. A man, who had just entered, doffed his hat, made her a small bow and held the door open. She inclined her head in acknowledgment of the politeness and stepped through the portal into the afternoon sunshine.

One chore completed. And she had a little less than an hour to accomplish the others. Sarah moved into the shadow cast by a large brick building, walked to the corner, turned left and made her way up Main Street, scanning the storefronts. She had spotted what seemed a suitable establishment along the way to the post office. Where…? Ah, there it was. Mrs. Westerfield, Milliner & Mantuamaker and dealer in Millinery and Lace Goods and Embroidery. She moved closer and read the smaller print of the sign.

Keeps constant on hand a splendid stock of Leghorn, Tuscan & Straw Bonnets and Florence Braid, artificial flowers, Paris ribbons, plain & figured silks, satins & etc. suitable for bonnets and dresses which she is prepared to manufacture in the most fashionable style.

Sarah checked her reflection in the window. The flowers adorning her silk hat trembled slightly in the warm breeze. She adjusted the tilt of the hat, smoothed the lace at her throat and entered. A cluster of women examining trimmings displayed in a glass case, and two women seated on a settee studying a book of patterns, glanced up at the discreet tinkle of the small bell on the door. The women looked at her with varying degrees of curiosity, gave small, polite nods and returned to their business.

"If you will excuse me a moment, ladies." The woman behind the glass case smiled and came forward. "Welcome to Mrs. Westerfield's salon. May I help you?"

"I would like to speak with Mrs. Westerfield please."

"Certainly. I will be a moment. If you would care to have a seat?" The woman gestured toward a grouping of chairs, walked to a door at the back, gave a light tap and disappeared into another room.

Sarah strolled over to look at a display of paintings on the wall. Bits of conversation from the women at the counter drifted her way as she studied the drawings of the latest fashions.

"—heard that Rose Southernby has taken to her bed?"

"Oh, I do like this red silk braid!"

"Did you say Rose is ill?"

"Yes. Dr. Lambert has been making daily calls. She is not at all well, and— The red silk braid is a little… bright, Charlotte. Perhaps the gold…"

"You were saying, Gladys?"

"I beg your pardon? Oh. Yes. I heard the Southernby children are stricken also."

Children. Sarah moved a step closer to the women.

"I'm becoming frightened by all this sickness!"

"I share your fear, Isobel. I have ordered the servants to open our country home. It is early, I know, but I am not going to stay in this city and—"

"Mrs. Westerfield awaits you, miss."

Sarah walked to the back of the room and stepped through the door the woman held for her. A tall woman in a beautiful day dress of ecru pongee with a cross-over shawl collar banded in white stood behind a desk. She swept an assessing gaze over Sarah's hat and dress, smiled and came forward. "That will be all, Jeanne."

The door closed. Sarah waited.

"I am Mrs. Westerfield. You wished to see me?"

"Yes. I have recently come to Cincinnati and I am interviewing dressmakers as I find myself in immediate need of a few gowns."

A faint flush appeared on Mrs. Westerfield's cheeks. "I assure you, Miss…"

"Randolph."

"—Miss Randolph, I make the finest, most stylish gowns in Cincinnati. If you will permit me to show you a few of my recent designs." Mrs. Westerfield turned and led the way toward a settee.

Sarah smiled and seated herself, looked with interest at the sketches the dressmaker handed her. "And was your gown made by you or a seamstress in your employ, Mrs. Westerfield?" She eyed the excellent workmanship of the woman's day dress.

"I designed my frock, and Miss Bernard, my highly skilled head seamstress, crafted the dress. I would not wear the work of another, Miss Randolph."

"Nor will I." Sarah handed Mrs. Westerfield three sketches. "These are the gowns I have chosen. Please have Miss Bernard make them in your highest quality fabrics, one in ecru, one in brown, and one in dark blue. But I do not want the lavish adornments, only simple trims suitable for a nanny. I want them commissioned immediately and delivered to Stony Point when they are completed."

"I shall select the fabrics and trim myself, Miss Randolph." Mrs. Westerfield smiled. "And please forgive my confusion. I thought the gowns you have ordered were for you. Miss Bernard will begin work on them as soon as the nanny comes in for a fitting."

"You have made no error, Mrs. Westerfield. The gowns *are* for me. I am the new nanny at Stony Point." Sarah ignored the look of astonishment that flashed over the dressmaker's face and rose to her feet. "I have another appointment, so if you will direct me to Miss Bernard for my fitting…"

Only fifteen minutes left. Sarah hurried into the Franklin House, nodded to the desk clerk and rushed up the stairs to her room. "Ellen?"

"Miss Sarah! Oh, Miss Sarah, I've been so worried about you what with the storm an' all!" Her maid set aside what she called "busy work," bustled over, pulled her into a strong hug, then stepped back and studied her face. "Are you all right, child?"

Sarah blinked a rush of tears from her eyes and nodded. "I am fine, Ellen. But I have missed you." She gave a little laugh. "I have a new appreciation for how hard you work. You have always made everything look so easy. Whenever I needed anything I simply called for you. Now…" She laughed again, gave a helpless little shrug.

"Miss Sarah—"

"Don't scold, Ellen. There is no time. I must meet Mr. Quincy in a few minutes to—"

"You're going *back?* You're going to *continue* being

a nanny?" Ellen's eyes clouded. "I thought you'd come to your senses." She shook her head. "Your mother and father are not going to be happy about this. They—"

Sarah placed her hand on the older woman's arm, halting her words. "There is no time for a lecture, Ellen. I only have time to say goodbye, and I do not want to waste it in useless debate."

The maid studied her for a moment, drew herself up straight. "You're sending me back to Randolph Court?"

Tears surged into Sarah's eyes at the hurt in Ellen's voice. She forced a smile. "I have no choice, Ellen. I shall miss you dreadfully. But whoever has heard of a nanny with her own lady's maid?" Her voice caught. She took a breath. "This little girl needs me, Ellen. And right now I need her."

"And when I'm not here and the nightmare comes?"

"I will imagine you hugging me and pampering me with warm blankets and hot tea. Now—" Sarah cleared her throat and swept her hand through the air toward the trunks stacked against the wall. "Take my clothes with you. I have commissioned new gowns suitable for a nanny." She glanced down at her watch, reached into her reticule and pulled out a small packet of money and a folded letter. "This will cover the expense of your journey and answer any questions that might be asked of you. Now I must go. Safe journey, Ellen. Oh, I shall miss you so." She gave the older woman a quick hug and hurried toward the door, blinking back tears.

"And I'll miss you, Miss Sarah. May the Lord bless you and watch over you."

The soft-spoken words—the last words Ellen spoke to her every night—followed her down the hall.

Now she was truly alone.

* * *

Clayton put down his pen, stretched his arms out and to the back and rolled his shoulders to get rid of the kinks caused by the hours spent drawing on the blueprint. He had worked longer than he intended, but it was of no consequence. No one waited for him to finish. All he faced was an empty house and another lonely night.

He shoved back from his desk, rubbed at his tired eyes and snuffed the lamps. The silence of the late night closed around him. Moonlight poured in the windows. Candlelight painted a yellow stripe under the door. Time to go to bed.

He reached for the jacket he had hung on the back of his chair, paused and glanced toward the door at the sound of soft footfalls. A shadow blocked out the gold of the candlelight, passed on. Eldora? No—she was heavy on her feet. And sound asleep by this time.

Clayton slipped on his jacket, tugged his waistcoat back in place and opened the door. There was no one in sight. He stepped across the hall and looked into the drawing room. Sarah Randolph was standing in the center of the room and something in the slope of her shoulders and the tilt of her head spoke to him of deep sorrow. He stepped back to go his way and give her privacy. But his movement must have caught her attention for she glanced in his direction. Their gazes connected. For a moment she neither moved nor spoke, then her chin lifted and her shoulders straightened. The melancholy on her face disappeared as quickly as smoke before a strong wind. Except for the shadow that dulled the golden glints that usually sparkled in her brown eyes. The brightness in them now was caused by the glistening moisture of unshed tears.

Clayton stood frozen in the doorway, wanting to leave but knowing a hasty exit would reveal he had seen her moment of vulnerability. And he knew, too well, how important it was to cover that inner vulnerability with a facade of normalcy to protect your heart and save your pride. He moved into the room, pretended he did not see her tears, did not recognize her sadness. "Did you wish to speak to me?"

"No, I—" She blinked rapidly, turned away. "I was feeling restless, unable to settle for the night. I hope I did not disturb you."

"Not at all. I was finished with my work." He sought for an innocuous subject, something that would give her time to compose herself. "Is there a problem with your room? Are you uncomfortable or—"

"No, the room is quite satisfactory. I—" She took a breath, turned back to face him and gave a rueful little smile. "The truth is, I posted a letter to my parents today, and I have become a little homesick. We are very close. Especially since—" Her voice broke. She hurried to the fireplace and looked up at the two portraits that hung side by side above the mantel beam. "What a lovely lady. And the gentleman…" She glanced at him, looked back at the picture. "You have the look of him."

A distraction so he would not question her about what she had left unsaid or comment on her tears? Clayton nodded, went along with the change of subject. "Not surprising. That is my grandfather and grandmother, Ezekiel and Rose Bainbridge. They built this place back when this area was the frontier. It served them well. The neighbors used to fort up here when there was an Indian raid."

Her eyes widened. "Truly?"

Clayton smiled at her awed tone. He had captured her attention. Perhaps he could do a little distracting of his own, give her something to think about that would hold her sorrow at bay through the long night hours. He knew the anguish of troubled, sleepless nights. "Truly. Stone doesn't burn, and most of the other homes were made of log back then. Have you noticed the deep gashes in the front door? They are from Indian tomahawks."

"Tomahawks." She looked toward the entrance hall. "I cannot imagine…"

But clearly she did. Clayton strode to a window, reached behind the drapes and pulled the solid wood shutters that were folded up against the deep walls of the window well into view. He pointed to the small square holes in them. "These holes were for their rifles. If they had enough warning, they opened the windows—if not, they broke the glass out. Grandma hated that because it took so long to get the glass to replace the broken panes and the flies and mosquitoes always found the holes."

He folded the shutters back and indicated a large chest that sat against the wall beside the window. "My father used to stand on that chest so he could load my grand-father's long rifles during battles. He used to tell me the stories of those battles when I was young. It is one of my fondest memories. That, and my mother singing me to sleep at night."

He moved to the fireplace, ran his finger over the hole where a cartridge had buried itself in the heavy beam. "There are many reminders of those days in this house. And a story behind every one of them." A smile tugged at his lips. He gave it free rein. "I inherited my grand-parents' stories and memories along with their house."

"How lovely for you. I never knew my grandparents."

Or my parents, either. She looked up at him. "And your parents?"

His smile faded. "They died in a smallpox epidemic at Fort Belle Fontaine when I was four years old. My grandparents raised me."

"Oh." Compassion warmed her eyes. "I'm sorry you lost your parents. But how fortunate that you survived."

"I was here." Clayton looked away. The vision of Sarah Randolph standing beside him with the candlelight highlighting her delicate features and playing with the golden strands of her light-brown hair was disconcerting. "It was a new posting and my parents decided to leave me here until they discovered what sort of living quarters were assigned them. I was to join them when they were settled in."

"But they died. And your drea—your plans to join them died with them."

"Yes." His wife's face flashed before him. The acrid taste of bitterness spread through his mouth, tainted his words. "It happens that way sometimes."

"Yes. Yes, it does."

The words were little more than a whisper, but something in her voice… Clayton looked back. A fresh spate of unshed tears glimmered in her eyes. She blinked, looked down and smoothed at her skirt.

"The hour is getting late. I believe I shall retire now." She raised her head and smiled. It was the saddest smile he'd ever seen. "Thank you for sharing some of your family history with me, Mr. Bainbridge. It has made Stony Point come alive for me. I shall wonder over every mark I see. Good evening."

Clayton dipped his head in response, clamped his jaws shut and held himself rigidly in place as Sarah Randolph left the room. He did not want to let her go. He wanted to keep her here with him. He wanted to learn what caused that sadness in her eyes and take the sorrow from her. He wanted her company.

Clayton scowled, strode to the front door and stepped outside. Moonlight fell in cool silver radiance from the night sky, chased the darkness into shadows. He walked down the slate path to the gate, stepped out into the road and looked back at the house. Thin strips of golden lamplight showed through the slatted shutters in the front bedroom. He turned and strode off toward the tree-covered hill. Sleep would not come quickly for him tonight. It would not be easy to rid himself of the image of Sarah Randolph's beautiful face smiling that sad smile.

Chapter Six

"God in heaven, save us!" Wind tore the words from her mouth, slapped at her long, sodden skirts, whipped them into a frenzied flapping that knocked her off her feet. A sulfurous yellow split the dark, flickered, streaked downward with a sharp crack. The planking of the deck heaved, shuddered. The ship tilted. She groped for something to cling to, found only emptiness, slid. Lightning flashed, threw flickering light over a gaping hole where the ship's rail had been, over Aaron clinging to the broken end and reaching for her. She stretched out her hand.

The world exploded. Brilliant light blinded her. Thunder deafened her. She fell through a black void, battered by wind and rain. Frigid water swallowed her, drowned the scream trapped in her throat.

Sarah jerked upright in bed, heart pounding, pulse racing. She wrapped her arms about her ribs and rocked to and fro, shivering, waiting. The terror of the nightmare would pass. It always did. All she had to do was wait. Alone.

Tears surged. Why did Aaron have to die? She had

prayed. She had— No. There was no sense in going over the same old questions. There were no answers. Sarah shoved her feet into her slippers and pulled on her robe. Even its quilted warmth couldn't stop the cold inside. Her teeth chattered. Her body shook. Her fingers trembled so she could not turn up the wick of the oil lamp. If only Ellen were here to bring her some hot tea. Oh, she *hated* the night! The darkness, the solitude, the long hours with nothing to distract her from her thoughts.

The nightmares.

Sarah shuddered, rubbed her upper arms, looked toward the door to the right of the fireplace. A longing, too strong to be denied, welled. She snatched up the lamp, opened the door and started down the narrow winder stairs, her shadow floating on the wall beside her. A step creaked. Another. She paused, listened to hear if Nora woke, then continued down into the kitchen.

The darkness of the large room swallowed the meager light of her lamp. She put it on the center table, removed the globe and lit the candles on the table and in the sconces that hung over the fireplace. The dark withdrew to shadowy corners. Another shudder shook her. She glanced at the hearth, yearned for a fire, but had never started one. Hot tea would have to do.

She rubbed her cold hands together and shivered her way to the big, black iron stove. The weight of the teakettle surprised her. It fell from her shaking hand, clanged against the stove. She gave a guilty start and glanced toward the stair door. All was quiet. Defeated, she put the kettle back in place. The stove was cold. So was she. Cold, and helpless, and inadequate, and lonely. She could not even make tea. Why ever had she sent Ellen home?

Sarah fought the constriction in her chest for breath.

The answer was simple—because it was easy to be brave during a warm, sunny afternoon. But in the darkness when the memories returned and the nightmare came... Tears burned behind her eyes, clogged her throat. She clenched her hands and fought them with all her strength. She was tired of tears. Of grief. She wanted to be happy again. How would she ever be happy again?

Clayton opened his door a crack and listened. Yes, there it was again. The squeak of a step on the winder stairs. Dim light flickered against the wall. A sound of stealthy movement reached him. He tightened his grip on his pistol, eased the door open, pressed into the shadow against the wall of the landing and looked down. A frown drew his brows together. Sarah Randolph was descending the steps, light from the lamp in her hand illuminating the downward spiral, glinting on the silky mass of brown hair loosely restrained at the nape of her neck and spilling down the back of her quilted robe. The sight of her struck him breathless.

She paused, glanced toward her open door. The terror on her face froze him in place. She blinked tears from her eyes and continued on her way down the stairs.

Clayton rushed into his room, put the pistol away and pulled trousers on over his cotton drawers. What could be wrong? What could have put that look of terror on Sarah Randolph's face? He shoved his arms into his shirtsleeves, fastened a few buttons and tucked the tails into his pants on the way to the door. Barefoot, he started down the stairs, driven by a need to help her. To protect her. From what? How could he help her? Would she even want him intruding into her personal life? He slowed his steps, approached the kitchen door cautiously.

"Was it tea you was wantin'?"

Eldora. Clayton stopped, stood undecided. The sight of his half-fastened shirt and bare feet determined his path. He turned and made his way back up the stairs to his room. The unexpected sight of Sarah Randolph on the stairs had given him a jolt that left him shaken. He was better off staying as distant from her as possible.

He left his door open a narrow slit, finished buttoning his shirt and pulled on his socks before he stretched out on top of his bed—in case. Eldora would call him if he was needed.

A clanking sound, a soft murmur of feminine voices from downstairs filtered in through his slightly open door. Moonlight flowed through his windows, a haunting silver radiance. Clayton frowned. There was something about moonlight that made him lonelier. He folded his hands on his chest and stared at the ceiling overhead, ignoring the ache in his heart, dreading, *hoping,* that his housekeeper would call him.

"Was it tea you was wantin'?"

Mrs. Quincy! Sarah's throat constricted. She couldn't speak to answer the woman's question. She compressed her lips to hold back the rising sobs and nodded.

The housekeeper waddled forward, the hem of the blue robe she wore swishing back and forth around her slippered feet dusting her path. She neared, squinted up at her from beneath the mobcap covering her gray hair and gave a brief nod. "Havin' a bad night, are y'? Well, there's no problem a good hot cup of tea can't make better." She removed the tool from the wall, lifted a front plate from the stove, set it aside and nodded toward a box on the floor. "Hand me some of that kindlin'."

The shock of the enjoinder stabbed through her emotions. Sarah stared. At the woman's second nod, she came to herself, bent and gathered a handful from the box.

The housekeeper crumpled newspaper, stuffed it in the stove and placed the kindling on top. She reached up and turned a knob protruding from the side of the chimney pipe. "Now light this spill from that candle and set this a burnin' whilst I fill this kettle."

Obviously, she was not going to be coddled. Sarah quashed a twinge of offense at not being pampered when she was so upset, took the long, slender piece of wood and hastened to obey. In a moment the kindling was blazing. The warmth felt wonderful on her icy hands.

Mrs. Quincy returned with the filled kettle, glanced at the fire. "You've got that goin' proper. Now add a few of them sticks o' wood. An' lay 'em in easylike. You don't want sparks to fly up and singe your hair." She waddled away to the cupboard.

Sarah did as she was bid. The wood caught. The fire blazed.

The housekeeper returned with a tin of tea in her hand, nodded approval, lifted the iron plate back in place and set the water over to heat. She reached up and fiddled with the knob on the chimney pipe again. "We'll need cups 'n' saucers."

Sarah moved to the shelves on the wall and took down two cups and two saucers, surprised to find her hands were no longer shaking. She took an experimental breath, then another—the pressure in her chest had eased. The activity had made her feel better than being babied ever had. She looked toward the housekeeper who was spooning tea into a china pot. "Thank you for asking me to help, Mrs. Quincy."

The housekeeper nodded, put the cover back on the tin of tea and gave it a sharp rap with the heel of her hand to seal it. "Most times when I'm feelin' plagued by somethin' it helps to keep busy. Keeps me from stewin' on the trouble." She pointed toward a cupboard with pierced tin doors. "Sugar's in the brown crock. I'll fetch some cream."

"Do you want to talk about what's botherin' you?"

Sarah weighed the offer, shook her head. "No. Thank you, but... I want to forget."

Mrs. Quincy nodded, stirred a spoonful of sugar into her tea. "I know how that can be." She reached for a piece of the bread and jam she'd prepared for them. "Mind if I ask how you come to be a nanny? I mean, you could sell one of them gowns of yours for more than a year's pay, so..."

"It is not for the money. It is—" Sarah blinked, looked down at the cup in her hand. "I lost someone I—" she swallowed hard, cleared her throat "—someone I shared a dream with." Tears streamed down her cheeks. She put down her cup and wiped them away. "That dream is gone and I need something to do. I need a purpose. Something to give—" She bit down on her lip, shook her head and picked up her cup. Her hands were trembling again. She put the cup down before she spilled the tea—waited for the commiseration, the comfort Ellen always gave her.

"Whatever your reason, 'tis a blessing for little Miss Nora you're here."

Once again shock pierced through her emotions.

Where was the sympathy? Sarah lifted her head, looked across the table at the housekeeper. "Truly?"

"Truly." Mrs. Quincy picked up the plate of bread and jam, offered it to her. "That little one wasn't never out of that room till you come. An' she cried all the time."

"How *awful* for Nora." Sarah shook her head at the offer of bread. Mrs. Quincy held the plate in front of her. She met the housekeeper's steady gaze, took a piece of bread. Still that steady gaze. She took a bite. Mrs. Quincy put the plate down.

"'Twas that, but she's laughin' and playin' like a young'un should now. An' that's thanks to you. You're a blessin' for her, all right. I wasn't sure that would be the way of it when you come—bein' late an' all. I figured you was another one like that uppish Miss Thompson, thinkin' only of her own self." Mrs. Quincy's gaze again steadied on her. Her lips curved in a rueful little smile. "I reckon I wasn't too welcomin'."

Amusement bubbled. Sarah's lips twitched. "You were so stern I almost turned away and ran back to Ellen." Curiosity flared in the housekeeper's eyes. "Ellen's my lady's maid." The amusement fled. Sarah sipped her tea, watched Mrs. Quincy's expression change to that of someone who had received an answer to something they'd been wondering about.

"Well, I'm glad I didn't scare you off. It's nice havin' another woman around the place."

Another shock. "One as helpless as I am?"

The housekeeper chuckled. "You're learnin'. You made the fire and helped set up our tea, didn't you?"

"Yes. I did." A warmth of satisfaction spread through her. Sarah smiled and took another bite of her bread and jam. It suddenly tasted wonderful.

"Tomorrow's Sunday. I was wonderin' if you'd like to go along to church with Mr. Quincy and me?"

Bitterness surged. The bread turned sour in her mouth. Sarah reached for her tea to wash away the rancid taste.

The housekeeper fixed another look on her. "Lucy goes to her church later on, so she can stay with the child."

That robbed her of the excuse that had readily formed on her lips. Sarah searched for another. Nothing suggested itself to her. She looked into Mrs. Quincy's eyes and gave up. The woman would see straight through any subterfuge and she didn't want to tell her the truth. Sarah sighed. After the housekeeper's kindness tonight, she couldn't simply refuse her invitation. "Thank you, Mrs. Quincy. I shall be pleased to accompany you. What time must I be ready?"

Mr. Quincy handed the reins to a young lad, moved up the steps and opened the door. Sarah glanced at the sign fastened to the white clapboard building—Fourth Street Chapel. Reverend William Herr—and followed Mrs. Quincy inside. Curious looks trailed their progress down the aisle. Sarah smiled and nodded a polite greeting to those who caught her gaze.

Quincy opened the door of the pew on his right.

A middle-aged man looked her way, smiled, bowed his head.

Quincy frowned and stepped back so they could take their seats. "At his age Granville should know church is not the place for tryin' to get a leg up on the rest of the young bucks in the city."

The warmth of a blush crawled into Sarah's cheeks at

the muttered remark. She gathered the skirt of her gold, watered-taffeta gown, moved to the far end of the pew and seated herself, feigning interest in the stained-glass window beside her in an attempt to ignore the stares aimed her way. Mr. Quincy followed his wife inside and closed the door.

"Can't abide Sherman Granville. Thinks every woman he sees will tumble all over their own feet runnin' to him just 'cause he owns half the county!"

"Hush, Alfred. You're in church."

"Don't make it any less true."

"Amen."

The whisper came from the pew behind them. Sarah snuck a peek from the corner of her eye as Alfred Quincy chuckled low and swiveled his head around. "Mornin', John."

A distinguished-looking gentleman with gray hair smiled. "Good morning, Quincy... Mrs. Quincy—" he glanced her way "—miss."

A man entered from a side door, stepped to the pulpit on the platform and bowed his head. "Almighty God, Thou who thunderest from heaven, yet speaketh in the tenderest, softest voice to Your servant's hearts. Speak to us this day, O God. Touch our hearts, our minds, our spirits with Your words, that we may be renewed in that which is Your will and purpose. Amen."

An organ sounded.

"Christ our Savior, Lord of all..."

Sarah glanced up at the man in the pulpit as he boomed out the first words of the hymn. The congregation joined in. She closed her heart and her mind to the meaning of the words and sang along. When they finished the last chorus, the organ music faded away and there was a general rustle as everyone settled in their seats.

Reverend William Herr cleared his throat. "Today I take my text from Psalms Eighteen, verse six. 'In my distress I called upon the Lord, and cried unto my God.'"

Sarah stiffened.

"'He heard my voice out of His temple, and my cry came before Him, even into His ears.'"

And He did not answer me. Aaron died. Anger pushed hot blood through her veins. Sarah gripped her gloved hands together on her lap and forced herself to remain seated when what she wanted was to rise, storm down the aisle and out the door and never, ever set foot in a church again. She blocked out the reverend's voice by surreptitiously glancing at the people within her view and trying to guess what their lives were like. To the men she assigned occupations, to the women a marital status.

A fist slammed against the pulpit. Sarah jumped, looked up at Reverend William Herr.

"Are you one who gets angry and walks away because God does not answer as you want him to? How prideful! How arrogant!" His voice roared at the congregation. "Were you there when God hung the stars?"

No. But I was there when He sent the lightning that killed Aaron! That exploded the deck beneath him and threw him into the raging ocean that claimed him forever! Anger lifted her chin, glared out of her eyes. The words crowded into her throat determined to be expressed—to be spoken and answered. Sarah choked them back, felt the pressure of them in her chest. Tears smarted her eyes. She blinked, willed the tears to stop. Willed the band of tightness around her chest to relax so she could breathe.

Determined not to make a spectacle of herself, she spent the rest of the service questioning why Clayton Bainbridge's servants occupied his family's pew. And why Clayton Bainbridge stayed home.

Chapter Seven

The weight of sadness pressed down upon her. Sarah took a deep breath to rid herself of the heaviness and hurried to her bedroom. A quick glance in the mirror told her she looked as wan and drained as she felt. It was the aftermath of the nightmare, of the upsetting message in church this morning. She needed some fresh air, some exercise to put some color back in her cheeks. She grabbed her straw sailor hat, opened the door wide and made her way down the winder stairs to the kitchen. The housekeeper was at the center worktable, kneading dough. Sarah plunged into her request.

"Mrs. Quincy, I've put Nora down for her nap. She should sleep for at least an hour or two. I know Lucy is at church, but I'm feeling a bit…undone…and I would like to go outside for a stroll. I wondered if you would mind listening for Nora? My door is open so you can hear if she wakes before my return, though I promise I shan't be long."

The housekeeper looked at her. Sarah fixed a smile on her face. Eldora Quincy nodded and went back to kneading the dough.

"Take as long as you wish. I'll bring Miss Nora down and give her some bread and butter should she wake 'n' you're not here."

"Thank you, Mrs. Quincy." Sarah stepped to a glass-fronted cupboard, put on her hat and exited the kitchen with a gay little wave she was far from feeling, and that likely did not fool Eldora Quincy for a moment. She strolled by the front of the kitchen ell on the stone path that led to the gravel carriageway and followed that out to the road.

The city beckoned from below, but she felt no inclination to be among people. She hadn't the energy or desire to put on a false front—this morning at church had been quite enough. She glanced to her left, felt the draw of the tree-covered hill and started up the road.

Clayton bent down, selected a stone and straightened. The pond was before him, still and waiting, its calm surface mirroring the blue of the sky, the brightness of the sun. An aura of serenity permeated the small clearing—the serenity he'd come seeking as he had all his life. But today it irritated him. It only emphasized his turmoil. What was he to do about Sarah Randolph?

Clayton scowled, fingered the stone, got it into the right position and curved his index finger around the back edge. The problem was his attraction to Sarah. He managed all right when he prepared himself to see her, chalked up the twinges as a result of his loneliness. But last night the sight of her on those stairs with her hair down had given him a jolt he was not ready for—and did not want. And his compelling need to go to her, to protect her from whatever caused her terror—that complicated things. What he felt for her was more than mere attraction—it was caring. And that involved the heart.

Clayton whipped his wrist forward and sent the small, flat stone skipping across the smooth face of the pond. Sunlight sparkled on the tiny sprays of water produced each time the stone skimmed the surface and highlighted the ripples that spread out from the point of contact.

Ripples. He knew about ripples. More than he wanted to know. And he had learned the lesson at the cost of Deborah's life. His face drew taut. One moment of weakness. One night of yielding to his wife's pleas and entice-ments…to his own need and— *Ah, Andrew, my friend, I am so sorry! I promised to keep your beloved daughter safe. I failed you.*

Clayton shoved his fingers into his hair and glared out across the water. He had no excuse. He never should have listened when Deborah begged him. When she said she wanted to know, at least once, what it meant to truly be a woman before she died. She told him she had taken precautions against pregnancy, but he knew precautions often failed. But he had given in. And the ripples had started.

Why? He was self-disciplined and strong-willed. Why had he given in to Deborah's appeals? Clayton lowered his hands and shoved them in his pockets. He hunched his shoulders and studied the ground as he walked along the edge of the pond toward the large, flat boulder that had been his fishing dock when he was a young boy. What did the "why" matter? Deborah had become preg-nant. The first ripple. A terribly dangerous one.

Clayton clenched his jaw, pulled back his foot and kicked a stone. It arced into the air and splashed down almost dead center of the pond. He stared at the circles spreading out in an ever-widening pattern from the spot where the stone broke the surface, and felt again the despair that had gripped him during her pregnancy. That was the second ripple—Deborah's health. With her weak heart she grew increasing frail. And no matter what he did for her, no matter how he coddled her, he could not make it better. Every time she had one of her spells, he prayed for her. Fervently. To no avail. Her health continued to decline. So did his faith. That was the third ripple—his loss of faith. And the fourth ripple was Deborah's death.

Clayton stared the fact square in the face, ignoring the pain that squeezed his chest, made his heart ache. And then there was the fifth ripple. The one that went on and on. The one it was becoming more and more difficult to ignore. The one he couldn't bear to look at, because all he saw was his guilt. The child.

Clayton leaned his hips against the boulder and glowered at the pebbles and stones littering the ground at his feet. It had been bad enough before, when he heard the child crying all day. But now, since Sarah Randolph had come, he saw the child daily. And the guilt was intensifying. That was the sixth ripple—his guilt, which enclosed all the others. But now there was a seventh ripple—Sarah Randolph. He would have to—

"Oh...*bother!*"

Clayton spun around, stared toward the path that led to the road. Patches of blue fabric showed through the gaps in the bushes. There was a snapping of twigs.

"Ouch!"

Clayton scowled, strode toward the path to warn off the intruder. This was his private sanctuary. He stepped around the bushes and stopped dead in his tracks. His heart slammed against his chest wall. Sarah Randolph stood in the path ahead trying to free a lock of her hair from a branch. He sucked in a breath.

She glanced his way. Surprise widened her eyes, erased the frown that had lowered her delicately arched brows into a straight line. "Mr. Bainbridge! Thank goodness. I seem to have become hopelessly entangled with this tree." A blush crawled along the crest of her cheekbones. "Would you please help me untangle— Ouch!" She yanked her hand down and stuck her fingertip in her mouth. "This tree has thorns."

An intense desire to take her finger in his hand and kiss the sting away shook him. He scowled and cleared his throat. "That's why it's called a thornapple." He stepped forward, reached for the branch holding her hair prisoner. Their hands brushed. She jerked back.

"Ow!" She grabbed for her hair, and her fingers closed over his, sprang open. Her startled gaze flew to his face, met his gaze and immediately lowered to somewhere in the region of the third button on his shirt.

"Hold still." Clayton moved closer, bent his head to study the entanglement of hair and thorny branch. The delicate scent of lilacs clinging to her hair teased his nose. He closed his mind to the fragrance, to the silky feel of her hair on his fingers, to the faint blush tinging her cheeks. "The branch is green and too thick for me to break without the possibility of my yanking your hair. I shall have to untangle it. It may pull a little."

"I understand. Do what you must."

He made the mistake of looking down. Their gazes met again. The blush on her cheeks increased. The gold flecks in her brown eyes warmed before she again lowered her lashes.

Clayton's mouth went bone-dry. He frowned and focused his thoughts on the job at hand. "It appears you have made everything worse by trying to free yourself." He unwound a few strands that were snarled by a thorn. "Tip your head back a bit." She complied. He leaned closer, bent his head to see around to the back side of the branch. She caught her breath. Lucky her. He had no breath left.

He worked swiftly, wishing he had brought his knife along so he could cut the branch and end the torture of being so near her. He stopped being careful, broke the last few strands of her hair and stepped back. "That got it. You are free." He stepped around her and picked her hat up off the path, slapped it against his thigh to rid it of any dust or tiny crawling critters and handed it to her.

"Thank you. It— I—" She whirled and started down the path. "Where does this lead?" She broke into the open and gave a little gasp. "Oh, how lovely! What a nice pond." She glanced up as he followed her into the open. "Do you come here often?"

Clayton nodded, moved to put space between them. "It has been a favorite spot of mine since I was a child. It is far enough off the beaten path to be quite solitary. Makes it good for thinking."

She glanced up at him. "Please forgive me, Mr. Bainbridge. I was out exploring. I didn't mean to intrude." She turned back toward the path.

He moved to block her way. "I did not mean to be rude, Miss Randolph. I was only trying to convey the special draw of this place for me." He smiled. "A young boy has a lot of things to puzzle through. Lots of weighty issues to come to grips with. He needs a quiet place to slip off to every now and again, where he can just sit and ponder the way of things. This was my place."

"I believe it still is, Mr. Bainbridge. The questions only become more difficult when we grow up." A shadow of sadness clouded her eyes, quickly dispersed by a bright smile. "And so, good sir, I shall leave you to your pondering. But first—" She gave a small laugh, walked to the edge of the pond and picked up a small, flat stone. With a quick flick of her wrist she sent it skipping out over the water.

He was still staring at the pond in amazement when she brushed off her hands and made her way back to him.

"Five hops. I can do better. James would be ashamed of me." She settled her hat more firmly, tipped her head up and gave him a polite smile. "I must be getting back to Nora. Good afternoon, Mr. Bainbridge. I hope you find the solution to whatever problem you are contemplating." She started off toward the path.

Solution. Clayton stared after Sarah, held back a roar of frustration. A beautiful, intelligent, sad but brave woman imbued with all the social graces who skipped stones! His problem had just become much worse. He blew out a gust of air, sucked in another. The torture was not over yet. Sarah Randolph was not the only one with social graces. His grandparents had raised him to be a gentleman.

"A moment, Miss Randolph. If you will allow me, I would be pleased to escort you home." Clayton fastened a polite expression on his face and strode forward, trying, unsuccessfully, to ignore the sudden bitter taste of jealousy in his mouth. *Who was James?*

Chapter Eight

"*Cincinnati?* I thought Sarah was in Pittsburgh visiting Judith Taylor." Justin Randolph frowned down at his wife. "I'll not have it, Elizabeth! Not after all Sarah has been through. She needs to be here with her family where we can love her and take care of her—help her through her grief over Aaron's death." He shook his head. "It is not like Sarah to act impulsively. I shall leave for Cincinnati tomorrow morning."

"To what purpose, Justin?"

He paused, searched her face. His wife did not ask idle questions. "To bring Sarah home, of course."

"Oh, *poof!*"

Laina. Justin pivoted toward the doorway, frowned at his sister. "Poof? What does that mean, Laina? And why are you eavesdropping on a private conversation?"

"Private?" His sister laughed and waltzed into the room. "I assure you, dearheart, there was no need to eavesdrop. I could hear you roaring about Sarah being in Cincinnati the moment I entered the house." She laid the book she was returning on the table by the settee, hugged Elizabeth, went on tiptoe and kissed his cheek.

"Stop glowering, dearheart, it is most unbecoming. And 'poof' means Sarah very much wanted this position as nanny and you should stop being a bear about it and let her be."

Justin glanced at Elizabeth, saw his own bewilderment written on her face and looked back at his sister. "You do not seem surprised by this news, Laina. How do *you* know Sarah 'very much wanted this position'?"

"Because she told me so when she wrote asking me for a reference."

"A reference." Justin lowered his voice to an ominous tone. "And you gave her one?"

"Well, of course I did. Sarah—"

"Without *speaking* to us about it? Laina Allen, sometimes I—" Justin stopped, glanced down at Elizabeth's hand on his arm. A wifely gesture to calm him. It would have worked better if she was not holding the letter. The sight of it exasperated him anew. He scowled at his sister.

"I would have spoken with you about it, Justin, had I thought the matter serious. I thought it was but a whim to provide Sarah diversion from her grief. I certainly did not know she would go through with it, or be accepted in the position. I am as surprised by that news as you." Laina shook her head. "Imagine Sarah a *nanny*. I have no doubt she will be an excellent one. She has a way with children."

"That is *not* the issue, Laina." Justin released a growled litany of concern. "What of Sarah's grief? Her nightmares? Who will comfort her when the memories overwhelm her? When there is a storm?" He blew out a breath, looked at his wife. "Dear heaven, Elizabeth, what will she do without us if there is a *storm?*"

Elizabeth gazed up at him, her eyes awash with tears.

"Perhaps, dearest, without us to console her, to ease her every problem, Sarah's need will overcome her bitterness and she will again seek her heavenly Father. Perhaps she will regain her faith. Surely that blessing is worth the heartache and concern having our daughter at so great a distance will cost us."

Justin watched her force her trembling lips into a smile he knew was for his benefit and covered her hand, still resting on his arm, with his own. Her smile steadied, warmed at his touch.

"And perhaps this position of nanny will carry another blessing from the Lord as well." She blinked the tears from her eyes and stepped back. "Try to clear your heart and mind of your anxiety for Sarah, Justin, and listen to this last part of her letter." She glanced at her sister-in-law. "And you, Laina."

Elizabeth unfolded the sheet of paper, scanned down and cleared her throat.

"'And so, Mother and Father, quite by accident I have found a purpose for my life. Little Nora is an adorable toddler. I grow more fond of her every day. She is a precocious child, and has already learned every game suitable for her tender age that I remember. I am forced to invent games to hold her interest. Yet all is not well for her. Her situation is a sad one. For reasons I have yet to discover, Mr. Bainbridge will not allow his daughter in his presence. He will not even acknowledge her by name. And adorable little Nora needs her father's love.

"'Please do not worry about me. Stony Point is a lovely house, and, other than the treatment of his daughter, Clayton Bainbridge is a thoughtful man, careful for my comfort and every inch a proper gentleman. And though he is young and handsome with much to recommend him, there is no danger of romantic involvement. Mr. Bainbridge still grieves for his wife, and, though he is gone, my heart remains loyal to Aaron. And even if that were not so, who can abide a man who will not even *look* at his own child? I am safe here.

Your loving daughter, Sarah.'"

Elizabeth looked up at him. Justin stared down into her beautiful, deep-blue eyes and read their silent message. *Remember?* How could he ever forget? He closed the space between them and pulled her into his arms. "Safe? I think not." Memories curved his lips into a slanted grin. "Not if God has another plan."

"Then you will stay home?"

He kissed the top of her head and nodded. "I will stay home."

She smiled up at him, her eyes still overbright with tears. "Oh, Justin… I know it will be worrisome and painful to have Sarah stay in Cincinnati. But I truly think God is answering our prayers. I think He is using that little girl to bring about Sarah's healing."

Justin tightened his arms, drawing her close, still crazy in love with this woman he had married by accident eighteen years ago. "And I think, Elizabeth—if history repeats itself—Sarah and Mr. Clayton Bainbridge may both be in for a wonderful, blessed surprise."

Clayton frowned down at the report he was working on for his meeting with the canal commissioners in Dayton the day after tomorrow. No matter how hard he tried to concentrate it wouldn't come together in a cohesive whole. The sound of the child's happy giggles and Sarah Randolph's laughter drifting in through the window kept intruding on his thoughts.

He rose from his chair and stretched to relax the muscles in his back. A dull ache had developed across his shoulders, no doubt from the rigid posture he had maintained to keep from looking out the window. A frown creased his brow. It was unsettling how much he wanted to go to the window and watch Sarah Randolph playing with the child in the yard. But his equally strong guilt held him back. If it weren't for him, Deborah would be the one outside his window. It would be her laughter that enticed him.

Clayton tilted his head, scrubbed his hands over the tense muscles at the nape of his neck. If only he could find peace. But how could that be when he had a living, breathing reminder in his life?

Maaaa, maaaa.

"No! Get away! Leave her alone!"

Clayton pivoted at the outcry and stepped to the window to see Sarah Randolph snatch up the child in one arm while trying, with her free hand, to fend off a sheep intent on butting her. He frowned. A woman hampered by long skirts and the weight of a child was no match for an angry, determined sheep. Not even a young one. Where was Quincy? He swept his gaze over the portion of yard visible from his window.

Maaaa, maaaa.

"Go away! I sai— Oh!"

Clayton jerked his gaze back to see Sarah staggering backward, her free arm flailing as she tried to maintain her balance. She lost the battle and sat down on the ground—hard. And no sign of Quincy. *Blast!*

Clayton whirled, slammed out the doors, leaped off the stoop and ran to place himself between Sarah and the child and the rampaging sheep. He barely had time to plant his feet before the animal charged. He balled his hand into a fist and thumped the black nose. The sheep jumped back. Clayton moved to the side, drawing the animal's attention from its intended targets. The sheep lowered its head and leaped toward him. Clayton thumped its nose again, harder, and harder yet, then stepped in front of a tree. The sheep again drew back and lowered its head to butt. Clayton tensed, waited. When the sheep charged, he jumped aside. The sheep's head rammed solidly into the tree. Clayton slipped behind the trunk, scanned the ground behind the tree for a weapon but spotted nothing. He pressed back against the trunk, rubbed the edge of his hand and watched the irate sheep. It looked around, let out a few challenging bleats, made a halfhearted feint at the tree, then, having lost its target, turned away.

Clayton edged out from behind the tree on the other side.

"Bad sheep." The child, lower lip protruding, pointed a tiny, pudgy finger at the now grazing animal.

Clayton's lips twitched. He jerked his gaze away from the child to Sarah Randolph and stepped over to offer his hand. "Are you hurt?"

Sarah shook her head. "Only my dignity. Thank you so much for rescuing us. I'm afraid I was not much protection for Nora. Would you please lift her off me so I can rise?"

Clayton sucked in a breath, everything in him refusing the idea of touching the child. He closed his hands around her small chest, felt his own constrict with an emotion he immediately squelched. He lifted her to one side, released her and again offered his hand to Sarah. This time she accepted his help. Her hand felt soft and warm in his.

"What happened?" Quincy came hurrying across the yard. "Is anyone hurt? I was in the loft and heard Sarah cry out."

"No one is hurt." Clayton helped Sarah to her feet, forced himself to release her hand. He turned his back as she bent to pick up the child and focused his attention and anger on Quincy. "But that is not to say they were not in danger. Get rid of that hoggerel, it is getting too frisky. You should have known that."

He turned and made his way back to the house, furious at the emotions tearing at him, at his inability to stop them. He strode through the still-open door, yanked it closed behind him and went to his study and stuffed the report into his waiting saddlebags. He would finish it when he reached Dayton. It was impossible to work here with Sarah Randolph so close. With her ignoring his orders to keep the child out of his sight.

Clayton scowled, slung the saddlebags over his shoulder, slammed out the door and took the stairs two at a time. The faint sounds of Sarah entering the house with the child followed him as he crossed the upstairs hall to his bedroom to grab the clothes he would need for the next few days. He paused, struck by an idea. Perhaps he could employ Sarah Randolph to take the child back to Philadelphia and care for her there. Yes. That would solve all his problems. He continued into his room, packed his clothes and toiletries and hurried downstairs. He would consider the possibility while he was away.

Sarah roamed around the drawing room feeling restless and at loose ends. Clayton Bainbridge had gone to Dayton and would not return for a few days. He had not even told her he was going away. Not that he owed her an accounting of his movements, but she *was* Nora's nanny. At least he had told Eldora.

Sarah frowned, glanced at the various objects decorating the shelves in the alcove by the fireplace and moved on. It was odd how empty the house felt without Clayton's presence. She stopped in front of the fireplace and looked up at the portraits of his grandparents. Ezekiel Bainbridge was a very handsome man, with a square jaw and a look in his eyes that led one to believe he could well have fought and won battles against hostiles. But there was a tilt at the corners of his mouth that spoke of warmth and good humor. A pity his grandson had not inherited those traits along with Ezekiel's good looks. Most of the time Clayton looked as if he were walking around with a sore tooth.

Sarah shifted her gaze to Rose Bainbridge, studied her refined features. There was a touch of sadness in the woman's eyes, but nothing like the ill humor that darkened her grandson's. If it was not inherited, what had caused his sour disposition? Was it his wife's death? Aaron's death had certainly changed her. The joy had disappeared from her life, sucked down the same vortex of swirling water that had swallowed him. All that was left was pain and grief and darkness. The light in her world had been snuffed as surely as a candle doused by water. Perhaps it was the same for Clayton Bainbridge.

No. No, it was not the same. He had a child. A part of his wife lived on. She had nothing of Aaron but memories and a dead dream.

An overwhelming longing for home and the way things had been before Aaron's death rushed upon her. Tears blinded her eyes, clogged her throat. It could never be. Not ever again. She collapsed onto the sofa and buried her face in her hands, unable to stop the flow of tears.

The wave of anguish passed. Sarah pushed herself erect, wiped the tears from her cheeks, clenched her hands and made her way from the room. She hated crying. Hated the feeling of hopeless— She stopped, arrested by her reflection in the hall mirror, startled by the anger and bitterness that glittered, cold and brittle, behind the glisten of tears in her eyes. She turned away, lifted her skirts slightly and started up the stairs. It seemed she and Clayton Bainbridge had more in common than first appeared. But he had Nora. Pain stabbed sharp and deep. *Why had God taken Aaron?*

Sarah caught her breath and hurried down the hall to prepare for bed—for another lonely night filled with nightmares, startled awakenings and unanswered questions.

Chapter Nine

"Excellent report, Mr. Bainbridge. Work seems to be progressing nicely."

"Thank you, sir." Clayton noted the looks exchanged between the commissioners seated at the table, and a shaft of worry speared through his pleasure in their approval. Something was in the wind. He sat a little straighter.

"So you judge you will be through with the remaining necessary repairs to the Cincinnati locks in three months' time?"

A warning flag waved in his mind's eye. Had he built too much leeway into his report? No, not nearly enough, given the unskilled laborers he had to work with. "Barring emergency situations, yes, sir."

"And the aqueduct you report in emergency condition?"

"I inspected it yesterday on my way here. It's near collapse and must be repaired immediately." Clayton glanced at the other three commissioners seated at the table, including them in his answer and assessing their reactions. "I'll start a crew of men working on it as soon as I return, though it will stretch workers on the locks too thin—which could add two weeks to my timetable." He took a chance. "Unless you authorize the funds I requested to hire more men."

The head commissioner looked around the table. Clayton's hopes surged at the unanimous nods of affirmation. He held his face impassive as the head commissioner again looked his way.

"Very well, Mr. Bainbridge. We will give you authorization to hire the extra men you need—within reasonable bounds. In return you will complete all the needed repair work on the entire southern section by the end of June."

"Two months! Gentlemen, what you ask is unreasonable—"

"But not undoable, Mr. Bainbridge—given adequate funds and sufficient numbers of workers. Under those conditions, and given your talents and capabilities, we are certain you will manage to accomplish the task."

Clayton took a breath, weighed his words. "I appreciate your faith in me, gentlemen." He shot another assessing glance around the table. "But even under the favorable conditions you outline the undertaking will be a formidable one. The time constraints—"

"Are necessary—and not of our doing." The head commissioner scanned around the hotel dining room and leaned closer. So did the others.

Clayton responded in kind.

"As you know, Mr. Bainbridge, July fourth will mark the tenth anniversary of the opening of the Miami Canal from Cincinnati to Dayton. The governor intends to commemorate that occasion with a special celebration. There will be speeches and public entertainments in

Cincinnati on the third. On the fourth, the governor, the mayor and councilmen of Cincinnati, and those of us gathered around this table, along with everyone's families, will board a passenger packet the governor has ordered specially outfitted for the purpose and travel to Dayton. There will be stops and speeches at the various towns along the way, of course. That is the reason all repairs must be completed by the end of June. The canal must be in excellent condition for the anniversary trip."

"I see." Clayton sucked in a breath, thankful he had added in those two weeks of leeway. By subtracting that time and adding more men he should be able to get the jobs completed on time. "I shall start hiring immediately, sir."

The head commissioner nodded, leaned back against his chair and smiled. "That brings us to our last piece of business, Mr. Bainbridge." His smile disappeared. "We are not pleased with the quality of construction, nor the rate of progress being made on the new, northern section of the canal. The present chief engineer of the project is unequal to the job. Therefore, we are offering you that position—beginning when your repair work on the Miami Canal is finished in June and the celebration trip is over."

Clayton stared, hoped he didn't look as surprised as he felt. "I am flattered, gentlemen. Beyond that I do not know what to say. Knowing the position was filled—I was not expecting such an offer to be tendered, and there is much to be considered. I should like the opportunity to inspect the project before I respond."

"Perfectly understandable." The head engineer smiled. "You needn't give us your answer now, Mr. Bainbridge. We will talk more about it onboard the packet during the anniversary trip. That should give you ample time to make your decision."

"On the anniversary trip?"

"Yes. I thought I had made it clear that you and your family are expected to come along. It's the governor's way of expressing his gratitude for your excellent work in engineering the repairs and keeping the Miami Canal functioning at optimum capacity."

Family. The word settled like a stone in the pit of his stomach. Clayton forced a smile. "I am flattered by the governor's favorable opinion of my work, and I will be pleased to join you on the celebration trip to Dayton. But as to family…my wife is deceased."

"Yes. We are aware of that. You have our sympathies. But you have a daughter, do you not?"

Clayton nodded, kept a pleasant expression on his face. "I do." He sought an acceptable excuse, offered it with relief. "But the child is not yet three years old—too young to be away from her nanny."

The commissioner frowned. "Then bring the nanny along. There will be ample accommodations, and the governor was adamant about all family members being present." His tone of voice made it clear he would brook no argument. The frown smoothed to his previously friendly expression. "That concludes our business, Mr. Bainbridge. Would you care to join us for a glass of port?"

"Thank you for the kind offer, Commissioner, but I must decline." He forced his lips into a smile. "Time is of the essence, and I intend to retire to my room and go over the needed repairs to discover how many laborers I must hire to accomplish our goal. If you gentlemen will excuse me?" He rose, inclined his head in a polite bow to all present and left the table.

Now what was he to do? *Pray?* Not likely! Clayton flopped down on the bed and stared up at the plaster ceiling. "I wish you were here, Grandma and Grandpa. I could use some advice. I don't know what to do, how to get out of this snare I find myself in. I had thought to be rid of Sarah Randolph and the child. Now I *have* to take that anniversary trip on that packet. I want that job as chief engineer on the northern Erie section of the canal. It will mean a real advancement in my career, and— Ahh!"

Clayton bolted out of bed, strode across the small room and yanked open the window. Sounds of revelry from the hotel's barroom floated up to him on the night air. Too bad he wasn't a drinking man. He could go downstairs, get drunk, then come back up to this room and sleep the night away. As if that would help anything. His problems would still be here when he woke tomorrow morning. At least this way he had a clear head to think things through and come up with a solution. And the first step was to define the problem. To admit it was not only the child anymore. It was Sarah Randolph, as well. She was so beautiful. So vibrant. So warm and caring and spirited. And when she had looked up at him the day her hair got tangled in that limb... And again yesterday, when she put her hand in his...

Clayton gripped the window frame and stared out at the night. Why had a woman like Sarah Randolph come into his life? And why was it impossible for him to be rid of her?

Bitterness rose, acrid and sour in his mouth. He stared

up at the ebony sky. Did it amuse God to see him writhing in the pain of his guilt over Deborah's death? Is that why He took her, even though he had offered himself in her stead? Why He allowed the child to live as a daily reminder?

Clayton shoved back from the window, rubbed his hand over the back of his neck. He was without excuse or defense. He had known carrying a child would likely kill Deborah. He stared into the darkness, filled with remorse, helpless to change what was.

He loathed himself. Every time he saw Deborah's child, his shame and guilt grew. And now there was Sarah. Beautiful, warm, spirited Sarah, who stole his breath by simply walking into a room.

Was she a test sent by God? Clayton turned his back on the night, walked over and flopped on the bed. It would take every bit of strength he possessed, but he would not fail this time. He stared up at the ceiling, the pain in his heart swelling. "Do You hear me, God? I will not fail this time."

Sarah scanned the yard, spotted no sheep and, laughing at herself for being a coward, hurried to the front gate. Clayton Bainbridge had been gone four days, and each day left her feeling more restless. A good brisk walk should help.

A quick, longing glance toward the city below brought a sigh. There was so much of Cincinnati she was eager to explore. And she dearly wanted to go to Mrs. Westerfield's and see how her new gowns were progressing— and visit that shop on Fifth Street, the one opposite the Dennison House. N. L. Cole, that was the name. They had such lovely umbrellas and parasols in the window.

But after all the talk of sickness she had overheard on her first visit to town, she was afraid to go again for fear of bringing the illness, whatever it was, home to Nora. She could not bear the thought of the toddler becoming ill.

Sarah pushed open the gate, turned her back on the city and started walking along the road, enjoying the fresh air, the response of her body to the demand of the hill. Unlike most of her lady friends and acquaintances, she enjoyed exercise, thanks to James. She had spent countless hours as a child playing outdoor games with her baby brother. A smile curved her lips. How he hated to be called her baby brother, but age gave one some privileges.

Sarah picked up her pace, her mind leaping from James to skipping stones to Clayton Bainbridge's private pond. Where was that trail…? Perhaps around this next bend? Yes! There it was. She started down the narrow path, careful to avoid the thorny branches that had ensnared her the first time. Clayton Bainbridge was not here to rescue her today. Heat stole into her cheeks. She had been so awkward and bumbling that day, so…inept. But Clayton had not said a word about her foolishness. He had simply untangled her, and very gently, too. And when she had looked up at him…

Warmth rushed through her in remembered response to the look in his eyes. Their blue color had deepened to almost black, and there had been tiny lights, almost like flames, flickering in their depths. For that one unguarded moment he had looked…dangerous. Had made her nervous.

Sarah replaced the disturbing thought with the memory of Aaron's quiet, respectful kiss the day she had accepted his proposal of marriage. Clayton Bainbridge was not at all like Aaron Biggs. Aaron had always made her feel safe and comfortable. Cared for. Not…restive and uneasy.

Sarah rounded the curve in the path and stepped out into the small, open space. The pond shimmered in the sunlight, bright and tranquil. The rocks and pebbles along its shore invited her to skip them across the still surface. The large rock beckoned her to sit and rest in the sunshine. She stood staring at the beautiful little glade, at the serene beauty of Clayton Bainbridge's special place, and tears welled into her eyes, made the pond's calm surface quiver, the trees shimmer and blur. She should not have come here.

She whipped around and rushed back up the path to the road, sobs filling her throat. She did not want to see that pond ever again. Nor the path. Or that thornapple tree! She did not want to remember being there with Clayton Bainbridge. She wanted Aaron. And the safe, undisturbing harbor of his love.

Chapter Ten

Eldora Quincy jumped at the quick, sharp raps of the front door knocker and scowled in the direction of the entrance hall. "How's a body supposed to get any work done with someone bangin' to be let in every five minutes!"

"Would you like me to answer the door for you, Eldora?"

"No. You're busy with Nora, Sarah. I'll go." The housekeeper dropped the stalk of rhubarb she was slicing into the bowl, wiped her hands dry on the towel tucked into the waist of her apron and hurried from the kitchen.

"More berries?" Nora held up her dish.

Sarah fixed her with a look.

"Pwease?"

"Good girl." Sarah smiled, sliced a few strawberries into the dish and placed it in front of the toddler. "You must remember to be polite and always say please and…"

"Tank you!" Nora piped the answer, beamed a smile, then stuffed a pudgy little handful of the sliced berries in her mouth. Her cheeks bulged.

Sarah laughed and wiped the red smear from around

the toddler's lips before it stained her fair skin. "Small bites, sweetie. It is impolite to stuff your mouth."

"'Twas another man t' be interviewed fer workin' on the canal." Eldora came plodding back to the table. "Seems like all I got done all day is to answer that door. I would never get this rhubarb put up without you lendin' a hand, Sarah."

"I am happy to help, Eldora. I only wish I could do more." Sarah placed the washrag on the table, picked up the knife and resumed slicing berries. "I have been thinking..." She glanced over at the housekeeper. "I know how to manage a household, Mother taught me that. But, as you well know, I am at a loss in the kitchen. Would you be willing to teach me how to cook and bake?"

Eldora stared at her for a moment, then picked up the rhubarb, finished slicing it into the bowl and started on another piece. "I might could do that. You can start by adding them berries you cut up to this rhubarb an' tossin' in a couple handfuls of sugar." She pushed the full bowl across the table. "Then I'll show you about making crust. Mr. Bainbridge's favorite dessert is strawberry and rhubarb pie."

Sarah paused in her slicing and looked up. Eldora turned away from the table, but not before she had seen the woman's smile. She frowned and dumped the berries in with the rhubarb. What was amusing Eldora? Did the housekeeper think because she had been pampered all her life she was incapable of learning to cook?

Determination stiffened her spine. Sarah wiped her hands on the cloth, dried them on the towel and reached for the crock of sugar.

* * *

She had baked a pie. And helped Eldora put up the rhubarb. How surprised everyone at home would be when she wrote them about it. Sarah laughed, crossed the porch and walked down the stairs. She was finding it quite satisfying to learn how to do things for herself. But in spite of her baking lesson and the success of her pie, today had been disappointing. She had waited and watched, but no opportunity had presented itself for her to bring Nora into her father's presence. Clayton Bainbridge had been ensconced in his study all day. He was there still, interviewing potential laborers for the canal. And she had kept Nora far from the front of the house. Some of those applicants looked very rough and ill-bred, and she did not want the toddler frightened.

Sarah sighed and plucked a leaf from a bush, shredding it with her thumbnails as she ambled down the path toward the pagoda. A full week she had been disappointed in her purpose. What would her mother do?

She frowned and brushed the bits of leaf from her fingertips. She knew the answer to that question. Her mother would pray. But she had no intention of doing so. Nothing seemed to shake her mother's faith, but her own had been shattered by Aaron's death. She was not interested in communing with a God that turned a deaf ear to her cries. She cast an angry glance upward and caught her breath. Layers of vibrant red streaked across the cerulean sky, each tier outlined by the glittering golden rays of the hidden sun and diminishing in intensity as they touched the wooded hill. Sunset. She had not realized it was so late. She did not want to—

"Breathtaking, isn't it?"

And heartbreaking. Sarah blew out a breath to rid

herself of the onrush of bitterness and turned toward the house. Clayton Bainbridge stood on the porch looking at the sky. "Yes, it is." She did not elaborate on her answer. He was talking about the beauty of the sunset, not her reaction to it—let him think she agreed. She tensed as he descended the steps and came down the path toward her.

"It feels good to be outside, to breathe fresh air after being cooped up in the house all day." He stopped beside her, looked up at the sky and fell silent.

Why didn't he say what he wanted? Surely he wasn't planning to stay out here with her. Sarah went rigid. She did not want to share the sunset with him...or anything else for that matter. It intruded upon her memories of Aaron. She launched a change of subject. "Are your interviews going well?" The question drew Clayton's gaze to her and the expression in his eyes made her stomach tighten. She could not tell what he was thinking. Did he resent her crossing the servant/employer line by asking about his work? She reached for another leaf, began slitting it with her thumbnail.

"They are going well enough. Though they are taking time from my work I can ill afford to lose. I hope to finish them tomorrow, but it will be difficult. I need at least ten more men."

Through her lowered lashes, Sarah watched him lift his hand and rub the nape of his neck, a gesture that brought her father to mind. Justin Randolph did the same thing when he was troubled. Compassion welled, unbidden and unwanted.

"You see, the commissioners have set time constraints. All the repair work is to be completed by July first." Clayton's gaze sought hers. "And without enough laborers..."

There was concern in his voice, worry in his eyes. She tried to ignore the compassion but it was too strong. She tossed the mangled leaf away, brushed off a shred clinging to her skirt. "Perhaps if you explain their time-table is unreasonable they will grant you an extension." Something flickered in his eyes. Astonishment? Not surprising, he probably thought she was simply a mindless piece of social froth. He could not know the education and respect given the women in the Randolph family.

"Unfortunately, that is not possible. July fourth marks the tenth anniversary of the opening of the Miami Canal and the governor is planning a big celebration. Unreasonable or not, the work must be finished by that date. But, I did not come out here to bore you with a discussion of my work, Miss Randolph—except as it concerns you." He paused, looked off into the distance.

Sarah studied his face. He looked…uncomfortable. "I do not understand, Mr. Bainbridge. How does your work concern me?"

Clayton's gaze swung back to her. "The governor's celebration I spoke of—" He looked away again. "There is to be a trip to Dayton aboard a specially outfitted packet boat. I am invited—" he frowned "—nay, *ordered* to go along. The head commissioner made it quite clear that I must do so." He looked straight at her. "The trip will no doubt assure that I receive the position of head engineer for the new northern extension." He paused again.

Why was there such tension in his voice and posture? Sarah hesitated, but he had said it concerned her. "And is this a position you covet?"

He nodded. "Very much. It will mean great advancement in my career."

She studied his taut face. He certainly did not *look* pleased. "Then I offer my felicitations. But, I confess to confusion. I do not grasp how this concerns me."

His face took on that stony look she so disliked. "The governor has requested that those accompanying him on the packet bring their families along. I explained my wife was deceased and protested the child was too young to be away from its nanny, but I was informed there are ample accommodations for that circumstance. You are to come along to tend the child."

"Oh. I see." So that was what was troubling him. He would be forced to acknowledge Nora. Anger surged. But also excitement. It was the perfect opportunity to bring father and daughter together.

"Of course I will give you extra compensation for caring for Nora during the excursion. And also pay for two suitable gowns." He cleared his throat. "You do not look like a nanny—" he waved a hand toward her "— your gowns, I mean."

Sarah glanced down at the full, rosette-and-lace-trimmed, long skirt of her rose-colored silk dress. "I know my gowns are inappropriate and give people the wrong impression, Mr. Bainbridge. But I had no time to order suitable ones before I came." She looked up at him. "However, your offer is unnecessary. I have already commissioned several new gowns. They should be ready soon."

"I see. In that case, I shall bid you a good evening, Miss Randolph. I will explain more about the excursion as the time nears." Clayton gave her a small nod and turned back toward the house. She watched him walk away, again feeling that odd connection to him she had experienced that day in the garden. She and Clayton

Bainbridge both were plagued by loneliness and painful memories.

Like long walks in the sunset.

Sarah swallowed hard and looked down at her lengthening shadow on the lawn. One shadow. Aaron's taller, broader silhouette was gone forever. She would never know the comfort of his presence beside her again.

A sudden glow of candlelight spilled through the slatted shutters of an upstairs window brightening the dusk. Sarah stared up at it, her throat tight, her heart aching. Her pain seemed unbearable at times, but how much worse must it be for Clayton Bainbridge who had to sleep alone every night in his marriage bed?

Sarah blinked tears from her eyes and clenched her hands. A walk in the garden had lost all appeal. She closed her mind to the fading sunset and headed for the porch.

She would have to board a boat!

Sarah froze. Panic squeezed her lungs. Her stomach roiled, her body shook. She forced her legs to move, made it to the porch before they gave way. She dropped onto the seat of the wooden bench and stared out into the garden, forcing her mind to concentrate on something else in order to gain control before going inside.

Were those high stone walls surrounding the garden built by Clayton's grandfather? She placed herself in that earlier time, and gave her imagination full rein. What would it have been like to suddenly see Indians pouring over those walls? To see painted, half-naked, yelling savages racing toward you with tomahawks raised? Her skin prickled. Her shoulders stiffened. She stared into the deepening shadows of the night, saw movement and edged along the seat toward the door.

A dark shadow swooped down out of the night sky straight for the porch, sent a screech shrilling through the air.

Sarah shot to her feet and stumbled to the door. She jerked it open, leaped inside, slammed it shut and sagged against the wall, listening to the roar of her racing pulse.

"What happened? What is wrong?"

She started, looked up. Clayton Bainbridge was hurrying toward her from across the library, a scowl on his face and a book in his hand.

"Indians." She meant it to be light, amusing. To distract him from her appearance and the fear she knew was reflected on her face. And it might have worked— if she had not burst into tears.

"Feel better now?"

Sarah nodded, longed for her mother and father, Ellen, the comfort of home. She could not stop shaking.

"Would you like another sip of wine? It always seemed to help Deborah when she was…discomposed."

"No. No more." She gathered her courage and looked up. "I apologize, Mr. Bainbridge. I— It—" She took a breath, swallowed, looked into his eyes and knew she would have to tell him at least part of the truth. "The sunset brought back some painful memories and I tried to suppress them by imagining what it was like during the Indians raids on this place. And then the owl—" She stopped; it sounded so foolish, but it was the best she could do given the state of her tangled emotions. She gave a helpless little wave. "There is no excuse for my actions. But I am sorry."

Clayton nodded, placed the glass in his hand on the table beside the wine decanter. "There are times I think it must be fortunate to be a woman and have the outlet of tears for inner turmoil." He smiled down at her. "Men are not permitted that luxury, though we are allowed to punch a wall—or each other. Or fight Indians."

"Of the 'Owl' tribe?" She tried again to make it sound light, humorous.

"Especially them."

The understanding in his voice brought tears welling. Sarah blinked them away and gave up all pretense. He was very good at calming a woman. He must have had a lot of practice with his wife. "And have you done so? Punched a wall, I mean—not fought Indians." That must have been too personal. A frown creased his brow, was quickly erased.

"On occasion."

"And did it help?" Her heart beat furiously at her temerity, but something compelled her to ask. She looked into Clayton's eyes, waited. At last he shook his head.

"No." He looked away, looked back and smiled, but the smile never reached his eyes, and she knew he only did so to lighten the tense atmosphere for her. "At least not always. Only when you punch so hard your hand hurts and you forget the other pain."

Sarah gave a light laugh to reward him for his effort. "Then perhaps I shall try it your way should I again have a need of release, Mr. Bainbridge. For tears never work. They merely give you a headache, a stuffy nose and red, puffy eyes—most unattractive." She rose and gave him a genuine smile. "Thank you for your care, *and* for your understanding, Mr. Bainbridge. It is most appreciated. Now I shall bid you a good evening."

"Good evening, Miss Randolph—and rest easy. No

Chapter Eleven

Sarah made a slow turn in front of the pier glass in the dressing room. The gown was perfect. It was made of lovely, yet sensible, fabric with no flounces or ruffles, its only trim a touch of dark-red roping at the neck, waist and sleeves that enhanced the red in the material's deep-chestnut color. A plain and serviceable dress—exactly what she had requested. And the workmanship was excellent.

Sarah smiled and patted the matching red roping that held her hair in a loose knot on the crown of her head. There would be no more confusion as to her nanny position due to her elegant, unsuitable gowns now. They were stowed away in her trunk. It was a shame she could not pack her painful memories away with them. But the faint crescents of fatigue under her eyes testified to the impossibility of that.

She sighed and went to her bedroom to open the shutters and let in the morning sunshine. She had not slept at all well. But this time it was not only memories of Aaron that had kept her awake. A vision of Clayton Bainbridge's face, his eyes shadowed with pain, had kept her tossing and turning all night. That, and this strange connection she felt to him. A connection that grew stronger with each encounter.

Sarah frowned, moved over to the desk, sat in the chair and slipped on her shoes. She did not *want* these feelings. She did not want to sense Clayton's grief and pain. Did not want to understand it. Or to feel compassion for him. She had enough pain and grief of her own. All she wanted was to feel safe. That is all she had ever wanted since her mother abandoned her. It seemed little enough to ask.

No harm will come to you in this house. It was built stout and strong to keep out enemies.

Oh, if only that were so. But Randolph Court was built of brick, and she had learned that stout walls could not protect one from the worst enemies, the most painful hurts. Nor could wealth, or social position. Death and grief came to all.

Oh, Aaron, I miss you so. Sarah closed her eyes to conjure the face of her dead fiancé, but it was Clayton Bainbridge's countenance that came into view. She snapped her eyes open, rose and hurried toward the nursery, wiping the frown from her face and curving her lips into a smile as Nora stood in her crib and held up her arms.

"Good morning, sweetie."

"Mornin'." Nora yawned, rubbed her eyes. "Me go outside?"

"After we get you cleaned up and have breakfast." Sarah lifted the toddler into her arms, blinked back tears at the rush of love overflowing her as Nora's small, sleep-warm arms tightened around her neck. How was she ever going to give up this child? But she didn't have to think about that now. Nora would not be taken from her in a moment's time. She would be able to prepare herself for this loss. And meantime she had a purpose for her life.

Clayton rose from his desk chair and held out his hand. "Most impressive recommendations, Mr. Wexford. The job is yours."

"Thank you, sir." The man stood and shook hands. "I'll not disappoint you, Mr. Bainbridge." He picked up his hat and moved toward the door. "When and where shall I report for work, sir?"

"Come here to the house at eight tomorrow morning. I want to go over some blueprints with you and familiarize you with the various projects."

"Very good, sir. I shall be here promptly at eight o'clock."

Clayton nodded, faced the group of men gathered outside the door. "There will be no more interviews. The positions have all been filled. Thank you all for coming." He closed the door on the mumbling, disappointed men and turned back to the study, his steps quick and light. A grin split his face. At last! He had finally found an engineer qualified to oversee the repairs. The man could actually *read* a blueprint. He could put Wexford in charge of the minor projects, freeing himself to oversee the difficult jobs. He would have no trouble meeting that July first deadline now.

A muffled, childish giggle, coming from the direction of the back of the house, wiped the grin from his face. Clayton reached to close his study door, paused at the sound of soft, feminine laughter. His exhilaration swelled, pushed at him. He scowled, fought the strengthening urge, the memory of the understanding on Sarah Randolph's face as he had explained his deadline plight last night in the garden.

Another burst of muffled laughter reached him. He tightened his grip on the door latch, glanced around his empty study, then stepped back into the entrance hall and closed the door. What good was this elation if he could share it with no one? Surely there would be a moment when the child was off playing by itself when he could speak to Sarah and tell her of his good fortune. There was no harm in that.

He strode down the hall and into the library, slowing at sight of the open door. No wonder he could hear their laughter. He stepped onto the back porch, spotted Sarah marching, shoulders back, arms pumping, around the trunk of the maple tree at the side of the garden. The child, imitating her posture and giggling, was following close behind. Clayton's face drew taut. This was not a good time. In fact, it was a bad idea altogether. What had he been thinking? He turned to leave, pivoted back at a sudden squeal. The child was running toward the pagoda, chasing after a squirrel.

"Good afternoon, Mr. Bainbridge."

Clayton looked down. His heart thudded. The sun bathed Sarah's upturned face, highlighted her delicate features, the golden strands among her light-brown hair—especially those strands that had worked loose from the restraint of the red cord and now dangled from her temples to rest against her cheeks. Cheeks pink from her exertions playing with the child. Why did the woman not wear a bonnet? He dipped his head in greeting, not trusting his voice. Was that plain gown supposed to hide her beauty? It only enhanced it.

He stood silent, watched her walk to the porch and climb the stairs, all grace and beauty.

"Were you looking for me?"

All my life. The unbidden answer crowded all other thought from his mind. Guilt assailed him. Would he betray Deborah's memory? Bitterness rose, washed through him. Clayton frowned, shook his head. "Someone left the door open. I could hear your laughter all the way to my study. Please make certain the door is closed in the future."

He stepped back through the door, closed it firmly and headed back to his study, his elation replaced by a grim determination to avoid Sarah Randolph from now on.

That had not gone as planned. Sarah glared at the closed door, itching to open it again—to march down the hall to Clayton's study and demand that he come back to the yard and at least *speak* to his daughter. She clenched her hands, turned and hurried down the steps before she gave in to the desire.

"Nora…come with me, sweetie." She held out her hand, and the toddler came running. Sarah took hold of her tiny hand, opened the gate and started down the gravel way toward the carriage house, hoping Quincy would not be offended if they invaded his territory. She needed a change of scenery. She looked around the far side of the building, but spotted no one.

"Hello?"

No answer. Sarah released Nora's hand, tugged one of the wide, plank doors open a crack and peeked inside. Cool, musty air carrying a hint of oiled leather, feed, hay and manure flowed out of the dim interior, tantalizing her and bringing back childhood memories. She and Mary and James had spent many happy hours in their father's stables. And it had been one of Mr. Buffy's favorite places. Her lips curved at thought of the huge black dog that had been a gift to her from Justin Randolph. It was the day Justin gave her the puppy she first felt he loved her, and she began to talk that very day. Tears filmed her eyes. Mr. Buffy had been her constant companion for seven years. She had been ten years old when he died. Her smile ebbed. That had been her first experience with grief. She had never wanted another dog.

Sarah pushed away the memory, lifted Nora into her arms in case there should be an unfriendly animal of some sort lurking about, pulled the door wider and stepped inside. "Mr. Quincy?" A low nicker was her only answer. She looked toward the far wall. A dark roan with powerful shoulders extended its neck over the stall door, flared sensitive nostrils, snorted and tossed its head. Clayton Bainbridge's mount. The shoulder muscles bunched, a hoof thudded against the floor. The roan tossed its head again, stared at her out of dark-brown eyes separated by a white blaze.

"My, you are a beauty." Sarah kept her voice pitched low and soft. "And I think you know it, too." The roan's ears twitched, pricked forward. Its stable mate nickered. Sarah shifted her gaze to the smaller bay with a white star on its face that occupied the next stall. The carriage horse. What had Quincy called her? Sassy. Yes, that was it. "Yes, you are a beauty, too, Sassy."

She started forward. Nora wiggled, tightened the arm she had wrapped around her neck. Sarah looked at the toddler, who—thumb stuck securely in her little mouth—was staring wide-eyed at the horses. Anger gushed. She kept forgetting the little girl had been kept caged in the nursery before she came. "See the pretty horses, sweetie? They will not hurt you. Shall we go pet them?"

"Horse." Nora pointed at the stalls, stuck her thumb back in her mouth and squirmed closer.

Sarah gave her a reassuring hug and started toward the smaller bay—stopping as she caught movement out of the corner of her eye. Heart pounding, her gaze locked on a grain box that sat on the floor along the side wall, she backed toward the doors. Something small and gray darted out of the empty stall beside Sassy's and ran behind the chest. A rat? She swallowed a scream, stared at the spot where the rat had disappeared and felt behind her for the door.

"Mew." A tiny gray face with green eyes poked out from behind the box, drew back. *"Mew."*

"A kitten!" Sarah laughed and hurried to the grain box, her long skirts sweeping a trail through the dust and bits of hay and straw covering the puncheon floor. She sat Nora down on top of the chest and peered behind it. Four pair of green eyes gleamed up at her. "Oh, Nora, look! There are four baby kittens."

She reached down. Kittens darted from behind the box and scattered every direction.

"Kitty!" Nora squealed, wiggled to the edge of the chest, flopped over onto her stomach and pushed. Sarah made a grab for her and missed. The toddler landed with a thud on the spotless seat of her white ruffled pantalettes, pushed to her feet and chased after the kitten that had run into the empty stall.

"Wait, sweetie! He will scratch you." Sarah rushed inside the cubicle, pulled the door shut and stooped to pick up the tiny, spitting and hissing, furry ball of feline fury crouched beneath the manger.

Clayton frowned at the rap on the door. He had told Eldora to turn away any further applicants. "Yes?"

The door opened. Eldora Quincy stepped into the room. "Not wantin' to bother you, sir, but—" She stopped, glanced toward the window as light flickered through the room and a low rumble sounded in the distance.

Clayton followed her gaze. Raindrops batted at the leaves on the trees, danced on top of the low, stone wall and tapped at the window. "When did it start raining?"

"A bit ago, sir. 'Tis why I come. Miss Randolph and the child…they are still outside."

"Most likely on the back porch." He returned to his work of assigning men to the various repair jobs.

"No, sir, I checked."

"Eldora, Miss Randolph is perfectly capable of caring for the child. She will come in when—" Lightning flashed, thunder growled. The image of Sarah's frightened face during the last storm popped into his head. Clayton frowned, looked up. "The pagoda?" It was a foolish question. He knew the answer before his housekeeper shook her head no. He fought the urge to rise and go search. The child was safe in her care, and Sarah Randolph was not his concern. "Have Quincy look in the stable, perhaps she took refuge there."

"Mr. Quincy went to the farm early this morning."

"Then send Lucy!"

Eldora started at the snap in his voice, gave him a curious look. "Lucy has been home these last two days tendin' her sick family. An' I've food on the stove and in the oven needs watching. 'Tis almost supper time. That child is goin' to get almighty hungry." She turned with a swish of her long, gray skirt and left the room. He could hear her shuffling down the hall toward the kitchen.

How could footsteps convey disgust? Eldora's clearly did. Clayton shoved his chair back and lurched to his feet. So much for avoiding Sarah Randolph and the child! He peered out the windows, scanned the front and side yards. Lightning flashed. Rain poured down. He snatched an umbrella from the brass stand by the front door and ran down the hall to check the backyard and stable.

Sarah caught her breath at the glint of lightning, brushed at the dust clinging to Nora's frock and plucked bits of hay from the toddler's golden curls. How was she going to get Nora to the house? She had delayed as long as she could, hoping the storm would move on. Instead it was growing more intense. She gave the hem of the long skirt of her gown a vigorous shake. Dust flew. Nora sneezed. "Sorry, sweetie."

Her voice shook. Sarah took a breath to gain some control, pushed at her mussed hair with her trembling hands. Thank goodness Nora was too little to guess she was terrified.

Lightning seared across the darkening sky, threw its light in the window. Thunder cracked. Sarah jerked. The roan snorted, tossed his head and thudded his hoof against the stall floor. The bay shifted position. Clearly, the horses were sensing her fear. She had to leave. Right now.

"Time to go, Nora."

The little girl shook her head, tightened her grip on the ball of fluff in her lap. "Kitty."

"We will come play with the kitty tomorrow. But now we have to go get cleaned up for dinner. Your tummy is getting hungry."

"And my mouf."

"Yes. And your mouth." Sarah settled the toddler's sunbonnet in place, tied the strings and took the purring kitten from her lap. "I do not want you to get wet in the rain so I am going to run really fast." She lifted Nora into her arms, gathered every bit of courage she possessed, walked to the door, slipped it open and waited. She would go after the next flash of lightning and, hopefully, reach the house before it came again.

Lightning streaked against the darkened sky. "Hold on tight, Nora!" Heart pounding, Sarah bent forward to cover the toddler with her body, leaped outside, kicked the door closed and ran, terror driving her every step.

They were not in the backyard. Clayton lowered the umbrella to block the slanting, wind-driven rain from his face and opened the garden gate. *If they were not in the stable—* He refused the worry trying to squirm its way into his thoughts and broke into a loping run toward the carriage house. Something hard slammed into his chest just below his breastbone.

"Ugh!" The breath burst from his lungs. He dropped the umbrella, grabbed his assailant by the shoulders. Sarah Randolph lifted her head, stared up at him out of eyes wide with fear. Her shoulders trembled beneath his hands. He tightened his grip, felt something squirm between them and glanced down.

The child lifted her bonnet-clad head and giggled. "We runned fast!"

Lightning rent the darkness. Sarah jerked, shuddered.

Clayton picked up the umbrella, slipped his arm about her shoulders and guided her through the gate and up the path.

Light splashed across the glistening brick. He looked up. Mrs. Quincy stood at the top of the steps holding a lantern to light their way. "You all right, Sarah?"

Wisps of wet hair brushed his hand as Sarah looked up and nodded. "Yes. W-we are fine."

A gust of wind tugged at the umbrella, blew the rain beneath the porch roof. The lantern light flickered as the housekeeper stepped back. Sarah went rigid beneath his arm, her steps faltered as they reached the porch. Clayton stole a look at her face, glanced at his housekeeper. "Eldora, take the child."

Sarah stiffened. "I will care for Nora."

"'Tis only till you get into some dry togs, Sarah." The housekeeper sat the lantern on the bench and reached for the toddler. "Well, Miss Nora, what have you been up to?"

Nora leaned into Eldora's arms. "Me play with kitty. See horsy. And we runned fast!"

"Did you, now? That's just fine. Why don't you tell me all about it whilst I give you some supper." Eldora shielded the little girl with her broad body and waddled into the house.

Lightning sizzled, a brilliant yellow spear streaking to earth. Thunder cracked.

Sarah gasped, broke from his grasp and dashed for the door. She made it halfway across the porch before she collapsed in a heap on the floor.

"*Sarah!*" Clayton threw the umbrella and rushed to her side. She shook her head, pushed feebly at his chest when he reached for her. He ignored her protest, lifted her into his arms and strode to the door. The howling wind blew her hair loose from its restraint, whipped it across his face. The lantern banged against the back of the bench.

Sarah shuddered, tried to speak.

He shook his head, carried her into the library and lowered her to the settee. "Stay here! I have to get the lantern before it breaks and starts a fire." He ran outside, grabbed the lantern and rushed back. Sarah was sitting up, her wet hair spilling over her shoulders, a red cord in her trembling hands. Her face was the color of plaster. She winced and bit down on her lower lip as lightning flashed.

Clayton hurried to the windows and closed the shutters, then walked over and stood in front of her. "Are you all right?"

She nodded and looked up. He had never seen such fright on a person's face. He did not understand it, was helpless to take it from her. Could not even take her in his arms to comfort her. He jammed his hands into his pockets to resist the temptation. "Why did you not *stay* in the carriage house? Surely you knew I would come for you?" His concern made the words come out sharper than he intended. Color rushed into Sarah's face. She rose and faced him, shaking, her shoulders squared, the red cord dangling from one fisted hand.

"And why would I think you would care enough to come for us, Mr. Bainbridge? You will not even *look* at your daughter! And, as you refuse to allow her in your presence, how would you know we were missing? We could have been trapped in that carriage house all night!" Her chin lifted, she looked straight into his eyes, her own wide and shadowed. "I confess, had I been alone, that would have been my choice rather than go out in the storm. But Nora is my charge and I am not so selfish as to put my fear above her needs. Now, if you will excuse me, I must change out of these wet clothes. Good evening, Mr. Bainbridge." She whipped her long skirts to the side, stepped around him and hurried from the room.

Clayton stood silent and watched her leave, every fiber of his being screaming to go after her. He walked to the table by the door, picked up the lantern, opened the side and lowered the wick. The light sputtered and died. Darkness closed around him. He hung the lantern on its peg by the door, turned and walked out into the hall. There was no sound of Sarah's passing, not even her footsteps overhead. Only the storm—and solitude.

He drew his gaze from the stairs, set his mind against the sting of her indictment against him and walked down the hall toward his study. What Sarah had said was true—and the reasons did not matter. Explaining would not change anything. Things were as they had to be.

Chapter Twelve

Sarah hung her wet dress over the edge of the bathtub, grabbed a towel and rubbed at her dripping hair. Rain pounded on the roof, thunder grumbled. She shuddered, dropped the towel, pulled on her new blue gown and willed her trembling fingers to fasten the fabric-covered buttons that paraded from the prim collar to the narrow vee at the waist. How ironic that the dresses had been delivered when she would not be needing them. After her display of cowardice this evening, it was unlikely Clayton Bainbridge would trust her to care for his daughter—even if he did not love the child.

But for him to dismiss her would be unfair. It was *his* fault she had collapsed. Her legs would not have gone all weak and wobbly if he had not told Eldora to take Nora from her. Having to care for the toddler had given her the strength to face her fear. And when that strength was not required, her knees had given way.

Sarah frowned and shook out her long skirt over her petticoat. If she were summoned, what defense could she offer Clayton Bainbridge? She could hardly tell him the truth—that strong emotions struck her in the knees, a

silly weakness she had been plagued with since childhood. That would only further undermine his trust of
her reliability. Nor did it explain why she had attacked
him that way. She should have held her tongue instead
of lashing out at him. But the man was so incredibly
frustrating! And he had challenged her when she was
most vulnerable. The storm—

Lightning glinted between the closed slats of the shutters.

Sarah shivered, tugged her quilted robe on over the
dress, pulled it close about her for warmth and crossed
to the mirror. Her hair was a tangled mess. She brushed
it out, gathered it loosely at the nape of her neck and secured it with the blue ribbon edged in the same demure
scallops that graced her gown's collar and hem. Her hair
would dry faster falling free, and her hands were trembling too hard to manage her normal hairstyle. She was
having enough difficulty tying the ribbon.

A rush of tears blurred her reflection. Would she ever
again tie a ribbon in Nora's golden curls? If she were dismissed, who would care for the toddler? Eldora was too
busy. And Lucy was home caring for her family—may
have herself succumbed to the sickness going around.

The tears overflowed. Sarah wiped them from her
cheeks, turned from the mirror and pulled on her shoes,
concentrating on the activity as a defense against the
thought she did not want to entertain. But it hung there
in the dark recesses of her mind, refusing to be denied.
What if Lucy came back and brought the sickness to
Nora? What if— *No!*

Sarah jolted to her feet. She would not think that.
She would *not!* And she would not worry about being
dismissed. She still had tonight. And perhaps Clayton

would be too busy meeting his deadline for the repairs on the canal to think about replacing her. That would give her until July to prove her competency. Oh! And he needed her for the excursion trip in July.

Sarah grabbed on to the hope, hurried to her bedroom, tossed her robe onto the bed and opened the door to the winder stairs. Light from the kitchen lit the staircase. A smile trembled on her lips. Eldora must have opened the door at the bottom of the staircase to listen for her. And she had thought the housekeeper so harsh and uncaring. She started down the stairs, paused as Nora's baby voice floated up from below. "A horsy is big! Kitties are little. They scratch."

How endearing. Sarah's throat tightened. She cleared away the lump and started down the steep spiral, being quiet so she could hear Nora's conversation with Eldora.

"They do?"

"Uh-huh. See?"

The thought of Nora's pudgy little hand being held out for Eldora's inspection brought the lump came back to her throat. Sarah swallowed hard.

"My, my! That looks serious. Why don't you eat your last bite of peas like a good girl whilst I baste this roast, then I'll fetch my beeswax salve. That will fix you right up."

Sarah wiped away tears. Trust Eldora to have what was needed. If only she had a salve to heal a broken heart. Or an elixir one could take for a paralyzing fear. But no one could cure those ills. Not even time had lessened their grip on her, though loving Nora helped. Caring for the little girl had turned into a blessing.

Sarah caught her breath, tightened her grip on the railing. She had to keep her nanny post. She simply had to! But what could she do to secure it? Not even an apology could take back her rash words. Oh, she hated storms. And darkness. And fear. Why could she not simply be safe? And why could little Nora not be loved? What sort of God allowed such cruelty?

Her chest tightened, ached. Sarah blew out her breath, hid her trembling hands in the folds of her long skirts, counted to ten and stepped out into the kitchen.

Clayton shoved the last of the blueprints he would need for tomorrow into his leather pouch and crossed to the door. His work was finished and the study was crowding in on him. More accurately, his thoughts were crowding him. Dinner had been a nightmare of forcing food down his throat while trying to ignore the sound of Sarah's voice in the kitchen. And that glimpse he had caught of her carrying the child up the stairs—

Clayton broke off the thought and yanked the door open. He needed to move. His long strides swallowed the length of the hall, made short work of the library. He lit the lantern from a taper in a wall sconce, opened the back door and stepped out on the porch. Rain drummed overhead, ran off the eaves and splashed on the ground. So much for a walk. At least out here he had space around him.

He set the lantern on the table, leaned on the railing and stared out into the stormy darkness trying to empty his memory of the way Sarah Randolph had felt in his arms—of that one fleeting instant of trust he had seen in her eyes when she had looked up at him. He knew, better than anyone, he did not deserve a woman's trust. Deborah had trusted him and his weakness had killed her.

Lightning flickered in the distance. Thunder rumbled

in on a gust of wind. Something rustled behind him. Clayton turned. The opened umbrella he had discarded was trapped between the house wall and the table. He picked it up, grabbed the lantern and trotted down the porch steps and strode to the gate, slipped through it onto the gravel way.

Sarah had run into him right here—headfirst. Knocked the wind out of him.

We runned fast!

A smile tugged at his lips. The child was a brave one. Clayton scowled, squelched the frisson of pride that zipped through him. But the fact remained, dogged his footsteps—the child had been not fearful of the storm, only excited by the adventure. And she liked horses. He had always liked horses. Had never feared them.

Enough of that sort of thinking! Clayton leaned into the wind and picked up his pace. He had come outside to forget about tonight's events—not dissect them. He crowded under the stable's overhang, closed the umbrella and opened a door. The hinges squeaked. The roan snorted, neighed a challenge. "Easy, boy, it is only me." There was an answering whicker, low and welcoming.

The tension in his body eased. Clayton grabbed a handful of carrots from the barrel beside the door and crossed to the stalls. Both horses stretched out their necks, nostrils twitching. "Yes, I have carrots. Here, girl." He fed Sassy, stroked her velvety muzzle, patted her neck and moved on while she munched contentedly on her treat.

Pacer thudded his hoof, stretched out his head and bumped him in the chest. "I have not forgotten you, fella." Clayton scratched beneath the roan's throat latch and gave him his carrot.

Silence.

The sound of it surrounded him, emphasized by the drumming rain, the crunch of the horses' chewing. He opened the door and slipped into Pacer's stall, scratched beneath the black mane then slid his hand down over the roan's withers and back. Pacer turned his head, nudged him in the shoulder and went back to his munching.

Pain caught at his chest. *This was the sum of the affection in his life, a nudge from a horse.* Clayton patted the powerful shoulder and stepped back out of the stall. He gave each horse another carrot, walked to the grain box and sat, leaning back against the wall and studying the Wellingtons on his feet. A knot in a log pushed against his shoulder blade. He shifted his position, crossed his arms over his chest and listened to the rain.

And why would I think you would care enough to come for us, Mr. Bainbridge? You will not even look at your daughter! And, as you refuse to allow her in your presence, how would you know we were missing? We could have been trapped in that carriage house all night!

Clayton scowled. Could he find no peace from Sarah Randolph? Must thoughts of her intrude even here? It was his last haven.

Clayton jerked to his feet and paced across the carriage house. He could not escape the woman. Images of her appeared to him everywhere in the house, in the yard, even at his special, private place at the pond. Usually with her chin lifted and eyes snapping as she confronted him with some offense or other on behalf of the child. But there were those other few moments, when her eyes were warm and—

Clayton sucked in a breath and erased the vision by staring at his reflection in the window in front of him.

The woman was an annoyance. But she was excellent with the child. And she cared deeply for her—*it*. The way she had faced her fear of the storm to bring the child back to the house proved that. But she was also a temptation he should put out of his life. His attraction to her was growing and he did not want or need that complication. He wanted no part of love. There was too much pain, too much hurt when you let your heart become involved with someone. And he had already proven himself unworthy of a woman's trust.

He pivoted from the window, paced back across the dusty, puncheon floor and picked up the lantern. Trying to avoid her was not working. He had tried that this afternoon and she had ended up in his arms. He had to dismiss her. Be rid of her. It was the only answer. He reached for the door.

Nora is my charge and I am not so selfish as to put my fear above her needs.

The words stabbed deep. Clayton stiffened, tightened his grip on the bar. That was exactly what he was doing—putting his fears above the child's needs. What sort of man was he? Had he no strength of will? No honor? Sarah Randolph stayed.

He shoved the door open, stepped out, slammed it shut, dropped the bar into place and stalked toward the house, oblivious to the rain, the wind, everything but the turmoil inside him.

Wind slapped at her long, sodden skirts, whipped them into a frenzied flapping that knocked her off her feet. The planking of the deck beneath her heaved, shuddered. The ship tilted. She groped for something to cling to, found only emptiness, slid. Lightning flashed, threw flickering light over a gaping hole where the ship's rail had been, over Aaron clinging to the broken end and reaching for her. She stretched out her hand.

The world exploded. Brilliant light blinded her. Thunder deafened her. She fell—

Strong arms clasped her, lifted her, held her tight and secure against a solid chest.

Sarah opened her eyes, stared into the dimly lit room, disoriented…confused. Her heart pounded, her pulse raced, but something was different. She felt strangely calm. Why should that be? Usually the nightmare left her in a state bordering on panic. Perhaps she was finally getting over her fear—the terror that gripped her when she had almost drowned.

Shivers shook her. The calm disappeared. She would never forget the feeling of the icy-cold Atlantic waters closing over her head. Never.

Sarah pushed to a sitting position, slid her legs over the side of the bed and shoved her feet into her slippers. The storm had diminished. She could hear rain tapping at the window, but the pounding on the roof had ceased. She rose and pulled on her robe, watched for a telltale glint of light through the shutter slats, listened for the sound of thunder. There was only the rain. She took a deep breath, walked to the nursery door and peeked in at Nora. The little girl was sound asleep, her thumb in her mouth, her bandaged finger curled on her cheek.

She is so proud of that bandage. Sarah's chest filled. Her future was uncertain, but she would always treasure this time with Nora. She turned back to her bedroom, rolled up the wick on her bedside lamp and carried it to the desk. The letter from her parents Quincy had brought home with him earlier that evening lay on the polished wood. She picked it up and unfolded it, smiling as she caught sight of the salutation.

"Our dearest daughter,"

Sarah sat in the chair, pulled the lamp close and began to read. She knew what it said, had already read it three times, but tonight she needed the reassurance of their love.

The door at the bottom of the winder stairs opened, closed. Sarah lifted her head and listened, but heard no one calling. She rose, picked up her lamp and opened her door. "Did you want me, Eldor—"

She stopped, stared down into Clayton Bainbridge's upturned face. His features hardened. Her stomach flopped. "Forgive me, I heard the door and thought perhaps Eldora wanted me." She stepped back, closed her door and leaned against it, listening to Clayton's footsteps as he climbed the stairs. They paused on the landing. Her heart leaped into her throat. Would he knock? Tell her to pack and leave, that she was no longer wanted in her post in spite of the canal celebration? The door opposite hers on the landing opened, closed.

She released the air trapped in her lungs, crossed to the bed, adjusted the lamp and removed her robe and slippers. It was difficult to tell in the shadowy light from the lamp, but Clayton Bainbridge had looked angry. Was it only the late hour that had saved her from dismissal? She would know tomorrow.

Sarah sighed, slipped beneath the covers and nestled down into her pillows. She closed her eyes, sat bolt upright and stared at the stairway door. That was it! That was the difference in the nightmare. Clayton Bainbridge had kept her from falling in the water—had held her safe in his arms.

Chapter Thirteen

Clayton rode past the railed pens holding the mules and horses resting from yesterday's hard labor, stopped in front of the handler's shed and dismounted. "Unsaddle Pacer and put him in his pen and give him some hay, Murphy. I will be here the rest of the day." He handed over the reins, patted the roan's neck, then grabbed his leather pouch from behind his saddle and hurried toward the work hut. The work at this site would be finished today. Tomorrow afternoon at the latest. And then they would move to the next job.

Clayton glanced around. Workers were already hard at work cleaning up the site. Men were throwing construction debris from the bottom of the canal into skid wagons to be hauled up the high, sloping bank. On the towpath across the ditch, men with scrapers were lining up to smooth the surface. Things were moving apace.

He nodded to the men loading unused timbers onto a wagon to be moved to the aqueduct that was their next work site and quickened his steps. The canal repairs were progressing faster than he dared hope, thanks to his good fortune in hiring John Wexford. The man had proved himself wholly capable of bossing the easier jobs—and of controlling the hot-tempered, quick-fisted workers. He still had to check on Wexford's sites every couple of days, and his accelerated workload—dawn to dusk every day—was exhausting, but that was welcome. He had not had a glimpse of Sarah Randolph or the child in weeks. He left before they rose and came home after they were abed. Of course that would stop after the July first deadline. And then he would have to act.

Clayton frowned, stepped into the temporary, collapsible hut and tossed the pouch on the scarred tabletop. It still seemed the best solution would be to have Sarah take the child home to Philadelphia and care for it there. It would be well cared for—and they would both be out of his life. The only flaw in the plan was Sarah Randolph. She had not taken the nanny position to earn her living, so offering her increased wages to rear the child might not influence her to agree. If he knew why she—

Wild whoops split the air. Clayton pivoted and rushed back outside. Across the canal, the four men guiding the wooden scrapers were each urging their horses to greater speed, fighting for the lead position. In the dirt behind them were crooked grooves and ridges gouged out of the ground by the corners and edges of the wildly tipping scrapers.

Activity around him ceased as the workers stopped to cheer on their favorites in the impromptu race.

"Stop!" Clayton cupped his hands around his mouth. "You men on the far towpath—stop your horses!" His effort was useless, his order lost in the whooping, shouting din. The wild race went on. One of the scrapers slammed into another, sending it careening toward the edge of the bank. The worker hooted and urged his horse to greater speed, passing the worker trying to steady his wobbling scraper and get back in the race.

Fools. They were going to kill someone! Clayton ran to the edge of the canal and dropped over the side. Half running, half sliding, he charged down the sloping bank, hit the base running and sprinted across the canal bottom at an angle to intercept the racers, the workers he passed laughing and exhorting him to run faster. Heart pumping, breath coming in short gasps, he attacked the opposite bank, scrabbling for footing on the sloping ground, losing momentum as he neared the top.

The sound of pounding hoofs broke through the roar of laughing, shouting voices. He looked up, saw a worker rolling head over heels in the dirt, his wild-eyed horse panicked by the uncontrolled, crazily bumping and swaying scraper he pulled, bearing down on him. The scraper tilted, dropped over the edge. Clayton threw himself sideways. He flopped onto his stomach and hugged the ground. The scraper bounced, hit him in the back, grazed his head. Pain stabbed through him. Lights exploded behind his eyelids. The strength left his body, thought dissolved. Everything went dark and silent.

"Kitties are soft." Nora patted the black-and-gray-striped kitten in her lap, bent forward and placed her ear against the fluffy fur. "An' they go rrrrr-rrrrr."

Sarah laughed at the child's imitation. "That is called a purr. It means the kitty is happy." She reached over and removed Nora's bonnet. The ties were proving too much of a temptation for the kitten. One of the swipes of those tiny sharp claws might catch Nora's face instead of the bow beneath her chin.

The gray kitten, stalking imagined prey through the grass, jumped for the ribbon tie dangling in the air as Sarah placed the bonnet on the bench behind her. She laughed and lifted the wiggling kitten into the air, holding it so she could see its face. "I think these fluffy little bundles of energy need names." She looked over at Nora. "What do you think? What shall we call them?"

"Kitty!"

Sarah looked down at Nora's beaming face. How much Clayton Bainbridge was missing. For the past month he had left for work at dawn and came home after sunset. There had been no opportunity to bring father and daughter together. And it would probably continue that way until after that July fourth anniversary celebration. Three more weeks.

She sighed, pulled her attention back to Nora. "That is a good suggestion, but they are all kitties. They each need a special name—one only for them." Confusion clouded the toddler's shining eyes. "It is the same as Mrs. Quincy and I. We are both ladies, but her special name is Eldora, and mine is Sarah. And you are a little girl, but your special name is Nora." She looked back at the squirming kitten. "And I think this kitty's special name should be Wiggles."

Nora giggled. "I like Wiggles."

"So do I." Sarah pulled the kitten close and scratched behind its ears. It arched its back and rubbed against her hand. "And what about your kitty? What do you think its name should be?"

"Happy."

Sarah smiled at the quick response. "That is a very nice name." She glanced toward the other two kittens wrestling each other on the lawn. "And what about those two kitties? What shall we name the black one?"

"Fluffy."

"And the black-and-white one?"

"Bun'le."

"Bundle?"

Nora gave an emphatic nod. "Fluffy bun'les of engerny."

Oh. Of course. "Very clever. Bundle it is." Sarah laughed, leaned over and dropped a kiss on top of Nora's golden curls. The little girl was so intelligent, so eager to learn and to please. She was an absolute delight. Her family would adore the little sweetheart. And so would Clayton Bainbridge if he would—

A sudden screech of metal against metal jangled her nerves. Sarah tilted her head to the side, listening to the bump and creak of a wagon coming slowly up the road toward the house. And a rider with it. The wagon stopped out front, but the horse's hoofbeats grew louder, turned into the gravel way. Clayton Bainbridge must be home.

Sarah set the cat on the grass, rose to her feet, gave her long skirt a quick shake to rid it of any clinging grass or fur and reached for Nora's bonnet.

"Horsy!" Nora flopped over onto her hands and knees, pushed herself erect and ran toward the gate.

"Nora, wait!" Sarah rushed after her, stopped, stared. It was Clayton's horse, but there was a strange man leading him. Where was—

"Sarah."

There was urgency in the call. She jerked her head around toward the porch. "What is it, Eldora?"

"Come in, please. I need you." The housekeeper turned and hurried back into the house.

Sarah glanced from the still-open door to the riderless

horse. A sick feeling settled in the pit of her stomach. She turned and scooped Nora into her arms.

"Horse." Nora twisted round and pointed a tiny finger toward Clayton's mount.

The sick feeling worsened. "We will go see the horses later, Nora. Right now we have to go in the house." Sarah rushed up the brick path, climbed the steps and crossed the porch, uneasiness growing with every step. Maybe she was wrong. Yes, she was being foolish, allowing her imagination to run amok. She hurried through the library and into the hallway. "Eldora?"

"She said yer t' come up here, miss."

Sarah looked up. A dusty, dirty man stood at the top of the stairs. One of Clayton's workers? She wasn't wrong. Her heart lurched. Her legs wobbled. *Not now! Please, knees, do not give out on me now.* She shifted Nora onto her hip, took hold of the banister with her free hand and pulled herself upward.

"Would ya like I should carry the young'un up fer ya?" The man started down the stairs.

Nora stuck her thumb in her mouth and burrowed into the hollow of her neck. Sarah met the man's gaze and shook her head. The tightness in her chest made her too winded to speak. She continued to climb, every step making her more terrified of what awaited.

"In there." The man jerked his thumb toward Clayton's bedroom, doffed his dirty cap and clumped down the stairs.

Sarah stared at the gaping opening of Clayton's bedroom door, heard Eldora issuing orders but could not comprehend the words. Did not know who answered. She could not face another death. She could not. She tried to take a breath, gave up and forced her shaking legs to carry her through the doorway. Quincy was bent over a bed, a pile of dirty, bloodstained clothes at his feet. She closed her eyes, swayed, felt movement. *Nora.* She opened her eyes, forced away the light-headedness.

"There you are!" Eldora stepped out of a doorway on her left and waddled toward the bed. She put the large wash bowl she was carrying on the bedside table beside a stack of cloths, turned and fixed her with a look that said she would stand for no foolishness. "I need you to wash Mr. Bainbridge's wounds. Alfred has to care for the horse, and I have bakin' in the oven and food on the stove to tend." She held out her arms. "Give me the child, I'll keep her with me—leastways till Dr. Parker comes. He should be on his way if that man we sent to fetch him found him at home." The housekeeper took Nora into her arms and looked over her shoulder. "Bring them dirty clothes down to the wash room, Alfred, and I'll set 'em to soakin'. That blood'll never come out, else-wise." She padded out the door. Quincy gathered up the clothes and followed her.

Sarah held on to the door frame and fought for strength. *He is not dead, only hurt.* The reassurance did little to help. Clayton Bainbridge was as pale as the sheets on his bed. Except for the blood on his face. She shuddered, focused her attention on the steady rise and fall of the covers over his chest and took a tentative step to test her legs—moved forward with more confidence when her knees supported her. They quivered danger-ously when she reached his bed and took a closer look at him. The hair on the left side of his head was matted with dried blood that extended across his temple and covered his eyelid.

Sarah pressed her hand to her churning stomach and

glanced back toward the door. Where was that doctor? Anger surged. Eldora should not have left her here alone. She had no experience in caring for sick or injured people! She looked back down at Clayton, took a deep breath. Eldora said to clean his wounds, but what if she hurt him? She dipped one of the cloths into the bowl, squeezed out the excess water and dabbed at his matted hair. The blood was hard and dry. Her effort ineffective. She dropped the cloth back in the water and dried her hands on another. She had tried.

I'll set 'em to soakin'.

Eldora's words brought her to a halt. Sarah paused, looked back at the bed. If it would work for clothes, why not for hair? She sighed, squeezed out the rag again, laid it on Clayton's matted hair and wet another. It was not as bad with the gory wound hidden beneath the cloth.

The blood on his temple came off with a gentle scrubbing, but she was afraid to rub at his eyelid. She placed another damp cloth over his eye and dried her hands.

Sunshine streamed in the window above the table. Sarah leaned forward and peered out. Directly beneath was the porch roof, and stretched out beyond was the walled garden. So Clayton Bainbridge could see and hear Nora playing outside from here in his room. A smile curled her lips. She would remember that for when he was better. How long would that be?

She straightened, looked over at him so pale and still. How could he get better if no one cared for him? That wound needed cleansing. Her stomach rebelled at the thought.

Sarah took a breath to quell the nausea and picked up the moist cloth. Perhaps if she did only a bit at a time.

She moved the first cloth back an inch and began working at the blood at his hairline.

"You'll never get him cleaned up unless you put a little more effort into your work, young lady."

Sarah gasped, spun toward the open door. A short, stout man, dressed in a black suit and carrying a black leather bag in his hand, gave her a friendly smile. "Didn't mean to startle you. I'm Dr. Parker."

"Thank goodness!"

He chuckled. "Not used to caring for the sick and injured, eh, Miss…"

"Randolph. And you are correct, Doctor. I am a nanny, not a nurse. So, if you will excuse me?" She started toward the door, stopped when he held up his hand.

"I'm afraid not, Miss Randolph. I may have need of you."

Sarah's heart sank. She hoped with her whole being his prediction would prove false. She nodded, watched the doctor walk to the other side of the bed. He set his bag on the edge, leaned down and lifted the cloths away. Her stomach flopped. She took the cloths and dropped them in the bowl.

The doctor's lips puckered in concentration. His forehead furrowed. He reached down, palpated the flesh under Clayton's matted hair.

Sarah's knees threatened to buckle. She grabbed hold of the bedpost.

"Quite a lump there." The lines at the corners of the doctor's mouth deepened. He pulled a pair of glasses from his pocket, perched them on his rather large nose and leaned closer. He tugged at the bloody hair, exposing a long gash—and turned his attention to the eye.

Her stomach roiled. Sarah turned to the water bowl

and doused the cloths up and down, scrubbed them be-tween her hands to remove the red stains. Anything was better than watching the doctor work.

"Hmm, nothing wrong with his eye. Blood is all from that cut on his head. Strange things head wounds. Bleed like a stuck pig, but always seem to heal well."

Sarah swallowed, wished the doctor would not mut-ter aloud. She could have done without the image his words conveyed. She studied the green vine pattern that trailed around the rolled-over edge of the china bowl.

"Too swollen for stitches. Nothing to do but clean him up and wait to see if he comes around."

If. Sarah's legs trembled. She braced herself against the bedside table, dried her hands and again took hold of the carved corner post on the bed. "*If* he comes around?"

The doctor glanced at her, removed his glasses and stuck them back in his pocket. "Yes. Head wounds are chancy things. But we can pray and hope for the best."

Oh, yes, prayer. The usual balm for frightened, hurt-ing people. Anger took the wobble from her knees. Sarah released her grip on the bedpost and folded her hands in front of her. "Is Mr. Bainbridge in pain?"

"No. Not as long as he's unconscious. It may be a dif-ferent story when he wakes. The man that came to get me said some kind of wagon hit Clay in the back. I won't know if he has any injury from that until he wakes and can tell me if he has pain." He fastened a steady gaze on her. "Meantime, someone will have to stay with him day and night. He may have bouts of restlessness and he cannot be let to thrash around. He could do himself further injury."

There was no one but her! Panic clutched at her. Sarah caught her breath, cleared her throat. "Is there someone who does nursing care you could recommend, Doctor? I will pay—" She stopped as he shook his head.

"Diphtheria is going around the city. It's waning, but I wouldn't recommend you have strangers come into the house, Miss Randolph. It could be dangerous for all of you."

Nora. She could not endanger the little girl and the others because of her cowardice. Sarah straightened. "Very well, Doctor. What must I do?"

"Not much you can do. Clean Clay up, stay with him and keep him quiet. Cold cloths sometimes help with the swelling." The doctor picked up his bag and walked to the door. "If there's any change for the worse in his condition, send Quincy for me. Otherwise, I'll come by to check on him tomorrow. He comes from strong stock, and he may come around by then."

Sarah listened to the doctor cross the hall—his footsteps fading away down the stairs. Silence fell. She stared down at Clayton Bainbridge so still and white upon the bed. If he died, Nora would have no one—she would be the same as the children that filled her aunt Laina's orphanage in Philadelphia. Tears welled into her eyes. Sarah blinked them away, but more flowed down her cheeks. Fear for the toddler's future seized her, overrode her anger and drove her to her knees. For the first time since the shipwreck, she bowed her head and folded her hands.

"Almighty God, all my life I have been taught by my parents that You are a merciful and loving Father. That You hear and answer the prayers of Your children. Since Aaron's death, I do not believe that to be so." Bitterness rose, closed her throat. She took a breath and choked out words. "But my unbelief cannot change the truth.

Mother and Father say the Bible is true—and I know
Scripture says that You desire only good for Your children. Therefore, I ask You to have mercy on Clayton
Bainbridge. I ask You to heal him, not only in his body
but in his heart as well, that Nora may grow up knowing the love of her father." The anger edged back. "She
is only a baby, God. She needs him. Spare him for her
sake, I pray. Amen."

Sarah opened her eyes and rose, uncertain whether
she had done Nora good or harm. The prayer had somehow come out more of a challenge than a plea. How did
her mother always find faith in times of adversity? She
found nothing but doubt. A long sigh escaped her. She
wrung out a cloth, took a breath and began to wash the
blood off Clayton's eye.

Chapter Fourteen

Sarah wiped the last bit of red from Clayton's eyelid. Soaking the dried blood with the warm wet cloths worked. My, he had long eyelashes! And straight, dark brows—with dirt clinging to a few hairs. She scanned his face, leaned closer. And more dirt on his ear and jaw she had not noticed. No doubt because of all that blood.

She shuddered, rinsed the cloth and scrubbed gently at the dried mud, knowing she was only delaying the inevitable but unable to keep from hoping Eldora would return to cleanse the area around his wound. It was cowardly, but she kept putting off the task and hoping.

The bones of his face felt heavy and strong—so different from her own. She wiped the cloth over Clayton's rugged cheekbones, his long nose and square jaw. His shaved whiskers stubbornly resisted the cloth. She frowned and paused in her work to stare down at him. His whiskers did not normally appear in such contrast to his skin.

How would they feel? She touched his cheek. The dark stubble prickled her fingertips. Warmth rushed into her cheeks. She jerked her hand away and reached for a fresh cloth to dry his face. Worry settled its heaviness upon her. Clayton's complexion was dark and robust from working outside. How could a head injury cause such pallor? She uncovered his arms and checked his hands. Dirt was buried under his nails, ground into his fingers, palms and wrists. She soaped the cloth, washed one limp, unresisting hand, tucked it back under the covers and began on the other. Tears welled into her eyes. Clayton's thick wrists, broad palms and long fingers looked so powerful. They had been so strong when he had carried her into the house. And now—

Sarah gulped back a sob and finished washing his hand. It shouldn't be so. Clayton Bainbridge was a young, healthy man. Much younger than Aaron. And Nora needed him. She dropped the cloth into the bowl. "Must You take him, too, God?" She took a deep breath, fighting to steady her voice. "You shan't have him. Nora needs her father and I will fight to keep him for her." Her quavering words hung in the air, unchallenged, unanswered.

Sarah snatched the cloth from the bowl, squeezed it out and attacked the bloody, matted mass of Clayton's hair. She was so angry she did not even flinch when she reached the gaping wound. She snatched up a towel, tucked it around Clayton's head to catch the runoff and dipped cloths and squeezed fresh, clean water over the wound until there was not a bit of dirt, blood or hair left in it. When she finished, she marched to the dressing room, dumped the bowl, filled it with cold water and marched back. She grabbed up a folded clean cloth, dipped and squeezed it and placed it over the wound. There! He was clean and—and—*still*.

"Mr. Bainbridge? This is Sarah Randolph. Can you

hear me?" No response. She leaned over the bed, staring down at him. "Can you move? Open your eyes? Moan? Do *something?*" Sarah clenched her hands into fists to keep from grabbing Clayton's shoulders and shaking him. She whirled away from the bed and stalked about the room, quivering with anger. She was so afraid.

She walked to the door, listened. There was no sign of anyone coming to rescue her. She moved back to the bed, stood looking down at Clayton. He looked peaceful. And handsome. Softer than usual with his habitual frown erased and the tightness around his mouth relaxed. She wanted to slap him.

Laughter bubbled up, burst from her mouth. She crossed her arms over her stomach and sank to the floor, the laughter punctuated by sobs. She could not do this. She could not stay here in this room waiting for Clayton Bainbridge to die.

Her temples hurt. Sarah lifted her hands and rubbed at the pain. She always got a headache when she cried. It was so annoying, she—

Nora!

Sarah struggled to her feet and hurried to the window, drawn by the sound of the toddler's happy giggles. She shielded her eyes against the brightness and looked down into the walled garden. Nora and Quincy were chasing after kittens. She glanced up at the sun hanging low on the horizon. It was time the kittens were put back in the carriage house and Nora was— *What was she to do about Nora?*

Sarah turned from the window and glanced about the room. If she had to spend the night here watching over Clayton, where would she sleep? And what about

Nora? Gracious, what would she do about Nora? The nursery was too far away to hear her call. Oh, if only this headache would stop. She couldn't think straight. She hurried into the dressing room, splashed cold water on her face, then sat on the edge of the tub and held a cold cloth to her forehead. The pain eased, finally subsided to a dull discomfort.

Sarah hung the cloth on a brass bar and fixed her hair. She turned to go into the bedroom, stopped and glanced back at the cloth. How did the doctor know Clayton was not in pain? He could not tell them. What if he had a headache from that lump on his head? She remembered a few bump-related headaches she had when a child. One rather severe one when Mary had accidentally knocked her out of the hayloft. Of course the doctor knew best. Still, what could it hurt?

She grabbed the cloth and strode into the bedroom and laid it across Clayton's forehead. Perhaps the doctor was right and it would not help him, but it made her feel better. Now, for practical matters like sleeping arrangements and Nora's care.

She pursed her lips, pushed back a tress of hair that persisted in tickling her forehead. They would need the necessary toiletries, of course. And Nora would need cloths. And toys…books… What else? She looked at the deepening shadows in the room, glanced at the lamp on Clayton's bedside table. The lamp must be lit. She could not tend Clayton without light. And to sit alone in darkness waiting for— She shuddered, wrapped her arms about herself. That would be unendurable. But if she could not leave, how—

"How is he? Any change?"

Sarah gasped, swung around toward the door and

gave a little laugh. "You startled me, Eldora. I did not hear you come up the stairs. No, there is no change. He has not moved or spoken. But the doctor says someone must stay with him all the time, lest he become restless and injure himself further."

The housekeeper nodded, crossed to a table in front of the fireplace and set down the tray she carried. "Brung your supper. Roast beef and vegetables. There's broth for him if he wakes."

"When." Where had that come from? Sarah smiled to soften the correction. "Mother always says one should not entertain doubt."

"'Tis true." Eldora lifted the candle from the tray, carried it to the bedside table and lit the lamp. Black smoke billowed upward. She adjusted the wick, replaced the globe and shuffled to the bed. Golden candlelight spilled over Clayton's pale face and dark hair. Eldora lifted the cloth covering Clayton's wound and leaned down to examine it.

Sarah braced herself.

The housekeeper straightened. "You made a good job of cleanin' it." She looked her way, nodded commendation. "Got to go feed the others. I'll send Quincy for the tray." She started for the door.

She was not going to offer to spell her. Perhaps she had not thought about Nora. "Eldora, before you go…"

The housekeeper stopped and looked at her.

Sarah took a breath. "I have been thinking about what must be done. Please send Quincy to me when he is free. If I am to stay in this room tonight to watch over Mr. Bainbridge, I will need him to help me with sleeping arrangements. The nursery is too far from this bedroom. I shall have to keep Nora here with me."

The older woman's eyes gleamed, her lips twitched, firmed.

Sarah straightened. "What is it?"

Eldora shook her head, started again for the door. "'Tis nothin' of import. 'Tis only… The way you was speakin', you sounded like you was mistress of the house." She moved into the hall. Mumbled something under her breath.

Sarah, frowned, held back the apology readying on her lips. It sounded as if Eldora had muttered, "Grant it, O Lord." How *dare* she pray such a thing! She hurried after the housekeeper. If Eldora wanted a mistress of the house then she would have one until Clayton Bainbridge awoke!

"Eldora, wait!" Her tone stopped the housekeeper dead in her tracks. Sarah lifted her chin. "I need you to stay with Mr. Bainbridge while I gather a few necessities from my room. I shan't be long." She turned her back on the look of satisfaction spreading across the older woman's face, lifted her long skirts and sailed down the hall allowing her stiff posture and staccato steps to convey her displeasure with Eldora's attitude.

"Nanny!" Nora all but jumped out of Quincy's arms and came running across the bedroom, a big smile on her beaming face.

Sarah scooped her up, receiving a big hug from soft, warm little arms, and giving one in return.

"We catched the kitties. An' I petted the horsies. An' " Nora's eyes went wide. She stared down at the figure in the bed. "Him sleepin'?"

Sarah took a deep breath. "No, sweetie. Your papa is not feeling well, and I must stay with him." She ignored the shock that flashed in Quincy's eyes when she said "papa"—no doubt Eldora would hear of *that*—and kissed the toddler's cheek. "And you are going to stay here with me. Will you like that?"

Nora nodded, stuck her thumb in her mouth. "Does his tummy hurted?"

"No, he hurt his head." Sarah carried the toddler over to the chair by the window. "Now, you be a good girl and sit here and look at a book while I talk to Quincy."

She handed Nora a picture book and turned to Eldora's husband. "Quincy, I need you to bring Nora's crib mattress to this room and put it on the floor in that corner." She indicated the place with a sweep of her hand. "Then, I want you to bring the rocker from the nursery and place it there—beside the bed. That will be the perfect spot. I shall be able to watch over both of them at once."

Quincy nodded, ducked his head, stepped out the door into the hallway and hurried off toward the nursery. But not fast enough. She caught sight of his smile.

Sarah frowned, walked to the door and stared at Quincy's retreating back. What was he smiling about? There was nothing amusing about this situation—unless he shared the folly of his wife's wishes.

Sarah scowled, glanced back at Clayton in the bed and Nora by the window, suspicion growing that Eldora and Quincy had maneuvered her into this position on purpose. Well, she had no choice. But if they thought this was an indication of a permanent change, they were going to be sorely disappointed. Such a thing was out of the question. Her heart belonged to Aaron. She was only tending Mr. Bainbridge because there was no one else. She didn't even *like* the man. Who could abide a man who wouldn't even acknowledge his own child?

She dismissed the couple's foolishness, shook off her irritation and went back to studying the room. Had she forgotten anything? She had already gathered the toiletries for herself and Nora and placed them in the dressing room. She had brought picture books and a few of Nora's favorite toys. If Quincy would bring the dollhouse it should be enough to keep Nora content for a few days. She glanced at Clayton, lying motionless on the bed. Surely it would not be longer than that.

She walked to the bed, replaced the warmed cloth on his forehead with a fresh, cool one. Lifted the cloth off his wound.

"Nasty gash." Quincy put the mattress and pile of bed linen he carried in the corner and took a closer look.

Sarah placed a cold cloth over the wound. "I wish he would move or open his eyes or something. He is so still I keep looking at the covers over his chest to be sure he is breathing."

"He's a tough one. He'll come around."

"Yes." *One should not entertain doubt.* Sarah sighed, watched Quincy head back to the nursery for the rocker and walked to the corner to make up Nora's bed. It was not easy to believe good would happen. Not when her fiancé had been struck by lightning and lost in the ocean in front of her very eyes. Not when she had almost drowned.

Sarah replaced the cloths again, looked from her patient to Nora, who was sound asleep on her mattress. Clayton was a very handsome man, but she saw little of him in his daughter.

She frowned, picked up the wash bowl and carried it to the dressing room to get fresh water. This was not the time to be dwelling on Clayton's lack of attention or affection for his daughter. That would wait until he recovered from his injuries. She kept her ears tuned for any sound of movement from Clayton or Nora, dumped out the water, refilled the bowl and set it aside.

A quick glance into the mirror set her to amending the neglect to her own appearance. She looked tired. Not surprising. It was the small hours of the morning and she had not yet slept. She was afraid to. What if he woke, moved and harmed himself? It did not seem likely, but she was still afraid to sleep. Cool water would help. She washed her face, applied a dab of cream and tucked a few stray strands of hair back into place.

The light flickered. Sarah leaned down and adjusted the wick of the dressing-room lamp. The stained cloths she had rinsed clean and hung to dry over the edge of the tub caught her eye. She shook her head, a smile tugged at her lips. She must write her parents of her nursing efforts. They would never believe it. She was so squeamish as a child she was unable to look at a simple scratch without feeling ill. Even as an adult she averted her gaze from any sort of wound, no matter how small. Until now.

The smile faded. Sarah carried the bowl back to the bedside table, hoping all the cold cloths would help with the swelling as the doctor said. She yawned and stretched her back then roamed about the room, uncomfortable at being among Clayton's personal belongings. A frown creased her forehead. She did a slow pirouette, looking at the walls, the tops of his tables and desk. That was odd. There was no portrait or miniature of his wife in sight. Her father had—

"Unnnggh."

Sarah whipped around. Clayton was rolling his head from side to side. She gasped and rushed to the bed. "Mr. Bainbridge, you must lie still!"

He raised his hand, clawing at the cloth over his eyes, trying to lift his head.

"No, you must not move!" Sarah grabbed his hand, pulled it to her chest, pushed gently on his forehead.

He sagged back. Quieted. His arm went limp.

She tucked it back under the covers, replaced the cloth and stood there shaking. Had he been awake? He had not opened his eyes. She stared down at him, hoping he would move, terrified that he might. Oh, if only Eldora were here. But she was sound asleep downstairs.

She stood by the bed until her body screamed at her to move. She took a step, grabbing for the corner post as her numb legs collapsed beneath her.

Tears stung her eyes. Sarah pulled herself straight and made small circles with her ankles, wincing at the pains shooting into her calves. When the pains abated, she took a tentative step, released her grip on the bedpost and moved around the room.

A leather pouch full of papers someone had dropped on the floor beside Clayton's desk drew her attention. She picked it up and carried it to the cupboard by the fireplace. Clayton's clothes hung inside, his shoes and boots on the floor beneath them. Would he ever wear them again?

Sarah caught her breath, set the pouch on the shelf beside his hats where it would be safe from Nora's curiosity and quickly closed the door. The click of the latch was loud in the silence. The horrible silence of an endless night.

Sarah rubbed at her tired eyes, looked longingly at the rocker. She did not dare sit down. She was too tired. She might not wake if he started thrashing around again.

"Deborah—" Clayton rolled his head from side to side.

Sarah raced back to the bed. "Mr. Bainbridge, please lie still. You will hurt yourself."

"—died." Clayton dragged his arm from beneath the covers. His hand flopped against his chest. "My fault—my fault."

"Mr. Bainbridge, please! It's Sarah Randolph. Can you hear me?"

"Baby—" He rolled his head, the cloth crumpled into a wad. "Deborah— No…no—"

What should she do? He did not even know she was here!

His hand lifted slightly, moved toward his head.

Sarah grabbed it, held it in both of hers. He quieted. She fixed the cloth, covered his arm, pulled the rocker close and sat, too exhausted to stay on her feet a moment longer. She had to rest for a minute. Her eyelids slipped down. Her head dropped forward.

Sarah jerked upright, tried to focus. It was no use, she was simply too tired. She uncovered Clayton's hand, clasped hold of it, propped her arm on the bed so it could not fall off and rested her head against the rocker back. She should have thought of this earlier. She could sleep now. If he moved he would wake her. She sighed and closed her eyes.

Clayton opened his eyes, stared at the ceiling in the dim, yellow light. He had fallen asleep with the lamp on. He turned his head. Pain exploded behind his eyes, throbbed in his temples. His stomach churned. He took a couple of deep breaths, eased his head back to the former position. It helped. The pain was not quite as severe.

What was wrong with him?

There was a soft rustle on his left, something moved beneath his hand. Careful not to move his head, he shifted his gaze that direction. Sarah Randolph was asleep in a chair beside his bed. His heart lurched. *Why*— A jolt of apprehension set his pulse pounding, his head throbbing harder. He must be ill. He moved his hand slightly, felt a response. She was holding his hand. He must be very ill. He should ask. He opened his mouth, took a breath, then let it out slowly. She looked so tired, was sleeping so soundly. He would wait…ask… tomorrow…

He curled his fingers ever so slowly until her hand was snug in his grip and closed his eyes.

Chapter Fifteen

Clayton woke to birdsong and to pearl-gray light filtering through dew-kissed windowpanes. Dawn. His usual time to rise. But not today. His head throbbed. And beyond that pain was a discomfort, a weakness in his body. Something was wrong with him. Memory rushed back. Or maybe it was a dream. It had to be. Why would Sarah Randolph be sleeping in a chair beside his bed? He took a slow, deep breath, focused on his left hand, became aware of the soft, warm flesh it encased. It was no dream. Last night was real.

So what was wrong with him?

Clayton frowned, dredged through his memory but found no answer. Could illness cause such a thing? Could you be so sick you could not remember becoming ill? Fear brought a tightness to his chest. He fought down the temptation to seek comfort by tightening his grip around Sarah's hand. He had no right. No one knew that better than he. But he could not make himself release her hand—told himself it was only that he did not want to wake her. An excuse he could live with.

Perhaps he was trying too hard. Perhaps he would remember if he relaxed and let his mind drift.

Clayton forced down the fear, closed his eyes against the strengthening light and listened to the gentle sounds of morning's awakening. Nothing came to him but a growing certainty that he was creating a painful memory for the empty years ahead. His face tightened. He opened his eyes and slowly uncurled his fingers.

Sarah Randolph gasped. Her hand jerked free of his grasp. She surged to her feet, leaned over him and stared down into his eyes. "You are awake!"

The soft gladness in her voice, the sight of her relieved, happy smile brought a longing that stole his breath, constricted his throat. If only—

"You *are* awake?" Worry shadowed her eyes. "Can you hear me?"

"Yes." He forgot and nodded. The pain swelled, burst into splinters and speared him behind the eyes. "Ugh!" His stomach churned.

"You must not move, Mr. Bainbridge. *Please*." Tears welled into the beautiful brown eyes gazing down at him. "The doctor said if you move you could do yourself more harm. You must lie still."

The stabbing pain in his head held him mute. Clayton closed his eyes, gritted his teeth and fought a swirling darkness.

Fabric rustled, water splashed.

"If you can hear me—I have a cold cloth for your head, Mr. Bainbridge." Something cold and damp touched his forehead, rested there. "And another for your wound." The pillow beneath the left side of his head depressed slightly, cold touched the hammering pain centered there. He caught his breath, waiting for the spinning to cease, the pounding to subside to its former throb. The darkness deepened. He felt himself sliding in, reached out a hand, felt Sarah's soft hands grasp it just before he sank down to the place of unknowing.

"Hmm, you did a good job cleaning this wound. And the cold cloths seem to have helped with the swelling. It's no larger. Might even have gone down a tad." The doctor replaced the cloth, wrapped his fingers around Clayton's wrist and looked at his watch. He pursed his lips, nodded his head. "Pulse is good and strong."

Sarah folded her hands, stared at the doctor from across Clayton's bed. "And that is a good sign for his recovery?"

"It is favorable, yes." He gave her a tired smile, looked back at his patient. "You say he woke?"

"Yes. Early this morning. For a moment only."

"You are sure he was awake? In head cases like this, the person sometimes open their eyes and talks. Nonsense usually." He took a wooden tube out of his case, placed the flared end on Clayton's chest, leaned down and put his ear against the small end.

"I am quite certain, Doctor. He answered yes when I asked if he could hear me."

"That all he said?"

"This morning, yes. Last night he muttered a few words when he was restless."

"Thrash around, did he? I warned you he might." The doctor put the tube back in his bag. Pulled out a small bottle. "I'll leave this with you. Give him some for pain when he wakes up, if he wants it—but only when he's fully awake." He handed her the bottle, closed his bag.

"It makes people sleep and he's already sleeping too much, so half a spoonful should do."

Sarah nodded and put the bottle on the nightstand. "Is there anything else?"

"Keep putting the cold cloths on the wound—they seem to be helping. And continue to keep him quiet. Don't let him thrash around and hurt himself. And wait for him to wake up—if he's going to." He looked at her, frowned. "I think this household must be prepared, Miss Randolph. It is possible Clay will stay this way, even after his wound heals." He fastened the buckle on his bag and walked to the door. "If he does wake, don't feed him anything but a good strong broth till I come by again." He stepped out into the hall.

Sarah stood frozen in place, staring at the empty doorway. How dare he tell her such news and then simply walk away! How dare he say such a thing. "If he does wake." *If.* A horrible little word. She looked down at Clayton lying so still in his bed, and tears sprang into her eyes. He was so young. So vital. His whole life was before him. And what of Nora? Is this all she would ever know of her father—a lifeless form in a bed?

Death and life are in the power of the tongue...

The words of Scripture dropped into her mind—clung there. What did it mean? That she was to pray? Sarah stiffened. She knew better. The power of life and death was in a bolt of lightning, a raging sea—or a wound to the head. Not in prayer.

She turned her back on the bed and walked to the window. She looked down into the walled garden, slid her gaze to the carriage house. Memories of Nora poking a worm, chasing after animals, petting horses and kittens made her heart hurt, her throat tighten. What if the

Scripture was true? But how could it be? That day on the ship she had prayed "God save us!" and Aaron had died.

And all things, whatsoever ye shall ask in prayer, believing, ye shall receive.

A quietness came. A knowing. Sarah closed her eyes, faced the truth. Her words had only been an expression of her fear, not a call of faith. She had not believed. She had not expected God to save them. She had not *prayed*. She had only spoken empty words born of her terror and blamed God for not honoring them.

Tears slid from beneath her closed eyelids and coursed down her cheeks. This is what her parents had tried to explain to her—what she had refused to hear. But it was easier to be angry than to be honest. Easier to be haughty than humble. Easier to blame God than to admit Aaron should never had sailed out into the ocean that day. Sarah wrestled with her pride, sank to her knees and choked out words. "Forgive me, Lord. Please forgive me. And help Thou my unbelief."

She stayed there on her knees by the window, waiting, unable to rise though she did not understand why. A pressure built deep inside, grew in intensity. Words formed in her heart, rose to her mouth and poured from her lips. "Almighty God, Thou who hears and answers the prayers of Thy children, have mercy on Clayton Bainbridge, I pray. Restore him to fullness of health and richness of life for Thy glory, O God. For Thy glory. O God, have mercy on Mr. Bainbridge. Have mercy and heal him I pray in the name of Your beloved Son, Jesus. Amen."

Sarah drew a breath—a sweet breath, free of the bitterness she had harbored in her heart all these months. She wiped away the tears, opened her eyes and rose to her feet. She walked to the bed and looked down at Clayton. Nothing had changed—he was pale and still. Yet everything had changed. She knew it. Her fear was gone and in its place was a peace she had never before experienced. She replaced the cloths on his head with fresh, cool ones, crossed to the rocker, took hold of his hand, closed her eyes and yielded to her weariness. She would sleep while Eldora and Quincy cared for Nora.

"An' Wiggles jumped really, really high. Way up on the big box!"

The voice tugged at him. Clayton floated to the surface of the darkness. Struggled against heaviness, tried to summon energy to speak.

"Gracious! He must have been frightened."

Sarah. He fought to open his eyes.

"It was a big, *big* doggie! But Q'incy chaseded it away."

The child. What was the child doing in his room? Clayton stopped fighting the heaviness of his eyelids and listened.

"My! You had a busy day. But no more talking now. It is time for you to go to sleep."

Sleep? It was morning. Or had he slept the day away?

The rocker creaked, began a quiet, rhythmic movement that was peaceful and comforting in the silence. Sarah hummed softly, the sound conjuring a picture of what a family could be. Should be. But never would be. Not for him. Clayton took a long, slow breath and forced himself to think of Deborah.

The rocker stopped. He tried not to pay attention, but his will and his body betrayed him. His ears strained to pick up sounds, his brain to sort and identify them.

Dress fabric whispered and soft footfalls sounded. Would Sarah return after she put the child to bed? Or would she leave him to go through the dark night alone?

Clayton frowned, swallowed back the name he wanted to call out. He reminded himself again he had no right to keep Sarah near—that the very fact that he did not want her to go was proof that she should. He clamped his mouth shut, listened, judged direction and distance by the level of sound and followed Sarah's movements in his mind. Why was she walking toward the corner instead of the door?

"Good night, sweetie. Happy dreams."

The whispered words were followed by soft sounds he couldn't identify yet understood. The sounds of a woman tucking a child into bed. So the child was sleeping in his bedroom. He concentrated on the thought. Wondered at how little anger it provoked. He did not seem to have the energy for anger. No doubt because of the sickness. But he still knew what he wanted—no, what was *right*. What he *wanted* was wrong. He gathered his strength and opened his eyes to golden lamplight. "Miss Randolph?" It came out a raspy squawk.

There was a soft gasp, and then Sarah was beside the bed looking down at him, a smile trembling on her lips. "You are truly awake."

"Yes." It was so hard to frown when he wanted to return her smile. He needed to distance himself from her, did not want to ask her to do anything for him—but his throat and mouth were so dry his words were little more than a croak. "Water…please."

"Yes, of course." She started away, whirled back. "You must not move. It is very important that you lie still."

She disappeared. He heard her running water in the dressing room. A moment later she was back with a glass of water and a spoon in her hands. "You cannot lift your head, Mr. Bainbridge. The doctor said you could do further injury to yourself if you move. I will give you the water from a spoon."

Clayton scowled at the idea, but remembered the pain when he had moved his head and obediently opened his mouth when the spoon touched his lips. Cool water dribbled over his tongue, soothing the parched tissue. Water had never tasted as sweet. He swallowed the entire glassful, one spoonful at a time. "Thank you."

Sarah nodded and put down the glass. "Let me replace these cloths."

Before he could say no, she had lifted the warm cloth from his forehead. She replaced it with a fresh, cool one and repeated the process on the left side of his head. The throbbing ache eased a bit. Clayton took a relieved breath. "Thank you, that eases the pain."

"That pleases me." She smiled down at him. "I was not sure it would help."

He held his heart firm against that smile. "What is wrong with me? Did I take ill?"

"No, you were injured." Her eyes clouded. "You have a wound on your head."

"Injured? How did I—" A flash of a wooden scraper bounding over the earth and arching into the air behind a wild-eyed bay brought a surge of anger. *Those fools with the scrapers!* The throbbing in his head increased. Clayton took a breath, closed his eyes against the pain. "How bad is the wound?" He lifted his hand.

Sarah grabbed it, held it down. "Do not *move,*

Mr. Bainbridge." She covered his hand with the blanket. "The doctor said your wound is better. The swelling has gone down a bit. And—" She stopped, cleared her throat. "And I am certain your waking means it is much better."

Her voice sounded different. He opened his eyes. There were tears shimmering in hers. For him? The injury must be serious. His heart thudded. "How long did I sleep?"

She took a breath, blinked the sheen of tears away. "You have been unconscious, except for a few brief moments, since they brought you home in a wagon." She hesitated. He held her gaze. "That was yesterday afternoon."

"I see." He might as well hear it all. "Any other injuries?" His head pained so fiercely he had not noticed any other specific aches.

She took another breath. "You could have other injuries we are unaware of. One of your laborers told the doctor you were hit in the back by a piece of equipment of some sort, but the doctor did not want to move you to examine you while you were unconscious and unable to tell him what was wrong."

"Umm." The strength he had mustered was draining away. Clayton closed his eyes and garnered the little that remained. Other discomforts were now making themselves known. "I need… Quincy."

"I'm sorry, but I can't leave you to go after him."

The worry in her voice gave him the will to open his eyes. "I'll not…move. Please…get him."

She drew breath to speak, snagged her lower lip beneath her teeth and whirled away. He heard her run lightly across the floor, open the door to the winder stairs and start down at a hurried pace.

Chapter Sixteen

"I shall wait in my bedroom in case you need me, Doctor. It is there—" Sarah waved her hand toward the space beyond Clayton's open door "—across the landing." She glanced at Quincy, standing by Clayton's bed ready to help the doctor, bit back a plea for him to be gentle and left the room. There was no sense in giving him and Eldora fodder for their useless hopes. It was not that she *cared* for Clayton Bainbridge. It was only that she had witnessed the intensity of his pain when he moved his head, and she hated to see anyone suffer.

She left Clayton's door ajar, did the same with her own to better hear if the doctor called for her, then hovered there, close to the door, massaging the tense, tired muscles across her shoulders and listening to the faint sounds of Eldora working in the kitchen while Nora chattered in the background. A smile tugged at her lips. Nora had taken over the household. Eldora gave the toddler her meals in the kitchen, and Quincy took her to the carriage house when his work took him there—which seemed to be quite frequently of late. Her smile widened…faded. Of course, Clayton Bainbridge still held himself aloof from his daughter. But that would change when his health improved. On that she was determined.

The sound of the doctor's muttering, to Clayton or Quincy or himself, brought a shudder. Sarah moved away from the door, not eager to overhear any of his indelicate, gory comments. She walked to a window, wrapped her arms about herself and looked up at the white clouds dotting the azure sky. That one looked like a rabbit. And that one like a dog. Goodness, how one's mind wandered! She had not played the cloud game since she was a little girl. She would have to teach Nora. She smiled, leaned forward and searched the sky as she had when she was a child. But this time she sought a perfect fluffy-cloud pillow to give to Clayton so it could soothe his aching head.

"Ugh."

The utterance came, muted by distance and walls, but clearly conveying pain. Sarah sucked in a breath, abandoned her childhood game. "Please, Almighty God, help Mr. Bainbridge to bear the pain of the doctor's examination. And please, help them to not injure him further. Please do not let him be harmed in any way, Lord God Almighty, please. I pray this in Your Holy Name. Amen."

How horrid it would be if the doctor did Clayton harm. Such things happened. Sarah blinked sudden moisture from her eyes, chided herself for her cowardice and walked back to open her door a little wider. It was of no benefit to Clayton Bainbridge for her to stand around in her bedroom imagining awful things and suffering for him. She might better put this free time to good use. She took clean clothes from her cupboard and hastened to the dressing room. The doctor said his examination would take some time. If she hurried, she would have time to bathe.

That was better. The quick but thorough wash had chased away the stiffness from sitting and standing by Clayton's bedside. Sarah wound a towel around her wet hair, donned the chestnut-brown gown and stepped into her kidskin slippers, all the while listening for the doctor's call. There was only silence and an occasional murmur, the voices and words indistinguishable.

A few minutes work brushed the tangles from her hair. Sarah piled it on the crown of her head, secured it with pins and the length of red roping and gave it a last pat. She turned from the mirror and walked into her bedroom, a smile flirting with her lips. She had become quite adept at styling her hair—Ellen would be proud of her. So would her parents.

She halted on her way to the dresser, arrested by a sudden awareness of how much she had changed since coming to Stony Point. She was no longer the pampered and cosseted young woman who had arrived in Cincinnati. The circumstances she had faced—was still facing—challenged her in ways she had never imagined. And she had met those challenges. The old Sarah would have run home to be coddled. Indeed, she had almost done so when faced with Eldora Quincy's sternness on her arrival. Thank goodness she had stayed.

Sarah continued on to the dresser, took a lace-edged linen handkerchief from the top drawer and glanced at her partially open door. How different her life had become. If Ellen were here she would nurse Clayton Bainbridge and care for Nora in her stead. The maid would free her to go to town, to do whatever she chose. And

Ellen would indulge and coddle her when the nightmares came. She would certainly never make her build a fire and prepare her own tea. Why, Ellen would be outraged at the very idea. And a short time ago her own attitude had been the same.

Sarah walked to the window and looked out at the wooded hill across the road. She had been resentful of Eldora's lack of sympathy that night after the nightmare. And she had been shocked at being asked to build the fire. But the truth was, helping to make her own tea had given her a satisfaction she had never before experienced. She liked it. And she loved caring for Nora.

Clayton Bainbridge was a different matter. A frown creased her forehead. Nursing him filled her with trepidation. It frightened her. Yet, even though in the beginning she had nursed him against her will, she had come to a place where she would not want Ellen or anyone else to take her place tending him. That strange connection she felt to him had become—

"Miss Randolph?"

Sarah spun about, rushed to the door and looked across the landing at the doctor. "Yes?"

"You may take up your nursing chores again." The doctor disappeared into Clayton's room.

Sarah gathered her skirts into her hands and hurried after him. Clayton was propped up on pillows. His eyes were closed and he was very pale. They had hurt him! She drew breath to speak, blew it out again. It was not her place to know what the doctor had found during his examination. "Have you any new instructions for me, Doctor?"

"No. Continue on the same." Dr. Parker frowned, took his bag into his hand. "There's nothing to be done for Clay's head or back but rest. Keep him quiet." He dipped his head and walked out of the room.

So Clayton's back *was* injured. Was it causing him pain? Sarah stared down at Clayton. His skin was pasty white, his features pinched. He looked exhausted. Was he sleeping? Or unconscious? Or simply done in by his ordeal? She looked at his hands, limp on the coverlet, and a lump formed in her throat. He should not be like this. He should be at work directing the repairs to the locks on the Miami Canal. Or in his study drawing blueprints of the work yet to be done. He should be lifting his daughter and holding her safe in his strong arms.

Sarah blinked the film of moisture from her eyes, cleared her throat and headed for the dressing room to get cloths and a fresh bowl of water. It was all she could do to help him—to restore him to Nora. Except pray. And she would do that, too. She would pray without ceasing. And she would not allow herself to doubt. Not ever again.

It was like the thick fog that filled the mountain valleys before the morning sun burned its way through. Clayton turned this way and that, searching for a way through the cold darkness, struggling to reach the place of warmth and light. But the darkness closed in on him.

Sarah let go of Clayton's arm, lifted her weight off him and slipped backward until her feet touched the floor. Thank goodness that was over. He had been muttering and thrashing around so insistently, the only way she had been able to stop him was by throwing herself across him.

She shook out her skirts, sighed and pushed back a

few strands of hair that had worked loose in her struggle with Clayton. She missed Nora, but it was good that Eldora and Quincy were watching the toddler between her nap and bedtimes. She could never tend to both of them at once.

Sarah refreshed the cloths that had become dislodged, replaced them on Clayton's head and stood studying his face. He looked gaunt. Of course, that could be the result of the whiskers darkening his cheeks. But most likely it was weight loss. How long could he go without eating? At least he had been taking water when he was awake. She reached out and brushed the tip of her finger over the dark stubble of his beard. Did it annoy him? Or—

"Oh." Heat rushed into her cheeks. Sarah jerked her hand back and looked down into Clayton's dark-blue eyes. His clear, *aware* dark-blue eyes. "You are awake." An inane thing to say. "I mean, *really* awake."

"Yes."

Had he felt her touching his face? The heat in her cheeks increased. She wiped her fingertips against her skirt and cleared her throat. "How do you feel?"

"Thirsty."

"I have water here for you." Sarah lifted the glass from the bedside table and held it to Clayton's lips, her own parting slightly as he drank. "I am sure it is much more satisfying for you without the spoon. Are you more comfortable propped up on the pillows? Does it ease your pain?"

She frowned and clamped her lips together to stop her prattling. She always did that when she was embarrassed. She took a breath and held it. Avoided his eyes. When he finished the water she set the empty glass back on the table. "Is there something more I can do for you?"

"Nothing at the moment. And, yes, being propped up does ease the pain in my head…somewhat. But the cold cloths help the most." He lifted his hand off the coverlet toward his head.

Sarah's stomach flopped. "Do not move!" She grabbed hold of his hand, pulled it against her. Clayton went still. Had he lost consciousness again? She looked up at his face—met his gaze, and was suddenly acutely aware of their clasped hands—of the breadth and warmth of his palm, the calluses on the pads of the long fingers that were slowly uncurling, releasing their grip on her.

She looked down and yanked her hand free. It felt naked. "The doctor said you could harm yourself if you move."

"Not my arms. Not when I am awake. It is my head and back that are injured and must be kept still."

His voice sounded strained. Was he overtiring himself? Sarah chanced another look at him, relaxed in relief. His eyes now held their normal, cool expression.

Knuckles rapped softly against the hallway door.

Sarah jumped, hurried across the bedroom, grateful for the interruption that would give her a chance to regain her aplomb. "Yes, Doc—" She stared at the young man standing in the hallway, hat in hand. "Oh. I thought you were the doctor returning."

Dark curls tumbled forward as the man dipped his head. "John Wexford, at your service. The housekeeper—"

"Come in, Wexford."

Sarah glanced over her shoulder at Clayton, swallowed the protest she had no right to make and stepped back to allow the man entrance. She started to leave, took another look at Clayton's pale face, noted he had removed the cloths from his head. She left the door and moved to the far window, feigning interest in the view. With a slight turn of her head she could watch Clayton out of the corner of her eye.

"How are you, sir?"

Clayton scowled. "Never mind about me—how is the work progressing?"

"Work is finished at my present site. We will move to the upper lock tomorrow." The man stepped closer to the bed. "Your crew finished work at the lock the day you were injured, and all equipment has been moved to the aqueduct site. I was there today, overseeing the setup and the initial demolition." John Wexford frowned, slapped his hat against his leg. "That job requires close supervision, so I figure to boss your crew until you return. I set Thomas over my crew in my absence. Does that meet with your approval, sir?"

"It is your only option." Clayton's scowl deepened. "Thomas is a good man, but he has limited ability. You shall have to check the site often." Clayton's voice lost strength. The covers moved as he took a deep breath. "Keep the newly hired laborers under your control. And watch Maylor. He is…a fighter…troublemaker. He will try to run over Thomas…and you."

Sarah frowned, willed Mr. Wexford to leave. Could the man not see Clayton's pain and exhaustion—could he not hear it in his voice? She turned from the window, started for the bed.

"Thank you for the warning, sir. I will keep a wary eye on Maylor."

"Good. And do not hesitate to call upon me should

a problem arise, Wexford. Otherwise... I shall expect you to...report to me every other day. Good evening."

Finally! Sarah swerved toward the door to show Mr. Wexford out.

"Before I go, sir." She halted; John Wexford's voice held a hint of desperation. "The needed repair work cannot go forward without your blueprints. If you will tell me where to find them..."

"They were...in shack..." Clayton's voice faded. He took a breath. "In...leather pouch..."

"No, sir. They were not found—"

"I believe they are here, Mr. Wexford." Sarah went to the cupboard, opened the door and lifted out the paper-stuffed leather pouch she had placed there. "Are these the blueprints you are seeking?" She stood in front of the cupboard, which was adjacent to the hallway door, and held out the pouch as a lure to draw Mr. Wexford away from Clayton's bed.

The young man strode across the room, took the pouch and scanned the contents. "The very ones." There was relief in his voice.

"How fortunate."

"Yes." John Wexford lifted his head, smiled down at her. "Thank you for your help, Miss..."

There was an interested gleam in his eyes she did not care for. Sarah gave him a cool nod. "I am pleased to help. Good evening, Mr. Wexford." She cast a meaningful glance toward the open door. The gleam dulled. Good. The fact that she had ignored his invitation to tell him her name had not gone unnoticed. Nor had her silent invitation for him to leave.

"Good evening." He tucked the leather pouch under

his arm and left the room. A moment later she heard the thud of his boots against the stair treads.

Sarah hurried to the bed. Clayton's eyes were closed, his breathing slow and even. He had fallen asleep. She dipped the cloths he had removed in the cold water, put them back on his head, then sat in the rocker and closed her eyes. She had a few minutes to rest before Eldora brought her dinner.

Silence settled, punctuated only by the sound of Sarah's soft breathing. Clayton opened his eyes, studied her face. Her beauty stole his breath; her touch, his strength and determination. His face drew taut. Deborah's death and the child would always stand between him and any other woman. And Sarah Randolph deserved a better man than he.

Clayton closed his eyes, called back the image of John Wexford's face when Sarah had opened the door, the quick glances the young man had stolen of Sarah while he stood by his bed talking business with him, the softness in his deep voice when he spoke to her. There was no doubt the man was smitten. And John Wexford was a man of good character, with a promising future as an engineer.

Clayton set his mind against the sharp pangs of jealousy, relaxed his clenched jaw, and considered what he could do to foster a relationship between Wexford and Sarah. He would begin by extolling the young man's virtues when Sarah awoke. And by hiding his own feelings for her behind a solid wall of indifference. He would find the strength to do that somehow. For her sake.

Chapter Seventeen

"Me gonna play wiff kitties." Nora wiggled in her chair.

"Not if you do not finish your breakfast, sweetie." Sarah reached over and tapped the edge of the toddler's plate. "Eat your egg so you will be ready to go with Quincy when he comes downstairs." She cast a quick glance toward the open door at the bottom of the winder stairs. What was taking Quincy so long? Was something wrong? She frowned, nibbled at the soft corner of her upper lip. Perhaps she should go—

"That egg not t' your likin'?"

Sarah jerked her attention to Eldora. The housekeeper's expression was far too bland. It made her true thoughts very apparent. Sarah stiffened and picked up her fork. "The egg is fine." She took a bite and swallowed any explanation for her preoccupation along with the food. To offer one would do not one whit of good. The woman was determined to believe what she wanted to believe. It was most frustrating. Neither Eldora nor Quincy would accept the fact that her concern was only for Clayton's health—and for Nora's sake—that she had no personal interest in the man. No matter what she said they merely nodded and smiled at her with that *look* in their eyes.

Sarah took another bite of her egg, looked over at her charge and put down her fork. "You need a good wash, sweetie. The kitties will gobble you up if you go to the carriage house with bacon grease on your hands and egg smeared all around your mouth." She rose and wet a cloth.

Nora obediently lifted her face and held out her hands. "The kitties do this." She licked at her washed hand.

"No, the kitties would do *this*." Sarah bent and nibbled at Nora's pudgy little fingers. The toddler burst into giggles. Sarah smiled, got a towel and dried Nora's face and hands.

"Me see horsy. And me do—" The toddler bounced up and down on her chair.

What did *that* mean? "Eldora?" Sarah looked to the housekeeper for help.

Eldora chuckled and shrugged her round shoulders. "I've no notion what she means." She went back to fixing Clayton's breakfast tray.

Boots pounded against stair treads. Quincy was coming. Sarah looked back at the toddler. Surely Quincy would not allow her to do something that could be dangerous for her. Still, he might have a different idea of what construed danger to a child. She lifted Nora into her arms. "What will you do, sweetie?"

"Me do—" Nora bobbed up and down as best she could in Sarah's tight hold.

Deep male laughter erupted from behind her. "So you want another wheelbarrow ride, do you, missy?"

"So *that* is what she meant!" Sarah laughed and

turned to face Quincy. "I could not imagine…" She shook her head and kissed Nora's soft cheek. "You be a good girl for Mr. and Mrs. Quincy, sweetie. And I will see you at nap time." She gave Nora a last, quick hug and surrendered her to Quincy's arms.

Gracious! Sarah stopped beside the door and stared at Clayton. He was propped up against his pillows, clean-shaven, his hair brushed, and wearing a clean nightshirt. So that is what took Quincy so long. She tightened her grip on the tray and stepped into the room.

Clayton opened his eyes.

Sarah held back a frown. For all the improvement in his grooming, it was clearly evident he was still in pain. She could see it in the shadows in his eyes, the sallow tinge in his face, though his complexion looked more normal. And he *had* lost weight. Without the stubble of beard hiding his features it was obvious his cheekbones were more pronounced.

"Good morning." She placed the lap tray across his extended legs.

"Good morning." Clayton looked down. "What is this?"

"Your breakfast."

"Broth?"

Sarah glanced up, caught his frown. "Doctor's orders. You are to have nothing solid to eat until Dr. Parker gives his permission."

"Dr. Parker is not the one who has not eaten for two days."

Sarah let the faulty math stand. Judging from his disgusted tone, Clayton would not take correction kindly.

She shook out the napkin, spread it over his shirtfront and picked up the spoon. "Shall I feed you?"

Clayton's frown descended into darker regions. "I will feed myself—if I have the strength."

Her lips twitched. She pressed them together and handed him the spoon.

"I amuse you?" He scooped up a spoonful of the broth, swallowed it and scooped up another.

Sarah shook her head and poured him a cup of coffee. "I am not amused…exactly. I am pleased. Mother says, when a man who has been ill starts complaining it is a certain sign he is getting better."

"I see." Clayton gave her a sour look. "I shall endeavor not to improve too much."

The laughter broke free. She couldn't hold it in. "Forgive me. I did not mean—" she took a breath "—it is only…you sound like James."

"James?"

The word was a growl. Sarah stared at Clayton's face. His eyes had darkened to almost black and his lips were taut. He looked as if he could bite the spoon in half. He *was* feeling out of sorts. "Yes, James…my brother. The one who taught me to skip stones."

She studied his face. His mouth had softened, but still. "Is your pain severe? Would you like a cold cloth for your head?"

"When I am finished with my breakfast." He looked down and spooned up the last of his broth. "I ask your pardon, Miss Randolph. I should not have taken my frustration out on you." He tossed his napkin on the tray and looked toward the windows. "I should be working. There is much yet to be done, and instead I am confined to this bed." He put down the spoon and leaned back against the pillows.

She handed him his cup of coffee. "Mr. Wexford is not capable of doing the work with your help and supervision?" He met her gaze and something bitter came into his eyes. He looked away.

"Wexford is very capable—but he is a gentleman."

Sarah removed the tray. Her skirts swished softly as she carried it to the table by the stair door. "You make being a gentleman sound a disadvantage."

"Only when handling the tough men that make up our crews."

She turned back to face him. "You are a gentleman, and you handle them."

"There is a difference. I was raised here in Cincinnati, not in an eastern city." He held her gaze with his. "I am a gentleman with rough edges. Mr. Wexford is more refined than I."

His face had gone taut again. The pain must be increasing. His effort at conversation was taking a toll. "Then you shall have to help Mr. Wexford develop some rough edges, Mr. Bainbridge. But for now, drink your coffee." Sarah swerved toward the dressing room, looked back over her shoulder. "I shall be back presently with a cold cloth for your head."

Clayton scowled and watched Sarah disappear into the dressing room. *Help Wexford develop some rough edges.* She had missed his point about Wexford being an eastern-city-reared gentleman worthy to be considered as a potential husband entirely. And that little speech had cost him.

He sagged back into the pillows and closed his eyes

against the bright sunlight pouring in the windows. He would try again to make her look at Wexford with favor. Later. After the throbbing in his head eased…

"And did you have a ride in the wheelbarrow?" Sarah dried Nora's face and hands, brushed the last of the bits of straw out of her hair.

The toddler nodded, beamed up at her. "An' we founded the kitties' mommy. She does—" Nora hunched her little shoulders and imitated a hissing cat.

Sarah laughed and tugged a soft cotton slip over Nora's head. The little girl pushed her small arms through the banded openings, stretched them into the air and yawned. Sarah smiled, sat on the bench Nora was standing on and pulled her onto her lap. The toddler stuck her thumb in her mouth, leaned back and closed her eyes. Sarah dropped a kiss on top of Nora's golden curls and pulled clean stockings on over her small, bare feet.

Knuckles rapped against her partially open door—Quincy's signal that he had finished tending to Clayton's personal needs and she could return to his room. She rose. The rap repeated.

Sarah frowned. Was something wrong? She turned Nora in her arms so the toddler's head rested against her shoulder and hurried into her bedroom. "Yes, Quincy?"

"Wanted to let you know I have errands to run that will keep me busy all afternoon."

Sarah nodded. "Very well. Tell Eldora I shall keep Nora with me." The very opportunity she had been waiting for—praying for. She waited until Quincy had gone down the stairs and into the kitchen, then closed her eyes. "Please let this work, Lord. Please let Clayton Bainbridge accept Nora and learn to love her. Please—"

Do not entertain doubt.

Sarah took a breath and looked toward the ceiling. "Thank You, Lord, for giving me this opportunity to bring Clayton Bainbridge and his daughter together. He *shall* learn to accept and love her, by Your grace. For I pray it in Your Holy Name. Amen."

Sarah carried Nora across the landing and into Clayton's bedroom. Her gaze met Clayton's as soon as she stepped beyond the door. Surely he could not have heard her whispered words? Heat climbed into her face. She ducked her head to hide her burning cheeks, hurried to the corner and went onto her knees to put Nora down for her nap.

"Keep your right leg straight and *slowly* lift your foot six inches off the bed. Does it hurt?"

Sarah paused on the stairs to hear Clayton's answer to the doctor's question.

"A little."

She breathed out a sigh of relief and hurried up the last two steps.

"Do the same with your left leg."

"Ugh."

Tears sprang to her eyes at Clayton's grunt of pain.

"That one doesn't want to work, eh? Not surprised. That is a bad bruise on your back. Does it hurt if I press here?"

Sarah could hear Clayton's sharp, indrawn breath all the way out on the landing. She clasped her hands. *Please, Almighty God—*

"It's a piece of luck whatever hit you missed your spine."

"It does not feel lucky." The words were choked, breathless.

The doctor chuckled. "Nonetheless, I think you will be good as new if you stay still and let these muscles heal. Of course, that knock to your head will keep you quiet a few more days. Lump's almost gone. Gash is healing well, but there is no way to know what is going on inside your skull."

"Feels like someone is using a sledge to drive spikes behind my eyes."

Sarah's stomach turned over. She took a long breath to squelch a surge of nausea and blinked tears from her eyes.

"You will make it worse if you move around. Now let me fetch that pretty nurse of yours." The doctor's footsteps approached the door.

If Clayton saw her hovering on the landing, listening—Sarah whirled and dashed through her bedroom door.

"Miss Randolph?"

Sarah took a breath, counted to five and opened her door. "Yes, Doctor?"

"You can come back in now." He led the way to Clayton's bed and picked up his bag. "He's to stay in bed until I see him again in a few days."

"A few *days!* See here, Doc, I have responsibilities—"

Dr. Parker clamped his free hand on Clayton's shoulder. "Do as I say, son. If you do yourself harm, you could be in that bed for weeks." He glanced across the bed to her. "He's stubborn as his grandpap. Tie him there if you have to." He slapped his hat on his head and strode to the door.

Sarah glanced at Clayton's scowling face and hurried

into the hall after the doctor. "Excuse me, Dr. Parker, but what about his food? Is he to have only broth, or—"

The doctor paused at the top of the stairs and looked back at her. "No, regular food is fine. Keepin' him quiet is the main thing." His lips twitched. "I think you may have a time doing that, Miss Randolph. Good day."

"Good day, Dr. Parker."

Sarah watched him disappear down the stairs, squared her shoulders and marched back into the room prepared for battle. Clayton was sagged against his pillows, his face pale, his eyes closed. She hurried to the dressing room, wet a cloth and rushed back. She leaned down and placed it on his forehead. Her hands brushed his cheeks.

Clayton opened his eyes, looked straight into hers.

Her heart leaped, felt as if it might escape her chest. Sarah covered the spot with her hand, drew back, struggled for breath from lungs that refused to fill. "I—I have to get Nora." She groped for the corner post of the bed, turned and started toward the winder stairs, her need to be away from Clayton Bainbridge lending strength to her weak, shaking knees.

Chapter Eighteen

Sarah tuned out the murmur of the men's voices and cast a longing glance at the door to the hallway. How she would love to go outside for a walk. Of course that was impossible. But it had been so long since she had been alone. Since she had had time to think. That was her problem. She was quite certain of that. She loved Aaron. She did. So why could she not recall his face?

Sarah wrapped her arms around her waist and stared out the window. The sun was sinking behind the hill, throwing its golden light upward to outline the layers of clouds in a last defiant gesture to ward off the coming night. The lengthening shadows below the hill's crest announced it was a losing battle. It would soon be dark. She did not even shiver. She was too busy to have time to worry over the dark of night.

And that must be the reason she could not remember Aaron. She was simply too busy. The activity had chased all thought of him from her mind. Sarah sighed and closed her eyes. He had hazel eyes, with deep wrinkles at the corners from squinting out over the ocean in the sunshine. And thick, dark brows. And a neatly trimmed beard and mustache streaked with gray. His nose was long and— She frowned, pursed her lips. If she could remember his features one by one, why could she not see his face?

"Miss Randolph."

Sarah lowered her arms and turned. John Wexford stood a few feet from her with his hat in his hand and Clayton's leather pouch slung over his shoulder.

"Forgive me for interrupting your thoughts, Miss Randolph, but I am taking my leave and wanted to wish you a good evening."

"You have arrived at a solution for your emergency, Mr. Wexford?" She looked down and straightened a fold in her skirt to avoid his intent gaze.

"Yes. Mr. Bainbridge has been most helpful."

"How fortunate you have him to call upon." She looked up and gave him a polite smile of dismissal. "I wish you well as you endeavor to carry out Mr. Bainbridge's instructions."

The young man's warm smile faded. He gave her a puzzled look, dipped his head and left the room.

Silence fell. The light outside waned; the shadows in the room deepened. Sarah walked to the table and adjusted the wick on the lamp to give more light.

"An excellent man, John Wexford. Would you not agree, Miss Randolph?"

Sarah darted a glance at the bed. "I am sure he is very capable." She pushed a stray lock of hair into place and moved back to the window, unwilling to risk looking into Clayton Bainbridge's blue eyes again. She wanted to think about hazel eyes that looked at her with adoration, that made her feel comfortable and safe, not... discomposed.

"I was not speaking about work, I meant in a personal way. Would you not agree he is a very eligible bachelor who will make some fortunate lady an excellent husband?"

"Perhaps." Why did he not leave her alone? Could he not tell she was in no mood to converse? She did not want to think about John Wexford or any other man. She wanted to remember *Aaron*.

"You sound doubtful, Miss Randolph." Clayton's voice was quiet, insistent. "Have you an objection to Mr. Wexford?"

Sarah blew out a breath and pivoted. "I have neither objection nor opinion of Mr. Wexford, Mr. Bainbridge. You are a leader of men, and as such are experienced at judging character. I shall leave any decision as to Mr. Wexford's suitability as a husband to you and whatever lady you are considering as a possible bride for him."

"I was considering *you,* Miss Randolph."

Sarah gasped, went rigid. "You overstep your bounds, Mr. Bainbridge! You are my *employer,* not my father."

"That is true." Clayton stared into her eyes. "But I cannot help but notice Mr. Wexford's interest in you. And, as you are alone without family here in Cincinnati—and under my care as it were—I thought it prudent to offer a bit of guidance as to his recommendation as a possible suitor."

The gall of the man. Sarah clenched her hands. "Well, you may forget prudence, sir. I am *not* a child, nor am I your responsibility." She took a step forward, jutted her chin into the air. "And I am perfectly capable of choosing any possible suitor for myself. Indeed, I did so while residing in my father's house." *Oh, Aaron, why did you have to die? I had my life all arranged.*

Her ire fled. The starch left her spine and shoulders. Sarah blinked her eyes, turned back toward the window and stared at her blurry reflection against the darkness. "As for Mr. Wexford, he may take his interest elsewhere. I do not wish his attentions—or those of any other man."

Clayton stared at Sarah. That sadness he had noticed in the drawing room the night he had told her of his grandparents was on her again. So it had to do with a man. Who had hurt her? He scowled, fisted his hands, then slowly relaxed them. Sarah Randolph's life was not his concern. It was his feeling for her that created a problem.

He lifted his hands and rubbed at his throbbing temples. If only he were not confined to this bed. If only she were not the one caring for him. It was torture to have her so near him every day. And the *nights*—waking and seeing her sleeping in the rocker beside his bed…

Clayton gritted his teeth so hard his jaw cramped. Reminding himself Sarah was a test of his resolve did not help. And his plan to avoid her— An idiot racing a scraper had taken care of that. He threw a dark look toward the ceiling. *You must be amused at how well You destroyed that strategy, God. Were You laughing while I thought up the scheme, and the one to interest her in Wexford as well? That has come to naught, also.*

Clayton closed his eyes, hearing the fabric of Sarah's dress whispering as she moved. Those *gowns*. Their very simplicity enhanced Sarah's beauty, revealed in greater measure the grace of her movements. He tried not to, but the temptation to look at her was too great. He opened his eyes and watched her walk over to the corner, kneel down and straighten the blanket over the child. She would be a wonderful mother. If only—

Clayton veered his gaze to his open door. In the bedroom across the hall, on the far outside wall between the two windows, was where the bed had been. Deborah's bed. The one where she had given birth to the child he was responsible for—the bed she had died in. It was not there now. The bed was gone. As Deborah was gone. As his old bed was gone. He had taken an ax, chopped the beds to pieces and burned them. But the fire could not purge his guilt. The living proof of that was sleeping on a mattress in the corner.

Clayton sucked in a breath, forced himself to remember every detail of that night with Deborah. How he wished he could take back that night. But he could not. And he could not bring Deborah back. He had tried to keep her alive. Had prayed for God's mercy. Had offered himself in Deborah's place. But all his prayers, all his begging had changed nothing. Deborah had died.

Clayton's face tightened. He had to face that guilt every day. Had to endure the burden that grew every time he saw the child. But he did not have to add to the burden. And he would not. He would not allow himself to love Sarah Randolph.

"Deborah...*no*..."

Sarah jolted awake.

"...baby...mustn't..."

"Wake up, Mr. Bainbridge." Sarah caught hold of Clayton's flailing hand, held it in both of hers.

"...dead...no, take me..." He sat bolt upright in bed.

"Oh!" Sarah dropped his hand and grabbed hold of his shoulders. "Wake up!"

"My fault…"

Should she push him down onto the pillows, or would it hurt his back? She tightened her grip. "Mr. Bainbridge! Please wake up! You will hurt yourself."

He opened his eyes.

Sarah stared into Clayton's eyes, saw awareness returning and drew her hands back. "You were having a nightmare." She reached behind him, fluffed his pillows. Why was she blushing? She had done nothing wrong. "There. Can you lower yourself to the pillows, or do you need my help?"

"I will manage."

His voice was gruff, raspy. She nodded and stepped close, ready to do what she could if her help was needed.

Clayton placed his palms on the bed on either side of him, took the weight of his body on his arms and leaned backward. Pain knifed him on the lower left side of his back. He stopped the slow torture and let himself fall into the nest of pillows. "Ummph." He closed his eyes against the pain.

"Are you all right? Can I get you anything?"

"A new head and back would be nice." The words came out a little breathless, not jovial as he had intended.

"I wish I could grant your request. Or at least do something to ease your pain."

There was genuine concern in Sarah's voice. He knew it was unwise, but he opened his eyes and looked at her. "You have done more than I had any right to ask or expect, Miss Randolph. I am not your responsibility. The child is. But I thank you for your kind care. I do not believe I could have stood the pain without your cold cloths easing it somewhat." *Or your presence, which makes ev-*

erything better. And worse. Her answering smile stole the breath he had managed to regain.

"But you did not ask me, Mr. Bainbridge. I was ordered by Mrs. Quincy to care for you. And I confess to a great reluctance." She reached out and straightened his coverlet. "You see, since a little child, I have been sickened by the sight of blood." She glanced up at him. "I am quite over that now."

Her laughter was soft as the soughing of wind through the branches of trees. He would never forget it. Nor would he forget the way the dim lamplight made the golden flecks in her brown eyes shine and emphasized the shadows cast by her long, sooty lashes when she looked down at him.

Clayton drew himself up short. He moved his head to a more comfortable position and tracked her progress around the foot of his bed. "You said I was having a nightmare. Did I…say anything?"

Sarah paused, nodded. "You mumbled something about Deborah." She moved along the other side of his bed, straightening the covers as she went. "And you mentioned a baby." She looked down at him, her eyes warm with sympathy. "Nightmares are horrible things. I hope you do not suffer them often."

It would be so easy draw her close. To taste the sweet softness of her lips… Clayton clenched his hands and shoved them beneath the coverlet on his lap. "No, not often." He looked closer, noted the clouds in her eyes. "You sound as if you have experience with nightmares."

"Some." She looked away.

"From a childhood mishap?"

"No."

Her tone did not invite further questions. Intuition dawned. "From a thunderstorm?"

A shudder shook her. "I do not wish to discuss it."

Clayton gave a careful nod. "As you wish. But should you ever care to do so, I will be ready to listen. Sometimes, talking about a nightmare breaks its power over us and it goes away."

"Yours has not." Sarah offered a challenge in her stare. "Is that because what you say is false? Or because you do not discuss your nightmares, either?"

He should have let the nightmare topic die. His curiosity had him backed into a corner. But he could not lie to her. "I do not discuss it. My nightmare is true." Clayton sucked in air, spoke the words he had never before said aloud. "I made a terrible mistake. There were severe, irreversible consequences. Talking about it cannot make my guilt go away."

Sarah took hold of the bedpost beside her, blinked her eyes. "Forgive me, Mr. Bainbridge. I did not mean to bring the memory of a painful time back to you." She blinked her eyes again. "I know how devastating that can be. My nightmare is also real."

Sleep would not come. She was afraid to let it. Afraid the nightmare would come. Every time her eyelids grew heavy she got up and walked around the room. She remembered Aaron's face now. The way he had looked at his last moment on this earth—the moment before the lightning struck him. It was her last memory of him.

Sarah shuddered, rose from the rocker and pulled the blanket that covered her lap around her shoulders. It was a futile effort. The cold was inside. Nonetheless, she hugged the blanket close and wandered about Clayton's bedroom, wondering again why there were no paintings of his wife, no mementoes of her anywhere.

She strolled to the window and stood looking out into the moonlit night, mentally going through every room in the house searching for something that proclaimed Deborah Bainbridge had lived here. There was nothing. She was familiar with all of the rooms, except Clayton's study. Perhaps that was where Deborah's picture hung. Perhaps Clayton wanted it near him all day. Or perhaps he did not want to be reminded of Deborah.

Clayton had called out his wife's name while he was thrashing about in his bed. Was Deborah Bainbridge Clayton's nightmare? As Aaron was hers?

Sarah lifted the hem of the blanket off the floor and walked over to the corner. Clayton had also said "baby." Was little Nora involved in the nightmare? Was that why Clayton would have nothing to do with his daughter? And if he would not speak about it, how would she ever be able to bring father and daughter together?

Chapter Nineteen

Sarah carried Clayton's breakfast tray to the table by the stairs, came back and tugged the rocker away from the bed.

"What are you doing?"

She braced for battle, looked up at Clayton and launched into her prepared speech. "Quincy must go to the farm today, and Eldora will be putting up preserves. I will have Nora here with me. I thought it best to move the rocker away from the bed so we will not disturb your rest."

There was no display of anger. Clayton went absolutely still. His face had taken on that carved-of-stone look. She leaned down and tugged at the chair.

"Leave the rocker in place. Lucy will watch the child."

His voice was quiet, devoid of all emotion. *The child.* The words grated. As did his attitude. Anger would be better than cold indifference. At least it would show he had some feelings! Sarah lifted her chin. "Lucy is at her home. She has been taken with the sickness that is going around. And *I* am Nora's nanny." She took a firmer grip on the back of the rocker, glanced over her shoulder and backed toward the side wall.

"Stop! Leave the chair."

Sarah jerked to a halt at the barked words, looked up at Clayton. There was no indifference now. The expression on his face—the tightened lips, the pain, anger, *despair* in his eyes held back her defiance on Nora's behalf. That odd connection welled, stronger than ever. A desire to help Clayton, to see him healed. To see whatever caused him such pain erased. The longing rose, as strong as her purpose to give Nora her father.

She clenched her hands, hid them in the folds of her long skirt. Why did she have these feelings? How was she to help Clayton when her own heart was broken? What about *her* pain? Anger filled her eyes with tears. She ducked her head and blinked them away.

"The chair is too heavy for you. Get Quincy to move it."

Clayton sounded resigned. Well, she was *not*. She was grieving Aaron, and she did not have the strength to take on Clayton Bainbridge's burden. Sarah blinked her eyes clear and lifted her head. "Quincy has left for the farm."

Clayton's chest swelled. He blew out air. "Then leave the chair where it is."

"But—"

"Miss Randolph, do you not understand the roles of a servant and an employer? That was an *order*."

Sarah stared, bit back a retort. He was right. She was only a servant to him. She had forgotten that while caring for his wounds. Evidently he had not. And she had been concerned about him having a wounded heart? She ignored the pang of hurt. It was nothing but wounded pride.

"Very well." She lifted her hands from the chair and took a step back. "If there is nothing you need at the moment, I will go down to the kitchen and bring Nora back." She waited to a count of three, pivoted and sailed across the room. His dirty breakfast tray waited there on the table. She snatched it up and hurried out onto the landing before she gave in to the urge to throw his coffee cup at him, wound or no wound. It was a good thing for Mr. Clayton Bainbridge she was a lady!

Clayton leaned back against his pillows, bereft and hollow. He had accomplished his goal of distancing himself from Sarah. And all because he had been worried she would hurt herself moving that heavy rocker. He should have realized—should have challenged Sarah's pride earlier. Her stiff posture, lifted chin and flashing eyes were proof of a wall he would not be allowed to scale no matter how he longed to reach her heart and claim it for his own. All he had to do was make certain that wall stayed in place—and return to work as soon as possible. The less time he spent in her company the better.

Clayton lifted his hand and gently probed the wound on the back of his head. It was scabbed over and tender to the touch, but there was no eruption of pain, only a dull throbbing. He would not be bedridden if it were not for the injury to his back. He may not be in condition to supervise the work sites, but he would at least be able to care for himself, and work in his study. He would be independent. Sarah Randolph could return to being a nanny instead of his nurse. And he would be able to avoid all contact with her.

Clayton flattened his palms against the mattress,

braced himself and lifted his right leg a few inches off the bed. It hurt, but the pain was nothing he could not bear. He shifted his weight slightly, gritted his teeth and tried his left leg. "Ahhugh!" Pain thrust deep into his side, slashed across his lower back, agonizing and intense.

His stomach churned. Cold sweat beaded on his forehead and upper lip, moistened his palms. Clayton clamped his jaws together and sagged back against his pillows. Pain pulsated in the bruised area above his hip, traveled down his leg. For all his effort had cost him, his leg had not moved. Fear clamped his chest, squeezed his throat. What if he was crippled? That would make it certain he could not have Sarah. Ever.

"Mr. Bainbridge!"

Clayton opened his eyes. Sarah, the child in her arms, stared at him from the open doorway. He closed his eyes again, unwilling to let her see his agony.

"Sit here, sweetie."

The rocker squeaked. The blanket on his left pulled down. She was leaning over him. He kept his eyes closed.

"How can I help you?"

The sound of her soft voice was like balm, the fact that she cared, enough. But he could not tell her. He could never tell her. The wall had to remain firmly in place. Clayton rolled his head side-to-side, heedless of the healing wound, and waited for the pain to ease.

"And what is this?"

Sarah's voice, pitched soft and low—the whispering rhythm of the rocker in the background. Clayton frowned. He must have fallen asleep. He opened his eyes and looked toward the chair. Sarah was sitting with the child on her lap, holding an open book.

"A cow."

His lips twitched. The child was speaking in an exaggerated whisper. She must have been warned to be quiet.

"Very good! And what does a cow say?"

"Moooo."

"Yes. Now, what is next?"

The child twisted her head around and looked up at Sarah.

"A butterfwy!"

"Shhhh…" Sarah placed her finger across her lips and glanced his way. Her eyes widened. "You are awake." She rose, still holding the child, and stepped close to his bed. "How do you feel?"

"All right." Lamplight danced among the crests and valleys of the child's golden curls. *Deborah's hair.* He looked away, glanced out the window. The sky was gray. Layers of dark clouds foamed in the distance. "Looks as if we are in for some weather."

"Yes." Sarah took a breath. "Are you hungry? We ate some time ago. But Eldora will fix a tray for you."

Clayton nodded, tried not to notice the child who was staring down at him.

Sarah turned, lifted the picture book off the seat of the rocker and carried Nora to her mattress in the corner. "Now you be a good girl and look at your book, Nora. I have to go get your papa's food, but I will be right back."

Papa. Clayton's stomach knotted. "Take the child with you."

Sarah shook her head. "I have to carry your tray, and Nora cannot climb the stairs." She hurried out of the room. Closed the door behind her.

He was trapped! Clayton glared down at his useless leg.
"Duck...quack, quack."

Paper crackled—a page turning.

"Horsy!"

He pressed back into his pillows, closed his eyes and
willed Sarah to hurry. There were soft rustling sounds...
hesitant steps...a bump. He did his best to ignore them.
They grew louder, drew nearer. His heart thudded. Ridiculous to be frightened of a child. His blanket moved.

"Me petted your horsy."

Clayton sucked in a breath, opened his eyes. The
child was leaning against the bed staring at him, her tiny
hands holding on to the covers, her chin level with the
mattress. *How did she— The bed steps! If she moved—*
Clayton's heart leaped into his mouth. He shot a glance
at the closed stair door, looked back at the child. *Better
keep her talking.* "You did?"

Her blond curls bobbed with her emphatic nod. "Horsies are *big*." She let go of the covers and spread her little
arms as wide as they would go—teetered.

"Careful!" Clayton grabbed hold of her arm. *She was
so small.* He cast another look toward the door. Where
was Sarah? He looked back. The child was looking up
at him. There was something about her blue eyes... He
swallowed hard and held out his other hand. "Can you
climb up here and tell me about the horses?"

She nodded, slipped her tiny hand in his. His chest
tightened. He ignored the sensation, lifted her up onto
the bed and sat her down in the center, beside him, where
there was no chance she would topple off the edge.

"Horsy go—" She made a sound he interpreted as a
snort, dipped her head and pushed it forward.

He recognized Pacer's nudge. "That means he is glad to see you."

"Uh-huh. And kitties, too!" She wiggled into a more comfortable position against his legs. "Kitties go, rrrrr-rrrrr, 'cause they be happy when you petted them. And they gots special names."

"Oh." Rain pattered against the windows. A soft, soothing sound. He watched it flow together, form small rivulets and run down the panes.

"Uh-huh. They be Happy an' Fluffy an' Wiggles an' Bun'le."

Clayton's brow rose. Four kittens? He had told Quincy to take them to the farm.

"Me gots a special name. Me Nora." She yawned, stuck her thumb in her mouth and looked up at him. Blue eyes full of trust. Her eyes...

Clayton's heart lurched.

The stair door clicked open.

Sarah stepped through the door, leaned against it and pushed back until it clicked closed. She looked over at the bed and almost dropped the tray she carried. "Nora!" She rushed across the room. "How did you get up on your papa's bed?"

"She climbed the bed steps. I thought it prudent to keep her up here where she could not get hurt."

Sarah put down the tray and lifted Nora into her arms. The toddler snuggled close and closed her eyes. "I forgot about the steps, Mr. Bainbridge. I—" His raised hand stopped her apology. She searched his face. He had that stony look again. She could not tell if he was angry with her or— *O Lord, please do not let him blame Nora. It*

*was my fault. I forgot about the steps. O Lord, please,
please do not let him be angry with Nora.*

She gave the toddler a hug. "It is bedtime for you,
sweetie." She tucked her in, gave her a kiss and hurried
back to give Clayton his tray.

"Thank you."

Polite, expressionless. She could read nothing in his
voice. She walked to Nora's dollhouse, straightened the
furniture. Rain splattered the window beside her. The
tree branches outside tossed in a rising wind. Her hands
itched to close the shutters and pull the curtains, but it
was not her room and she did not dare. She finished her
work and turned her back to the window, looked toward
the rocker. It faced his bed and the window beside it.
There was nowhere for her to hide. Nothing for her to do.

Lightning flickered its white brilliance through the
room. Thunder rumbled in the distance, from somewhere
over the hill. She went rigid. The storm was coming.

"Would you remove my tray, please?"

Sarah whirled, walked to the bed. She lifted the tray
and carried it to the table by the stairs. *The stairs.* There
were no windows in the stairwell. Perhaps she could
sit—

"And if you would close the shutters, please?"

She glanced his way, read the understanding in his
eyes. She forced a smile. "Thank you. You are very
kind." She hurried from window to window, focusing
on her task, trying not to see the storm outside.

Lightning flared. Thunder cracked. She winced,
jerked away from the last window. It was coming closer.

"Come sit down, Miss Randolph."

Sarah glanced at Clayton and walked over to perch
on the edge of the rocker, unable to relax—ready to run.

"While you were down in the kitchen fetching my tray, I heard a tale of four kittens."

"Oh?" What did kittens matter?

"I had told Quincy to take them to the farm."

Oh. Had she gotten Quincy in trouble? "I apologize, Mr. Bainbridge. I asked Quincy to allow Nora to play with them. I hope any displeasure you may feel will be directed at me, not Quincy."

Something flickered in Clayton's eyes. "You are very quick to throw yourself on the sacrificial pyre, Miss Randolph. But you need have no concern for Quincy." A smile played with his lips. "I inherited him along with the property, and Quincy has his own quiet way of running things around here. I am quite certain, should I confront him with the situation, he would remind me that I did not tell him *when* the kittens were to be removed to the farm."

Light flashed through the cracks around the closed shutters. Thunder crashed.

Sarah gasped, jolted to her feet, clasped her trembling hands. How could Nora sleep?

"You see, Quincy worked for my grandparents and he considers it his 'boundin' duty' to ignore any orders I give that fall contrary to what he deems is best for this place. And Eldora—"

She could not listen any longer. Sarah took a breath, faced him. "Mr. Bainbridge, I realize what you are doing. And I thank you for trying, but distraction does not work."

"Nor does hiding." He glanced at the corner, looked up, caught her gaze and held it with his. "There is no place to run to—nowhere to hide from a...nightmare, Miss Randolph. And it seems we must both face ours today." She tensed as he drifted his gaze over her face. "What has made you so frightened of storms?"

Sarah looked away from the concern in his eyes. He had been so understanding of her moments of panic. And she *was* caring for his daughter. She owed him an explanation. She hid her trembling hands in the folds of her skirt and looked up at him. "When you were a child, did you have a dream for your life, Mr. Bainbridge?"

His countenance changed, became guarded. For a moment she thought he would not answer, but he nodded. "I wanted to be a soldier—like my father. But, having listened to stories of Indian attacks all my life, I wanted to be an army engineer so I could build strong forts that would keep other soldiers and their families safe."

There was disappointment in his voice. She forgot her own tale. "What happened to your dream?"

He took a long breath, looked off into the distance. "I became an apprentice to a highly respected engineer who became my mentor and friend—more so after my grandparents died." The muscle along his jaw twitched. "A short while before I was to leave my position with him to go in the army, he became ill. I delayed my departure and took over his work. His health failed quickly, and I promised, on his deathbed, to give up my dream of being a soldier and instead—" He shook his head. "I am going astray. We were speaking about childhood dreams. Mine did not come to pass." His gaze came back to her. "What was your dream?"

Sarah took a breath, forced out the words. "My father owns a shipping line and I grew up listening to talk of faraway places. My dream was to marry the captain of one of Father's ships and sail with him around the world on   " her voice broke "—on our honeymoon."

"And you found your ship's captain." Clayton's face went still.

She nodded. Lightning glinted. Thunder cracked. She gave a soft cry, hid her face in her hands and whirled away from the bed. Clayton's quick grasp on her arm stopped her from running for the stairwell.

"You have nothing to fear, Miss Randolph." His calm, deep voice washed over her. "You are with me, and—"

"And I was with Aaron also!" She yanked her hands from over her eyes, stared at him. "We were betrothed, and I felt safe with him. But—" She stopped, drew a long quivering breath and sank into the rocker. "We were to have married last Christmas. And to have set sail on our honeymoon voyage shortly after the first of the new year."

"But that did not happen."

How calmly he stated the fact.

"No." She looked down, smoothed a fold from her skirt. "Last October I went to Boston to visit my friend Elaine and engage her in the wedding plans. Father had ordered a new ship built at her father's shipyard. It was near completion. Plans were made for Aaron and his crew to come to Boston and sail the new ship home to Philadelphia." Her throat closed. She rose, walked to the bedside table and poured a glass of water.

"And he did not come?"

The words were gently spoken, but offensive nonetheless. "Of course he came!"

Lightning snapped. A sulfurous light invaded the room.

Sarah shivered, wrapped her arms about herself and hurried away from the window.

"What happened?"

She glanced over her shoulder at him. "Elaine and I were to travel home with him. But Elaine became ill. I had wedding preparations to make that could not await a more opportune time, and so, as it was only a day's sail down the coast and I was expected home, I joined Aaron aboard ship."

Her chest tightened. She could feel her face drawing taut. She turned away from his penetrating gaze. "It was a beautiful day, but as we were boarding a-an elderly sailor on the dock warned Aaron not to sail. He said there was a bad storm brewing." The pressure in her chest increased. That familiar cold hand squeezed her lungs.

"And he was right."

Another calm statement of fact.

She turned to face him, to defend Aaron against any blame. "The storm came out of nowhere. One moment the skies were blue and the sun was shining, and the next moment dark clouds rolled across the sky and shut out the light." Her voice quavered.

She moved forward, took hold of the bedpost and fought for breath. "Aaron tried to head for the open sea and outrun the storm, but the wind tore the sails to shreds. Waves, high as this house, threw the ship around like—like a toy. It plunged toward huge rocks in shallow water and there was nothing he could do. He—he ordered two of the crew to take me to the dinghy."

She stared off into the distance, lost in the horror of that day. "The rain came so thick and fast, breathing was almost like drowning. And the wind—it was impossible to stand. The sailors tried to hold me upright, but the ship was pitching so violently it tossed us about and I was wrenched from their grasp. I... I slid toward the side of the ship. I heard Aaron shout, and then—and then the lightning—"

A deep shudder shook her. She closed her eyes. "There was a h-horrible crack, and the deck in front of me disappeared. There was only a black h-hole and I could not stop sliding. And then I saw Aaron." The strength left her legs. She sagged against the bed. "He was clinging to the end of the broken rail and stretching his hand out to me. I... I reached for him but the lightning struck again. Aaron...the deck...everything vanished. I fell into the water. It was so c-cold and dark..."

She opened her eyes, stared down at Clayton's hand gripping hers, felt the strength and warmth of it. How had that happened? Had she reached out to him? She sighed, too emotionally spent to be embarrassed, too needy of his comfort to slip her hand from his, though she should.

"Thank God you were saved, Sarah." His grip tightened on her hand. "Forgive me. I should not have asked you about such a harrowing experience."

"You could not know." She gathered her inner fortitude and slipped her hand from his. Her remaining strength seemed to ebb with the broken contact. She glanced at the rocker, took hold of the corner post and started around the foot of the bed. She needed to sit down, before she collapsed in a weary heap on the floor. "When I awoke, I was in the dinghy. The skirt of my gown had caught on a piece of broken deck floating on the water, and two sailors saw it. They pulled me from the water and were able to get the dinghy over the rocks and into a small cove." Her lips trembled. She sank down into the rocker and closed her eyes. "We three were the only ones who survived. The sailors went on to Philadelphia, and a family who lived in the cove took me in until Father came for me."

Tears slipped from under her eyelids and ran down her cheeks. "The lightning struck Aaron, and the sea he loved claimed him. He, and my dream, died that day. But my heart remains loyal to him. I want no other…"

Clayton lay studying the ceiling over his head. The storm had played itself out. All was quiet, except for an occasional grumble of thunder in the distance.

He glanced at Sarah, asleep in the rocker. Telling him her story had exhausted her. But she had seemed calmer for having unburdened herself to him. He hoped he had helped to chase her nightmare away forever.

Clayton shuddered, cold knots forming in his stomach. It had been such a close thing. If her skirt had not caught on the jagged edge of that broken-off piece of the ship… If those sailors had not seen it through the rolling, crashing waves of the storm-tossed ocean and pulled her into their dinghy, she would have been lost forever. Swallowed by the sea along with her fiancé.

His hands flexed. He ached to wake her and tell her he loved her. But he was destined to remain silent.

…my heart remains loyal to Aaron.

Clayton compressed his lips, held back a bitter laugh. His struggles to deny his love for Sarah, to distance himself from her, were all for naught. Even had he yielded to his feelings for her and tried to win her for his own, it would have been useless. She loved another, though he was gone. He had been torturing himself needlessly. He closed his eyes and waited for sleep to claim him.

Chapter Twenty

Nora dropped her doll, gripped the windowsill and went on tiptoe. "Me go outside?"

Sarah shot a quick glance at Clayton. It was difficult keeping Nora quiet all day. But after yesterday's episode of the toddler's invasion of her father's bed, she dared not take the chance of offending him. "Not now, sweetie. Quincy is busy. Shall we look at a book?"

Nora's lower lip pouted out. She shook her head. "Me go see horsy." Her little chin quivered.

Oh, Nora, please do not cry! Sarah scooped her up into her arms and turned away from the window. "Can you find the horse in the book for me?"

Golden curls swung from side to side. The little lip protruded farther. Sarah's heart sank. Nora was not going to be easily distracted from her goal.

"Go see horsy. An' kitties."

Sarah kissed Nora's cheek. "I cannot take you outside right now, sweetie. Your papa—"

"Is fine."

Sarah turned toward Clayton.

"Take Nora outside, Miss Randolph. She wants to see the animals."

Nora. He had called her by name. Sarah squelched her elation. "But you may need something, and—"

"And if I do, I shall call for you. There is a bell on the table by the bed in the bedroom across the hall—bring it to me. The windows are open. You will be able to hear the bell from the garden."

Was he being considerate of Nora's wants—or did he want to be rid of her? Anger stiffened Sarah's spine. "Very well. I will be a moment. I have to also fetch Nora's bonnet." She turned toward the door.

"There is no need for you to take Nora. You will accomplish your tasks more quickly without her."

Sarah froze, her heart in her throat. *Had she heard him correctly?* She turned back, looked at Clayton.

"She will be safe here on the bed."

His voice was cool, his face impassive. Still... "Of course." Sarah held her own face expressionless, lowered Nora to the bed and forced herself to walk calmly from the room. She crossed the hall at the same sedate pace, entered the other bedroom and closed the door. The click of the latch set her free. She burst into laughter, spread her arms wide and whirled about the room, unable to contain her joy. "Thank You, Lord. Oh, thank You! You heard my prayers. You are giving Nora her father!"

Tears filmed her eyes. Sarah blinked them away and stopped her impromptu dance. She had to hurry back. She looked about the room. A bed, garbed in a woven tester and coverlet, the soft-blue color of the room's plastered inner walls, sat between two windows in the stone wall opposite the door. A brass bell sat beside a lamp on the table by the bed. She picked it up, jumped at its sudden sharp clang, clamped her other hand over it to stop its ringing and left the room.

The bell. He hated that sound. Clayton closed his eyes, fought an onrush of painful memories.

"Does your head hurted?"

"Only a little." He opened his eyes. The child was on her knees, staring up at him. His heart jolted, just as it had last night. He had not been wrong. She had his grandmother's eyes. And mouth. In fact, except for her coloring and curly hair—which were Deborah's— she could be a very young Rose Bainbridge. His heart squeezed, his chest filled. He had always thought of Nora as Deborah's child—when he was forced to think of her at all—but she was part of him. His daughter. Rose's great-granddaughter.

"Me make it better."

Before he realized what she was about, Nora placed her small hands against his chest, stood and kissed his forehead. Emotion rocketed through him, too complex, too mysterious to be defined, and he knew he would never be the same. His life had changed forever. This tiny waif in his arms suddenly owned him, body and soul. He pulled her close, kissed the soft, silky skin of her cheek. She slipped her little arms around his neck, hugged hard, then pushed back and looked at him. "Me make it better?"

Clayton blinked the tears from his eyes and cleared his throat. "Yes, you did. Thank you." *And I promise you, everything is going to be better from now on.*

Nora nodded and plunked down on his lap. "Me gonna go see horsy."

"So I understand. Will you give Pacer and Sassy a carrot for me?"

"Uh-huh. But not the kitties. Me gives kitties milk, an' soup, 'cause they go—" She stuck out her tongue and lapped at the air.

Clayton laughed, filled with sudden paternal delight at her precocity.

"What is so amusing?"

He looked up. Sarah stood in the doorway, smiling at him. His heart constricted. His mouth went dry. He looked away before she could read in his eyes what was hidden in his heart. His gaze fell on the bell in her hand. Deborah's bell.

Everything rushed back. Guilt stabbed his heart, soured his stomach. Clayton shook his head. "Nothing, really. It is only that I am learning what an unending source of information a child can be. For instance—it seems Quincy is feeding the kittens from the kitchen instead of letting the mother cat teach them to be proper barn cats that hunt for their food."

Sarah's smile disappeared. "I found the bell." She walked to the bed. "I will put it right here where you can reach it." She set it on the edge of the bedside table, turned and slipped the bonnet she held over Nora's curls. "Come, Nora, we will go outside and let your papa rest." She lifted the toddler into her arms and left the room.

His arms felt empty, his heart desolate.

Clayton stared down at the bed. This could not go on. Every day ate away at his resolve. He had to get out of this house! He set his mind against the void in his heart and threw back the covers. He gritted his teeth, braced his palms against the mattress and strained to lift his left leg. Daggers pierced his side, searing heat coursed down his leg. The agony was worth it. His foot had come off the bed. Not far. But it had definitely risen off the bed.

Clayton wiped the beads of cold sweat from his brow and sagged back against the pillows to gather his strength for the next try.

The room was barren. The mattress gone from the corner. The rocker and toys returned to the nursery. He had told Quincy to take them away after supper. A mattress on a floor was no place for a child to sleep. And a rocking chair no bed for Sarah. It was the right thing to do. But his heart ached nonetheless. His only connection to Sarah now was the bell.

Clayton stared at the dim area beyond his open door. The landing at the top of the winder stairs, lit only by the light flowing out from his room and Sarah's room on the other side—her door open to hear his call should he need her.

Need her? He was dying inside for want of her in his life. But that would stop now. She would no longer be caring for him day and night. He would see her as little as possible from now on. And when the strength returned to his injured muscles, not at all. Except for that celebration boat ride up the canal on July fourth. But, even on the packet, she would be busy caring for Nora, and he should not find it hard to avoid her company. He would manage some way.

Clayton scowled, picked up the book he was pretending to read and stared at the printing on the pages.

Sarah lifted Nora from the tub, dried her off and pulled the nightgown with tiny embroidered flowers on the smocking over her head. She had rejoiced too soon. Clayton Bainbridge had shoved his daughter out of his life as soon as he was able. Well, she would see about that! She brushed the tangles from the toddler's damp curls and lifted her off the small bench. "All right, sweetie, time for bed."

"Me see Papa?"

"Yes. You will see your papa tomorrow." She carried Nora toward her crib, swerved and headed for the rocker, back now in its customary place on the hearth. She did not want to let go of Nora yet. She would hold her for a little longer. She sat and cuddled the toddler close, hummed softly.

"Wiggles scratcheded me." Nora offered her arm for inspection.

"I know, but he did not mean to hurt you." Sarah kissed the red mark on the pudgy little wrist. "There. All better."

Nora yawned, wiggled closer. "Me made Papa's head better."

Sarah froze in midrock. "What did you do?"

"Me made... Papa's...head better..."

Sarah looked down. Nora's eyes were drooping. No. *Do not sleep yet, Nora.* "You kissed your papa's head?" She held her breath.

Nora's head moved up and down against her breast in a sleepy nod. She stuck her thumb in her mouth. Her eyes closed. Sarah released her breath, stared down at the smudge of brown lashes against round, rosy cheeks, the tiny nose, the soft pink mouth circling the small thumb. Why, you little sweetheart! She laughed softly, rested her head back and resumed rocking. She should have known Nora would not need her help to capture her father's heart.

Thought of Clayton brought the worry that had been haunting her leaping over the barrier she had raised against it. Was he all right? She frowned, rose and carried Nora to her crib, tucked her in and lowered the wick in the lamp. Clayton Bainbridge was no longer her concern. And he certainly did not want her fussing over him. He had dismissed her nursing services and rid himself of her presence at the first possible moment. His wishes could not be more clear. And she was thankful to be rid of the responsibility of his care. He meant nothing to her. Her concern for him was merely habit.

My, it was quiet.

Sarah closed the shutters, adjusted the slats to let in the warm night air and looked around the room. Everything had been put back in its place. It was good to have things settled again. She walked into her bedroom, glanced toward the landing. The lamp was burning bright in Clayton's room. He must be reading. He had requested several books from the library earlier.

She went to the cupboard in the fireplace nook and took out a nightgown, her robe and slippers. Should she change into them? What if he needed her during the night? That did not seem likely. He did not wake and thrash around anymore. It had been she that needed him yesterday, during the storm. He was very wise. She had taken his advice and it truly had helped to talk about what had happened to Aaron and to her. Last night was the first time she had slept through the night since that tragic day. And it had nothing to do with Clayton Bainbridge holding her hand. It was the unburdening of her spirit that helped. Still, he had been kind and understanding.

Sarah worried the soft cotton fabric of her nightclothes between her fingers and looked at the door. Perhaps she should go and see if he needed anything before she retired. She tossed the clothes on her bed, walked to the door and stepped out onto the landing. The light in Clayton's room dimmed and went out. She stopped, took another step, listened. Nothing but silence. He had no need of her.

A wave of emotion, a horrible feeling she did not understand, swept over her. She felt...*rudderless*...like one of her father's ships adrift on the ocean without course or direction.

She blinked and dragged in a deep breath. There was something horribly wrong with her tonight—but she would be better tomorrow. Yes. Everything would be better tomorrow. And right now the best thing for her to do was have a good wash and go to bed. She turned and went back into her room.

That was close. Too close! Clayton scowled into the dark. He had turned his lamp down just in time. Sarah moved so softly, if it were not for that squeaky board on the landing he would not have known she was coming until it was too late to feign sleep. And he was not at all sure he would have the strength to tell her he did not need her. He never had been a good liar.

Chapter Twenty-One

"Hmm, the bruise looks better. Still have a hard lump here above your hip bone though."

The doctor's fingers prodded his flesh. "Ugh." Clayton scowled, gritted his teeth.

"Still tender, eh? How's the head?"

"Fine. No pain at all."

"Good, good." Dr. Parker moved toward the foot of the bed. "You say you can lift your foot now?"

"Yes." Clayton braced himself for the test that was coming.

"Lift it up."

He held his breath, lifted his left foot, held it there, muscles quivering, until the doctor nodded.

"Good. You are doing better than I expected."

The doctor gave him an assessing look. Clayton relaxed his clenched jaw, smiled—though he feared it was closer to a grimace.

"Think you can swing your legs over and sit on the edge of the bed?"

"Doc, if it will get me out of this bed, I will do a somersault."

Dr. Parker chuckled, moved up closer to the head of the bed. "All right, then…easy now."

It took everything he had, but Clayton managed to move his legs to the side of the bed and hang them over the edge. He gave the doctor a crooked grin. "Victory."

Dr. Parker grinned back and gave him a clap on the shoulder that almost toppled him from the bed. "You're as tough as your father was, Clay. Now where is that cane your grandpap used when his rheumatism outdid his stubborn?"

Clayton's heart leaped. "In the cupboard by the fireplace—leaning in the back corner."

The doctor nodded, walked to the cupboard and got the cane. "I'll have your word that if I let you out of bed, you will not try it on your own. You only get up when Quincy is about to help you. A fall could do you a lot of harm."

"I understand."

"All right, then. Put your hands on my shoulders, brace your weight on me, and slide forward till your feet touch the floor. Good thing you got them long Bainbridge legs. You could never navigate them bed steps with a cane."

Clayton did as ordered. His leg threatened to collapse under him when he stood, but he willed it to hold.

"Rest a bit, then we will walk to the chair there by the window—one step at a time, and rest in between."

It took four steps with Dr. Parker's help to cover what was normally one stride for him, but he made it.

"Rest a few minutes, son, then we will get you back in—"

"Doc! Doc!" A boy burst in the room, laboring for breath.

"What is it, Willy?"

"It's Pa…he fell out the…haymow. He ain't movin'. Ma said I should…come fetch you back with me."

"Sorry, Clay, I have to go." The doctor picked up his bag, slapped on his hat and hurried for the door. "I'll tell Eldora to send Quincy up to help you back to bed."

Footsteps clattered down the stairs. Clayton blew out a breath and stared at the bed, which suddenly looked a mile away. Quincy had gone to help Zach Miller with a sick mare. And there was no telling when he would be home. He looked down at the cane in his hand and shook his head. "Looks as if it is you and me, Grandpa."

"Mr. Bainbridge."

Sarah. Clayton looked up, heart pounding. She was standing in the doorway to the winder stairs landing.

"Quincy is away, I have come to help you back to bed."

He stared, drinking in the sight of her—her slender form, her beautiful face, her light-brown hair piled high on the crown of her head. His mouth went taut, the knuckles on his hand gripping the cane went white. He was starved for her presence, and a man had only so much strength. He had already proven he was weak, and if he put his arm around her… He breathed deep, shook his head. "You are too slight, Miss Randolph. Your strength is insufficient."

She stared at him. His heart thudded, his pulse roared through his veins. He forced himself to look away, focused on her hand gripping the door latch. Remembered the soft warmth of it in his.

"We do not know when Quincy will return."

He nodded, stared down at his hand on the cane.

"Nonetheless, I will wait. You may return to Nora." He put dismissal in his voice.

"Very well."

Her skirts rustled softly. The sound drew nearer. The scalloped hem of her dark-blue gown brushed against his leg. He clenched his jaw, stared at the cane.

"Here is the bell." There was a clang as she placed it on the chest beneath the window beside him. "Should Quincy tarry, and you tire, I will be in the garden with Nora."

Her skirt billowed, disappeared from his view. He kept his gaze fixed on the cane until he heard her going down the stairs. When he heard the murmur of voices from the kitchen, he put his free hand on the chest, tightened his grip on the cane and pushed to his feet. His left leg quivered. He took his weight on his right leg, set his jaw and moved the cane forward. *Well, this is it. Sorry, Doc. I have no choice.* He let go of the chest, shifted his weight onto the cane, swung his left leg forward, and stepped forward with his right. He paused, stood there on his right leg, using the cane and his weak left leg for balance, and rested. One step accomplished—three to go.

"Diphtheria." James Randolph stopped pacing and looked at his parents. "I shall leave for Cincinnati immediately and bring Sarah home."

"No, James." Elizabeth smiled at the son, who was so like his father, but made her voice firm. "Your father and I agreed that we would trust Sarah to the Lord's care."

"So I did, Elizabeth, but diphtheria…" Justin Randolph scowled, clasped his hands behind his back and rocked forward on his toes. "I agree with James, I think we have to get Sarah out of that city."

Elizabeth shook her head, tapped the letter in her hand. "Sarah says the epidemic is on the wane. And time has already passed since she wrote the letter. By the time James arrived the epidemic would be over and all danger would have passed. And Sarah is needed to care for the little girl and, now, to nurse Mr. Bainbridge."

Justin's scowl darkened. "Common sense—most frustrating at a time like this. But, you are right, my love—" his scowl turned to a smile "—as usual."

"I could go to Cincinnati and care for the toddler." Mary cast a hopeful look at her father. "That will ease Sarah's burden. And I am good with children. Aunt Laina says so."

"No, Mary." Justin's voice was firm. "It is good of you to be concerned for your sister, but one daughter so far away is enough. You will stay here. Though your idea is a good one. I will send Ellen back."

Elizabeth looked at him.

Justin gave an exasperated growl. "You know how Sarah sickens at sight of the slightest injury, Elizabeth. Ellen can nurse the man and—"

"And destroy what the Lord may be doing, not only in Sarah's life, but in Mr. Bainbridge's and the child's, as well?" Elizabeth placed her hand on her husband's arm, looked at her children. "I know you all want to protect and help Sarah—as do I. But can you not see, bringing her home or easing her burden would be doing her a disservice."

"Mother, you always think the Lord is in everything that happens to one of us." Mary shrugged her shoulders. "Sometimes things simply happen."

Elizabeth eyed her daughter. "Mary, Sarah, our *Sarah,* is nursing Mr. Bainbridge. She has cleansed his wound, and cared for him day and night. And she is caring for the child, as well, because there is no other to assume the tasks. And she is praying for Mr. Bainbridge's recovery and asks us to pray for him. And to continue praying that God would unite father and daughter. You do not see the Lord's hand in all of that?"

Tears filled Elizabeth's eyes. "Sarah is *praying*. She is returning to her faith. And I believe the Lord—in His own mysterious way—is answering her prayers. And ours. And those of Mr. Bainbridge's housekeeper and her husband. '*Grant it, O Lord*.'" She laughed in sheer delight at the story Sarah had related in her letter, of Eldora's attitude and prayer. "Sarah is furious with the two of them. And, I believe, it is because she has growing feelings for Mr. Bainbridge and is frightened by them. But that will pass when the Lord has His way."

Elizabeth looked at her family, saw agreement in her husband's eyes, doubt in James's, and rebellion in Mary's. *If only you could deposit your own faith in your children.* She sighed and continued her explanation. "I see God's hand very clearly in this situation. I believe He has used the unfortunate circumstances of Sarah's grief over Aaron, Mr. Bainbridge's accident and the diphtheria epidemic to force them and the child into a…a *cocoon* of closeness that can bring about healing for them all." She looked up at her husband. "Would you send Ellen to free Sarah from her nursing duties and perchance destroy what the Lord is doing?"

Sarah grabbed her straw hat, plunked it on her head and hurried down the winder stairs. She had listened to Nora's chatter and Clayton's deep-voiced responses long enough. She would follow his suggestion and go for a walk.

She stepped out into the kitchen, redolent with the scents of a meal in progress, and strode to the door. "I am going for a walk, Eldora. I shall return shortly."

"No need t' hurry." The housekeeper buried her hands in the ball of dough on the table and pushed. "Now that Lucy's back, she can answer the bell and take care of things."

Yes. So I have been told. Sarah nodded and stepped outside. Rays of golden light beamed down from a sun riding high in a cloud-dotted, bright-blue sky. A breeze whispered through the air to rustle treetops. It was a perfect summer day.

She walked out the gravel way, glanced at the town and turned to follow the road up the hill. She was in no mood for people. She wanted to throw stones across a pond and cause the smooth, serene surface to splash and ripple. What she *really* wanted was to cause a ripple on Mr. Clayton Bainbridge's serene countenance. The man had no emotions! Except when it came to Nora.

Sarah slowed her ground-eating pace. It was amazing how Clayton had changed about his daughter. He spent time with her every morning and afternoon. And Nora loved being with her papa. And she was happy for Nora. She truly was. She was thrilled the little girl had her father's love and attention. It was only… Only nothing!

She glanced at the road ahead and turned down the path to Clayton's private place. She settled her straw hat firmly on her head and stayed as far away from the thornapple trees as possible. Tears filmed her eyes. She hurried past the spot where she had become entangled— where Clayton had freed her—and broke out into the open glade. The pond glistened in the sunshine, peaceful and calm. She gathered a few stones, walked to the large boulder and sat down. All desire to throw a stone into the smooth surface disappeared. She turned the stones over in her hand, studying the coloring and veining that made each unique.

Why was she excluded from Clayton's time with Nora? Why did he now call on Lucy if he had a need? He had banished her from his life. What had she done to make him so repulsed by her presence? And why did it matter so much?

Sarah lifted her gaze and stared at the water. Perhaps it was time to think about going home. She had accomplished her goal. Not the one for herself—she had come to escape grief and now suffered a greater hurt—but she had accomplished the purpose she had found on her arrival. Clayton loved his daughter. Nora had her papa. Yes. Perhaps it was time to go home.

She sighed, rose and walked to the water's edge. As soon as Clayton was completely healed and his life had returned to normal she would tell him she wanted to go back to Philadelphia. She would wait until then. For even though he no longer had need of her care and did not desire her company, she could not bear to go until she knew he was all right.

Tears flowed down her cheeks. Sarah dropped the stones into the water, lifted her hands and wiped them away. But still they came, faster and faster as the hurt in her heart grew and spread like the ripples on the water. She was unable to stem the tears, unable to restrain the sobs that burst from her throat in broken gasps. What had happened to her? She did not want to go back home. Did not want to leave Stony Point—or Eldora and

Quincy. And Nora. Oh, how could she endure to leave Nora? And—

Sarah caught her breath, refusing to think further, to give words to the ache in her heart. She looked down and studied the stones at her feet, picked up a small, smooth gray one and clasped it tight in her hand. It was a fitting symbol of Stony Point. She would keep it with her always. And whenever she looked at it she would remember.

Chapter Twenty-Two

"Here is the thread you asked for, Eldora. And I have something else for you." Sarah handed the housekeeper a paper-wrapped parcel.

"A present?" Eldora frowned. "There ain't no reason for buying presents." She picked up a knife and cut the string.

Only that I will soon be leaving. "I know, but I saw it in Mrs. Avis's store window and—" Sarah stopped at the housekeeper's gasp. "I hope you like it. I thought it would look lovely with your gray church dress."

Eldora lifted the black knit shawl out of the paper, fingered the wide lace edging. "I ain't never had nothing so fine as this."

"Then it is time you did." Sarah smiled at Eldora's pleasure. It took some of the sadness away. "And here is something for Quincy." She handed her a penknife with a bone grip. "I know little of such things, but I am assured by Mr. Jackson that it is a knife of finest quality. I hope Quincy will find it useful." *And that you will both remember me when I am gone.*

"Oh, my." The housekeeper turned the knife over in her hands, looked up. "Sarah, what—"

"Me gots a puppy!"

Sarah looked toward the door as Nora burst into the kitchen. Her gaze met Clayton's. He stopped in the doorway. She jerked her gaze to Nora, knelt to catch the excited toddler in her arms. "What is this?"

The toddler threw her arms about her neck and squeezed. "Papa gots me a puppy!" She leaned back, grabbed her fingers in her small hand and tugged. "Come see!"

"I would like to, sweetie, but…" She looked toward the door. Clayton was gone. And Eldora was watching. She fixed her mouth in a smile and kept her eyes down so the housekeeper could not read the hurt in them. "All right. I will come see your puppy." She took Nora's hand and walked outside.

"Hurry, Nanny!"

Sarah's throat closed at the feel of Nora's small hand tugging at hers. Tomorrow it would end forever. She blinked back tears. Everything she did today was so hard, so…devastating…because it was for the last time. There was no more clanging bell to be answered. Clayton was fully recovered. He had returned to his work on the Miami Canal last week. She had waited until she was sure he would not do himself harm, but it was only an excuse to delay her departure. Clayton was fine. It was time for her to go. Leaving would be excruciating, but staying was unendurable.

Sarah focused on the business at hand, lifted the bar and opened the carriage-house door. A small black-and-white bundle of fur barked and came running, tail wagging, ears flopping up and down. Nora plopped to the floor, giggling and squealing as the puppy jumped up and down licking her face and tugging on her hair.

Sarah closed the door so the dog could not escape and walked over to the horses. Pacer nickered a welcome, tossed his head and thrust it forward to be petted. She rubbed his silky muzzle and combed her fingers through his forelock. It was always tangled. He lowered his head and nudged her chest. She stepped back to keep her balance and something attacked her exposed ankle.

Sarah leaned down and scooped up the gray kitten who had flopped onto his back and was batting at her skirt hem. He was big enough to do damage now. She tucked him under her chin and scratched behind his ears. He purred his contentment. She reached out and patted Sassy's neck, then sat on the feed chest and stroked the kitten's fur. Wiggles was her favorite. Perhaps she would get a kitten when she went home.

Home. Not Randolph Court. Not anymore. Stony Point was her home. Her heart squeezed tears into her eyes. She wiped them away and held her breath to stop the flow. She would cry tomorrow. Today she must stay calm for Nora's sake. She fixed a smile on her face.

"What is your puppy's name, Nora?"

The toddler shrugged her shoulders.

"You have not named him? Well, that will not do. How will you call him to you if he has no name?" She put Wiggles down, walked over to Nora and lifted the puppy into the air to better see his face. He wiggled and twisted his body, trying to reach her cheek with his tongue. "What a rogue you are." She put him back in Nora's lap. "You could name him Scamper...or perhaps Trouble."

"Uh-uh." Nora shook her head, grinned up at her. "He be Rogue."

Sarah looked down at the toddler sitting on the dusty, straw-strewn barn floor, holding a wiggling puppy in her pudgy arms, and memorized the picture she made. Every detail, from the bits of straw in her golden curls, to her happy smile, to the smudge of dirt on the stockings covering the short little legs sticking out from under the yellow-checked cotton play dress. This was the image she would remember when she thought of Nora in the years to come.

Sarah straightened the books and rearranged the stuffed animals that sat neglected on the shelf. Nora had lost interest in them since she was now free of the confines of this room and could go outside and play with live animals.

She turned and glanced around. So much had changed since she first walked into this room and was greeted by a harried young maid and a squalling toddler. *She* had changed. And she could not go back to simply being a pampered daughter in her parents' house. When she returned to Philadelphia she would work full-time at the Twiggs Manor Orphanage. Her aunt Laina would be glad of the help. And there were always so many children in need, it would keep her too busy to dwell on memories. Her shoulders drooped. It seemed all she did was run from memories.

Sarah swallowed back a rush of tears and walked to the dressing room to check her appearance. It was time. Delaying the moment of truth only increased the agony. She brushed a few stray hairs into place, pinched some color into her pale cheeks and headed for the hall-way door.

It seemed strange to use the main stairs. She had become accustomed to using the winder stairs that opened directly into the kitchen. They were much more convenient when Clayton was ill and she had carried food trays up and down at every meal.

A strip of golden lamplight gleamed under Clayton's study door. He was still working. Sarah stopped, gripped the railing and held her breath for a count of ten. It helped. She continued down the last few steps, lifted her hand and knocked on his door.

"Come in!"

Tears stung her eyes. She blinked them away and lifted her chin. *Almighty God, please help me not to cry. Please. I know pride is a sin, but right now it is the only weapon I have to keep my feelings from being revealed.* It was a prayer unlikely to be answered, but it still made her feel better. She squared her shoulders and opened the door.

"Put the—" Clayton glanced up, rose from his chair, snatched his jacket off the back and shoved his arm into the sleeve. "Sorry, I thought you were Eldora with my coffee." He shoved in his other arm and shrugged the jacket into place on his broad shoulders.

She did her best to ignore the frown furrowing his forehead. And his eyes. Though she need not have bothered. He seemed not to want to look at her. Well, she would be out of his life soon enough. "Forgive me for disturbing your work."

"Not at all. I was going to talk with you when my report was finished."

How ironic if he was about to dismiss her. Well, he

would not do so! Sarah clenched her hands at her sides and dug her fingernails into her palms. "I have come to tell you I wish to return home to Philadelphia—immediately." She took a breath, dug her fingernails in deeper. "Lucy can care for Nora until you can hire another nanny." *Thank You, Lord. I said it without breaking down.* "I will leave tomorrow." She stared up at Clayton. His face had that stony look again.

"I am afraid that is impossible, Miss Randolph." He looked down, straightened his suit coat. "I believe I once mentioned to you that the fourth of this month is the tenth anniversary of the opening of the Miami Canal. And that as the engineer in charge of the repair work, I am to accompany the governor on a gala celebration trip up the canal to Dayton aboard a specially outfitted packet." He looked up. "If you remember, I told you, the governor has requested that all those accompanying him bring their families along, and that provision has been made for young children and their nannies."

So once again he was forced to accept her presence. "I thought Lucy—" She stopped, stared at the muscle twitching along his jaw.

"Lucy is not capable of this undertaking." He picked up a book from his desk, turned and placed it atop the pile on the mantel. "The journey will take two days. You will need to include bedclothes for Nora in your packing. Please have everything ready by tomorrow afternoon. Directly after supper tomorrow night, Quincy will transport everything to the packet. We will board at nine o'clock the following morning."

Sarah stood staring at his rigid back, torn by the conflicting needs of her heart. She should refuse. She should leave tomorrow as she had planned and end the torture of being where she was not wanted. But she could not go away knowing Nora was on a *boat*. A canal boat to be sure, but still a boat surrounded by water. She shuddered. "Very well. I will do as you ask. But I will have my possessions packed, and I will leave for Philadelphia as soon as we come back to Stony Point." She turned and left his study, the curt nod of agreement he gave her stuck like a sword in her heart.

Nora was beside herself, trying to see everything at once. It was her first ride in the buggy, her first trip away from Stony Point, and she peppered Sarah and her father with questions. Sarah welcomed them. The short ride seemed endless.

"Here we are." The buggy rolled to a stop. Clayton stepped down and held out his arms. "Come here, Nora." The toddler leaned into his arms, stared wide-eyed at the commotion at the boarding site, and stuck her thumb in her mouth. Clayton shifted Nora to one arm and offered his hand.

Sarah steeled herself and placed hers in it. It was as she remembered, broad and warm, with calluses on the pads of the long fingers—but strong. Not flaccid and weak now, but so very strong. *She should have worn gloves.* She looked away from their joined hands, stepped from the buggy and held her arms out for Nora.

Clayton yielded his daughter to her, placed his hand at the small of her back and guided her through the crowd of people milling around a bandstand where a man was holding forth on a topic that was lost in the din. He urged her toward a packet boat decked out in red, white and blue streamers, with a large yellow banner that read Miami Canal—Ten-Year Anniversary, stretched along the pristine white railing that enclosed the open deck. A broad boarding plank slanted upward from the ground, spanned the narrow space of water between the packet and the docking area and continued its climb to the packet's deck.

Sarah's steps faltered. Her stomach knotted. She stopped walking and stared down at the water, felt the blood draining from her face, the strength leaving her legs. "Take Nora." The words were a whisper, forced from her constricted throat.

"No. She is your charge, Miss Randolph. And 'you are not so selfish as to put your fear above her needs'— are you?"

The challenge in Clayton's voice firmed her will. "No. I am not." Sarah lifted her chin, flashed a look up at him and stepped onto the gangplank.

He lowered his head. "Close your eyes. I will guide you. I promise, I'll not let you fall. You are safe with me."

His whisper fell soft upon her ear. His hand pressed more firmly against the small of her back, drew her ever so slightly closer to his side. It was amazing the courage his touch gave her. She braced herself against her response to his touch, to his nearness and hurried up the gangplank.

The courage left the moment she stepped onboard and felt the slight movement of the deck beneath her feet. She closed her eyes. *Help me, O God. Take away—*

"Bainbridge! I have been watching for you."

Sarah snapped her eyes open at the hail. A short, stout man, wearing a gray suit with a brocaded, maroon vest, separated himself from a small group of men on the forward open deck area and hurried toward them.

"Good morning, Commissioner Thomas." Clayton

smiled and shook the man's offered hand. "It looks as though we will have fine weather for our trip."

"Indeed. Yes."

The man skimmed his gaze over her, lingered for a moment on her face. Did her fear show? She lifted her chin. He flushed and focused his gaze on Nora.

"Is this your child, Bainbridge?"

Clayton nodded. "This is my daughter, Nora, yes. And—"

"Beautiful child." The man clapped Clayton on the shoulder. "We have to hurry, Bainbridge. The governor wants you with him when he speaks, and he is about to begin." He turned toward the front deck area, filled with people, then turned back. "Have your nanny get the child settled. Little ones get restless at these sort of ceremonies—and we will be on our way after the governor's speech." He gave her a cursory glance. "The children and nanny quarters are that way." He pointed toward the narrow deck that ran along the left side of the centered cabin area.

Sarah glanced over the side of the boat at the water, caught her breath.

Clayton stepped to the outside edge of the narrow deck. His broad shoulders blocked her view of the water.

"I wish to see my daughter settled, Commissioner. I will join you in a moment."

He thought she was too frightened to care for Nora. Sarah straightened, squared her shoulders. "Nora will be fine, Mr. Bainbridge. I will bring her to you after the governor's speech." She glanced at the short man waiting for him and dipped her head. "Commissioner Thomas." She lowered Nora to the deck, took hold of her small hand and, gripping the rail on her left and fastening her

gaze firmly on the highly varnished deck, walked down
the narrow passageway.

"But I want to go see Mama and Grandpapa, Nanny
Alice."

Sarah paused at the sound of the young child's voice
and glanced at the open door of a room on her right.

"If you are searching for the children's quarters, you
have found them."

The voice was soft, kind.

Sarah led Nora into the room. The cabin was small,
with white painted walls, dark-blue coverlets on narrow
berths attached to the walls and matching curtains at the
windows that marched in a row above the beds. A small
table with two chairs and two high children's chairs con-
stituted the furnishings. A plump, buxom young woman
knelt beside an open door at the far end of the room
straightening a little girl's dress.

"So you have been banished to the nether regions
with your charge until the festivities are over, also."
The woman motioned toward the wall beside her. "I
have claimed these berths. Those on the side wall will
be yours. And this—" she indicated the room behind
her "—is a very small, but adequate, dressing room."
A smile warmed her round face. "There will be only
the two of us sharing these quarters. I am Alice Gardner, and this—" she rose and took the child by the hand
"—is my charge, Miss Portia Holbrook. The governor's
granddaughter."

Sarah smiled. "I am Sarah Randolph, and this is my
charge, Miss Nora Bainbridge. Her father is the engineer in charge of the canal repairs." She glanced down at
Nora, who had leaned back against her legs, then smiled

at the other little girl. "We are pleased to make your acquaintance, Miss Portia."

Nora stirred, took her thumb from her mouth. "Me gots kitties an' a puppy."

"You have a *puppy?*" Portia tugged her hand from her nanny's grasp and ran across the room to Nora. "What is his name?"

"He be Rogue. An' the kitties be Happy an' Wiggles an' Fluffy an' Bun'le. An' we gots horsies, too."

"We have horses. And I have a pony." Portia leaped into the conversation, clearly not to be outdone in the pet department. "His name is Noodles. And he is gray with white spots…"

"It looks as if our charges are going to enjoy each other's company."

Sarah looked at Alice. She was peering out a window, looking up and down the narrow walkway outside. "Yes, it does." She stepped to the two berths on the side wall. Their trunks rested on the floor beneath them. She leaned down and patted the mattress of the small one with the rail around it. It was softer than it appeared to be. "How old is Portia?"

"Almost four years."

"Miss Gardner?" The voice was low and soft, somewhat urgent.

Alice's face lit. She spun away from the window and hurried toward the open door. "Did you wish to speak with me, Mr. Adams?"

A young, brown-haired man, of medium height, stepped into the room. "If you have a moment, I am free until after the governor's speech and I thought perhaps   " He stopped. His face flushed. "I see you are busy." He backed toward the door.

Sarah looked at Alice, noted the disappointment wiping the smile from her face. "Pardon me, Miss Gardner. I do not mean to intrude on your conversation, but, if you feel comfortable with the suggestion, I would be happy to care for Portia while you speak with your gentleman friend."

"Oh, I could not impose—"

"It is no imposition. I am sure Nora will be happy for the company."

"Well…" Alice glanced at Mr. Adams. "Let me fetch my hat." She hurried to a trunk, grabbed the hat resting on top and headed back for the door. "Thank you, Miss Randolph. I shan't be long."

There was a burst of cheering and applause. The boat moved. Sarah caught her breath, glanced at the children happily engrossed in picture books and stepped to a window. People on shore were milling about, calling and shouting to each other and those onboard. White handkerchiefs and small flags fluttered goodbye from the hands of old and young alike. Crew members shouted to one another. Young boys ran on the towpath, cheering and keeping pace as the packet began its slow-moving progress up the canal.

The excitement of the moment overwhelmed her apprehension. She bent down and snatched up the small sunbonnet resting on Nora's berth. The little girl should not miss this occasion. And she had told Clayton she would bring Nora to him when the governor's speech was finished. Sarah frowned and glanced toward the door. She could not leave Portia. Where was Miss Gardner?

The plump, young woman rushed through the door as if her thoughts had conjured her.

"Come, Portia. You are to join your mother and grandfather." Alice Gardner lifted a bonnet out of Portia's trunk, tied it on the child's head and hurried toward the door. "Thank you, Miss Randolph." The words floated over her shoulder as she disappeared in the flow of people walking by on the deck outside the cabin.

"You are most welcome." Sarah laughed and turned to Nora.

"Me go see kitties." Nora's lower lip trembled. She held her arms up.

Sarah scooped her up and hugged her close. Poor little tyke, she was no doubt feeling overwhelmed by all the noise and excitement, the strange place and new experiences. "No kitties today, sweetie." She infused her voice with excitement. "But I will take you out to your papa and perhaps he will let you watch the horses pull the boat. Would you like that?"

"Horsies?"

"Yes." Sarah kissed Nora's soft, silky cheek. "But first you need to visit the dressing room."

The slight breeze played with the strands of hair that had escaped the red cord. Sarah frowned and lifted her hands to tuck the locks back under their restraint, saw Clayton glance her way and lowered them again. Perhaps he would not notice she had forgotten her bonnet again if she did not call attention to the fact.

"Who him?" Nora pointed a pudgy little finger toward the man walking alongside the horses on the towpath.

"That is the man who makes the horses pull the boat."

Clayton smiled at his daughter. "They call him a 'hog-gee'—it is his special name."

Nora nodded, twisted round in her father's arms, looking at everything. "Who him?" She pointed.

"That is the man who pushes the boat away from the banks of the canal."

"What he special name?"

"He is called a 'tripper,' and, yes, he has a big stick. It is called a pole."

Clayton grinned and looked her way. "Is she always this inquisitive?"

Sarah met his gaze. Her stomach fluttered. "Yes, she is." She looked away, looked back. *His eyes!* Her heart stuttered, and her tongue followed its lead. "I... I must answer at least fifty questions a day."

"You are very patient."

"Mr. Bainbridge?"

Sarah started. The young man who had come to the cabin asking to speak to Alice Gardner stepped up beside them. "The governor requests you join him at his table, sir." He glanced at Nora. "He also suggests it would be too adult an occasion for your child."

"How opportune." Sarah stepped forward, avoided Clayton's gaze. It was too unsettling. "It is time for Nora to eat. And then she must have a nap. All of the excitement has tired her." She reached for Nora. "Tell your papa goodbye, sweetie."

"Bye, Papa."

Clayton leaned down, received Nora's kiss and gave her one in return. He lifted his head, looked at her. "Goodbye, Miss Randolph."

Her voice deserted her. Sarah dipped her head, turned and walked away. But when she reached the corner, she could not resist a backward glance—and immediately wished she had. Clayton was at the governor's table, smiling as he bowed over the offered hand of a very attractive young woman. She eyed the woman's gown of shimmering green silk trimmed with rows of lace-edged flounces, looked down at the serviceable material, the plain full skirt of her own gown and wished fervently she had brought along one of her own elegant, fashionable gowns.

Sarah pulled the coverlet up over Nora's arms, moved over to the other wall and did the same for Portia. Alice Gardner had disappeared the moment she put her charge to bed. Not that she minded. The children were both fast asleep, exhausted by the day's excitements. And it was little wonder. There had been so much enthusiasm and fervor when the boat stopped and the governor spoke briefly to the people who lived in the small settlements along the canal.

She had lost count of how many stops they had made. Or of how many cannons had boomed in respectful salute or wild celebration. But she remembered how handsome and distinguished Clayton had looked, standing with the commissioners during the speeches. And how the governor's daughter had hovered nearby. The pretty, stylish, *widowed,* newly out of mourning, governor's daughter. Alice said Portia's father had died a year ago last month.

Sarah frowned, walked to a window and looked out. The narrow walkway was empty of people. The constant hum of voices had ceased. It must be late. She should go to bed, but the berth was uninviting. She was too restless to sleep. Where was Clayton now? Was he abed?

Or was he standing out there on the moonlit deck with the governor's daughter?

Soft whispers caught her attention. Sarah glanced toward the door. Alice Gardner walked into the room, the glow in her eyes and the flush on her face visible even in the dimmed lantern light. It made her own loneliness unbearable. "I feel the need of some air, Miss Gardner. Would you please watch over Nora while I step outside for a few minutes?"

"Of course. It is a lovely night, Miss Randolph."

It was. A warm, gentle breeze caressed her face, teased the tresses of hair at her nape and temples as Sarah walked along the narrow passage to the now-deserted open deck at the front of the boat. Moonlight streamed down from the ebony sky to light her way. The night was soft and still. So quiet she could hear the clop of the horses' hoofs against the dirt of the towpath, the rustle of the streamers overhead. Footsteps.

Sarah whirled about. Clayton Bainbridge crossed the deck to stand beside her. "Good evening, Miss Randolph. You are up late." Concern shadowed his face. "Are you unable to sleep? Is it your fear of the water?"

Sarah shook her head, brushed a strand of hair off her face. "No. The canal boat is very different from a ship. And I find the water does not frighten me if I stay on the side of the boat by the canal wall. And, of course, the boat being towed by horses is very reassuring." She was babbling! Why did the man make her so *nervous?* She took a step back, put some space between them. "I simply came out for some fresh air before I retire." She took a chance and glanced up at him. "And what of you? Why are—"

"Hey! Hey! Lock!"

Sarah started at the crewman's shout and turned back toward the front of the boat. Light illuminated the darkened canal ditch, glimmered on the water.

A bugle blew.

"This is why I came out. Watch." Clayton spoke softly, his deep voice little more than a whisper.

A crewman ran by them to the front of the boat—waved a red lantern.

She looked up at Clayton. He had closed the distance between them again. She edged forward. "What is he doing?"

"Telling the lock keeper we are here."

The boat slowed, stopped. Men came into view, running on top of the stone wall. A minute later there was a rushing, swishing sound.

"Hear that? They have opened the first set of gates."

He had stepped up beside her again! Sarah wiped the palms of her hands against her long skirt and looked at the small space between her and the rail. She was running out of room to move away from him.

"As soon as the water level is even, they will unhitch the towrope, and we will enter the canal chamber. The captain will steer us through while our crew helps the lock crew."

The boat moved forward, floated between thick walls of stone so close crew members jumped to them and joined the other men already on the walls.

Sarah stared at the massive walls. Had Clayton built or repaired them? She looked up to ask, but the question died on her lips. Clayton was looking down at her, his blue eyes dark and smoky with tiny flames burning in their depths. Everything in her went as still as the night. He moved closer. Her knees quivered.

"Locking through!"

The shout ripped through the air. Sarah jerked, came back to sanity. Water rushed and surged. Crew members leaped back onboard and went about their tasks. She groped behind her for the railing before she fell in an embarrassing heap at Clayton's feet, and watched them hitch the towrope to a fresh team of horses, grab their poles and take up their positions. She fixed a polite smile on her face and looked up him. "That was very interesting. Thank you for sharing your expertise with me, Mr. Bainbridge. But it is late, and I need to check on Nora. Good evening."

He did not move. He just stood there, looking at her. Heat climbed into her cheeks. He was probably wondering why she was acting so strange. She straightened her spine, let go of the railing, inched by him and walked down the passageway to her room.

Everyone was sleeping. Sarah went to the dressing room and changed into her nightgown and robe. She draped her gown over a chair, walked to the empty berth, slid beneath the covers and stared out the window at the dark night sky.

She loved him. She could not deny it any longer. With all her being she longed to be Clayton's wife. To have his children. But it was impossible. He still loved his wife. And he barely tolerated her presence.

Tears welled, flowed down her cheeks. What was she to do? How was she to get through tomorrow without giving her feelings away? *Oh, dear God, help me to stay calm tomorrow, to not reveal my love to Clayton.*

Sobs threatened. Sarah took a deep breath and wiped the tears from her cheeks. Tomorrow. One day. She could manage that. She would simply stay as far away from Clayton as possible for the rest of the journey.

Stony Point. It wrenched her heart to think of leaving, but the time had come. Sarah looked in the dressing-room mirror a last time. Lavender half circles stained the skin below her eyes, a testimony to the last two sleepless nights. But there was nothing to be done about them. At least they would not be so visible in the shade of her hat's deep brim. She settled the yellow, flower-bedecked bonnet in place and turned away. The deep ruffle around the bottom of her yellow silk gown whispered across the plank floor as she walked to the bedroom.

The bare space on the rag rug increased the lump in her throat. Her trunk was waiting in the carriage. Quincy had carried it down earlier, right after Clayton had been called away on business.

She would never see him again.

Sarah's steps faltered. She stopped, held her eyes wide and took a deep breath to stop the tears pushing for release. *Do not cry! For Nora's sake, do not cry.* She hurried through the bedroom, refusing to think about the woman who would live here in her place, and started down the winder stairs to the kitchen.

Nora's voice floated up to her. She set her mind against the horrid ache in her heart, fixed a smile on her face and stepped into the kitchen.

Eldora looked her way, disappointment on her face, censure in her pose. "So, you are really going." It was not a question. It was an indictment.

Sarah steeled her heart and nodded. "I must, Eldora. I hope someday you will understand and not judge me too harshly." She swallowed, forced herself to go on. "I will always remember you with gratitude and affection."

"Me go bye-bye?" Nora stopped petting Rogue and scrambled to her feet. Her blond curls bounced as she ran across the slate floor.

Sarah closed her eyes, took a breath, then opened them and knelt to take Nora in her arms. The last time. *Dear heavenly Father, help me! For Nora's sake give me strength.* She leaned back and looked into Nora's blue eyes. "Not this time, sweetie. Nanny Sarah has to go away. Far away." She cleared the tears from her throat. "And you must stay here with your papa, and Eldora and Quincy. And Lucy."

Nora's lower lip pouted out. She shook her head. She leaned close and put her arms about her neck. "Me wants you. Me go, too."

Sarah blinked hard, hugged Nora as tight as she dared and rose to her feet. She smiled and forced a playful note into her voice. "Now, what would your papa do if you went away with me? And who would play with the kitties and Rogue? Gracious! They would be very, very sad without you." She glanced at Eldora, sent a silent plea for help.

"And who would I have to make cookies for?" Eldora shook her head, walked over and held out her arms. "And you know what else? I have a job for you to do. I promised your papa I would make him some ginger cookies. But I am almighty busy. Would you help me?"

Nora nodded and leaned into the housekeeper's pudgy arms.

Sarah whirled and ran from the kitchen. Tears blinded her. She wiped them away, fumbled with the front door and stumbled to the carriage. Her chest ached with

Chapter Twenty-Three

"How are you feeling this morning, Sarah?"

"I am all right, Mother." Sarah put down her book and summoned a smile.

"You did not eat any breakfast." Her mother eyed her, as only a mother can. "And you ate very little last evening."

"I was not hungry."

"And you were pacing around in your room until the wee hours this morning because you were not tired? Sarah, dear, you are talking to your mother." Her mother reached down and touched her cheek. "Did you get any sleep at all?"

"A little." Sarah took a breath, rose from her chair and walked over to look out the French doors. "I did not mean to disturb your rest, Mother. I did not realize you could hear me."

"That is not my concern, Sarah. You are." Her mother came up beside her, put her arm around her shoulders. "Do you want to talk about Mr. Bainbridge, and why you suddenly decided to come home?"

Sarah bit down on her lower lip and shook her head.

"Sarah, the Lord…"

"I am not blaming God for anything, Mother. I know now I was wrong to blame Him for Aaron's death. It was not God that decided to sail home on the *Seadrift* that day. It was Aaron. And he did so against the advice of a sailor who was familiar with New England weather. He warned Aaron of a coming storm. But it was such a beautiful day when we set sail Aaron was certain the sailor was wrong."

She shuddered, walked to the mantel and stared up at a painting of a clipper ship under full sail, her rail almost plowing the water as she skimmed across the waves. Her father had painted it. He often painted his ships. She hated the painting that hung over the fireplace in his study. It showed a ship, mast broken, rigging fallen and trailing in a raging ocean. He had been aboard that ship during the hurricane that so damaged it. But he had survived. Just as she had survived the storm that swept down on the *Seadrift*.

"I did not realize how dangerous sailing upon the ocean can be." She sighed. "Since I can remember, all I wanted was to marry a ship's captain and sail with him around the world on our honeymoon. I… I never thought further than that."

Sarah turned, looked across the library. "Is it possible to get a man mixed up with a dream, Mother? I mean, to think you loved a man when it was what he stood for that you really loved?" Tears blurred her vision. She wiped them away. "I… I thought I loved Aaron—and I did. He was always so calm and kind and respectful. But now I do not believe I was *in* love with Aaron. I just wanted to be safe. And I always felt safe with him. Not…nervous."

She took a breath, plunged. "Mother, when Father…

looks…at you, do you go all breathless and weak in the knees, as if you are going to fall?"

"No, dear." Her mother shook her head, smiled. "*I* always go all breathless and feel as if I am going to melt."

Sarah stared, gulped, ran across the room to the safe haven of her mother's arms. "Wh-what am I going t-to do, M-Mother?"

Her mother held her close, stroked her hair. "A very wise lady once gave me some excellent advice when I was in a similar situation, Sarah. The same advice I am going to give you—go to Mr. Bainbridge and tell him you love him."

Sarah lifted her head, drew back out of her mother's arms and shook her head. "No. No, I cannot do that, Mother. *Ever.* You see, Mr. Bainbridge has made it very clear that he does not want me in his life."

"Him a *big* kitty." Nora pointed at the picture on the right side of the page.

Clayton smiled at her sleepy tone and looked down. His daughter was losing her battle against sleep. "Yes, a *very* big kitty. He is called a lion."

"What him special name?" She snuggled closer against his chest. Yawned.

"He does not have a special name. Why don't you give him one?"

She nodded, closed her eyes. "Me likes…"

Clayton chuckled, set the book aside and rose from the rocker. "That is one lion who will never have a special name." He kissed Nora's warm, rosy cheek, laid her in her crib and pulled the coverlet over her. She would soon be too big for the crib. He should go into the attic and see if that small child's bed he had slept in was there.

His child. The fact still had the power to knock him
slightly off-kilter when he thought about it. The guilt
over causing her mother's death lingered, hovered in the
background, when he looked at her, but no longer consumed him to the degree he would not even acknowledge his own daughter.

He frowned, brushed Nora's curls back off her face.
Was he doing her a disservice by not hiring another
nanny? They seemed to be managing all right without
one. Eldora and Lucy, even Quincy, watched over her
while he was working. And he had breakfast with Nora
every morning, and tucked her into bed every night. He
had been the only one that could calm her enough to go
to sleep when Sarah had left.

Sarah.

Clayton turned from the crib and walked into the
adjoining bedroom. Sarah was the real reason he did
not seek another nanny. He missed her. Longed for her
presence.

He stepped through her door onto the landing, glanced
at his own door, both open now as they had been when
she was caring for him, and his face tightened. No, he
would not hire another nanny. They would continue on
as they were. The idea of another woman across the landing, so close to his own room, was intolerable.

He checked to make sure the gate he had built for the
top of the stairs was latched. The bedroom doors had to
stay open all night so he could hear if Nora needed him,
and he wanted no possibility of his little daughter taking a fall down the winder stairs. He glanced down the
stairwell, sucked in his breath at the memory of Sarah
descending the steps, light from the lamp in her hand
illuminating the downward spiral, glinting on the silky

mass of brown hair loosely restrained at the nape of her neck and spilling down the back of her quilted robe. The mere thought of her struck him breathless.

Clayton fisted his hands. *Men are not permitted that luxury, though we are allowed to punch a wall—or each other. Or fight Indians.* Another memory. The house, his mind, his heart was rife with them. They had been talking about her crying, because she was upset by memories of the man she loved. The man who had so captured her heart she wanted no other. He stared at the wall, quivered with the desire to punch his fist through it. But it would solve nothing. And it would only, once again, prove his weakness. His lack of self-control. And it would show that he had been right to let her return to Philadelphia.

Clayton strode into his bedroom, the muscle along his jaw twitching. Letting Sarah go was the hardest thing he had ever done, but she deserved a man of honor and moral strength. A man like her fiancé, who had died in that storm at sea. A man who betrayed a deathbed promise to his best friend did not qualify.

"What is it, Eldora?" Clayton looked up from the cost estimations he was figuring for the northern canal extension.

"You have a visitor. She's waitin' in the drawing room. I'll bring tea." The housekeeper threw him a look and trudged off down the hall toward the kitchen.

She? Clayton frowned, rose and shrugged into his suit coat. Whoever it was, he would get rid of her quickly. He had work to do. Three long strides took him across the hall to the drawing-room doorway. A slender, dark-haired woman sat in an upholstered chair, facing away from him. He fixed a polite smile on his face and strode into the room. "Good afternoon. I am Clayton Bain-bridge, may I help you?"

The woman rose, turned and held out her arms.

"Victoria! My dear friend." Clayton rushed forward and gave the older woman a hug. "I am astounded by your visit. I had no idea you were back home. When did you return?"

"Charles resigned his post in England two months ago. But we only arrived in Cincinnati last week. I would have come sooner, but my mother is ill. Let me look at you." She drew back and studied his face. "You are hand-some as ever, Clayton."

"And you are just as lovely as I remember."

"Flatterer!" She laughed and took hold of his hand. "Now that the polite niceties are out of the way—" She pulled him toward the settee. "Come and talk to me. I have not had a chance to catch up on all that has happened since we left, and there is so much for you to tell me. Do you realize I have been gone over three years?"

"Yes. I know."

She stopped arranging her skirts and looked up at him. "That sounded grim." She studied his face so intently he wanted to squirm. "Are you not over Debo-rah's death?"

"There are some things you do not get over, Victoria."

"Bosh. Deborah was beautiful, Clayton, but it has been almost three years since her passing. She would want you to marry again. Especially as your marriage was…well…*chaste*. Except for that one time."

He went rigid. "You know of that?"

"Now do not go all offended on me, Clayton. I am old enough to be your mother, and you know my repu-tation for boldness." She placed her hand on his arm.

"Of course I know. I was the closest thing to a mother Deborah ever knew. She confided everything to me."

"I see." Clayton surged to his feet, stepped to the fireplace and looked up at his grandparents' portraits so he did not have to face Victoria. "I am surprised you treat me with such affection."

There was a small gasp behind him. "What an astonishing thing to say. There has always been fondness between our families. Why would I not?"

He turned to face her, the muscle along his jaw twitching. "Because if Deborah told you everything, you must know I am responsible for her death." It was the first time he had said the words aloud. The first time he had spoken with anyone about his wife's death. It was painful, but there was something freeing about it.

"I know no such thing!" She peered up at him, gave his face a close perusal. "I do not follow your reasoning, Clayton. Please explain."

"How can you not understand, Victoria? I am the one responsible for the baby that took her life."

"That is preposterous, Clayton. Many women die of childbirth. Do you hold that their husbands are responsible for their deaths?"

"Of course not. But that is different." The bitterness and self-loathing poured out of him with his words. "Deborah had a weak heart and I knew it. I knew having a child could kill her."

"And so did she."

"Yes. But Deborah was innocent of such things. *I* knew that birth precautions often fail." There, he had admitted it all. Victoria looked stunned. He braced himself for her disgust.

"*What* birth precautions?" The words were quiet, reflective.

"The ones Deborah got from Dr. Anderson."

Victoria drew in a breath, released it. "She never told you."

Clayton scowled down at her. "Never told me what?"

"Deborah lied to you, Clayton. She knew you would never agree to treat her as a real wife because you were afraid she would become with child. But that is what she *wanted*." Victoria rose and came to stand facing him. "When Dr. Anderson told Deborah she had only a year, perhaps a year and a few months left to live—"

"*What?*" Clayton stiffened. "I never—"

Victoria touched his arm. "Listen, and you will understand."

He stared at her, gave a curt nod.

"Dr. Anderson told Deborah she was soon to die, and she decided the only way she could live on was through a child. She had nothing to lose but a few months' time. Either way she was going to die. So she planned, and she lied." Victoria took a breath, exhaled. "She swore Dr. Anderson to secrecy about her limited time to live and tried to convince you to treat her as a wife. I know how long you withstood her pleas, Clayton. But Deborah was nothing if not inventive when it came to getting her own way. You know that better than anyone. So she lied to you. She begged you to treat her as a real wife for once—only once—because she knew if she said *once* you would be more likely to yield. And she told you Dr. Anderson had given her birth precautions and assured her it was perfectly safe. She won." Victoria's gaze locked on his eyes. "Deborah knew exactly what she was doing *and* the risk she was taking with her life in doing it. You are not guilty of Deborah's death, Clayton. *She* is. It is all in the letter she wrote me."

Victoria turned and walked back to the settee, opened her purse and pulled out a letter. She came back and held it out to him. "I saved the letter because I thought your daughter—when she is grown—would like to know her mother wanted her so much she was willing to give up her life for her."

Deborah's death was not his fault. Clayton shook his head, lit the lantern and walked to the door in the upstairs hall. He could not grasp it. He had blamed himself for so long. But it had been Deborah's choice. Dr. Anderson had said her frail heart was about to stop beating, even without her having a child. It was only amazing that she had lived long enough to give birth. But Victoria believed that God had granted Deborah the desire of her heart, and part of her lived on in Nora. And he agreed. For the first time he understood why Deborah had named her baby Nora *Blessing*.

The sadness that had been with him all evening swelled. A cleansing sorrow. For the first time he was able to grieve Deborah's passing without guilt and anger. He only wished she had not lied to him. But that, too, he understood. He had been so determined to honor his promise to Andrew to keep Deborah safe, he would not have agreed to shorten her life by even one day.

Clayton set aside his musings, held the lantern high and climbed the attic stairs. The child's bed he wanted for Nora had to be up here somewhere. He ducked beneath a half-log rafter and swung the lantern to his right. The circle of golden light flowed over dusty trunks and pieces of furniture. Old toys.

He stopped, shoved a large crate aside and moved the lantern closer to a bench with a broken armrest, stared at the toy that sat on the seat. *Noah's ark.* His father had made the ark and carved the animals for him. He had forgotten all about it. He set the lantern on the bench seat, squatted on his heels and picked up one of the animals that crowded the deck of the ark. A deer.

A smile tilted his lips. His fingers had remembered what he had forgotten. The deer had been his favorite—which probably explained the missing antler. He put it down and picked up the bear, the fox, the beaver and otter. He looked inside and found the buffalo and horse, squirrels and rabbits. Crows, turkey and grouse perched on the flat roof, a cat and dog nearby. He grinned, blew off the loose dust and carried the ark over to the top of the stairs. Nora would love it.

Nora. He had Deborah to thank for Nora. It had been her choice to have a child. And if she had not lied to him about the birth precautions, Nora would not exist. The truth settled deep in his soul. He was not *guilty.* And all the torment he had suffered over the past three years had been self-inflicted. It had come from him—not God.

Clayton's heart almost stopped. Sarah was not some sort of punishing test from God, as he had believed. He frowned, brushed the dust from his hands and walked back to get the lantern. Even at his most angry moments, he still believed in God. Still believed in His sovereign power. And that He controlled the things that happened to those who accepted Him as their Lord. That truth had been ingrained in him by his grandparents from the time he could walk and talk. So what was God's purpose in bringing Sarah to Stony Point? To care for Nora because he had turned his back on his own flesh and blood?

Clayton reached for the lantern, glanced at the small chest the ark had sat on and opened it instead. Small balls of multicolored fine wool rested on a folded piece of fabric. He touched them, tears filming his eyes at a sudden flash of his mother, sitting in a chair by the hearth working needlepoint. He lifted out the fabric, stiff and yellowed with age, unfolded it and smoothed it out across his knee. A green vine with purple flowers formed a border around a needlepoint verse.

For thou wilt light my
candle: the Lord my God
will enlighten my
darkness. Psalm 18:28
Joann Bainbr

A length of black wool trailed from the *r* in his mother's name. She had never finished the sampler. Clayton blew out a breath to release the pressure in his chest and read it again. And again. A sureness grew in him. Sarah had not been a test from God, she had been a gift sent to enlighten the darkness he carried in his heart. A darkness of his own creation. And in his hurt and anger and pride, he had sent her away.

Clayton's chest and throat ached. How many mistakes he had made. He closed his eyes and cleared the lump from his throat. "Forgive me, Lord. Forgive my arrogance…my pride…my anger. Forgive me for blaming You, instead of seeking Your wisdom. For holding control over my life, instead of yielding to You. I made a mess of things, Lord. And I thank You for Your mercy in waking me up before it was too late and I lost my daughter forever. Please help me not to make those mistakes again. Amen."

Clayton opened his eyes. Lamplight glowed on the sampler. He stared at it, smiled, then folded it and put it back in the small chest. A quick search discovered a small trunk that would hold all his treasures sitting on the floor beside the bed he was seeking. He placed the chest and the Noah's ark inside, tucked the trunk under his arm and picked up the lantern. Light flowed around him, soft and golden, as he walked down the stairs.

Chapter Twenty-Four

She missed Nora. So much. Sarah tugged a leaf off a boxwood and pulled it apart strip by tiny strip as she walked down the brick path to the pavilion. She had not realized how deeply it would hurt to leave the toddler. But Nora had conquered her heart so completely it felt as if a part of her was gone. It was.

Sarah sighed, threw away the bit of stem that remained of the leaf and tugged off another. Her heart was back in Cincinnati, at Stony Point. She missed Eldora and Quincy. And the house. It was not grand like Randolph Court, but it was…home. She blinked, swallowed and thought of something else. The carriage house. How she longed for the carriage house, and Pacer with his welcoming nickers and head nudges. And Sassy. And Wiggles and Happy, Fluffy and Bundle. Tears overflowed. A sob caught in her throat. Who ever heard of naming a kitten Bundle? It was an absurd name for a cat.

Sarah threw away the leaf and wiped the tears from her cheeks. Crying did no good. She simply had to wait for time to take away the horrible hollowness inside. That empty place that only—she jerked her mind from the name it wanted to utter and searched for an acceptable substitution—that only Stony Point and all it stood for could fill.

She rounded the curve in the path and paused, looking at the garden bench that sat in its own little nook, created by the brick paving and the hedges that surrounded it. It was there, right there on that bench that Elizabeth had broken through all the hurt and fear harbored in her little girl's heart and become her mother. She had been only a little older than Nora at the time. And Elizabeth had been showing her how to make a tea set for her dolls from clay. And then that woman with the cane had come around this very curve and frightened her. Elizabeth had taken her in her arms and she had felt loved for the first time. What had the woman called them? *Urchins.* Yes, that was the word she had used. *Urchins.*

Sarah smiled and walked on to the pavilion. That woman had been her father's good friend, Abigail Twiggs. And she had grown to love her—after she had discovered the warm heart beneath the stern exterior. Aunty Abigail. She would have loved Nora.

Sarah gripped the railing, lifted her long skirts with her free hand and climbed the steps into the pavilion. This is where Justin Randolph had become her father, not her guardian. He had brought her a puppy—in a wicker basket with a lid. And he had hugged her close and kissed her cheek and she had felt safe at last. That was the day she had spoken for the first time since her mother had died. She had named the puppy *Mr. Buffy.* He was a wonderful dog that had been her constant companion from that day on. And now Nora had a puppy— Rogue. And she would not get to see Nora grow up with him. And she would never know the sort of love that existed between her mother and father because the man she loved cared nothing for her. He did not want her.

Tears spilled from her eyes. The pressure in her chest broke into sobs that clawed their way up her throat and gained freedom in painful gasps. She covered her face with her hands and rocked to and fro, giving vent to the pain she had been holding inside until she could be alone where no one would see her cry.

"I have found you."

Sarah turned and smiled at her younger sister. "I did not know I was lost." She sobered. "Did Mother send you after me? I fear I have caused her great concern since I arrived home."

Mary's lips curved in a wry smile. "You should have seen her and Father while you were away." She climbed the steps and sat on the bench.

"Oh, dear." Sarah let out a long sigh and leaned back against the railing that enclosed the pavilion. "Was it very bad for them? I tried to ease any concern they may have felt in my letters."

"Well, let me see… Father *and* James wanted to rescue you from Cincinnati and bring you home where they could make sure you were safe and well cared for. And Mother, though she talked them out of doing so, has spent hours praying for your safety and well-being, and that you would return to your faith in God."

Sarah exchanged a look of sisterly understanding with Mary. "I feared as much. Well, it seems Father and James have gotten their wishes. And Mother's prayers have been answered—as always."

"Truly? Is that why your eyes are all red and puffy? Because of your well-being?"

Sarah stared at her sister, shook her head. "You are circumspect as always, I see."

Mary smiled. "You have not been gone long enough for me to change. I fear that would take a lifetime." Her brown eyes darkened. "I am still as bold and forthright as ever, and it is very off-putting to young men. Especially since I have little physical beauty to overcome my character flaw."

"Mary!"

"I am only speaking the truth, Sarah. It is a fact of life you have never had to be concerned about, as men fall willing victims to your beauty and charms."

The words stung like salt in her wound. "Not all men." She spun around and gripped the railing, stared out at the garden, willing back tears. She had cried enough.

"Forgive my blunt and hurtful words, Sarah. I did not ⸺ " Mary sighed. "I thought you were sad over the child."

"And so I am." Sarah pasted a smile on her face and turned to face her sister again. "Nora is absolutely adorable and I miss her dreadfully. Now, shall we go in and find Mother and have some tea? It has been a long while since I have talked about fashion and the latest styles."

Clayton sat in the chair in front of Justin Randolph's desk and waited for his answer.

"And why should I grant your request to court my daughter and seek her hand in marriage, Mr. Bainbridge?"

"Because I love Sarah, and I want to care for her and share the rest of my life with her." Clayton met Justin Randolph's gaze squarely. "And while I am not as financially prosperous as you obviously are, Mr. Randolph, I do quite well. I own a farm, in addition to my home. And I have invested in several growing businesses in Cincinnati which are prospering. I am well-respected and on the rise in my field of endeavor, and have recently accepted the position of head engineer for the northern Miami Canal extension to Lake Erie."

Clayton watched Sarah's father's face, tried to gauge his reaction to his litany of assets. There was not so much as a flicker of an eye to betray what the man was thinking. *Please, God, grant me favor in this man's eyes.*

"On the personal side, my home is solid and comfortable, not large but of adequate size with property enough for any additions we would choose to make in the future. I have a housekeeper, who is also my cook, and a maid to keep things tidy, so Sarah would not be overburdened in running our home.

"I also have a toddler daughter, Nora, who loves Sarah, and whom Sarah loves in return. I want only the best for Sarah, sir, and I believe I can make her happy." *Nothing. No reaction.* Clayton took a breath. "*And* last, because, though I want to do this right, *want* your blessing and that of Sarah's mother—if you withhold that blessing and refuse me the right to court her, I will defy you and climb the very *walls* of this brick mansion to see her and beg my case before her."

"I see." A smile broke across Justin Randolph's face. "*That* is the reason I was waiting to hear, Mr. Randolph. I wish you well in presenting your petition to Sarah." He rose and extended his hand.

Clayton grasped and shook it. "If I may ask a favor, sir?"

"Already?" Justin's eyes narrowed. "You are not in

the family yet, son. My daughters will choose their own mates."

"I ask nothing more than that, sir. It is only—" Clayton cleared his throat. "I have some explaining to do to Sarah, and if you could arrange our meeting without mentioning my name it might be helpful."

Justin stared at him. A grin slanted across his mouth. His eyes crinkled at the corners. "Got yourself in trouble with her, did you, son? Well, that's easy to do with women. Do it myself on a regular basis." He chuckled and clapped him on the shoulder. "You stay here, Mr. Bainbridge, and I will arrange the meeting."

Clayton waited until Sarah's father left the room, then walked over and stared out the French doors that opened onto a porch, and from there to formal gardens as far as he could see. Could he make Sarah happy? Was what he had to offer her enough? Stony Point was certainly no Randolph Court. He turned back to the spacious room, glanced at the furnishings and thought about the tomahawk gashes on his front door and the bullet holes in his mantel at home. What right had he to ask her to give up all this elegance? What made him think he could compete with her dead fiancé? She had said she wanted no other.

His stomach knotted. His palms turned moist. What if she said no? How would he ever live the rest of his life without her? He glanced at the floor beside the chair where he had been sitting, swallowed and closed his eyes. "I have made enough mistakes, Lord. Thy will be done."

The library door opened, closed.
"You wished to see me, Father?"

Clayton turned. His heart, his very life stood in front of him.

Sarah gaped. Stared at him. A flood of emotions washed over her face so rapidly he couldn't identify them. And then there was only one. Fear. Her hand went to the base of her throat. The blood drained from her face. Her mouth worked, but nothing came out. He started toward her. She tried again, and one word came out on a breathless gasp.

"Nora?"

It stopped him. He had not considered— "Nora is fine."

"Oh." Sarah's shoulders sagged. "Oh, thank goodness." She closed her eyes, sighed. "I thought—" Her eyes opened, widened. She averted her gaze and glanced around the room, looked back at him. "What are you doing here, Mr. Bainbridge? And where is Father? I was told he wanted to see me here in the library."

"I am the one who wanted to see you."

Her gaze touched on him, confused, disquieted, then skittered away. "I do not think that is wise. If you will excuse me—"

"Sarah—"

Her gaze jerked back to him. She took a breath. Her hand went to the base of her throat again.

"I have come all the way from Cincinnati to speak with you. Will you please listen—without interruption?"

She stared at him a minute, then gave a polite nod. "Very well." She moved to the front of a leather chair, sat, rested her hands in her lap and lifted her chin.

His heart thudded. She was so beautiful. Proud, defiant and beautiful. *Lord, please give me the words to say to make her understand.* He looked down at the floor and gathered his thoughts. "Do you remember the night we talked about our childhood dreams? I told you about my mentor and best friend. What I did not tell you was that Andrew was an older man who had an only child he adored. A daughter who was sickly from birth and unable to do the things other children did. Andrew gave her every thing within his power. But he could not give her a healthy heart. And so he centered his life around making his daughter safe. And then he became seriously ill."

Clayton glanced Sarah's way. She gave a polite nod, but remained silent, as she had promised. "Andrew did not fear dying. But he feared leaving his frail daughter unprotected. So he called me to his bedside and asked me to marry his daughter, Deborah, and keep her safe always. I promised to do so."

Sarah stiffened. "I am sorry, Mr. Bainbridge, I know I said I would listen, but I do not see—"

"Please. Let me finish. It will not take long. And I promise I have a purpose." That caught her interest. Clayton went back to his story. "Deborah and I were married at Andrew's bedside. He died two days later." He paused, uncertain how to go on. "Some of what I must say is…indelicate. I will be as circumspect as possible." He turned toward the windows to spare her embarrassment. "The doctor informed us that, due to Deborah's frail condition, having a child would probably take her life. I was determined that should not happen and so we occupied separate bedchambers. In spite of visiting many doctors and employing every effort known, Deborah's health continued to decline."

He heard movement behind him and glanced in the window. Sarah had risen and walked around to stand behind the chair. At least she was still listening. He braced himself for what was to come. "We continued on as before. But Deborah changed. She became insistent that she did not want to die without knowing the…intimacies…of marriage. I was not willing to risk her life with a child and refused. But one night—"

"I have heard enough, Mr. Bainbridge!" Sarah whirled and swept toward the door.

Clayton hurried around the desk and blocked her way.

"Let me pass."

"Not until you have heard what I have to say." He tried to hold her gaze but she refused to look at him. "Sarah, I realize you are a maiden and this is difficult for you to hear. But I promise you, if you do not feel what I have to say is important to you—to your life— when I am finished, I will allow your father to have me horsewhipped!"

Her lips quivered. She spun away and walked back to stand behind the chair. "Very well. If you will not let me pass, say what you must and say it quickly. Or I will have Father do as you suggest!" She looked the other direction.

Clayton clenched his hands and cleared his throat. "That night Deborah told me the doctor had given her precautions, and I yielded. Her wish was granted. Though she grew weaker daily she lived to give birth to the baby conceived that night. Her heart stopped beating a few minutes later.

"To my shame, I could not look at the child. She was, to me, a living symbol of my guilt, my failure to uphold the deathbed vow I had made to my friend. I was consumed with that guilt. I lost sight of anything good and saw only the shame of my weakness. I blamed God for everything and turned away from him. My heart, my life, was full of darkness."

Sarah had turned back to face him. The anger was gone, her eyes shimmered with tears.

"And then you came to Stony Point."

She did not move, her expression did not change, but he could feel a sudden tension emanate from her.

He took a step closer. "I did not understand, Sarah. I was so consumed with my own ugliness I thought you were a punishment from God. A test of my will. I was drawn to you from the start, but I was determined that this time I would not fail—I would not give in to my feelings for you though they grew stronger every day. And then you told me you still loved your dead fiancé and wanted no other. I determined then my only course was to avoid you. And when you asked to go home, I let you go. It was the hardest thing I have ever done."

She raised her hand, pressed the tips of her fingers against her lips.

To still an outcry? To protest his mention of her beloved? Clayton took another step toward the chair. "I have made so many mistakes, Sarah. But God in His mercy has forgiven me and set them right. All but the last. That is for me to do."

He bent down and picked up the small chest he had polished until the wood gleamed, sat it on the chair cushion, opened it, unfolded the unfinished sampler and handed it to her. "God showed me the answer to why He sent you to Stony Point, Sarah. You hold it in your hand." He took the last step that separated them as she read it. "You are my gift from God, Sarah. The light that brightened my darkness. I love you, Sarah, with all my heart and soul. Please forgive my foolishness, marry me and come home."

Sarah blinked away tears, looked up. Flames burned in the dark-blue depths of Clayton's eyes. Her knees buckled. She gave a little cry, dropped the sampler and grabbed for the chair back.

Clayton caught her. He lifted her up, drew her close against him and lowered his head. "I told you I would not let you fall." His warm breath whispered across her skin. He brushed his mouth against hers. "I told you you are safe with me."

Safe? Calm, comfortable, serene safe?

Clayton's arms tightened, his hand slid up and cupped the back of her head. His mouth claimed hers.

Sarah sighed, slipped her arms around his neck and answered his kiss, quite certain she would never be safe again.

Epilogue

The carriage climbed over the break of the hill and there it was, Stony Point. Her home. Every nerve in Sarah's stomach fluttered to life. She leaned out and drank in the sight of the rectangular stone house, with its set-back kitchen ell, sitting square in the middle of the point of land that forced the road to curve. It was not large. And there was nothing ornate or fancy about it. Its solid wood-plank front door had deep gashes in it from Indian tomahawks. But it was her home, and she loved every inch of it.

Clayton squeezed her hand, smiled when she looked back at him. He reached up and cupped her cheek, leaned down and kissed her lips. "Welcome home, Mrs. Bainbridge."

Sarah's heart overflowed into her eyes and blurred her husband's handsome face. He kissed the tip of her nose, then climbed from the carriage and offered her his hand. She placed hers in his, reveling in his touch, and stepped out of the carriage. He placed his arm about her shoulder, leaned down and opened the gate sandwiched between the two lamp-topped stone pillars that anchored the low stone walls enclosing the front yard.

Maaaa.

One of the sheep grazing on the lawn lifted its head and followed their progress up the slate walk. Sarah's pulse quickened. Her new life was starting.

The front door opened. Sarah caught sight of a smiling Eldora standing in the opening, and then a small figure darted out of the dim interior onto the stoop.

"Nanny!" Nora held up her pudgy little arms and bounced up and down, beaming a smile that rivaled the sun overhead.

Sarah laughed through her tears, scooped the toddler into her arms and hugged and kissed her until Nora squealed.

"I misseded you, Nanny!"

"She is not your nanny, Nora." Clayton wrapped his arms about them both and kissed Nora's rosy cheek. "She is your mama."

Mama. How wonderful that sounded. Sarah smiled up at her husband. He looked down at her, blue flames flickering in the depths of his dark-blue eyes, and her knees turned to water. Clayton's strong arms stopped her from tumbling backward off the stoop. He lowered his head, covered her lips with his, and her heart melted. No. She would never be safe again.

* * * * *

SPECIAL EXCERPT FROM

Love Inspired HISTORICAL

*Widowed father Boothe Powers needs a wife in order
to retain custody of his son. Emma Spencer was sure
to see the practicality of such an arrangement.
Emma's heart yearns for marriage and children.
But she has her own secret anguish…*

Read on for a sneak preview of
The Path to Her Heart *by Linda Ford*

"We don't even like each other. Why would you want to
marry me?" At the untruthfulness of her words, heat left a
spot on Emma's cheeks. She'd tried to tell herself otherwise,
but she liked Boothe. Might even admit she'd grown slightly
fond of him. Okay. Truth time. She might even be a little
attracted to him. Had been since her first glimpse.

"I like you just fine."

"I'm a nurse. Have you forgotten?"

He hesitated. "Well, as nurses go, you seem to be a good
one."

She snorted in a most unladylike fashion. "I'm thrilled
to hear that."

"Surely we could work around that."

"I think not. Can you imagine how we'd disagree if I
thought one of us or—" Her cheeks burned. She'd been
about to say *one of our children*, but she couldn't say it
aloud. "If I thought someone needed medical attention?"

"I'm desperate."

"Well, thanks. I guess." Just what she'd always dreamed
of—the last pick of someone who was desperate.

"Wait. Listen to what I have to say." He pulled a battered envelope from his back pocket.

Nothing he said would change the fact they were as unsuited for each other as cat and mouse, yet she hesitated, wanting—hoping—for something to persuade her otherwise.

He waved her toward a pew and she cautiously took a seat. "This is a letter from a lawyer back in Lincoln informing me that my brother-in-law and his wife intend to adopt Jessie."

She gasped. "How can that be?"

He looked bleak. "I needed help after Alyse died and Vera offered. Only then she wanted to keep Jessie."

Emma pressed her palm to his shoulder. "Surely they don't have a chance?"

He slowly brought his gaze toward her. At the look of despair in his eyes, her throat pinched closed.

"I went to see the lawyer in town and he says the courts favor people who have money and their own home, but especially both a father and mother. My best chance is to get married."

She settled back, affronted to be no more than a means to an end, and yet, would her dreams and hopes never leave her alone? "And I was the only person you could think of?"

He shrugged. "You're fond of Jessie."

A burning mix of sympathy and annoyance shot through her. She withdrew her hand from his shoulder even though she ached to comfort him. She sat up straight, folded her hands together in her lap and forced the words from her mouth. "Yes, I'm fond of Jessie but I can't marry—not you or anyone."

Don't miss
The Parson's Christmas Gift & The Path to Her Heart
by Kerri Mountain and Linda Ford,
available December 2018.

www.LoveInspired.com

SPECIAL EXCERPT FROM

Love Inspired

*With her family in danger of being separated,
could marriage to a newcomer in town
keep them together for the holidays?*

Read on for a sneak preview of
An Amish Wife for Christmas *by Patricia Davids,
available in November 2018 from Love Inspired!*

"I've got trouble, Clarabelle."

The cow didn't answer her. Bethany pitched a forkful of hay to the family's placid brown-and-white Guernsey. "The bishop has decided to send Ivan to Bird-in-Hand to live with Onkel Harvey. It's not right. It's not fair. I can't bear the idea of sending my little brother away. We belong together."

Clarabelle munched a mouthful of hay as she regarded Bethany with soulful deep brown eyes.

"Advice is what I need, Clarabelle. The bishop said Ivan could stay if I had a husband. Someone to discipline and guide the boy. Any idea where I can get a husband before Christmas?"

"I doubt your cow has the answers you seek, but if she does I have a few questions for her about my own problems," a man said.

Bethany spun around. A stranger stood in the open barn door. He wore a black Amish hat pulled low on his forehead and a dark blue woolen coat with the collar turned up against the cold.

The mirth sparkling in his eyes sent a flush of heat to her cheeks. How humiliating. To be caught talking to a cow about matrimonial prospects made her look ridiculous.

She struggled to hide her embarrassment. "It's rude to eavesdrop on a private conversation."

"I'm not sure talking to a cow qualifies as a private conversation, but I am sorry to intrude."

He didn't look sorry. He looked like he was struggling not to laugh at her.

"I'm Michael Shetler."

She considered not giving him her name. The less he knew to repeat the better.

"I am Bethany Martin," she admitted, hoping she wasn't making a mistake.

"Nice to meet you, Bethany. Once I've had a rest I'll step outside if you want to finish your private conversation." He winked. One corner of his mouth twitched, revealing a dimple in his cheek.

"I'm glad I could supply you with some amusement today."

"It's been a long time since I've had something to smile about."

Don't miss
An Amish Wife for Christmas *by Patricia Davids,*
available November 2018 wherever
Love Inspired® books and ebooks are sold.

www.LoveInspired.com

Love Inspired®

Inspirational Romance to Warm Your Heart and Soul

Join our social communities to connect with other readers who share your love!

Sign up for the Love Inspired newsletter at **www.LoveInspired.com** to be the first to find out about upcoming titles, special promotions and exclusive content.

CONNECT WITH US AT:

Facebook.com/groups/HarlequinConnection

 Facebook.com/LoveInspiredBooks

Twitter.com/LoveInspiredBks

LISOCIAL2018

Reward the book lover in you!

Earn points on your purchase of new Harlequin books from participating retailers.

Turn your points into **FREE BOOKS** of your choice!

Join for FREE today at
www.HarlequinMyRewards.com.

Harlequin My Rewards is a free program (no fees) without any commitments or obligations.